THE GOOD
BARRISTER

THE GOOD BARRISTER

DIANE COIA-RAMSAY

ARCHWAY
PUBLISHING

Copyright © 2023 Diane Coia-Ramsay.

All rights reserved. No part of this book may be used or reproduced by any means, graphic, electronic, or mechanical, including photocopying, recording, taping or by any information storage retrieval system without the written permission of the author except in the case of brief quotations embodied in critical articles and reviews.

This is a work of fiction. All of the characters, names, incidents, organizations, and dialogue in this novel are either the products of the author's imagination or are used fictitiously.

Archway Publishing books may be ordered through booksellers or by contacting:

Archway Publishing
1663 Liberty Drive
Bloomington, IN 47403
www.archwaypublishing.com
844-669-3957

Because of the dynamic nature of the Internet, any web addresses or links contained in this book may have changed since publication and may no longer be valid. The views expressed in this work are solely those of the author and do not necessarily reflect the views of the publisher, and the publisher hereby disclaims any responsibility for them.

Any people depicted in stock imagery provided by Getty Images are models, and such images are being used for illustrative purposes only. Certain stock imagery © Getty Images.

ISBN: 978-1-6657-4839-1 (sc)
ISBN: 978-1-6657-4838-4 (hc)
ISBN: 978-1-6657-4840-7 (e)

Library of Congress Control Number: 2023915170

Print information available on the last page.

Archway Publishing rev. date: 08/14/2023

CHAPTER 1

Sophie Sullivan was seated at her favorite table by the window in the Willow Tea Rooms, on Sauchiehall Street, Glasgow. The Willow Tearooms were very popular with stylish ladies and Sophie very much aspired to become one of these exceedingly fortunate women.

It was Monday afternoon, and Sophie's day off from her father's haberdashery on Springburn Road, which now belonged to her older brother Jack and his wife Norma. Her father had finally passed away after a painful, debilitating illness and her mother was long since gone. As Norma had told her so often, there was only so much of a living to be made in Sullivan's Haberdashery, and only so much room in her father's tiny bungalow in Bishopbriggs, which had now passed to his son, who of course was Norma's husband.

Sophie did not much care. She had her own plans. She had been invited to stay with her Aunt Loretta and Uncle David Carlisle, who were childless and eager to assist their beautiful niece in beginning a new exciting life in New York. Sophie understood her sister-in-law was jealous of her much remarked upon beauty. Norma often accused Sophie of putting on airs, since Sophie was paying for elocution lessons with Miss Patterson, instead of spending her wages on having good times with friends and going to dance halls to meet boys. Sophie felt her brother could have done better than Norma McMahon, but that indeed was his problem and not his sister Sophie's.

Sophie had little interest in the boys in her sphere of acquaintance, and thus, having attained the grand old age of twenty-three, she was considered by Norma of already being a spinster. Norma didn't fully comprehend that her sister-in-law had taken care of her mother and afterwards her father during both of their long illnesses and had been doing so since she was only sixteen. Sophie had little desire to spend her remaining young years looking after a man of limited means and even less ambition.

However, those years of caring for her parents were all in the past now and Sophie had a second class, Atlantic crossing steamer ticket booked for August 18, 1910. Consequently, as she sat sipping her tea and watching the passersby on the busy city street, she dreamed about what wonders awaited her in America.

Sophie Sullivan, like many others in 1910, was convinced the streets of New York were paved with gold and she would meet and marry an American millionaire—if not by Christmas—then certainly very soon thereafter. She knew her beauty and grace were much admired and complimented in her small town and that she could probably win the attention of any boy in Bishopbriggs, should she so desire to do so, which she most certainly did not. In Scotland, rich men only sought out rich girls with dowries—or so Jack had often told her, and he said she was so special, he was happy for her being given this chance to better her life. Also, failing Sophie finding and marrying a millionaire in New York City, their uncle owned property in Upstate New York, in a small town by the name of New Chestnut. Sophie liked that name, so if it turned out that American millionaires were rather thin on the ground, she would persuade her uncle to allow her to open a little gift shop in New Chestnut. There she could make her own modest living, in the beauty of the North American countryside and with no husband to have to please and put up with. The more Sophie thought on it, this alternative option for her future appealed to her the most, and she sat smiling to herself as she made out imaginary lists of the merchandise she would need to purchase—with her uncle's money—in order to stock her little shop. He was certainly indulgent, and her aunt was the very best of women.

Sophie was suddenly roused from her blissful reverie by a commotion taking place, just a few tables away from her, in the delightfully appointed tearoom.

It seemed a lady had forgotten her purse and the waitress was being extremely disrespectful toward her. Sophie had seen the lady in the tearoom on several previous occasions and even one time in the haberdashery. It was Norma who waited on her, and she purchased a card of mother of pearl buttons, as well as needles and matching thread. Sophie was in the back shop, stocktaking, but she noticed her kind and soft voice when she addressed Norma, and Sophie had watched her through the window as she left and walked up the main street. She was very finely dressed, and Jack said she was one of the Cochranes who lived in the mansion high above Springburn Road, which many people said was haunted. He said she lived with her brother, whom he had often witnessed speeding up and down Springburn Road. He called them snobs and that was the end of the matter.

Therefore, although Sophie had noticed Miss Cochrane in the Willow Tea Rooms on previous occasions, she never chanced to greet or make herself known to her. She was certain Miss Cochrane would have little interest in making the acquaintance of a shopkeeper's daughter, even though they both lived in the same small town, on the outskirts of Glasgow. Jack had called them snobs, and even dressed in her Sunday best, the lady's clothes were visibly finer, and she never appeared to notice Sophie, not even to nod her head. Miss Cochrane had a faraway look in her eyes, so that Sophie almost felt sorry for the well refined and expensively dressed lady.

Miss Cochrane was becoming more and more embarrassed and agitated and Sophie felt so sorry for her and infuriated at the nasty waitress, who surely should have seen that this was a very fine lady, who had simply made a mistake.

Sophie looked down under her table and patted the shopping bag which contained her navy-blue suit, brand new underclothing, and a white silk blouse. A purchase made possible by her aunt Loretta which was meant to be safely put aside as her traveling suit, which she would require in a little less than two months. Sophie had not found a hat she particularly admired in Pettigrew and Stephen's department store and therefore had enough money left over to render her assistance to this fine lady, who by now was almost in tears.

She walked over to the lady's table and said, "Miss Cochrane, I hardly recognized you! Please allow me to join you in a fresh pot of tea."

Sophie turned to the discourteous waitress, standing with a suspicious look upon her face and said, "I shall speak to the manager about this outrage, if you do not quickly fetch a fresh pot of tea and some scones with butter and strawberry jam for my dear friend and I! How dare you insult a customer in such a manner!"

Miss Cochrane looked stunned, and then so grateful that Sophie almost felt she wanted to embrace her. Sophie sat down and said, "It could happen to anyone, and I know you to be a very fine lady. I saw your distress and hope you do not mind my intervention. I just hate nasty people, and that waitress was beyond nasty to you. My name is Miss Sophie Sullivan, from Bishopbriggs. You might know the haberdashery that my family owns on Springburn Road. I believe you may have purchased buttons there in the past. However, I will soon be on my way to begin a new life in New York where waitresses would never dare address a lady in such a manner."

Finally, the other woman gathered herself together enough to speak to this most unusual girl.

"How do you do Miss Sullivan. I am Miss Euphemia Cochrane and yes, coincidentally, I am also from Bishopbriggs. I have been in the haberdashery once or twice but never saw you there. You are so kind and lovely I would surely have remembered you had I done so. My brother will be furious if he hears of this. Please allow me to reimburse you as soon as possible, and please do not tell my brother of this extreme humiliation."

Sophie was somewhat surprised. This woman was clearly in her early thirties and to be so afraid of her brother. What type of man was he? What type of woman was this poor lady's sister-in-law?

Sophie said, "Clearly, this has nothing to do with your brother—or his wife. I have a frightfully horrid sister-in-law too, which is why I rarely serve in the shop, and why I am anxious to be on my way to America. We have not met otherwise, because you are of a social class above me. However, I speak very well, and I have certain ambitions. One day I intend to be a fine lady and to wear expensive clothes. I expect I will achieve this in New York, and I am biding my time until then. However, I would like to be your friend and to tell your brother and his wife where to go! I can tell you are not a snob, and I am certain that they are. My brother detests snobs. He often says so."

Euphemia laughed and sipped her fresh tea that had been quickly brought to them. This girl with her long, lustrous blonde hair, brilliant blue eyes and clear complexion was stunning. Her figure was perfect, her speech, her spirit, her self-confidence, although only a shopkeeper's daughter—quite extraordinary. Euphemia thought of her brother, the arrogant and ill-disposed, well-renowned barrister, and wondered what he would make of Miss Sophie Sullivan. She said, "Oh no!" As she laughed, "He has no wife. My brother is two years my senior and a barrister in the Glasgow High Courts. His disposition is such that I cannot imagine any woman would ever want to marry him, and yet he has had several of them setting their caps at him. He is very good looking you see. As the saying goes, tall, dark and handsome. He was given all the family's good looks, since I know I was not. He is, however, haughty and contemptuous, and since our parents are both deceased, I must abide by his rules and standards, having no husband of my own who could override his demands and opinions."

Sophie Sullivan was immensely diverted. She was delighted that she rescued this lovely lady. She was even more delighted that Miss

Cochrane required rescuing in the first place, since by their mutual honesty they had struck up an immediate friendship. She said, "Do you have many friends, Miss Cochrane? I do not have any since I have very much kept to myself and spent my spare time on self-improvement. My sister-in-law hates this about me and calls me a spinster, although I am but twenty-three. Not that being a spinster is such a terrible thing—well unless you have a horrid brother or sister-in-law. My brother is nice. He simply married the wrong woman. This of course is his concern and not mine, although I can see it in his eyes sometimes. They have no children."

Euphemia responded, "Well at thirty-two, I am most certainly regarded as a spinster. My brother is rarely home, so I suppose that is not such a bad thing—being a spinster I mean. I dislike his friends and their wives and have no friends of my own. My brother would most likely disapprove of anyone I would even desire to be my friend. Your brother is right about Benedict; he is a complete and utter elitist and thinks himself smarter and far above the rest of us mere mortals."

The two women spent a wonderful afternoon together and spoke so freely that they agreed that their unusual manner of meeting must have been destiny. Miss Cochrane laughed when she explained that in all her years of taking tea in Glasgow, she had never on any previous occasion forgotten her purse. They arranged to meet the following Monday. That would be Miss Cochrane's treat and they would go shopping together. Sophie was still in pursuit of a new hat and Euphemia stated that she would be very glad to render her opinion.

They parted, eventually having drank yet another pot of tea and eaten more sandwiches and scones so that neither woman expected to eat a morsel at dinner that night.

Sophie took the tram car home, having refused a lift in Miss Cochrane's carriage. She used the excuse of merchandise that she needed to collect before going home. "We have completely run out of candy pink ribbon, and it is selling so well. I fear my sister-in-law will accuse me of tarrying if I do not bring it home with me."

This was, of course, nonsense, however, Sophie felt that her new friend might be quite set upon by her odious brother, if he discovered that she had allowed herself to be placed in the position of relying upon the kindness of a shopkeeper's daughter.

It was the first time that Sophie felt lesser, even though Euphemia had not treated her as such. It was quite clear that she feared her brother finding out about her newfound friendship. Despite their arrangements for the following week, Sophie fully expected that she would be stood up and let down, with some ridiculous made-up excuse.

～

Mr. Benedict Cochrane was a man of strong opinions and little time for the excesses of the female sex. He was, however, saddled with the responsibility of his sister, since at thirty-two, she had little expectation of attracting any man by her own merits as a woman. He had no intention of selling her off for her fortune, so he accepted that she would remain his responsibility for life.

At thirty-four, he had little intention of marrying and as a highly paid and well sought-after barrister, in a city where there was no shortage of crime, and no lack of interesting cases to defend; why on earth would he ever want to permanently saddle himself with a wife? He thought of his sister as entirely feeble-minded and consequently, she was enough for him to have to tolerate.

Mr. Benedict Cochrane was surprised to find his sister still out when he returned home a little early that Monday afternoon. "What kept you so long?" He said upon her return home. "How long does it take to drink tea in the Willow Tea Rooms?"

He was sitting behind his evening paper as was his usual behavior, but Euphemia felt so light and happy. She felt optimism that she was quite unused to, and she said, "I met a young lady today. She is so lovely, quite the loveliest girl I have ever seen, and we drank tea together. I believe I have made a true friend. However, she is sailing to New York in less than two months—more is the pity."

This got her brother's attention. "What are you talking about? Euphemia? What is this all about?"

Euphemia was forced to confess. "Benedict, I am embarrassed to say that I forgot my purse. This girl rescued me, and we drank tea together and ate sandwiches all afternoon. She is so very beautiful, inside and out, and next Monday is her day off. We are meeting again to drink tea, and I will assist her in choosing a hat for her voyage to America. She is the daughter of old Mr. Sullivan who owned the haberdashery on Springburn Road, which her brother and his wife have taken over."

Benedict was outraged. "You took tea paid for by a shopkeeper's daughter and you dare to tell me she is your new friend? Euphemia, it seems you have even less sense than I supposed, and there will be no friendship. I will reimburse this woman tomorrow morning. Let that be the end of the matter."

That was the exact moment when Euphemia's trepidation of her arrogant brother turned to contempt. He was indeed such a hateful and disdainful man—always believing he was so much smarter and better than everyone else. However, something inside of Euphemia's heart told her that whatever her brother expected at Sullivan's Haberdashery, he was not expecting Miss Sophie Sullivan, who would certainly give him a run for his money. In addition, Euphemia would be paying a call at Sullivan's later in the week, to reassure Miss Sullivan that their luncheon date was still on—with or without her brother's approval.

She said, "She is a young lady. Kindly refer to her as such."

And her brother responded, "Do not be ridiculous Euphemia. She is a shopkeeper's daughter. Unquestionably not a lady and most certainly not about to become your new bosom friend. I will see that she is made aware of this tomorrow. By the way, how much do you owe her? I will not allow her to profit from her supposed kindness. She no doubt has that in mind."

Euphemia said, "One hundred pounds," and laughed at the ridiculous sum, as she left the room and her brother to his evening paper.

～

Tuesday morning, and the shop opened its shutters and Jack turned around the sign on the door from 'Closed' to 'Open' at precisely 9 a.m... They were open each day until 6 p.m. except Wednesday, which was half-day closing, and Sunday, when they of course did not open for business.

It seemed on this Tuesday morning, there was an early customer. He had driven up in a shiny new Wolseley Tourer—or so it was, according to Jack Sullivan, who knew his motor cars. The man parked outside the shop and hopped out, without opening the driver's door.

He was indeed tall, dark and handsome—devastatingly so—and was very well turned out, in a black silk suit, expensively cut to fit his muscular frame. Sophie knew exactly who he was. It would seem his sister confessed everything to her unpleasant—yet so very well favored—brother, and he had turned up with the idea of paying back what his sister owed Sophie for her tea and sandwiches, not forgetting the scones and strawberry jam. In truth the total bill for lunch took all the money Sophie had allocated for her new hat. However, when she told her brother of her rendezvous with Miss Cochrane, he was so impressed that he promised her an extra two pounds in her wages to make up for her loss. Neither Sophie nor Jack mentioned the matter to Norma.

Norma hurried to the front shop to wait on the handsome gentleman. However, she was soon disappointed when he asked for

Miss Sullivan and said, "From my sister's description, my assumption is that you are not in fact, Miss Sophie Sullivan. Of course, I might be mistaken."

Sophie had been hiding in the back shop. This man certainly wasted no time in coming to pay off his sister's debt, which meant that he disapproved of their new friendship. She straightened her hair and then walked out front, proudly, and with her nose in the air. She wasn't about to be intimidated by this most unpleasant man. However, she wondered why he had to be so exceedingly good looking.

~

Mr. Benedict Cochrane thought to give this young woman a couple of pounds and be on his way. He would inform her that Euphemia had thought the better of their plans the following week, since she had too many commitments—or some such nonsense.

Then he saw her. She walked right up to him with her nose in the air, and he had to fight back the impulse to take her in his arms. She was, quite possibly, the loveliest girl he had ever seen. Her lustrous blonde hair was thick and plentiful and fell almost to her waist. He thought, *a man could lose himself in that hair.* Her brilliant blue eyes stared at him impertinently. She instinctively knew who he was and why he had come. However, he was having trouble forming the words he planned to say to her—not a problem he usually suffered from—inability to speak. She was of average height but there was nothing else average about her. She had the body of a goddess, the face of an angel, and an expression which revealed she was ready to go to battle with him.

He found himself, almost struck dumb. He felt as if he was losing control of his mind and his body. He thought, *what the hell is wrong with me?* And then she first spoke.

"I am presuming you are Mr. Benedict Cochrane, am I correct?"

He nodded his head and suddenly remembered he was holding two pound notes in his hand.

Sophie excused herself from her awestruck brother and sister-in-law—uncertain as to what exactly was going on—as she opened the door and led him outside, saying, in a most superior manner, "Kindly follow me, sir."

Benedict Cochrane followed this uppity little madam, whom he felt had bewitched him, without opening his mouth.

Once outside she said, "Do not even try to pay me for rescuing your sister! How dare you come into my family's shop to berate me or tell me to know my place? I know my place and the problem is that you do not. You are too used to defending thieves and murderers and you are incapable of appreciating a kind and decent act, even if it hit you in the face."

Benedict had finally recovered himself. This girl was the most delightful creature on earth. He changed his mind. He changed his mind entirely.

"Miss Sullivan, it seems my sister did not speak very kindly of me. I came into your shop, to buy something suitable for my secretary's birthday. It is today and I quite forgot about it. I also came in to thank you for your kindness and to invite you to afternoon tea, this Sunday at 2 p.m..."

Benedict had to restrain his laughter as he watched the lovely Sophie Sullivan's face go scarlet. He waited for her to speak—to profusely apologize for her outrageous behavior, but all she said was, "Oh, I see. I will happily accept your kind invitation to afternoon tea with my new friend Euphemia. Please allow me to assist you in choosing a suitable gift for your secretary. She then led him back inside and asked, "What colors does your secretary favor?"

She was very well spoken, not a trace of a Glaswegian accent, which he expected. She spoke better than he did. There was no secretary's birthday. He made that up. He said, "I have no idea Miss Sullivan, perhaps you could provide a few suggestions."

∽

Sophie Sullivan couldn't quite believe that she was so rude to this handsome gentleman. She may have jumped to conclusions but possibly she had not. She saw the attraction in his eyes. He was attracted to her, the shopkeeper's daughter, Sophie Sullivan. However, Sophie knew enough to be wary. She knew quite enough to doubt his intentions.

Norma approached them and asked if she could render some assistance to the gentleman. He waved her off with his hand—a very arrogant gesture—and Sophie proceeded to select some pretty blue ribbon, but before she went further, she asked, "What color hair and eyes does she have? Is she young or middle-aged?"

Benedict was bemused, not an emotion he was familiar with. "She has your coloring, and she is young—like you."

Sophie said, "Then I will select what I would like to be given. How much do you want to spend—on this secretary of yours?" By now Sophie was convinced there was no secretary. This man was merely backtracking on the insult he intended toward her, until their eyes met.

He said, "No matter, wrap up what you like, and think might be suitable."

Sophie took full advantage. She wrapped up six lace handkerchiefs, three yards each of candy pink, duck blue and black velvet ribbon. She threw in three cards of fancy buttons, some lavender and rose bath salts, rose scented soap, and finally a tiny flowered enameled mirror and matching comb. She wrapped it all up and said, "One pound nineteen and sixpence, plus two and sixpence for the wrapping and colored string. Two pounds one shilling and sixpence please."

She did it deliberately because at Sullivan's, they never charged for wrapping, and because this fascinating man was still holding the two pound notes, he had no doubt intended to use to reimburse her for his sister's lunch.

Benedict Cochrane handed her his two pounds, and she said, "Sir, that is not enough. You still owe me one shilling and sixpence."

He said, "You charge a lot for a white sheet of paper and a piece of string," but he was smiling as he reached into his pocket.

Sophie said, "If you don't have it, you can pay me back on Sunday, the one and sixpence, I mean."

Benedict handed her a crown and said, "You owe me three shillings and sixpence change."

Sophie rang up the overpriced purchase in the cash register and presented him with his change, which she counted out in five sixpences and four thruppenny bits, saying, "I apologize but we are a bit short of change this morning. My brother still has to go to the bank."

Benedict laughed, he knew she was having fun at his expense, and said, "That's alright, I will give the coins to the valet who parks my car." And he was off, speeding down Springburn Road, with Sophie Sullivan, dreamily watching after him.

She said to Jack and Norma, "Oh my, isn't he so very handsome! That dimple on his chin just finishes him off perfectly. So expensively attired, so debonair, and according to his sister, so completely obnoxious and full of himself. "Afternoon tea on Sunday? You know he came in to berate me for saving his sister. I wonder why he changed his mind. I think he has taken a shine to me." And Sophie's nose was again back up in the air.

Jack said, "Well remember he is a Cochrane. There will be nothing honorable in that man's brain."

Just then Norma realized he left the package behind.

Jack said, "I know where they live—the Cochranes—Sophie, perhaps you should deliver the package to his housekeeper?"

Norma said, "I will be happy to do it."

But Jack said, "That gentleman had no interest in you, my dear, but it seems to me, he was rather interested in our Sophie," and then he turned to Sophie and said, "you make sure you mind yourself with him. He will not have marriage in his mind."

Sophie said, "Possibly not yet, but I intend to make him fall madly in love with me, the shopkeeper's daughter. Wouldn't that be so funny? I mean him being such a stuck-up snob! I wonder if I can manage that on Sunday afternoon." Of course, she was joking, but only somewhat so.

Jack laughed and said, "Thank goodness you will soon be on that ship to America, sister Sophie! Although I had to prevent myself from laughing out loud when you charged him two and sixpence for the paper and string."

That afternoon Sophie freshened up and made her way to their small town's most imposing house, high above the main street and surrounded by such a huge wall and tall hedgerow that one could hardly see it from the road. Sophie was told that Miss Cochrane was not at home and so she left the package with the housekeeper, who promised to give it to her mistress upon her return.

Sophie practically skipped back to the shop. She felt somehow elated. Of course, nothing would come of it, but she had clearly interested Mr. Benedict Cochrane enough, that instead of paying her back the money he felt his sister owed to her, he invited her to Sunday afternoon tea, and purchased a ridiculous selection of gifts for a secretary who did not exist. Every item that Sophie selected was actually for herself. She somehow could tell he knew this. She was not particularly sorry she was so rude to him. Had he not found her pretty, he would have most certainly insulted her. However, it seemed that the unattainable and arrogant Benedict Cochrane was indeed as attracted to Miss Sophie Sullivan as she was, most unquestionably, to him.

That Tuesday, Sophie Sullivan did not consider their difference in social status. She did not even consider that as a shopkeeper's daughter, he thought her to be far beneath him. Her thoughts were entirely wrapped around Benedict Cochrane's piercing grey eyes, his muscular frame, his height, his dimple and his carelessly groomed black hair.

Sophie Sullivan had never felt this way about any man, and yet she knew she must keep these thoughts and desires to when she retired each night to her lonely bedroom. Perhaps there were men just like him in New York? That thought cheered her a little, because she was well aware that Benedict Cochrane was out of her league, and well he knew that too, no matter the attraction between them.

Benedict Cochrane went quickly on his way to the High Court. He was in the process of defending a man accused of assault with a deadly weapon. To Benedict, all men were innocent until proven guilty, and he only took on the cases he was certain he would win. He had a fine reputation, as one of the elite barristers in Scotland, to maintain. However, after his brief encounter with the lovely Sophie Sullivan, he found his mind was not particularly on the law.

He could not quite understand the effect this young woman was having on him. He felt distracted and left the court as soon as he successfully wrapped up his case. His client walked free, presumably to commit another crime—or possibly he had learned his lesson. Benedict Cochrane did not much care either way because his mind was on another matter. He was bemused. He did not believe in love at first sight, and he had most certainly never been in love. However, is this what it felt like? He found himself growing angry with his sister for placing him in this preposterous situation.

When he arrived home, he briefly greeted his sister on his way into his office, as was his usual habit. However, Euphemia waylaid him. "When did you employ a secretary? Benedict?"

Benedict then noticed his sister was holding the package

Miss Sullivan had wrapped up for him that very morning. He had forgotten all about it—thought he threw it in his motor car. She said, "Unfortunately, I had gone to the park—such a lovely day—and I missed my new friend. She dropped off the gift you had purchased for your secretary's birthday."

He felt quite ridiculous, as was the situation his sister had put him in. "I changed my mind. I do not think she had any bad intentions after all. Therefore, I needed a reason to be in that shop at 9 a.m... It was the first thing that came into my head." He paused, embarrassed, "Another thing, I stupidly invited her to tea on Sunday afternoon." Again, he paused, "Well I suppose you could send a note saying you have a cold—closer to the time—and that would take care of your date with her on Monday—having a cold, that is."

Euphemia Cochrane burst into peals of laughter. "Benedict, I am sorry, but I do not feel any cold coming on. You seem a little nervous? She is lovely, isn't she? She told you off, didn't she?" And she was still laughing when her brother took the package from her, and stormed into his office, closing the door behind him.

After much deliberation, Benedict Cochrane decided to also invite fellow barristers, Harvey Martin and John Nicholson and their wives. That would defuse the situation.

CHAPTER 2

Sunday morning dawned sunny and warm, and Sophie was concerned about this sudden change in the weather. It had been rainy and cool the past couple days, and that would have made her new suit the perfect option to wear to the Cochrane's afternoon tea. Now she either must wear her Sunday best dress, which was so out of style, or her new suit and pretend she wasn't too warm in it. Would it be rude to remove the jacket? She regretted not purchasing a new hat. She was nervous, since never having actually been to an afternoon tea with rich people, she wasn't sure what she was meant to do or say—even how long to stay. An hour? Half an hour? When she and Euphemia took tea together in the Willow Tea Rooms, they were on an equal footing. They sat as equals. Euphemia Cochrane was nice, and very much down to earth. Her brother was a tyrant and an utter snob.

Sophie almost regretted accepting his invitation—almost—however, if she were honest with herself, she very much looked forward to seeing Mr. Benedict Cochrane again, even although she knew he asked her upon impulse, and was surely regretting it, and even though she would likely never see him again.

In the end, she wore her new skirt and blouse, leaving the suit jacket at home, and tied her hair with a black velvet ribbon. She knew she should really wear it up, however, it was one of her best features, and she saw him admiring it in the shop since she had not had a chance to pin it up that morning.

Sophie Sullivan walked proudly up the pathway of the Cochrane's grand red sandstone mansion. She thought it to be very large for two people, siblings who would likely never need the extra bedrooms for future families.

After their housekeeper showed her in, Euphemia hurried out of the parlor and greeted her warmly and explained that her brother had invited a couple of his colleagues and their wives, and she introduced her to them as Miss Sophie Sullivan.

Benedict was standing with the other two gentlemen, and simply nodded a greeting and said, "Miss Sullivan." However, Sophie understood all three men were staring at her as she sat down to her tea which was served to her by Euphemia as hostess.

Then the interrogation began. These women, Mrs. Marsha Martin and Mrs. Audrey Nicholson, were nothing like Euphemia. They were hateful like their husbands and hateful like Benedict Cochrane. They were also completely overdressed on such a warm summer's day and looked like giant cream puff pastries—a day old and on sale.

Sophie told them she would be leaving for America in less than two months to join her aunt and uncle who owned a brownstone in Manhattan.

Mrs. Martin asked, "What do you suppose you will do there, my dear? Are you to take care of your aunt or are you seeking a rich husband?"

Before she could respond, Mrs. Nicholson said, "they say the streets of New York are paved with gold. I somehow doubt that, however, there are grand department stores and I gather you are currently employed in a haberdashery."

Euphemia was livid, but surprisingly, so was her brother. Clearly both these women were jealous of Sophie's sheer loveliness and annoyed at their husbands, since all three men stood enthralled with her good looks.

Sophie opened her mouth to respond, when again Mrs. Marsha Martin spoke, "We so despair of Mr. Cochrane ever settling down. He is so very discerning and there are no women of fine breeding on the Northside of Glasgow to even tempt him. We are trying to persuade him and Miss Cochrane to move their residence to the Southside of the city; Whitecraigs, where we both reside. Such a better class of people to be found there." She then shouted over to Benedict, "Mr. Cochrane, Mrs. Nicholson and I know a number of young ladies with fine breeding and grace. I do so wish you would allow us to introduce them to you."

She turned to her atrocious friend, "Audrey, what do you think? Miss Fiona MacBride? She is a beauty if ever there was one. Such elegance and refinement. Such pleasing manners."

Sophie wasn't sure which comment or question to address first. The absolute rudeness of these women astounded her. She could tell that Euphemia was embarrassed and upset, and Sophie smiled at her reassuringly, before opening her mouth to give as good as she had gotten.

Again, she was interrupted. However, this time, it was a most welcome interruption. Mr. Benedict Cochrane appeared to have had enough of such vulgarity. He approached Sophie and said, "Miss Sullivan, please allow me to take a turn with you around my garden. I can take no credit for it, that belongs to our gardener, Mr. Thompson, but nevertheless…." And he took Sophie's hand to assist her from her chair as they turned and walked out of the room together.

The look of utter shock and amazement on both Mrs. Martin's and Mrs. Nicholson's faces caused both their husbands to laugh and Euphemia to smile.

Then Harvey Martin opined, "Miss Cochrane, your new little friend is a cracker! I think your poor brother has just met his downfall."

Both she and John Nicholson laughed at such a statement, but the other ladies present did not. In fact Marsha Martin glared at her husband.

Benedict walked silently at first and motioned for Sophie to take his arm. Then he suddenly turned, "Why are you going to America so soon?"

Sophie said, "It is not so soon, Mr. Cochrane. It has been planned for several months now, ever since my father passed away."

He said, "Yes, sorry to hear that. I take it your sister-in-law wants you out. You are fortunate to have such a kind aunt and uncle. However, I think you are making a mistake."

Sophie turned toward him, "A mistake? What would you suggest I do, Mr. Cochrane? Come and work for you? Possibly as a parlor maid? Or perhaps your secretary—oh—but you already have one of those. By the way, did she like her gift?"

Benedict actually blushed a little, "Ah, I see I have been found out. Did my sister tell you?"

Sophie said, "No, I knew there was no secretary. I just picked out a few things that I would like for my voyage. I assumed you would return them and then how could I place them back into stock? Anyway, as far as mistakes go. I spent seven years looking after my mother and then my father and there is no longer anything or anyone for me in Scotland. I very much like your sister. She is remarkably kind. However, I am afraid that is not enough for me to give up such a wonderful opportunity."

He said, "You speak very well. You are also very lovely. I am told you are twenty-three, although you look younger—wearing your hair down—because you know it is magnificent. Why aren't you married?"

Sophie smiled, "You want the truth, the whole truth and nothing but the truth, Mr. Cochrane?"

He smiled too and his face softened so when he did. "Of course, Miss Sullivan, and well said."

"Well—this is embarrassing—no one has ever asked me. No that is not the whole truth. I aspire to more than a life spent behind the kitchen sink, feeding a husband and hungry children. The thought of it even makes me shiver. There is not the same class system in

America. My aunt has told me, and I have read it too. I might fall in love with a man of some means, considerable means. He might even love me back. I will not marry for money, but I want the man I do fall in love with—if there is such a man—to have money. Consequently, no one in my sphere of acquaintance quite makes the grade. I do not go to dances or out with friends. I study and I have even taken lessons to improve my speech, which, by the way, is better than that of those nasty women you also invited today—no doubt because you regretted inviting me."

Benedict was searching for a fitting comment to this most unusual and honest narration. However, she saved him the bother. "Then there is Plan B. My Uncle Carlisle owns property in a small Upstate New York town. It is called New Chestnut and it sounds so very delightful. Scenic and clean, and snowy in winter. I would like to open my own little gift shop that sells items like ladies' gloves, scarves, fancy buttons, possibly hats, handkerchiefs and fragrance. There is a flat above the shop and if I am perfectly honest, the second option appeals to me the most—particularly after meeting your friends. I am thinking possibly the women in New York are nicer but if not, I could never endure spending my time with the people with whom you prefer to keep company. I am sorry, sir, I think I talk too much. However, you did ask for the whole truth."

Benedict found his voice finally. "So, if you marry at all you must be in love with a man with money and that man must have to love you back? Do I have that correct? I don't approve of your Plan B."

Sophie was about to say a rebuke. It was not up to Benedict Cochrane to approve or to disapprove—that was until he shocked her.

"I have money, a decent occupation, not bad looking. My wife would never be tied to the kitchen sink. Miss Sullivan, do you feel two months is long enough to fall in love with me?"

Sophie blushed profusely and said, "Why are you making fun of me, Mr. Cochrane?"

He said, "I am not. I don't believe in love at first sight, or at least I didn't, until those hags started insulting you. I asked you that question because I am rather convinced that I am falling in love with you. I don't know why, or how this happened, but there it is."

Sophie was astounded. "This makes no sense. Less than a week ago, I wasn't good enough to take tea with your sister. You have made it quite clear to Euphemia, how inferior you consider my family to be, compared to yours. Actually, I am unsure? Are you proposing marriage to me in a roundabout way?"

He said, "I suppose I might be. This two-month thing hanging around my neck. I think you should put it off, at the very least. It might just be infatuation and let us face it, you and your family are not at all in my social class."

Sophie Sullivan was beyond indignant. She said, "Would you kindly collect my reticule, Mr. Cochrane. I left it in your drawing room. I am going home."

Surprisingly, he quickly went inside to fetch it, ignoring his sister's and guests' questioning looks. He came back outside and said, "Here. I will give you a lift."

Sophie said, "No need, I live just down Balmuildy Road. I can easily walk."

Benedict said, "Oh yes, the little bungalows. Not bad for a haberdasher." He followed her out to his driveway and as she was about to walk past his car, with once again her nose in the air, he opened the passenger door and basically pushed her in, saying, "Stop being ridiculous, Sophie."

She said, "I didn't give you permission to call me that. I actually believe you belong in the insane asylum."

He drove off laughing, and Sophie began to feel a little nervous. In fact, she started to feel afraid. "What were his intentions? Was he going to ravish her in the woods?

She began to cry, and Benedict pulled over to the side of the road. He realized he had frightened her. All her brave talk. He realized he was scaring this young girl and that made him ashamed.

He said, "I just wanted to kiss you Sophie Sullivan, no more than that, away from prying eyes. Then I will know."

She said, "What will you know? You crazy, nasty man."

"I will know for sure, because even as I couldn't get the image of you out of my head since our meeting, I somehow knew you felt the same way about me."

He then wiped her tears with his thumb, untied her ribbon, and wrapped her lovely hair around his hand. He kissed her tenderly and then as his passion increased, his kisses became more intense, and once again Sophie started to cry.

"Alright," he said. "Do you promise that as my wife, my kisses, my love for you will not make you cry?"

Sophie was bewildered. His conversation made so little sense to her. He then surprised her, "I might invite you to come watch me defend my client in the High Court this week. Would you like that, Sophie Sullivan?"

Sophie was bemused by the whole afternoon spent with this remarkable man and merely nodded her head, uncertain as to how to respond.

Benedict said, "Okay, you have a date with my sister tomorrow. I will take you there on Wednesday. Tell your brother you are taking the day off, with pay."

Sophie said, "Mr. Cochrane, you should probably ask him for my hand in marriage first. If indeed that is what you want."

Benedict said, "I will consider that. The idea of asking him I mean. Should I indeed decide to marry you. I am becoming convinced that possibly I should marry you, to keep you off that steamer to America. You love me, don't you? You would be overjoyed if I truly proposed marriage to you. Do you have a middle name sweet Sophie?"

She said, "Yes, Belle. It is stupid I know. And you are such a conceited man. I don't even know you so how can I possibly love you? Also, why would I be overjoyed?"

He said, "I like Sophie Belle, I will call you that, and I am assuming you will continue to address me as Mr. Cochrane. I am of the opinion that if you do not yet love me, you are falling for me, which is why you would be overjoyed."

Sophie said, "I will continue to address you as Mr. Cochrane until I actually believe one word you have said, since I don't know that I do. Nor do I know why you seem to think I am falling for you or would be so overjoyed if you proposed marriage to me. Of course, I do know you are an arrogant and conceited man. That could well be the reason."

He kissed her again and his kiss was awakening such desires in her that she regretted missing Sunday mass that morning. That was another thing. "I am Roman Catholic," she said, knowing full well that the good barrister would be Church of Scotland, which was Presbyterian.

And all he said was, "Good for you, Sophie Belle."

He then turned his car around and Sophie wasn't exactly sure what to make of the day's events.

Sophie endeavored to say very little about it, but her brother came to her room very late and said, "Did he try any funny business, Sophie?"

Sophie said, "He kissed me and said he might be in love with me. He is a bit scary I think but I have never known anyone like him. I will ask his sister more about him tomorrow and he is taking me to the High Court to watch him—I do not know—show off, I suppose, on Wednesday morning. Is that okay, Jack?"

He said, "Of course. We will not speak to Norma about it. However, that is another matter I would like to discuss with you, but it will keep."

Sophie was intrigued but she was also exhausted and those kisses. The way they excited her. She already knew she was falling in love with this awful man. She just couldn't understand the reason why. She also knew that she was on dangerous ground because he was so very different from anyone she had ever known. Miss Sophie Sullivan was way beyond her comfort level with Mr. Benedict Cochrane.

CHAPTER 3

Sophie was anxiously looking out the tearoom window for her new friend. She had so much to tell her. So much to ask her. It was Monday at noon, and the plan was a light lunch and then shopping for a new hat—or at least that was the original plan.

Finally, Euphemia appeared, looking somewhat harassed and as she gratefully sat down with her friend, she said, "Well, Miss Sophie Sullivan, what have you done to my brother?"

Sophie looked at Euphemia with some concern, until she realized that her friend was having great fun with whatever Sophie had apparently done.

"He came back home, after disappearing for several hours. He reassured me that he had dropped you off hours beforehand and *announced*—I can think of no better word for it—his intention of *possibly* marrying you. He asked me to convince you to give up your steamer ticket, so he has more time to consider, and to try you out in several social situations, to see if you pass muster—his words—not mine! My advice Sophie is, do not dare! My brother seems to feel you are his for the taking as if you have no say in the matter. I always knew he was a bit off; thinking he is so far superior to the rest of us mere mortals, but this is far beyond his usual ill-tempered behavior! So, tell me, Sophie, what happened!"

Sophie said, "I hardly know where to start. He sort of proposed marriage to me but was concerned that he might just be infatuated and having two months for him to make up his mind seemed to bother him. He told me I was making a mistake in going to America. I told him he belonged in an insane asylum."

Euphemia laughed, and Sophie carried on with her story. She left out nothing—not even the kisses and her fear that he planned to ravish her in the woods. Sophie was well aware this woman knew Benedict Cochrane better than anyone, and she asked, "Has he displayed this behavior toward other women, that you are aware of? Oh Euphemia, I think I am falling for him, and I don't know if that is a very good idea."

Euphemia exclaimed, "Never! I believe he has fallen hard for you and is much displeased with himself in so doing. I understand he is taking you to watch him show off in court on Wednesday morning. He also informed me he was considering taking you to lunch in some French restaurant so he could closely observe your table manners. This man might be my brother, but he is an absolute cad, and he was blaming me for bringing you into his life! The thing is now that I have done so, he is smitten, and how he hates being smitten. His behavior was always off the beaten track but now, it is quite ridiculous. Whereas another man might be thanking God for his good fortune in winning the love of such a wonderful girl; Benedict is cursing the devil. Unfortunately, I can see you are falling for him just as hard, and I am not sure that I see him as husband material. Well not unless you truly give him the runaround and please do not make this easy on him."

Sophie wondered how this could be achieved, and to what end? She mused, "He might just be planning to keep me off that steamer, and then to drop me like a hot potato. Euphemia, he won't stop me going. I have too long looked forward to it, and in the end, I fear Barrister Cochrane's evil brain will be the victor over his heart; if indeed he has a heart. I am sorry Euphemia, I sometimes forget he is your brother. You are so very different from him."

Euphemia said, "Don't you even consider not taking that steamer to America! In fact, the thought occurs to me, if your aunt and uncle don't object, I might be on it with you. I cannot imagine continuing with my lonely existence after knowing my little friend. You have brought so much life into my world. Now what will you wear on Wednesday?"

Sophie said, "My best attire is my navy-blue suit. However instead of a hat, perhaps I could purchase a new blouse? I saw a navy pinstripe the last time I was in Pettigrew and Stephen's but thought it a little too stylish for my aunt and uncle. However, I hope they still have it in my size! It has a blue silk bow tie and I will wear a navy blue ribbon in my hair. Oh, but I suppose I should really wear a hat."

Euphemia said, "Well, since I am paying for lunch, how much do you have to spend?"

Sophie said, "Four pounds, but it will wipe me out for the rest of the week. Still no matter. Do you think I can manage it?"

Euphemia said, "Yes, together we will manage it and you will be so lovely, that my brother will be at a complete disadvantage."

Sophie said, "Euphemia, I cannot take money from you. Well can I pay you back by buying our lunch next week?"

Euphemia agreed and it turned out that Sophie's blouse was on sale. There were only two left, one very petite and one very large and Sophie purchased the petite blouse and also managed a navy-blue top hat with a blue feather and navy veil. Euphemia told her she looked magnificent and after the final transaction, Sophie was only indebted to her for one pound.

On this occasion, Sophie was dropped off at her house by the Cochrane horse-driven carriage and although Sophie noticed a decided atmosphere between Jack and Norma, her heart was too full to set much store by it.

∼

Wednesday morning at 9 o'clock sharp Benedict Cochrane drove up to the Sullivan's little bungalow on Balmuildy Road. He almost did not come—almost—but he felt his soul was on fire. He had to see her again. Perhaps on this occasion, she would not appear as delightful as on the last two occasions—possibly it was just a momentary whim.

Sophie Sullivan walked outside and up to his motor car and waited for him to open the door. She assumed his hesitancy in so doing was bad manners.

It was not that. Sophie Belle Sullivan looked like a duchess, not a shop girl, and Benedict wondered how this could be. Had she somehow bewitched him? Would he one day wake up and come to his senses? He helped her into his car and drove off, too fast, and very little was said between them both until they reached the High Court.

He then said. "I hope you are not squeamish, Sophie Belle. The case is rather gruesome. A woman hacked her husband to death. However, it was self-defense—or at least it was, according to my argument."

Sophie shook her head and when they walked into the grand edifice, her appearance with Barrister Cochrane caused much whispering and covert smiles. Benedict nodded at a few of the men but introduced her to none of them. He just led her up to the back of the courtroom gallery and disappeared until eventually appearing in his black gown and white wig, just before all were told to rise for Judge Hicks.

The judge saw Sophie, and she assumed the gossip had spread. He gave her a kind look before proceeding with the case.

The accused was brought out and she looked so wretched that Sophie almost felt sorry for her. What did this poor woman have to endure before she was driven to such a desperate act? The woman looked at Sophie several times and Sophie wanted to smile at her in reassurance, but she dared not.

Benedict was brilliant. So much play acting. He consulted his notes several times but for some reason Sophie knew he was not reading them, and as far as posturing, he was masterful at it. Sophie Belle Sullivan watched this man, fully aware that likely, he would never belong to her, but oh, how she dreamed that he would. She had never longed for a man before; yearned for a man, but she knew that day in court she had unwisely given her heart to this man, who would never be hers.

She wondered if he thought to make her his mistress. But then why take her to the High Court where all his colleagues would know his plan. Perhaps he did not care? Then she remembered how he spoke about falling in love with her. He almost proposed! Almost—but he felt she was beneath him and he consequently back-tracked upon it. He was quiet on their way to the High Court. Would he speak to her at lunch? Would he still be taking her to lunch? When the court session concluded, Sophie left the court room and sat down on a bench in the grand vestibule, where men dressed in suits—many wearing white wigs and black gowns were passing or gathering in hushed conversation. There were no other women present and several of the men smiled at her. She began to feel uncomfortable and out of place and it seemed Mr. Cochrane was gone for too long. Sophie decided she should leave.

She stood up and was about to exit the building when he came after her. "Where are you going?" He asked.

She responded, "Home, I suppose. Mr. Cochrane, you were brilliant. But you already know that. Actually, I am uncertain as to why I am here."

He said, "I invited you to come. Don't you remember? Anyway, there was a plea bargain, involuntary manslaughter. She will do just a year, maybe two."

Sophie said, "Well of course. You are incredibly brilliant, but you do not need the likes of me to tell you that. Goodbye Mr. Cochrane."

He grabbed her arm, "Wait! Why so downhearted? We are going to lunch together as planned."

Sophie could not quite shake the feeling of being lesser than this enigmatic man she now knew she loved. Benedict took her hand to lead her down the steps outside the High Court. Confused, Sophie tried to pull her hand away, even though her hand held in his felt thrilling, but he held on fast, and she could not do so without causing a scene. She blushed profusely and he laughed and bade her to take his arm instead, as they walked several blocks up St. Vincent Street to the highly acclaimed and well renowned French restaurant, La Bonne Auberge. He was pointing out several buildings and the architecture, almost as if she was a tourist, and he, the tour guide. She was about to mention that she had walked up and down that street many times, but then she chuckled to herself as she pondered the term, streetwalker, and she decided against making such a remark.

Benedict looked at her quizzically and was about to ask her what was so funny, when he instead decided she was no doubt nervous to be on her way with a gentleman to such an expensive eating establishment. When they finally reached the restaurant, he gallantly led her inside. Then came the test.

Sophie was glad French was her best subject in school and when Benedict Cochrane began to order fish for her, without enquiring as to what she would like, Sophie asked the waiter about the menu items which contained chicken. He responded to her in French, and she made her selection. The waiter then asked Benedict what the lady would prefer to drink.

Sophie felt this was the end of the line so why not? She said, "The lady would prefer champagne."

Benedict said, "Best make that a bottle of your finest." And then turned to Sophie.

"Sophie Belle, you are sad. Something is wrong. Okay, I am impressed you speak French. I am impressed with so many things about you. You are the most unique girl I have ever known. What did I do wrong?"

She said, "Yes, quite impressive for a shopkeeper's daughter. Something for you and your friends to laugh about."

He said, "That isn't even remotely true. Why are you saying this to me? Sophie Belle, I repeat, what did I do wrong?"

Sophie decided to be honest. "You made this shopkeeper's daughter fall in love with you. There I have said it. Go now and tell your friends about this foolish girl you met."

Benedict Cochrane's face lit up. He thought she hated his court room antics, but she didn't. She loved him and his heart was so full.

Before he could say a word in response she said, "You have spoiled my chance of falling in love with an American millionaire, so it will indeed have to be Plan B. However, although I have been long considering Plan B as the most appealing to me, I would have preferred to be taking on my new enterprise with a full heart, and not pining for some conceited barrister back in Scotland."

Benedict was intrigued by this beautiful, unusual girl, who somehow in her sadness was even lovelier to him. "I am flattered to be the cause of such misery. However, the matter is easily solved. Give up your steamer ticket and stay in Scotland. Perhaps we can find a solution—together."

Sophie felt she knew exactly what he meant and was not afraid to say it, most especially when he freshened her glass of champagne. "No, Mr. Cochrane, I will never be anyone's mistress—not even yours. Do you think you can rent a small flat—inexpensive of course—and install me there until you tire of me? I have not kept myself free and pure at age twenty-three to throw everything away on a man who finds me pretty at this moment in time, until the next pretty girl comes along. What then? Pay me off? Or just send me back to my brother."

Benedict sat back in his chair and smiled and shook his head. He was about to reassure this extraordinary young woman of his intentions. He knew he had a mistress in Edinburgh that he needed to get rid of before moving on with his life and his determination to do so, just became stronger than ever.

However, Sophie was off again, "So how are my table manners, Mr. Cochrane? Have I passed the test? Shame you had to spend so much money on lunch since I could have told you French was my best subject in school and that I was first in my class of thirty girls. Also, I have studied many books on etiquette, which includes table manners. I was well prepared for my new life in America. I even took elocution lessons. So broken heart or not. I will be on that steamer. My gift shop will be a huge success and I will very soon become the next Mr. Selfridge. In fact, I will be so rich that you and your cronies will be vying to be part of my circle of friends, but you will be the ones that don't pass muster, not me!"

Sophie stuck her nose in the air. She felt she had spoken brilliantly to put the brilliant barrister in his place, even though she wanted to slap that silly smile off his face.

She waited for him to speak and finally he did. "Well said, Miss Selfridge! However, you have gotten everything all wrong. I imagine that is something you are often guilty of, getting things all mixed up in that beautiful head of yours. Possibly all that lovely hair is the culprit. Anyway, I have decided that I might be prepared to marry you. Despite our class differences, and the fact that I cannot expect a dowry. I thought of marrying a titled lady, to elevate my status, which of course is much greater than yours, however I find you very entertaining. I think whichever lucky man wins your heart, whom it seems is me, will find you a delightful companion in bed. All that passion. What a waste to use it all on that nasty temper of yours."

Sophie was staring at him wide eyed; this magnificent man was in love with her. She could tell. Why else would he be sitting here with her? The mention of the word, "bed," made her stomach spin. Benedict Cochrane's black hair always seemed a bit messy although his manner of dress was impeccable. She felt she wanted to push back the lock of hair that had fallen on his forehead. She also wanted to kiss her finger and press it into the dimple on his chin, which she so adored. She waited for him to continue. Was he seriously about to propose marriage to her? Would she accept? What if he became a monster after her ship sailed? What if he changed his mind? And why did she so mistrust him? Was she being over-dramatic? Perhaps it was she, herself, who felt she was not good enough for the good barrister, and not the other way around.

Then he said, "I actually put together a list one night in my office. A list of pros and cons about making you my wife and there were more cons than pros. Your beauty and appearance are definite pros, along with your intelligence, and you have certainly worked hard at self-improvement. However, your background and upbringing are completely unacceptable, or they should be at the very least. Also, the years you spent looking after your sickly and dying parents? That makes you into a sad little creature. You would have to keep that to yourself. You probably shouldn't have even told me. Then there is your brother and his wife. I could hardly invite them to my home when I was entertaining friends. However, I find myself so drawn to you that I am seriously considering marrying you. The thing is, why? Am I simply infatuated by your beauty? Is it merely a very strong desire that I feel for you? Then again, I might just want to keep you in Scotland. I don't want you to take off to America at any rate; not while I am so strongly considering making you, my bride. However, you must surely understand such indecision, for the reasons I have given you."

For a moment Sophie was shocked, flabbergasted at such absolute rudeness. She had told this man she was in love with him, and he just spouted out everything that was wrong with her—things he would need to overlook in order to make her his wife. The arrogance of this man. Surely, he must be the most unpleasant man in Scotland. She thought, *what on earth is wrong with you, Sophie Sullivan? Stand up now and leave him sitting here. You saw him nod to a few fellow diners, although he didn't speak to them, and he certainly didn't introduce you. Stand up and proudly walk out the door. Surely even Mr. Benedict Cochrane is capable of embarrassment. A woman walking out on him in the middle of her expensive French lunch. Do it! Get up and walk out the door.*

Sophie Belle Sullivan was glad of her new hat. It made her feel especially elegant. She stood up, lifted her purse and said, "Go to hell,

Mr. Cochrane," before proudly walking out of the restaurant without a backward glance, to the utter astonishment of her fellow diners.

Once she was well away from the restaurant, she ran and grabbed a tramcar home. The tramcar was almost empty in the middle of the afternoon, and she sat upstairs and cried her eyes out, all the way to Bishopbriggs. She needed to talk to Euphemia and hoped to persuade her to walk to the park—just in case he came home. Barrister Cochrane was the last person on earth Sophie ever wanted to see again.

Benedict stood up and shrugged his shoulders and a fellow barrister shouted over, "This will be some apology. I am sure of it!"

Benedict laughed and paid the bill. He proceeded around the corner to the Cock and Bull pub where he ordered a pint of lager and a large whisky chaser. He sat down and wondered about his own sanity. He ripped that beautiful girl apart. He had been kinder to the procurator fiscal in the past. He knew exactly why he did it. He felt he was in so deep. He was besotted with Sophie Belle Sullivan. However, he needed to get Carlotta Ramirez off his back. He had stopped seeing her even before Sophie, but she had taken to writing him letters and was threatening to come and seek him out in Glasgow. She lived in Edinburgh—just a short train ride away. He needed this woman to never contact him again. He had to see her in person, for that to occur. He felt he hated her now and she needed to see that in his eyes. And then in six weeks this new woman whom he could not get out of his head, was leaving for America, unless of course he stopped her, and the only way to stop her would be to marry her. He knew she was in love with him. Theirs was truly the ridiculous 'love at first sight' situation but he had known her less than two weeks, seen her three times. He felt rushed and as if his life was tumbling out of control. Benedict Cochrane was used to being very much in control. If only his feeble-minded sister did not forget her purse. If only Sophie Belle Sullivan hadn't rescued her. Then he thought, *if only what, Barrister Cochrane? You would still be in the process of removing Carlotta from your sinful life and would possibly never know what it felt like to be in love. Well, you have made it into torture, Barrister Cochrane, now it is up to you to fix it.*

Benedict Cochrane staggered back to the flat in Kelvinside; the one his sister did not know he owned. It was a short ride on the subway from the High Courts and he often left his car there since it was a much nicer and safer place to leave it. He preferred his flat to the family mansion. He remembered Sophie Belle's words about him installing her in a tiny flat as his mistress. He smiled to himself, and thought, *if only, I would have those voluptuous curves stripped naked in five minutes, less than that!*

He decided—roses—six dozen delivered to the shop tomorrow late morning. He then congratulated himself on such an inspired and romantic gesture. She was bound to forgive him, most especially since he was quite certain that the girl who had never been kissed would never have been sent roses, let alone six dozen of them.

∽

Sophie was grateful to find Euphemia as she was just walking out of her front door. "Sophie?" she said with a questioning look. Sophie's face was tearstained, and Euphemia very well knew the culprit. "I was just about to take a walk to the park. Come along with me. Sophie, tell me what that stupid man has done or said to you now."

Sophie ran through her entire day right up to him listing all the cons against her, which included her nursing her sick parents and her background and upbringing being completely unacceptable.

Euphemia surprised her, "Good grief, Sophie, my brother really has it bad. Even for him, this behavior is utterly outrageous. I could never imagine him sitting in a fine expensive French restaurant, rhyming off everything he found, "unacceptable," in the beautiful woman seated across from him. He certainly blew this one. I cannot imagine you forgiving him very easily, and you mustn't do so."

Sophie was appalled, "Forgive him? I hate him! I hate him with every fiber of my being, my soul. I…"

And then she began to cry and Euphemia shushed her. "Well, all I can say is, I have never before come across two people—a man and a woman—so much in love and so very opposed to it."

Sophie said, "Euphemia how can he say such things if he loves me? He is positively insane!"

Euphemia patted Sophie's hand, "Well, I daresay he must have been astonished when you walked out on him. And you didn't say anything insulting? Other than telling him to go to hell?"

Sophie thought about it. "Well, I accused him of wanting me as a mistress, until someone prettier came along and he grew tired of me and of then paying me off or sending me back to my brother. I suppose some other things too; but I told him I was in love with him and that he had ruined my life."

Euphemia laughed, secretly she felt that one day this tempestuous couple would come together. However, that would not be on this side of the Atlantic. She said, "Sophie, my brother is in love with you, and he doesn't know what exactly to do about it. A normal man would find the solution easy enough and sweep you off your feet."

Sophie said, "As opposed to under the carpet," and both women laughed. Sophie felt the better for speaking with Euphemia. Perhaps it was not over with Benedict. Maybe he would regret what he said to her. Possibly she should not have walked out on him at lunch. After all, she started it. She was the one feeling lesser, most especially after watching him in the courtroom.

Then she said, as the two women parted company. "Well, I am not expecting an invitation to afternoon tea, this Sunday anyway."

And Euphemia shouted back, "Well let's just see what tomorrow brings!"

CHAPTER 4

Sophie Sullivan was forlorn as she stood in the front shop awaiting customers. She wasn't much in the mood for tidying shelves and Jack was quiet. He had something serious on his mind, and Sophie assumed, Norma. They had been fighting and arguing and it was all easily heard in the small bungalow. Sophie was more than anxious to get away and if the flat above the shop wasn't already rented out, she would have begged her brother to allow her to move in.

Of course, this wasn't the reason for her sadness. Through the course of her sleepless night, she was by now taking most of the blame for what had occurred the previous day with Benedict Cochrane. She had watched him weave his magical web in the courtroom. He was so very brilliant and charismatic, and she felt like little miss nobody. That was her issue all along. Of course, the fact that he reinforced the opinion she already had of herself by the things he said, was being explained away in her head by now. He was the most fascinating and handsome man she was ever likely to come across and for a moment she fully had his attention. Then she decided to act like a spoiled child.

Without even asking for it, it seemed Benedict Cochrane's appalling behavior was forgiven, and for no other reason than Sophie Sullivan was head over heels in love with him.

This did not change her plans to go to America. How could it? She could not really trust him, couldn't understand him and she had to get away from Norma. Jack was foolish in marrying her. He knew that now. He had been used. Sophie wondered briefly if he would do anything about it.

That was until she heard the bell on the shop door and saw a rather portly man carrying in several bunches of red roses. Sophie counted them, and there were six dozen. He said, "Miss Sophie Sullivan?"

Sophie nodded her head. These had to be from Mr. Cochrane.

The man said, "There is a gentleman outside parked on the side of the road and I am told to ask you to go out to thank him."

Sophie was bemused. She tidied her hair but was wearing one of her oldest summer dresses, so old fashioned and careworn. She chided herself for feeling so depressed that morning that she wore the worst thing she could find. However, she would carry the roses and he might not notice the dress.

She walked out, carrying all six dozen roses, with her nose in the air. She said, "Thank you, Mr. Cochrane. The roses are beautiful. Is this an apology?"

He pushed open the passenger door, still seated in his car and said, "No, because it is you who owes me one. Hop in."

She immediately obeyed gently laying the roses in the back seat of the car, and he sped off, without saying anything further to her.

She wondered where they were going but sat quietly, miserably conscious of the awful dress she had on. Eventually she said, "I did not expect you. I was tidying shelves and just put on this old dress. Besides it is so very warm today."

He looked around at her and felt his heart melt. He was reminded of the fairy tale, 'Cinderella' that Euphemia used to love as a child. Both times he was with her, she was wearing the same blue skirt. The previous day she had added a matching jacket and jaunty new hat, and he suddenly felt so tender towards this beautiful young girl who owned his heart and was attempting to explain away her careworn old dress.

He lied, "It is very pretty Sophie Belle, so colorful."

Sophie cringed; oh, why didn't she wear something a little more presentable? And then she thought, *well Sophie Sullivan, surely not the blue suit again. Jack needs to give you a raise or a bonus or something, you need some new clothes.*

He carried on, "It is a bit small for you. I mean up top. Perhaps you should undo a few of those buttons."

Sophie looked down and indeed they did appear ready to pop open. She repeated, "It is very warm today. Why don't you take off your coat and tie then?"

He said, "I will, if you will," as he pulled his car over to the side of the winding road which led the way through the Campsie Hills, and he proceeded to do so. It was the first time Sophie saw him not so buttoned up and perfect, and she liked him better. As an added bonus, he removed his gold cufflinks and handed them to her, as he rolled up his sleeves and opened the top three buttons of his silk shirt.

Sophie was awestruck by the sight of his black hair showing now on his arms and the top of his chest, and Benedict caught her admiring him. "My great-grandmother was Italian. The coloring came through on me. Do you like dark hairy men, Sophie Belle?"

Sophie blushed profusely and that answered his question. He said, "Your turn now, Miss Sophie Belle Sullivan."

She made to give him back his cufflinks, but he said to keep them. "Wear them with your blue and white pinstripe blouse. I liked that."

Sophie just looked at them and said, "Really I shouldn't," and he laughed when she wrapped them in her handkerchief and put them in her pocket, even upon saying this.

She felt brazen yet exhilarated. The dress was too tight and uncomfortable. She undid three buttons and then realized her décolleté was revealed. She quickly made to button herself back up, but Benedict stopped her. He then pulled down her hair, wrapped it around his fist with one hand and pulled her to him with the other. His kiss was soft and loving. Sophie could think of no other way to describe it. He opened his eyes and told her to open hers as he proceeded to kiss her while they stared into each other's eyes. Sophie felt as if she was losing control of her senses and finally jumped up.

Benedict laughed quietly and said, "I know you do not believe this, Sophie Belle Sullivan, but you will never be in safer hands than mine. I have brought a blanket and a picnic basket. Are you hungry?"

They spent a glorious afternoon, and it was such a lovely spot, not far from Bishopbriggs, but in the middle of the Campsie Hills, it could have been a hundred miles away. The weather was perfect, and Benedict told Sophie that the Campsie's averaged considerable rainfall every year, and in fact it rained there almost every day. Therefore, today was a gift.

He spoke softly and romantically of the beauty of the Highlands, he seemed to love so dearly. He described the Grampian Mountains which occupied almost half of Scotland and included the Cairngorms and Scotland's highest mountain, Ben Nevis, at almost a mile high. He told her there were over thirty thousand lochs in Scotland, ranging from small lochans to the most famous lochs, such as Loch Ness, fabled to be the home of the Loch Ness Monster, Loch Lomond, which was over twenty-five miles long, and Loch Katrine, which provides Glasgow's fresh drinking water. He talked of the Western Isles and of his favorite, the largest, the Isle of Skye. He spoke of the wildness of the unforgiving North Atlantic Ocean, and of the Outer Hebrides, and in particular, St. Kilda and how he once sailed there in a fishing trawler, in trepidation of being swept into the ocean. He said one day he would like to take Sophie to see the real Scotland and the majestic beauty it contained.

Sophie sat enthralled by the sound of his voice and the magical way he was describing the land he loved so well. She told him that if he ever grew tired of defending villains, he might consider taking up poetry, and he surprised her by saying that he sometimes penned a few lines to help him relax. He said they were nothing wonderful, but Sophie said she would love to read them anyway. He said one day he would write one especially for her.

They ate chicken salad sandwiches and vanilla sponge cake, and then Benedict opened a bottle of wine. He was an absolute gentleman, that whole afternoon, in a way she had never before seen him, gentle and relaxed. Sophie laid back and he kissed her lovingly, murmuring wonderful things in her ear. There was no mention of America nor of their difference in social status. He kept it light and romantic and by the time he dropped her home just around 6 p.m., Sophie Sullivan was completely in love and positively confused. She put the cuff links under her pillow and folded up her dress which would always hold sweet memories. She had the feeling that this was Benedict Cochrane's way of saying goodbye the more she thought about it, and her happiness turned to sorrow. Surely the good barrister was too good for her. He knew about so many things, and Sophie felt she knew so little.

Jack and Norma were soon home from the shop and immediately the arguing began. Sophie was counting the days till she left but she still had five weeks to go. She would have to endure. She was quite certain by now that there would be no offer of marriage—no further afternoons filled with love. Sophie went to bed early and left her brother and sister-in-law to it, as she placed her pillow over her head and cried into the handkerchief that contained the gold cuff links. She thought, *my payment for all those kisses.*

It seemed Sophie was correct in her interpretation of that wonderful Thursday. The haberdashery was busy that Saturday, although as usual, Sophie was hiding in the back shop. In the mid-afternoon, Jack appeared with a package wrapped in brown paper and tied with string. He told her a young lad had dropped it off for her.

He said, "Books, I will wager. Open it and see."

Sophie opened the package, and sure enough, the contents were a collection of poetry by Lord Byron and a pictorial history of Scotland.

Both books were beautifully bound, and although there was no note to identify who the books were from, Sophie knew it must be Benedict Cochrane.

She ran outside fully expecting to find him in his motor car, but he was not there. Saddened and confused, she walked back inside the shop. She told Jack she didn't feel well, and he allowed her to go home.

As soon as she got home, she opened the book of poetry first and inside the pages which featured the poem, *She Walks in Beauty*, was a pressed yellow rose—the meaning of which Sophie thought to be, "Thank you."

She now knew for sure that Benedict Cochrane was saying goodbye, or why else yellow?

Sophie gathered all the red roses, which were scattered around the tiny bungalow, and threw them onto the compost heap in the garden. They were still in bloom, but Sophie felt her heart was broken.

Jack came home that evening alone and Sophie thought, *good, no arguing, Norma must be away with her pals to the Crow Tavern in Bishopbriggs*. He went straight in to see if Sophie was okay. She showed him the books and the yellow rose.

Jack said, "Most men do not know the meaning of flowers. At least I do not. Do you mind if I borrow the pictorial. I cannot be bothered with poetry."

Sophie handed him the book and said, "He talked about Scotland on Thursday afternoon. He spoke beautifully and I told him he should be a poet. He mentioned that he had dabbled with that. He must believe I am totally uneducated and stupid. I should have said we read Lord Byron in school, although I found that poem a bit depressing. Also, I do not have raven hair, as written in the poem. I should have also told him that I studied history and not geography. I could have questioned him on the Battle of Culloden and the Highland Clearances—although I am sure he is an expert on all that stuff too. I don't believe Euphemia went to university either."

Jack said, "Well I am sure he thinks very little of her intelligence, although you are much smarter than her, and of me, sister Sophie. You are doubtless cleverer than many in these parts, most especially my wife. I'm away to look at your book. I do need to talk to you; but not now. It is important, however."

Sophie was too wrapped up in her misery to care. She placed the book of poetry under her pillow, along with her other farewell gift—his cufflinks.

She was to meet Euphemia at the Willow Tea Rooms that Monday at noon, as had become their usual routine, but she did not really expect her to come. She was by now quite certain the Cochranes had grown tired of slumming with Sophie Sullivan—old Sullivan the haberdasher's daughter.

⁓

Jack again mentioned that he needed to speak to her that night. Sophie asked where Norma was, and he just said, "At her ma's," and gave Sophie a couple of pounds to buy a new summer dress. He knew she was once again depressed about Cochrane, but that was nothing new.

Sophie looked anxiously out of the window. Would Euphemia simply stand her up? Then suddenly she appeared, rushing and looking harassed, as was her usual, and Sophie's heart was gladdened. Sophie said, "I thought you weren't coming. I had a wonderful afternoon with your brother on Thursday and he gave me his gold cufflinks, a volume of Lord Byron's poetry and a pictorial history of Scotland, as parting gifts. Well actually he didn't give me the books. Jack told me a young lad dropped them off at the haberdashery. He included a yellow rose, which means 'thank you.'"

Euphemia said, "I knew I should have come to see you. In fact, I almost stopped by on Sunday afternoon but could hear arguing, so I just kept on my way past your house. Anyway, I doubt my brother has studied the meaning behind the colors of roses. We have a beautiful yellow rose bush in our garden, however."

Sophie said, "Jack wants to speak with me tonight and Norma wasn't there this morning. Whatever he wants to talk about, I cannot imagine it to be very pleasant."

"Not to change the subject, Sophie, but my brother disappeared all weekend. Not so unusual for him, but he came back last night and informed me of a white tie ball at the City Chambers, Saturday next. He told me he would be taking you to see how you got on. He also told me to ensure you have something "decent" to wear and not some old "flowery frock" as he put it. I told him you can hardly afford to waste money on some fine fancy ball gown, in order that he might again test your manners. I hope that I haven't offended you?"

Sophie said she was far beyond being offended, when it came to Benedict Cochrane, but inside she could feel her excitement build up again and thought, *confound this man and the effect he has on me.*

Euphemia excitedly continued, "Sophie. You will not believe it. He gave me a one-pound note, to pass along to you, along with his *secretary's* birthday present."

Sophie was aghast. "A pound? Oh Euphemia, please give it back to him and tell him to use it to purchase some manners!"

Euphemia said, "I hoped you would say something like that but still, I think you should buy a new dress. If you don't mind me asking, do you have any money with you? Lunch is on me today."

Sophie added it up in her head, "I can go as high as four pounds since my brother gave me an extra couple pounds to buy a new dress—isn't that a coincidence? Although he didn't have a ball gown in mind. Still it is much more than your brother allowed for such an undertaking. My brother is having some major problems with his wife. Another nasty woman, different kind of nasty than your visitors that Sunday, at afternoon tea. It was rather sweet of your brother to rescue me. Sometimes he is almost human in his behavior. A pound?

Well, I will keep the birthday package, since I picked everything out for myself anyway."

Euphemia said thoughtfully, "Oh yes, he invited those two couples intentionally. I dislike both of those women, and well he knows it. Sophie, you are in love with him, I can see it in your eyes when we speak of him. I am not so sure that is a good thing—although I would adore you to be my sister, but he really is a dreadful man. He is concerned that you are not of his social class. He actually said that and berated me for bringing you into his life."

Sophie said, "Well that is his fault. Had he not come to the shop to insult me, we would never have met. He is very good looking. I am sure he has considered many women of his social class, not to be good enough either. I wonder what he sees in me—I mean other than another pretty face. I cannot believe I am talking this way to his sister, but it is the truth. Anyway, this whole white tie thing. He knows I have never attended such an affair. I am sure he wants me to struggle and blunder, so he can be free of me, as not good enough for him."

Euphemia said, "I am sad to say I agree. Although I am surprised and a little confused by him sending you poetry and the history of Scotland. What a peculiar thing to do? His behavior has become most uncommon. Anyway, we will do the best we can with your gown and here." She took a small package from her purse, "I have brought you a pair of white silk gloves. I have never worn them."

Sophie opined, "Perhaps he wishes to further my education," as she opened the package and took out the gloves. "Euphemia, these are exquisite. I surely cannot accept them?"

Euphemia said, "Nonsense, it is the least I can do for bringing my brother into your life. Your manners, speech and self-confidence are all excellent qualities to go along with your beauty, however, I am sure Marsha and Audrey have put it about that you are a shopkeeper's daughter. They were so clearly jealous of how their husbands, as well as Benedict, stood that Sunday afternoon, enraptured by your beauty and charm. In fact, after you walked outside with my brother, Harvey

Martin called you a "cracker." That was indeed quite a compliment coming from him. He also opined that Benedict may well have met his downfall. Think of it as a test. I know that is exactly what my horrendous brother is considering it."

"Oh my, I cannot quite believe this, such self-important and pompous men, paying me, Sophie Sullivan, such compliments." Sophie was bemused by the whole situation. "Euphemia, how could I have fallen so badly for a man who may have fallen for me, but would prefer if he hadn't done so?"

Euphemia said, "Well believe it you must, and I can tell you truly want to attend the ball, so let's go and see what we can find for you to wear."

The ladies walked across the street to Copeland and Lye department store. It was known to sell the latest Paris fashions; however, Sophie's choice of gowns was extremely limited with only four pounds at her disposal. Soon Euphemia had her trying on gowns that cost ten pounds and more, and when Sophie protested, she said, "I have an account in this store. By the time my brother gets the invoice you will have already triumphed at this silly Glasgow City Chambers annual ball. Now for underclothing and shoes."

In the end they had spent almost thirty pounds and since Sophie still had her four pounds, she treated her new dear friend to dinner at the Corn Exchange Restaurant. They both ordered haddock and chips and a half pint of shandy. They felt mischievous, although Sophie wondered about Benedict's reaction when he received the bill from Copeland's. She said, "Euphemia, I cannot believe I allowed you to talk me into this. It will take me years to pay back such a huge debt! Oh, but I have never seen such beautiful clothes, never mind owning them. I wish you were coming too. What if he finds out that these things were not purchased for you?"

Euphemia said, "One pound? The effrontery of that gesture! Believe me, he may never admit it, but once he sees you in that gown—he will be truly beaten! Just make sure he doesn't see anything else. Well perhaps a glimpse of your ankle."

The women ordered a second shandy. By now it was six o'clock and both knew they might soon be in serious trouble with their brothers—most especially Euphemia—so why not make the most of it?

Suddenly Euphemia quietly exclaimed, "Oh dear goodness Sophie! Cripes! Look who just walked in with a few of his colleagues? Hide! Let us see if we can sneak out. Oh, confound it! What is he doing here?"

Both women were a little tipsy—the consumption of two half pints of shandy to blame—and Sophie was giggling, hiding her head behind the menu which was standing on the table. "I still have to pay the bill. I have to ask the waitress! Oh dear! What are we to do?"

Euphemia was giggling too, and grabbed the menu from the next table which was empty. She also hid behind her menu; never could she remember having such a fit of the giggles.

Sophie whispered, "Perhaps he will just have a quick pint and leave."

Then both women really lost it. They heard a voice, and he was standing right at their table.

"Did you both get lost? I don't believe this to be the Willow Tea Rooms. Miss Sullivan, I fear you are a frightfully bad influence upon my sister. Ah, such a shame, I see shopping bags. You may as well return the dress; in the event it was for the City Chambers ball. I fear you would be an embarrassment to me. I have decided not to take you after all. Sorry about the misunderstanding but I fear I must find a more suitable young lady to escort to this prestigious annual event. I hope you aren't too disappointed."

Sophie went from a fit of the giggles to abject humiliation. She was certain other diners heard every word he said to her, including his colleagues.

Euphemia wanted to slap her brother's face—right there and then. She was about to tell him off when he said, "Okay Euphemia, let's go.

I will take you home." He took her arm, quite forcefully, and threw a few pounds on the table. He said, "For dinner," and marched his sister out of the restaurant to the curious and outraged stares of the other diners, all looking at Sophie with shock and sympathy.

One of Benedict's colleagues offered Sophie a lift home. She thanked him and declined. She picked up the money, grateful that she had sufficient in her purse to pay the bill. She gave it to the gentleman and said, quite loudly, "Please return this money to the good barrister tomorrow, if you would be so kind."

The man took the money and promised that he would do so and said, "Miss, I am horrified at Mr. Cochrane's behavior this night to a delightful young lady. I will be sure to tell him that when I return his money. Will you allow me at least to pay the bill? It would be my pleasure. My name is Sir Alfred Hicks, and forgive me for saying this, but you are so very lovely."

Sophie's heart was lifted by this man's kindness, and she recognized him as the judge who presided at the trial that past Wednesday morning. He was a titled gentleman and seemed appalled at Benedict Cochrane's behavior. This helped to mend her damaged heart—and she felt such gratitude towards the kindly judge.

Sophie politely declined and paid the bill herself. She lifted her purchases, which she would need to return to Copeland's and ran to catch the tramcar home. She was looking out the window crying. Never had she been treated so by anyone—and by the man who had kissed her so lovingly the previous Thursday? The man who spoke so romantically of his native land? To throw money on the table and leave her to find her own way home at 6 p.m.? To announce to the world that he was breaking their date—that she should return the dress she had purchased for it— because he *feared* she would embarrass him? To declare openly that he deemed it necessary to find a more suitable young lady to escort to such a *prestigious* event?

She got off the tramcar a stop before her regular one. There was a park in the center of Bishopbriggs, within walking distance of her house. It was July so the sun was still high in the sky, even at half past six. Sophie Belle Sullivan sat on a bench and cried her eyes out, oblivious to passersby. Then she realized her brother was standing looking down upon her. She blurted out her sad and sorry tale between sobs and Jack Sullivan said, "Right. That is enough. I am taking you home and then I will go and call on this scoundrel."

Jack looked in the bag. He saw the pretty white gown, and ladies silk underclothing and his heart broke for his sister. He said, "He can return it all. Or his bloody stupid sister can. She should have stood her ground, instead of leaving you there."

Sophie was so grateful to her brother. She said, "I spent almost a whole week's wages on dinner. I gave his money to his colleague. I think the man felt sorry for me, and he was a titled gentleman, Sir Alfred Hicks. He offered to pay for my dinner and even to give me a lift home. Of course, I thanked him, but declined."

Jack said, "Never worry, bonnie lass. You and I have a few things to discuss—tomorrow when you are rested. Turns out Norma has a fancy man and has been giving him money out the till! I wondered why the books weren't balancing."

This statement surely took Sophie's attention away from herself. She was shocked. She was never fond of Norma. She knew there was something amiss in her brother's marriage—but this?

He continued, "I threw her out this morning. She is away home to her ma's. She said she was going to get her brothers to set about me. They already paid me a visit—to ask if there was any chance of reconciliation. I chased them. Anyway, we will talk tomorrow about everything. I am shutting the shop for the day. I will hang a sign, family bereavement or some such hogwash. Come on. I am taking you home."

Sophie was aware that her brother had gone back out and took the shopping bag. It was nice to have someone on her side and she thought she would stay awake. However, all that crying, and emotion took its toll, and she was soon fast asleep.

Jack Sullivan was livid. His lovely sister, treated in such a shameful way. Jack was as tall and well-built as Benedict Cochrane. He intended to throw every pretty item contained in that bag right at him and his sister. How could a so-called gentleman be so cruel to such a sweet young girl who so recently rescued his sister from embarrassment and humiliation at the Willow Tea Rooms?

~

Benedict Cochrane immediately turned his car around. What the hell did he just do? However already Sophie was gone, and an extremely rude, Sir Alfred Hicks, the High Court judge he had been trying to impress, called his behavior shameful—which of course it was.

He handed Benedict his few pound notes and told him that although he offered, the lovely young lady paid for both meals herself. "I am quite certain it took all of her wages, since she didn't seem like one of these idle women who will be attending this City Chambers ball." Sir Alfred turned to Euphemia and said, "Miss Cochrane, would you be so kind as to give me the young lady's address? I intend to call upon her with an invitation to accompany me to the ball, since I have just decided to attend. I do hope she will oblige me. It will be such a treat—to walk in with such a beauty upon my arm. Hopefully it might cheer her up a little. Cochrane, why don't you take your sister. Nice of you to rescue her tonight." The man then turned his back on him, and Benedict left and drove silently home, feeling sick inside, cringing at the unpardonable things he had said to this lovely girl, whom he knew deep inside he was in love with, as his sister cried and berated him, all the way to Bishopbriggs.

When he pulled into his driveway, Euphemia was about to run out of the car, but was stopped in her tracks. Her brother shouted, "Why did I do that? Why did I leave her there? Why did I say such terrible things to her? What man would do that? My God Euphemia, what have I done? You were both laughing—laughing at me—no doubt about her making a man in my position fall for her—my clumsy attempts of romance. She thought it a big joke—and now she has traded up and found herself a judge and knight in shining armor. Sir Alfred Hicks to the rescue."

Euphemia looked at him in puzzled amazement. "Romance?" She shouted back in shock. "What attempts of romance are you referring to? Giving her a couple of old books from your library? Taking her to a fine French restaurant, where you could verbally list everything, you found unacceptable about her background and life? Well, you have most certainly lost her, if indeed you ever had her in the first place, and you have caused me to lose a very dear friend. We had a wonderful day—until you showed up. We were laughing because we were hiding from you behind our menus. We expected a sarcastic rebuke. Actually, I don't really know what we expected but it certainly wasn't your shameful behavior toward such a lovely girl. That was your humiliation, brother, not Sophie's."

They had gotten out of the car, and he was standing leaning on it with his head down.

Euphemia shouted back, "I had the impression that your attentions to her had been very well received. I told her that I thought she had quite fallen for you, and she didn't disagree. I should have included a stronger warning, Benedict, you are not a very nice man. I do not see how I can stay here now. I have my inheritance. I will be looking for alternative accommodation."

~

They were home less than an hour when the doorbell rang, and Jack Sullivan did not wait to be invited in. He was holding the Copeland's carrier bag. He had murder in his eyes. He could see that Sophie's friend had been crying. As for Cochrane, he had clearly gone home and hit the whisky bottle, since he looked like hell.

Benedict said, "Go ahead. I deserve it, I will not even fight back. I will stand and take my just desserts. We went right back for her. She had already left. Sullivan, I went right back for her. Oh my God, what have I done?"

Jack said, I was about to throw these clothes at you piece by piece. I looked through the bag. A lovely white dress and all the trimmings. She would have looked like a princess, you arrogant, pompous bastard."

Euphemia interrupted, "No please have her keep them. Sir Alfred Hicks intends to call on her tomorrow to see how she is. I gave him the address of your shop. He also intends to take her to the ball at the City Chambers. He suggested that I go with my brother, and I now intend to do so. I am looking forward to watching him suffer through the night since I feel quite certain that Sophie Belle will be the belle of the ball."

Jack Sullivan could easily tell that this Cochrane chap was suffering—his own fault—maybe it would all work out for him in the end.

Benedict asked, rather hesitantly, "How is she?"

Jack said, "Well considering I found her on a park bench, crying her eyes out. My impression is that she has been better. Still, I will tell her…no maybe not, in case he turns out to be a lying bastard like you, Cochrane. If he comes it will be a nice surprise. I was going to shut the shop. I will keep it open—for him. We shall see. Miss Cochrane, is this knight in shining armor a handsome fellow?"

Euphemia responded, "Yes, he is not at all bad looking and he is a judge in the High Court. Possibly a little old for Sophie, must be forty—at least. Still, that is only six years older than my brother. Perhaps he is too old for her too. So set in his ways."

Benedict finally recovered himself. "Pray tell me where did Miss Sullivan get the money for these fancy clothes? Most especially, since she got stuck paying for dinner?"

Euphemia answered easily, "I put them on my account. So, I suppose that means from you, dear brother."

Jack left after that. He felt better. This barrister chap absolutely had feelings for his sister. Just a bit soft in the head. How he prayed this Sir Alfred turned up. He also surprised himself by having gotten rid of Norma. He would never take her back. He would divorce her. Once he and this Cochrane fellow were on speaking terms, he would ask him for some free advice or possibly he could ask this judge, if he shows up. Jack thought, *I might be the one to move to America*. He would sell the shop and the house. Give some money to his sister, since she well deserved it, looking after their parents all those years. Even when Norma came on the scene, she never lent a hand.

CHAPTER 5

Miss Sophie Sullivan was a nervous wreck. She was attending a ball at the City Chambers with a judge! Sir Alfred Hicks, the gentleman who had been so kind to her that awful night.

She and Euphemia were friends again. Euphemia had called around to see her the next day. She was in tears in her shame and explained that she and her brother went back for Sophie, but she was already gone. She further explained that he was wretched.

"Make the most of this ball. You will be the belle of it. I just know it! He thought we were laughing about him. It occurs to me that my brother has simply no clue about women—young ladies at the very least. Still tell me something, Sophie...."

Sophie interrupted her, "I can't imagine a future without him in it—nasty, dreadful man that he is. I do not know what that says about me. Oh Euphemia, I only want to dance with him at the ball, and of course, I cannot."

Euphemia said, "Why not? Sir Alfred no doubt fully expects that. Unless of course Benedict prefers to dance with his sister all night!"

Sophie told Euphemia about her brother, "Jack is happier than I have ever seen him. He hasn't yet filed for divorce. He said he was waiting until the big romance was back on. I told him, he might have a long wait!"

Euphemia invited Sophie to come to her house to get dressed and that she should stay overnight. The ball would go on until the wee hours, and this way her brother, Jack, wouldn't worry.

The women knew that their plans were of great interest to Benedict. He said not a word of approval or disapproval. They felt that in truth, he didn't know what to say.

~

Benedict Cochrane was consumed with the thought of this ball. He should have been taking the most delightful girl in the room as his partner but instead, he was taking his sister, and Miss Sophie Belle was going with Judge Hicks—and it was all his own fault.

He knew Hicks was doing this to him deliberately because on that same day, when he made such a fool of himself in the Corn Exchange, Judge Hicks had asked him who was the delightful creature he had brought to the High Court the previous week. Benedict had admitted that she was indeed delightful but added that she was not of his social class and therefore he must tread carefully. He still believed that, and now it seemed her brother was getting divorced. More scandal. It was all a total mess, but he knew he had to get her back, or his life may as well be over. His desire was consuming him along with the thought of the ball. He was in a mental tangle, and now right at this very moment she was down the hallway, taking a bath. Sophie Belle was naked in his house. He thought *I could need something and have to ask Euphemia where to find it. My brush!* He messed up his hair and knocked so quietly that his sister didn't hear him. He walked into her room and said, "Have you seen my new hairbrush? It has gone missing."

He heard a scream and the bathroom door slam shut.

"Oh," he said, "Forgot you had a visitor. Possibly she has my brush. Shall I ask her?"

Euphemia was beside herself. "Benedict, why would I take your brush, or for that matter why would Miss Sullivan take it? And why are you in my chamber? I have a guest who is currently bathing, with the expectation of privacy. Would you mind GETTING OUT!"

Benedict shouted, "This is my house, and I installed the plumbing with hot water. I hope you are enjoying your nice warm bath, Miss Sophie Belle Sullivan!"

Sophie was so amused. Her heart was singing. Whether this man liked it or not, he was in love with her. She had already dried herself with the towel which was now wrapped around her head. She was wearing her dressing gown and was therefore *almost* decently clad, although she was naked underneath, and her feet were bare. She decided to walk into Euphemia's chamber, emitting the pungent aroma of roses.

"Oh dear, Mr. Cochrane, I never thought. Do you charge for hot water? I did not bring my purse, since my escort would never require me to carry money. I am afraid that I do not have your brush. I am sure it is where you left it. If not, you can purchase one at the haberdashery on Tuesday, since Monday is my day off, and I might be able to sell you one for half price, in exchange for your hot water."

Benedict knew she was naked under that dressing gown, a fact that was torturing him. Her bare feet were delightful and he so desired to see the rest of her. He knew she felt exactly as he did. He was quite certain of that, or else why was she teasing him?

Euphemia again told him to get out and then Benedict thought he had an inspired idea.

He said, "Euphemia, I think you should attend the ball with Sir Alfred. He is too old for your friend. And then I don't mind taking her instead of you."

Sophie had taken off her towel and was brushing her long blonde hair and Benedict was prolonging this, since he didn't want to leave that room with the smell of roses, and the utterly delicious Sophie Belle Sullivan, deliberately primping in front of him.

Euphemia said, "Don't you recall Benedict, you were concerned about being embarrassed by Miss Sullivan? I am not sure why, since she will be the loveliest girl in attendance. So, the answer is no. Go away."

And finally, he left saying, "I will be watching you Sophie Belle Sullivan. Keeping a check on your behavior."

Euphemia rolled her eyes and walked over and whispered to her friend. I think my brother is completely smitten. Good thing—that whole incident—and Sir Alfred rescuing you. It seems he has a rival! Here let me brush your hair. It is so beautiful and my, you have so much of it!"

~

An hour later, Sir Alfred arrived, fully rigged out in his white tie and cutaway as indeed was Benedict, who offered the judge a whisky. He said, "You know you are too old for her, Sir Alfred. She is only twenty-three. She looks younger with her hair down, although I suppose it will be up tonight. She is also totally innocent in the ways of men, clueless, since I am the first man who ever kissed her. Anyway, they have been getting ready for hours. Using up all the hot water and the upstairs smells like a whorehouse. I don't know why my sister is bothering with all this primping. I will not be dancing with her. I will be in the gaming bar."

Sir Alfred was very amused. "You know, Cochrane, I prefer you when you are not making up to me and trying to impress. I am now in the company of the real Benedict Cochrane. The good barrister who has grown tired of setting guilty men free and aspires to be a judge. I was aware all that affability was put on for my benefit. Anyway, I agree. I am probably a bit too old for the lovely Miss Sullivan. The first man who ever kissed her. You should be honored since I'm quite sure she could have her choice of any of the young bucks at the ball tonight. You are indeed most fortunate, although I doubt you will be the last one to do so, and I doubt you will be given another opportunity to kiss the lovely lady after your atrocious behavior toward her. How old are you by the way, Cochrane?"

Benedict said, "Younger than you. You know this is complete and utter nonsense. I should be the one taking Sophie Belle Sullivan. Whether she knows it or not, she would be much happier in my company."

Sir Alfred was enjoying himself, "In the gaming bar? What? Drinking whisky? Although more is the pity. Your sister, Euphemia, as she has allowed me to call her, is quite delightful and with such a keen wit. I am surprised that I have never met her before. I would have been honored to escort her. However, I am of the understanding that you fear embarrassment—should you escort Miss Sullivan—so I will be more than happy to risk it."

Benedict thought, *perhaps I can persuade him,* and said, "Possibly more embarrassing to attend such an event with one's sister. I know you set me up. I was angry about my sister frequenting pubs with this new friend of hers. I have gotten over it. Euphemia may go to pubs if that is what she cares to do. She is past thirty and can take care of her own virtue. She got me into this predicament in the first place, with this new bosom friend, and as far as kissing, I will need to keep an eye on her. She will not be kissing anyone tonight, unless of course it is me. I have already told her I will be watching her and keeping a check on her behavior."

Sir Alfred laughed. Benedict Cochrane was clearly besotted with the young lady, whether he cared to admit it or not. "I hear Miss Sullivan will soon be off to New York. Cochrane, the world is changing, and we must move with the times. You do realize that many of the wealthiest men in New York—dollar millionaires—grew up with no shoes on their feet. Miss Sullivan is hardly that—although I am quite certain her feet are as pretty as the rest of her."

Benedict was reminded of earlier that evening, "I saw her bare feet earlier. I was looking for my brush in my sister's chamber and she appeared barefoot. Well actually, I was just pretending to be looking for it. I know, abominable behavior. They are indeed delightful. Sir Alfred...."

Sir Alfred interrupted him, "She might prefer to go to the ball with you—rather than me. However, there is the whole possibility of embarrassment for you to consider. Were you about to ask me to switch partners? Well, I am quite certain that your sister has little desire to accompany you, and I find her charming. I also prefer not to partner a young lady who would prefer to be escorted by another man. Therefore, I suppose the decision rests with the young lady in question. Why not ask her? I will not be offended. Not now when I see how the land lies."

Benedict said, "What do you mean? How the land lies...."

Sir Alfred said, "I thought you were so well educated, the eminent barrister, Mr. Benedict Cochrane. Why not just accept it. You are in love with her. Of course, she might still hate you. Such horrendous behavior. But perhaps not."

Benedict said, "So you will allow me to accompany her? You are willing to take my sister?"

"Sir Alfred laughed, "Cochrane, you surprise me. The tough talking barrister needs another man's permission to approach the woman he loves. Wait, I hear the ladies coming down. We should go meet them at the stairway."

The two men walked out, and Benedict Cochrane could hardly believe his eyes. He already knew how lovely she was. However tonight she was positively radiant. She looked at him and then quickly away to the man she supposed was to be her partner. But he saw it. She loved him as he loved her, and in that moment nothing else mattered.

∼

Sophie was aware that Benedict Cochrane was staring at her, as she made her way downstairs. She had taken Euphemia's arm for which she was grateful. Sophie was so nervous that she could feel herself shaking. Benedict Cochrane was so handsome, so completely captivating and how she wished he was to be her partner. Then she felt she was being unkind to the gentleman who had rescued her and asked her to the ball. However, she could not help herself. For all that he might be the most disagreeable man in Scotland, she had fallen in love with him. She would never want another man. She almost felt like crying and then they reached the bottom and Euphemia squeezed her arm and turned towards Sir Alfred who approached her and kissed her hand.

Sophie stood in shock, not sure what to do. She looked wide-eyed at Benedict, and he was smiling at her. He approached her, and said, "Miss Sullivan, there has been a change in plans. It seems I am to be your escort this evening."

She turned to Euphemia and Sir Alfred, a shocked look upon her face, and they were both smiling at her.

Euphemia said, "Sophie dearest, did you honestly believe I had any intention of spending the evening with my odious brother? Sir Alfred and I agreed to change partners almost from the beginning; providing of course he passed the test."

Benedict turned, "What test? What are you both talking about?"

Then he turned back to Sophie, smiling at him and he could feel her love for him. Despite everything, his dreadful behavior, and he smiled down at her and said, "Never mind. Who cares? A sherry for the ladies before we depart. My lady seems a little nervous although there is no need. You will outshine every other lady in attendance."

Sophie could not resist, "So you are no longer afraid that I will embarrass you, Mr. Cochrane?"

Benedict said, "Actually I am still afraid of that. Where is your dance card?"

Sophie took the card hanging with the little pencil—the first one she ever had—and handed it to her handsome escort. There were two sides with sixteen dances listed, with two breaks for repast.

Benedict took the pencil and wrote Benedict on one side and

Cochrane on the other. Then he filled in both sections that were titled "repast" with the words dinner with Mr. Cochrane. He handed it back and said, "There, less chance for embarrassment."

Sophie was shining with happiness and said, "But Mr. Cochrane, you have filled your name in for the entire evening."

He just said, "You may call me Benedict tonight. I think I will allow that."

The two couples drank their aperitifs and set off in separate cars, Benedict going in the opposite direction from Sir Alfred, who said to Euphemia, "I'll wager he plans to propose to her first. I have rarely seen a man more besotted with a woman. Who would ever have believed it of Benedict Cochrane."

Euphemia said, "Certainly not I, Sir Alfred."

He said, "Euphemia, we are co-conspirators. Please drop the "sir," and Euphemia smiled happily.

~

Sophie exclaimed, "Where are you taking me? Odious man? We are going in the wrong direction. Are you taking me to Torrance?"

He said, "Possibly. There is a pub there and now that I know you like pubs. Actually, I intend to be nice to you this evening, but first I want a kiss."

He pulled over to the side of the road and she said, "Don't mess up my hair again."

He promised he would not since he would have to be seen in public with her. Then he suddenly grew serious.

"Sophie, will you do me the honor of," he paused, she was looking at him expectantly. He became hesitant, and all he could manage was, "accompanying me to the City Chambers annual ball?"

He could see she was disappointed. He was disappointed in himself. He should have at least told her he loved her, but was that truly enough? Their difference in circumstances, upbringing really. He was attending Glasgow University with top marks. She was attending Catholic school by day and caring for sick parents by night—working at the haberdashery in-between.

She was quiet on their way into Glasgow. He felt she could read his thoughts. He felt guilty and ashamed all at once. What was wrong with him? He knew it. He desired her beyond reason. He wanted to make love to her so much that the thought of it was consuming him—keeping him awake at nights. However, being seen in public with her? He always thought he would *trade up* when he eventually married. He was handsome enough to have his pick of the litter. He thought, *what a terrible expression, Barrister Cochrane. Shame you ever went to that shop. Shame your feeble-minded sister ever forgot her purse.*

He said, "Sophie, do you know how to dance?"

She said, "A little, but I have never been to a dance. Only what I learned in school."

He just said, "Great," and laughed, somewhat cruelly.

∼

The couple arrived at the City Chambers a little after Euphemia and Sir Alfred, who right away, noticed the change in Sophie's demeanor. She was no longer radiant. She looked scared and depressed—like she just wanted to get away.

Benedict had left Sophie to give her wrap to the cloakroom attendant, and he walked in the ballroom without her. He approached his sister and Sir Alfred. He said, "It seems the only time she has ever danced was when she attended Catholic school. She has never been to a dance, let alone a formal ball. This should be fun. I suppose I best go find her."

They were both blaming themselves and Sir Alfred said to Euphemia, "I should have stuck to the arrangements. If he hurts that girl again tonight, Euphemia, I promise! He should have accompanied her into the ballroom, instead of leaving her to find her own way in. What sort of gentleman does that?"

Euphemia patted his hand, "We saw his love for her. I am sure it will be fine. Although he should have taken care of her wrap. I wish I had asked her about her dancing skills. That was careless of me. I didn't even consider it." Euphemia was angry at herself. Of course, Sophie would have had little opportunity to learn to dance. She had never even attended a ball before. Euphemia berated herself for not considering this. She could have taught her a little—If only Sophie had mentioned it.

Sir Alfred and Euphemia decided to sit out the first dance and watch. Benedict led Sophie onto the dance floor for the first waltz. She wasn't terrible, but she was slow and deliberate. An obvious beginner. She must have been trying to teach herself. Then the next dance began, and it was a fox trot. This time Sophie could see Euphemia and Sir Alfred skillfully dancing across the dance floor, and Benedict said, "Who would have thought my sister was such a fine dancer? Well done, Euphemia." He smiled at Sophie, but she could see the embarrassment written all over his face.

This dance was more difficult, and Sophie had never danced it before, not even when she practiced by herself in her bedroom. She felt so nervous and clumsy that she stumbled a little and then apologized to her charming dance partner who smiled and said, "Think nothing of it," as he then led her back to her seat in the middle of the dance, excused himself, and made his way to the gaming bar in the next room.

Sophie sat by herself, feeling humiliated, and as soon as the dance ended, Sir Alfred and Euphemia joined her. They had both seen what had happened, but tried to make light of it, even although they both wanted to seriously berate the man. Sir Alfred asked Sophie to dance, since it was another waltz, but she thanked him and said, "I would rather not Sir Alfred if you do not mind. I am so sorry, but I would like to go home."

Euphemia said, "Let's give him a few minutes, wait and see if he re-appears after the next dance. Possibly he met someone and is talking at the bar."

However, it was obvious to Sophie, that wasn't what Euphemia and Sir Alfred believed. She knew no one there. The young women were skillfully twirling around the dance floor with their partners and Sophie wanted the ground to open and swallow her. She was out of her depth and well she knew it.

The fifth dance was halfway through, and she said, "I am leaving. I am sorry, but I cannot stay. After all my escort abandoned me in the middle of a dance and went to the gaming bar. I wonder how many watched with sheer amusement and delight."

Several young men had approached Sophie to fill in her dance card. She may not have been the best dancer in the room, but she was without a doubt the prettiest. However, when they saw Benedict Cochrane's name written upon every dance, despite him spending the evening in the bar, Sophie felt she could see the sympathy in their eyes as they took their leave.

One man muttered, "What a bounder," to himself as he walked away.

Euphemia and Sir Alfred stood up and said they would take Sophie home.

Euphemia said, "I still want you to stay with me tonight. You are upset and your brother, well he has enough on his plate."

Sophie said, "You mean, he might murder your brother? No worries, he never declared himself to me—in case that is what you are concerned about. He never even told me he loved me. I will be leaving for America soon, and I will never return. In time I will forget him and meet a gentleman, because Euphemia, your brother is not a gentleman. He is not even a nice or decent man. He is the devil. I will stay tonight because my brother will want to kill him. I will be composed tomorrow morning. I will tell Jack I had a nice time, but I still prefer to go to New York, which indeed I do."

Euphemia sat in the back of the car with her little friend. She was ashamed, embarrassed, angry—so many emotions that she could hardly put into words.

Sir Alfred was much affected too and knew he would never recommend such a man to be a judge of his fellow man.

Then Euphemia shocked both him and Sophie. "Sophie, do you think your aunt and uncle would put me up for a little while? Until you and I sort ourselves out? I am coming with you. I have my own inheritance, and I cannot continue to live under the same roof as my brother. He has thrown away so much this day. Such a sad and foolish man."

Sophie said, "Of course! And we can surely obtain another ticket. Do you have long enough to take care of your affairs?"

Euphemia felt a little lighter. Sophie seemed so much better than an hour before. "Indeed, I do!"

∼

Euphemia gave Sophie a glass of brandy and helped her to bed. She and Sir Alfred intended waiting a while to see if Benedict came home. However, if the hour grew late, it was decided that they would retire and Euphemia had another spare room prepared for Sir Alfred, since he had drunk several whiskies in his anger and care of this young girl he barely knew, yet had to rescue twice, due to Benedict Cochrane's appalling behavior. He also felt guilty for not keeping to his plan of taking Sophie to the ball. It was just that Cochrane seemed so very taken with her. Sir Alfred said several times, "Your brother's a damn fool."

∼

Benedict Cochrane had gone to the gaming bar for a large whisky to help him make it through the night, and there he came upon Harvey

Martin. He bought his friend a drink and himself another and said, "Dutch courage. It seems my dance partner does not know how to dance. Bloody embarrassment. She actually stumbled during the fox trot, and I was terrified that we might both fall onto the dance floor."

Harvey said, "Benedict, that girl, Miss Sullivan, is it? She clearly has all the other ladies well and truly out-classed, most particularly my wife. The young bucks are all asking who she is and her lack of dancing skills makes her so sweet and adorable. You can surely teach her to dance, Cochrane, I would not let that one get away. She seems quite taken with you, but I am told she will soon be off to New York. She will be quickly snapped up over there by one of those American robber barons. She did not learn all that refinement that she appears to have, so she could marry anyone less. Come to think of it, perhaps a Scottish barrister isn't wealthy enough to win her hand, even if his legal fees are beyond ridiculous."

Benedict pretended he did not care one way or another, however, after three whiskies, he decided to go back out and risk Sophie Belle's dancing again, because he did care—and he cared very much.

He walked into the main ballroom, only to find that all three of them had left—his sister, Sophie Belle and Sir Alfred Hicks—Sophie's knight in shining armor.

He was immediately approached by Mrs. Marsha Martin, who was eager to tell him this good news and also to inform him that Miss Fiona MacBride might still have a few dances available on her dance card.

Benedict simply said, "Excuse me," and rudely pushed past the woman, as she once again glared at her husband, who had exited the gaming bar with Benedict. He told her she was wasting her time.

~

They were not home very long, perhaps an hour, when Benedict appeared. He had been visibly drinking and said, "Why did you leave?

I came back in for the seventh dance. Needed a little Dutch courage—three large whiskies. Did you see her dancing? I swear, I think she was counting dance steps during the waltz and I feared us both landing upon the floor during the fox trot. One would expect that all young ladies know how to dance." He stopped thoughtfully, "But then again, Sophie Sullivan is not really a lady, is she? She puts on a good show of it, but the truth will out."

Euphemia and Sir Alfred sat stunned at such an unkind remark. It made little sense after his earlier behavior. Then Benedict, who was standing at the drawing room entrance, looked up and saw her. His face went bright red, and he said, "Sorry, Sophie, didn't know you were still here."

∽

Sophie was beyond hurt. She had cried quite enough over this man, since the day she met him actually—just a few weeks previously. She felt such an anger inside, that she strode down the stairs and physically attacked him, beating him on his chest, while the others watched in astonishment.

He was holding his arms up to protect himself, but she would not stop, and certainly no one came to his rescue. She was crying out, "Clearly your mother never taught you manners or how to behave among your fellow human beings. We are not all thieves and murderers. However, you are a big nasty imbecile! Furthermore, I have news for you! You are indisputably not a gentleman—even although you think you are—you are not—in fact you are hardly even a man!"

She was on a roll and Euphemia and Sir Alfred were trying to hold in their laughter, when all he was shouting was, "Stop hitting me, you crazy Irish ragamuffin!"

As he was attempting to hold her off, she shouted, "That is right, my father was an Irishman. Much better than you, stupid Scotsman," She turned, "sorry Sir Alfred."

Sir Alfred said, "Actually Sophie, I am English."

And she was off again, punching Benedict's arms and chest till he finally took a hold of her wrists and said, "Get out of this if you can," and he was laughing.

So, she started kicking him instead, still shouting, "I attended St. Margaret's Academy for girls, because I was first in my class! Not like you, stupid dunce—you probably cheated all the way through your fancy university. And as I already told you—I am Catholic. A Roman Catholic of Irish descent. Stupid Benedict Cochrane falls for an Irish Catholic ragamuffin. And where did you get that dumb name? And in case you think you are so handsome. You are not even a little good looking, not even a tiny bit and I HATE YOU!"

Benedict was still laughing, even as he was protecting himself from the crazy woman, whom he now absolutely intended to marry."

He shouted over, "Judge Hicks, can you fit in a wedding next month? I have decided I might marry this crazy woman, so I can teach her to dance and how to address a gentleman. Euphemia, we will arrange a dinner party. Invite our friends, all cultured ladies and gentlemen. I need to assess Sophie Belle's table manners, see if she knows what silverware to use—that sort of thing. See what the gang makes of her."

Sir Alfred said, "Are you so certain that Sophie Belle will want to marry you. She doesn't seem to think too much of you, at the present time at least."

Sophie started laughing, "Marry you? I would sooner marry an alley cat! As for cultured friends? You might mean, unpleasant ill-mannered persons, if they are at all like those ignorant people, I met for afternoon tea."

Benedict said, "No you would be marrying a gentleman. Lucky you! I will be marrying an Irish Catholic ragamuffin who must learn to be more respectful towards her betters."

He then lifted her over his shoulder, as she continued to kick him. He was laughing and said, "Have you tired yourself out, Sophie Belle?

None of that hurt. You are too little and weak," and to the others he said, "the night is still young since you left the ball so early. I will bring the ragamuffin back down in half an hour. That should be enough time, to reprimand her on tonight's totally outrageous behavior! And then we have a wedding to plan—and a dinner."

Euphemia and Sir Alfred had been sitting in shock and then, after Benedict took Sophie away, they started laughing so hard, and Sir Alfred said, "I swear, in my entire life I have never had such an entertaining evening."

And Euphemia stated, "Seems I may not be going to America after all. Well, I still might be, since it's not over yet!"

~

Benedict threw Sophie down on her bed. Sophie grew wide-eyed, watching him, wondering what was coming next and already aware that she would positively marry this extraordinary man—if indeed he was serious."

He unbuttoned his formal shirt and said, "So, Sophie Belle, what do you think? Not a man, you said. Still not handsome enough? I hope you like hairy men. Do you like hairy men, Sophie Belle?"

She stood up and said, "I have never given it much thought. I suppose your appearance is pleasing enough, although your behavior is insulting and most inappropriate."

Benedict was vain enough to know he was very well favored, and he could easily tell that Sophie was of the same opinion, and said, "My legs look great in a kilt. Would you like me to show them to you?"

Sophie blushed profusely, "Absolutely not! I expect you are a man, although not particularly a gentleman. Some women might even call you handsome. A bit too smug however."

He laughed, "What about you? What do you have to show me, so that I may be tempted to overlook your lack of manners."

"My ankles. Your sister said no more than that."

He said, "Is that it? I offer to marry you and give the rest of Scotland a break, and all I can see is your ankles?"

She said, "What comes next sir, a proper proposal, which I may consider? I already know you are insane, and mean and cruel. In fact, you are loathsome. And yet...."

He was drawing her to him, "And yet?"

But he did not give her a chance to answer. He took her into his arms and began to kiss her so passionately that she thought she might swoon. They fell onto the bed and Sophie realized she was half naked. She pushed him away and said, "Not until you marry me. I do not trust you one bit...and even if I did. I want to have a proper wedding night."

Benedict said throatily, "I can already tell certain things about you and the rest I imagine. Though I hate to admit it. I am exceptionally fond of every bit of you, Sophie Belle Sullivan. You know I fought against it—the difference in our circumstances, but now I am completely at your disposal, if you still want me after all my bad behavior. Do you, Sophie Belle? Do you still want me?"

Sophie was captivated, "Yes, I believe that I do. I am in love with a crazy man but I don't know that I would want him any other way."

"So," he said, "we are to be married—three weeks next Saturday—assuming all goes well at the dinner party—cannot invite your brother to that. He can come to the courthouse. No fuss, just us, the judge, your brother—thank God not his soon to be ex-wife—and my sister. We can perhaps invite a few friends in afterwards to drink our health. Sophie Belle, do you have any friends?"

She said, "No, none that I would want."

Benedict seemed relieved, and Sophie thought. *I am marrying a man who thinks he is my better. I wonder who these friends are he is referring to. Hopefully not the ones he invited that first Sunday I came to tea.*

She Said, "Why the dinner party, Benedict? Two weeks before the wedding. Isn't the wedding enough to plan at such short notice? Also, my wedding dress, trousseau and that sort of thing. Are you planning a honeymoon? Are you fixing up a bridal suite for me? Can I choose the colors?"

He said, "You can talk to Euphemia about those things. She has an account in several stores, which I pay for. Why not the dress you wore tonight? It was white. You can also wear it for the dinner party. White dresses—they all look the same. Let me think about your bedroom suite. As far as a honeymoon, maybe later. I am in the middle of an important case. Perhaps we can go somewhere in October, depending on my caseload."

Sophie ventured, "Like Paris? It is supposed to be lovely that time of year."

Benedict said, "Whoa, you are already spending a fortune and we haven't even walked down the aisle. I do not believe you have a dowry to give me?"

He saw her face, sheer and utter fear and regret. "Sophie Belle, I am only fooling with you. I know you are poor. Let us go downstairs and tell them our news."

Sophie said, "I will be down in a minute. I will see you downstairs."

He left and she thought, *or in hell!* Sophie looked inside the little secret compartment in the traveling bag she brought, since she was staying overnight. There was the steamer ticket. It was dated five days after her planned wedding day. She also had one hundred and fifty pounds hidden in there. Her father had given it to her shortly before he passed away, along with his gold signet ring, and he told her to keep it a secret—which indeed she had done—having no intention of ever spending it. It was her father's secret stash and now it was hers. Also, Jack promised her something when the shop and house sold. Between this and her aunt and uncle's benevolence, Benedict Cochrane could indeed go to hell, after she left him, hopefully to suffer for all his unkindness and cruelty toward her.

She knew one of two things would most likely occur and both involved her getting on that steamer. Either he would marry her and immediately become the monster, she was starting to fear. Or they wouldn't marry at all. He never mentioned a ring. He told her to wear the dress she wore that night to his dinner party and as a wedding dress and to purchase anything else she needed on his sister's account. No honeymoon was planned either and no plans of where she would sleep or of fixing up her own private bedroom suite, like Euphemia's. Really, it was the worst marriage proposal in the history of time. Why did she accept? No matter, married to him or not, she was leaving on that ship. She thought, *Sophie, then why marry him at all?* She knew the answer. If this was all that he intended for his bride, his bride would leave him after five days and he would be a laughingstock in the High Court.

Sophie did not go downstairs, and feigned being asleep when Benedict and Euphemia checked in on her. He said, "She was asking me about wedding gowns and trousseaus. You can see to that Euphemia, but I already got her a white gown. They all look the same to me. I suppose I will need to give her one of the en suite rooms. We can discuss that later. Same thing honeymoon. I am a bit worried she thinks she is on to a good thing. At least she did not ask me for a diamond ring."

Euphemia could not quite believe her ears. She expected both of them to come downstairs basking in their love for one another. How could she let this sweet girl marry her brother? What was to be done? He left and she sat down on the bed and patted Sophie's hair. She felt responsible.

Sophie was not asleep. She said, "It is okay Euphemia. I heard him. I will be on that steamer, five days after the wedding, if there is a wedding. I can never forgive him. Not this time."

Euphemia said, "My darling girl, why marry him?"

Sophie said, "To humiliate him as he has done me. I would have loved that man forever, but Euphemia, I used to joke about it, but I truly do believe he is evil. To treat a young innocent girl, the way he is treating me. Euphemia, will you sleep with me tonight—in case he comes back? He showed me his bare chest so I could admire him. That man is in love with himself."

∽

The next morning Sophie was told Benedict had already left for Chambers, when she joined Euphemia and Sir Alfred for breakfast.

Sir Alfred said, "Sophie, why are you going through with this wedding? Euphemia has spoken to me. It makes no sense. Benedict Cochrane makes no sense."

Sophie said, "The good barrister had the idea of marrying a lady with lineage, but stupid him—he fell for a poor Glasgow lass—a nobody—dirt beneath his feet—unworthy of a diamond ring. Unworthy of her own room in his house, a proper church service, a wedding gown, a honeymoon. My goodness, he didn't even declare his love for me. I am going along with it but one way or another, I am leaving on that ship. My brother has also booked a ticket. He sold the shop and has an offer on the house. He is grateful, Sir Alfred, for your kind advice."

Again, Sir Alfred asked, "But Sophie, how will you get through it? Why put yourself through it?"

Sophie's voice was flat in her response, "Sir Alfred, I hate him. I finally hate him. He destroyed an innocent girl full of optimism and hope and who was so very much in love with him. I will pay him back for all his kindness."

Sir Alfred was exasperated and said, "Euphemia, what is all this about a dinner party?"

Euphemia said, "Another ill-advised idea of his. You will come, Sir Alfred. Sophie and I will need your support. I cannot see it going at all well. I am wondering about his motivation in so doing with his wedding two weeks later."

Sophie said, "Oh, he is hoping I let myself down with my table manners. I do hope someone asks to see my ring, so I can tell them he can't afford one."

She thoughtfully continued, "If I am to wear my white dress to the dinner party, I may as well simply wear my navy-blue suit to my wedding. No veil, no wedding dress, no something borrowed and something blue. Well, I suppose my suit is blue. He probably has a mistress. After all, and as he is very aware, he is an exceedingly handsome man, in his prime of life. He has no doubt promised to go to her that night. As you have asked, why marry him? So, I can do to him what he has done to me. He knew I was staying at his house. It is Sunday morning. Why is he at Chambers? I am quite sure he is in a chamber but not at chambers. I am thinking she must be married or some such thing, some impediment, or why bother marrying me. Why do you suppose he is marrying me? And so quickly? I think possibly his mistress is older than he, unable to provide him with an heir, due to her age or possibly her husband? Anyway, I gave him the incorrect date for my steamer ticket. At first, I just got it mixed up. I said the 14th. It is not until the 18th. I meant to rectify my mistake and tell him the correct date. However, somehow, I never got around to it. He therefore believes it to be the day after our wedding, which of course would necessitate me leaving for Liverpool the night before—my wedding night at the very latest—in order to board the ship the next morning. However, I will not need to leave until Wednesday, and my brother and I are booked on the 10 o'clock train—long after Mr. Cochrane has left for Chambers."

Sir Alfred asked, "I know it is not my place to raise the question, but what if he comes to you? Surely, he will. What if there are consequences? What then Sophie? I would never speak this way, but I feel enough has passed between us to allow me to do so?"

Sophie said, "Of course I have considered that. It is quite possibly the only reason he is marrying me."

She saw Euphemia blush at this statement and continued, "I might be innocent in the ways of men, however, when most girls began courting and thinking of marriage and children, I was too busy nursing both of my parents. First my mother and then my father. Afterwards, I had quite gone off the idea until my aunt put the notion of a wealthy American man into my head, with the option of my own little shop in Upstate New York, if I cannot find a wealthy man who wants to marry me. The shop is what appeals to me now. After Benedict, I want no other man. He has cured me of that idea. If there is a little consequence, which somehow, I doubt because…well I just doubt it…the baby will be born in America, and as I said, good luck to the stupid Scotsman if he attempts to get him. Frankly, if he is she, he probably won't even try."

Sir Alfred said, "My advice, Sophie, as a judge and as your friend, and if you want to get him back for breaking your heart, is to change your mind at the altar, so to speak. Please reconsider throwing your life away on such a man. I do not understand his rush anyway. He should be planning a church wedding several months from now. He should be buying you a ring, planning a honeymoon with his beautiful bride, fixing up your new bedroom suite. Despite his odd behavior, I am still convinced he is in love with you, and I am unconvinced that there is a mistress. Surely, he is not as vile as that. Nonetheless, why the hurry?"

Sophie said, "So I miss the steamer. I will not leave him free to marry a fine lady that he may prefer. That would be bigamy. I believe he loves me too. However, he hates himself in so doing. My uncle Carlisle is a prosperous attorney in New York City. My aunt tells me he enjoys a good fight and again I say it—good luck stupid Scotsman in the American courts. My uncle is my mother's brother. My mother was English. She met my father on holiday in Inverness and in essence she married beneath her station. That explains why the shopkeeper did not live above the shop, although my brother also owns that flat. My mother's family purchased the house on Balmuildy Road as a wedding gift. My father made my brother promise to always take care of me after he passed, and Jack gave him his word. Jack is a good man.

He will always see me right. He will disapprove of my plan to marry the good barrister but will go along with it and ensure that I get on that ship safe and sound."

Sophie thoughtfully added, "You won't tell Benedict any of my story, promise me! Until after I am gone, and then, please do. He has never asked me about myself. My aunt and uncle Carlisle are very well placed. Strange that Benedict assumes they cannot possibly be so."

Euphemia said, "Well tomorrow is your day off. I am taking you shopping on my brother's account. Possibly, a peignoir, more likely some fine fashionable clothes for your new life ahead. I intend to join you in New York, once I have settled my affairs."

Sophie said, "I am so excited that you are truly coming with me, Euphemia. Even if it is a little later. I will be anxiously awaiting your arrival!"

Sophie stood up, placing her napkin on the table. "I truly love you both. You have been so kind to me. Yes, Euphemia, I would like that. Small price for him to pay for breaking a poor girl's heart. However, I still intend to embarrass him in my suit on our wedding day. Possibly a new hat?"

~

Sophie was in a tangle of emotions when she left the Cochrane's house that day. She and Euphemia were traveling to Glasgow the next morning and since she had no future arrangements to see Benedict, all the better. Sophie Sullivan realized that hate was as powerful an emotion as love. Perhaps it was even more powerful.

That night Benedict didn't come home, and Euphemia started to wonder about a mistress. Was that possible? Was her brother so immoral? She always believed him to stay in his club in Glasgow on the nights he didn't come home. However, it was Sunday, and he should have spent the day with Sophie. Euphemia hesitated to call Sophie her brother's fiancée. He certainly wasn't acting like a man who had just promised marriage to the woman he declared he was in love with—just the night before. She had no fortune—so it wasn't that—and it almost seemed as if he hated sweet Sophie. Sophie said she hated him. What was this all about and why on earth did she ever confess to her brother about forgetting her purse and her new little friend? Still, how could she ever have imagined this turn of events.

⁓

Both ladies were a little more optimistic when they traveled into Glasgow that Monday. They took the train in together, earlier than their usual rendezvous. Their first stop was Copeland and Lye, where Sophie bought two new dresses, three skirts and blouses, a pair of boots, shoes, a new carpet bag, a smart jacket and fashionable raincoat, lingerie, modest nightgowns, a new dressing gown, slippers and one peignoir. The bill was over one hundred pounds and a small price to pay for Sophie's pain, however, she promised to pay it back because her brother was giving her money and of course her aunt and uncle were very well placed.

She said, "Euphemia, I will try to get the money to you before he knows it is gone and then you can pay him back. I shall have my uncle wire the money as soon as I arrive in New York. It is funny, isn't it? A girl should be excited about marrying the man of her dreams, I am excited about leaving him."

Euphemia said, "In truth, I don't understand you Sophie and I certainly don't understand Benedict. Is he the man of your dreams, Sophie? Are you taking the chance he is devastated you leave him and comes to New York to bring you back to Scotland? He might do that, but I really don't comprehend his behavior. He would need to change significantly, surely, for you to return with him."

Sophie said, "In truth, I love him madly and hate him even more. I could never stay with a man who is so cruel and uncaring toward me. I will leave the pretty peignoir for him because somehow, I doubt, he will come to me on our wedding night, which is why he has allowed so many of his friends to stay over. I am not exactly sure why, yet I am certain he has his reasons. I am glad I told him the incorrect date for us setting sail. He will believe I have missed the steamer, so no need to worry that I would be on it. Also, he sees me as unable to afford another passage if indeed I did miss the ship's departure. Possibly, if we had more time? No, he thinks I am beneath him, not good enough and hates his own weakness in loving me. He does love me. He shows it so clearly, only the next minute to do a complete about turn, as if he realizes he has displayed some sort of frailty. What was your father like, Euphemia? And your mother."

Euphemia was thoughtful, "My father was very much in love with my mother and spoiled her completely to win her favor. However, I do not think he ever really did. She was somewhat aloof—unreachable. She died of an internal complaint, and he was dead a few months later. I always felt it was from a broken heart. Benedict despised what he perceived as his father's weakness. He told me more than once that my mother only married my father for position and money. My mother was the daughter of an impoverished clergyman. She was beautiful but had no fortune. My father was besotted with her and didn't care about receiving a dowry. Perhaps that is what this is all about. His fear of weakness if he gives in to these feelings, he has for you."

Sophie said, "I see. Perhaps he thinks history is repeating itself. That would certainly explain his lack of generosity regarding trinkets and baubles. Well, he will not have to worry about it for much longer, will he? He can keep his money. I have no need of it."

That day, it was straight home after their afternoon tea in the Willow Tea Rooms—no Corn Exchange, they decided; a little sadly.

CHAPTER 6

The week went by quickly and the bridegroom had pretty much disappeared. Sophie was hurt by this. How could a man love a woman and decide to steer clear of her. However, Sophie acted as if this was somewhat of a relief. Whether anyone believed her, she cared not. Most brides would have been preparing for their nuptials. Sophie was preparing for her voyage and a completely absurd dinner party. She started to question her reasons for marrying the good barrister. The dinner party was getting more attention, as far as food and table settings, than the wedding buffet that was so soon afterwards.

The wedding was barely mentioned except there were to be cocktails and canapés served on the terrace if the weather stayed warm.

Benedict had mentioned nothing about a hotel room for their wedding night. In addition to that slap in the face, several of Benedict's cronies were expected to stay overnight.

Sophie and Euphemia were invited to the High Court by Sir Alfred that Thursday. Judge Hicks was presiding, and Barrister Cochrane was brilliant. They were both wearing white wigs and black gowns and the good barrister looked magnificent in his. He saw his sister and Sophie, who gave him a little wave which he ignored. Judge Hicks then took both ladies to lunch at the same French restaurant that Sophie had walked out from, during that dreadful lunch with her future bridegroom. She wondered if Benedict intended to accompany them, but it seemed not, since he left the courthouse, somewhat in a hurry, while they were awaiting the judge, and told her and Euphemia to enjoy their lunch. At least on this occasion, Sophie did indeed enjoy her lunch, and Sir Alfred ordered champagne without being prompted to do so.

On Friday, Sophie stopped by to see if anything had been prepared for the bridal suite. Euphemia took her along to a guest room that contained an en suite and Sophie was thrilled with it. New bed linens and fine fragrances in the bathroom, and vases that would be filled with flowers. She turned and suddenly realized, this wasn't Benedict's doing, it was Euphemia's.

Euphemia said, "I showed it to him. He did not really say anything. But somehow, he seemed sad. I do not understand him. Oh! I have said that to you so many times. It is like he is afraid to be happy, to let down his guard. He is about to lose you because of it."

Sophie said, "He will not come to me on our wedding night, but I will enjoy sleeping in here anyway. But first the dinner party. I will not be staying over that night. I have a feeling; I won't make it until the end of the evening."

∽

The guests were complimenting Euphemia on the sparkling crystal and polished silverware. An abundant assortment of flowers was displayed on every tabletop and the dining room table was magnificently laid out with the very best china dishes and crystal glasses. Sophie gasped at the splendor displayed throughout the entire downstairs. She felt somehow disregarded and dishonored by such extravagance. This should have been the plan for her wedding day, and not some silly dinner party, created to show off the Cochranes' wealth and importance. Sophie's heart was broken by the opulence that surrounded her. It was beyond comprehension. She was in no way impressed. She was depressed.

Sophie was wearing her new beige summer skirt and linen blouse. She wore her mother's pearl necklace, which was the only jewelry she possessed, and the brand-new beige kidskin boots her brother surprised her with earlier that day. She wore her hair down, tied with a beige velvet ribbon—almost the color of her hair. She was fully aware that the other feminine guests would be dressed up like cream puff pastries, and the men like penguins in their white tie dinner ensembles, but she did not care. She arrived unaccompanied and no car or carriage had been sent for her. There were two footmen employed to assist the guests with their wraps and hats. Sophie wondered if Benedict was paying them by the hour, in order to impress his guests, since she had never before seen them.

She looked over at Benedict. He was standing laughing with a few of his cronies. It seemed that was his usual behavior, but what upset Sophie, was Euphemia's role in all of this.

Euphemia immediately sought her out but before she could explain, Sophie said, "Well now at least I understand why my wedding is to be such a small and insignificant affair. All the funds have been spent on the dinner party. Such opulence. Most impressive. Is there a special occasion, Euphemia? Such as a real betrothal? I think I should leave."

Euphemia said, "Oh no, please do not go, Sophie, and do not censure me. I am as horrified as you. This is all Benedict's doing. Why? I cannot even imagine. We never hold dinner parties like this. He has had Mrs. Thompson in tears since I refused to play a part in this travesty. He has also moved your place setting to the middle of the table since I had of course placed you on his right-hand side."

Sophie said, "What am I supposed to have done this time? To deserve such treatment?"

Euphemia said, "Possibly, the fact that Judge Hicks has taken a shine to you? He will not give Benedict his recommendation and I cannot say that I blame him."

Sophie was served a glass of champagne and Euphemia moved

along to greet some of the other guests. Sophie was standing alone, wondering why she had even come, and shortly thereafter everyone was called into dinner. Sophie watched incredulously as Benedict approached a rather mousy looking young woman, who took his arm and was seated beside him. The Martins were there, as were the Nicholsons, and it seemed the young woman who walked in upon Benedict's arm was the Fiona MacBride the old cats mentioned during that very first Sunday afternoon tea.

What was going on? Sophie walked in on her own and sat down at her place setting. She was working it out in her mind, the most crushing way to handle the situation. Euphemia was red-faced with anger, as was Sir Alfred Hicks. Sophie smiled over at them, but her heart was in her stomach. Clearly this was truly the end of the line. There was no going back from this.

Sophie had practiced her manners well. She had no difficulty in looking as sophisticated as the rest of these unpleasant people, even though she was dressed quite differently. However, she wasn't feeling particularly refined and though her preference would have been to sling some creamed potatoes at Miss Fiona MacBride, instead she turned and said to Euphemia, "Miss Cochrane, these candied fruits as table decorations are quite delightful. Such an unusual effect, I am sure."

Euphemia smiled and thanked Sophie for the compliment.

However, Benedict tore his attention away from the enraptured Miss MacBride, who was gazing at him with cow eyes, giggling like a schoolgirl at his flirtatious behavior, and he said, "Not so very unusual as a table decoration in our social class, possibly in yours, Miss Sullivan."

Sophie noticed a certain sympathy among her would-be fiancé's male counterparts, at such an unnecessarily rude remark, and decided she was going to let loose on Mr. Benedict Cochrane and his besotted dinner companion. At this point, she had nothing to lose.

"Oh, I see Mr. Cochrane. How utterly amusing? I would never

have imagined you to be a man who would take much to do with place settings and candied fruit. I am all astonishment. I should have given you the credit for this lovely table and not your sister. Forgive my thoughtlessness."

Sophie turned her attention to the insipid Fiona MacBride, "Excuse me, is it Miss MacBride?" The young woman, who had been gazing adoringly at Benedict Cochrane, turned and regarded Sophie with a haughty demeanor.

"I see you flirting—quite desperately actually— with Mr. Cochrane. You are perhaps unaware that he is already betrothed, and his wedding is a week next Saturday? Just thought to remind you. Possibly save you some embarrassment, since you are making rather a fool of yourself, mooning over him. This is just his way—to make fun of plain and mousy young women with money. I do not believe he is in actual need of your fortune, although one can never have enough money." Sophie paused thoughtfully, "Regardless, he is a fastidious man, with very particular taste —expensive motor cars, fine silk suits, beautiful women…" She again thoughtfully paused, "and my dear, he prefers beautiful blondes, like me, which is why you ought to behave yourself. Just a piece of friendly advice."

Mrs. Martin and Mrs. Nicholson looked as if they might choke on their venison wellington.

Fiona MacBride looked at Benedict in outrage, seeking some support but was offered none. He was sitting smiling at Sophie Belle's caustic statement.

Sophie changed tactics, "Mr. Cochrane, if I were you, I would instruct my kitchen staff to stick to beef wellington. I admire their sense of adventure, but clearly, they lack the skill."

Benedict sarcastically asked, "Do the Sullivans serve game often then, Miss Sullivan? I know several large estates have had major problems with poachers in recent years."

Euphemia and Sir Alfred could hardly believe their ears and Sir

Alfred said, in astonishment, "Mr. Cochrane, are you accusing your special guest's family of being poachers? Shame on you."

Sophie said, "Oh Sir Alfred, please do not be distressed, although I agree our host's table manners are very much in need of improvement. Perhaps he should educate himself on how to behave toward his guests, when he has put on such an elaborate dinner. I have several books I can lend him. Actually, I will allow him to keep them, since he has far greater need of them than I."

She turned back to Benedict, "Anyway, we very seldom serve game at our table. It is not a favorite of my brother nor of his exceedingly well-mannered friends. We are not poachers either since my family has long believed in earning an honest living. Possibly the culprits are among your other guests. At any rate, my brother prefers beef. I make a delicious beef wellington. I do so occasionally as a special treat for him and his friends. My beef wellington makes these men's mouths water. They tell me it is delectably delicious, and I am inclined to agree with them."

She turned, "Mr. Martin, is your mouth watering at the venison wellington before you, sir?"

Sophie knew he was the cheekiest of the whole lot of them. She almost even liked him.

He said, "Miss Sullivan, if my mouth is watering, I can assure you it has little to do with tonight's menu. Sorry, no offense intended, Miss Cochrane."

Euphemia said, "Oh think nothing of it. No offense was taken. This might well be a favorite of my brother's but not particularly of mine."

The gentlemen laughed out loud—except for Benedict, who was doing his best to maintain a serious demeanor.

And finally, Miss MacBride spoke up. "Oh golly! I've suddenly worked it out! You're only the girl who works in the haberdashery! I know that rumor is such poppycock. Of course, it is, and I don't think you are one bit beautiful, so you shouldn't think that you are," and she giggled—a habit that irritated Sophie since she sounded like a spoiled child.

Miss Fiona MacBride turned to Benedict. "Mr. Cochrane, I am quite certain that you do not find Miss Sullivan particularly attractive, most especially in her mode of attire."

He didn't answer her, and she turned back to Sophie, "I don't believe the gossip about your engagement to Mr. Cochrane. You are lying. Where is your engagement ring? In fact, I can't even imagine why you are here, seated at the Cochranes' fine dinner table. Clearly you are too poor to dress appropriately for such a grand occasion." And again, she was giggling as she put her nose in the air—proud of her discourteous retort.

Sophie declared, "How very kind and observant you are, Miss MacBride, however, I happen to know exactly why you are here—the perfect nitwit to suit Mr. Cochrane's sense of the ridiculous. You don't honestly believe he *admires* you? He is known to prefer beautiful women with brains in their heads, who present him with somewhat of a challenge. I mean as opposed to sitting gazing adoringly at him, as indeed you are doing. I am sorry you were so ill-used this evening. Just try to make the most of your venison wellington. Oh, and I do not care to wear a ring as yet, in the event that I change my mind, as I am often known to do. Mr. Cochrane has several rivals, and I may not have made my final selection. Either way, you stand absolutely no chance in winning his admiration and regard, most notably for reasons best not discussed at such a finely laid out dinner table."

Miss MacBride was outraged. How dare a shop girl address her in such a manner? She was red faced when she responded, "I cannot even imagine what a woman with no lineage nor fortune would know about what Mr. Cochrane, nor indeed any other gentleman would be seeking in a wife."

Sophie regarded Benedict, who was sitting with a smirk on his face, and announced, "Precisely Miss MacBride, however I have no need to imagine, because I am well aware of what Mr. Cochrane wants. On that final note, I have somewhere better to be this evening, but first, these candied fruits look delicious. She stood up to examine them more closely, "May I take away a few pieces of your fruit, Mr. Cochrane? I would like to bring them to my host at the soiree I am leaving to attend."

He said, "No, it will ruin the effect of my finely set table. I will be happy to send you over some rotten fruit tomorrow if you like, Miss Sullivan. However, you may certainly take your venison with you, should you so desire."

Euphemia and Sir Alfred, who had been watching this whole scene play out with barely disguised amusement, could not help their laughter.

Emboldened Mrs. Nicholson said in outrage, "What is all this talk about candied fruit and venison? Also, Miss Sullivan, I wonder about your table manners! Furthermore, you are dressed most inappropriately for such a fine dinner."

Sophie said, "Table manners? After our last meeting in this same home, I wonder if you know a thing about table manners. As for my clothes, I prefer not to be dressed up like some day-old giant cream puff pastry."

Mrs. Nicholson, by now truly affronted declared, "I say, Mr. Cochrane will you please put a stop to this repartee at your dinner table. This young woman is insupportably rude to your other guests!"

Sophie stood and declared, "No need for further alarm, Mrs. Nicholson. I am leaving. Oh, and Barrister Cochrane…." She walked over to him on the way out, carrying her glass of dinner wine. I thought perhaps this might improve the taste of the venison a little. Here, try it out." And she proceeded to pour her wine directly onto his dinner plate. "There; that might be a little better. I was about to pour it on your lovely head, but I recalled that you pay so very much for those nice silk suits."

She made her way out of the dining room, with her head held high, determined that she would never see any of these people again, not even Euphemia, not even Sir Alfred. She was free of them all! She would soon be off to America. She was being given her wrap when Benedict appeared. "Where do you think you are going Sophie Belle?"

Sophie said, "Oh dear, Mr. Cochrane, did I forget to ask to be excused from your most enjoyable dinner party? Well in that case, please excuse me. I have an evening soirée to attend with interesting people, and a fascinating man I just met."

He blocked her path, "What man? You are betrothed to me. I will sue you for every little penny you keep in your piggy bank."

Sophie became amused, her heart almost joyful—although she knew it shouldn't be so. "Mr. Cochrane, I see no ring? I saw you flirting with some insipid little girl while your would-be *betrothed,* sat ignored in the middle of the table? Anyway, Cyrus Hatter. My new love's name is Cyrus Hatter. He has excellent prospects and is so very much in love with me. I have decided upon him instead of you. He is more handsome, more manly, and certainly much more of a gentleman. He makes me feel…oh never mind how he makes me feel. It is really none of your business. Now Mr. Cochrane, why don't you run along and re-join your guests, most especially the not so lovely, Miss MacBride. She seems much taken with you, as I once was, but now I find I have completely gone off you. Women can be fickle you see—well I am anyway."

Benedict had not expected this. He did not expect such an enthusiastic description of another man either. What did his sister know about this, or did Judge Hicks know, for that matter?

Sophie preceded out the front door with her head held high and said, "Mr. Hatter had intended to come see you and demand you release me. I will tell him no need since you are a rake and a libertine and deserve no such courtesy."

Benedict Cochrane returned to the dining room. He pulled his sister's chair back and grabbed her arm to lead her out of the room. Sir Alfred excused himself and followed them.

Those remaining at the table, were in a mixture of shock and amusement.

Miss MacBride said, "Why does Mr. Cochrane even care if that woman leaves?"

Several of the men laughed at her remark, and at Harvey Martin's response, "Because he is besotted with her. He just does not care to admit it. Better get on with it though."

Another man said, "A cracker," and again the men were laughing.

Once Benedict got his sister outside, along with her ever loyal watchdog, Judge Hicks, he spat out. "Has she been two timing me all along? Who is Cyrus Hatter? So handsome and manly and so in love with her. More to the point, where is he? What is his occupation? Some uneducated brute with big muscles?"

Sir Alfred had to turn away in his amusement, but Euphemia kept her composure beautifully and said, "Mr. Hatter? He is a teacher, math or science, very intelligent and refined. I believe he came into her brother's shop one day and swept her off her feet. I couldn't object to this rapid change in her regard, because I can't say that I blame her for getting rid of you, brother dear, and if I was a bit younger…well he is quite a dreamboat. He is also closer to her age—several years younger than you."

Sir Alfred said, "Don't know about dreamboat, but damned interesting fellow, well-educated too. A fine man with remarkably good manners."

Benedict stood and looked at them both. Were they lying? All of a sudden, this epitome of manhood shows up out of nowhere. He said, "Euphemia, go see to your guests. I am going to find her and this handsome fellow, assuming he exists. And then we shall see how manly he is!"

Sir Alfred asked, "Are you intending a street brawl, Cochrane? If so, some of your cronies and I, would so enjoy watching it!"

Sir Alfred and Euphemia watched him jump into his motor car, leaving his guests—including the forsaken Miss MacBride, behind.

Sir Alfred said, "Well done Sophie Belle, quite a convincing load of codswallop—convinced your brother at any rate—the intended target. I have also never been quite so entertained at such a fine dinner. I am sure of it. However, I wonder why she appeared angry at us at first."

Euphemia said, "Well I for one should have prevented tonight's fiasco. I wonder what my brother will make of the handsome Mr. Hatter. I love the name!"

And laughingly, they both joined the others in the drawing room, since it seemed the venison wellington had been abandoned.

Benedict Cochrane was soon doubtful of the existence of this new suitor—his rival. Sophie Belle Sullivan was many things, but her heart was true, and he knew he was the man who owned it. And suddenly, some man with a ridiculous name appears out of nowhere? Two weeks before the wedding?

Benedict had been a little nervous of Sophie Belle being intimidated at her first dinner party, so as was in his nature, he set her very firmly to the test. Rather, he was incredibly impressed. Soon, his would be the most sought-after dinner invitation, with his captivating wife and him providing the entertainment. He would have to continually think of ways to set her up—for the rest of their lives, and the thought of it thrilled him.

All at once, his attention was caught by something beige in coloring, darting around a stone wall and apparently hiding behind it. He knew the folks that lived in that house, and they were certainly not called, Hatter. He grinned broadly. Sophie Belle was caught. He parked his car outside the wall and wondered how long it would take her to get fed up and show herself.

It didn't take very long. No more than a few minutes.

Sophie knew he saw her and felt ridiculous. She walked out to the sidewalk, and once again with her nose in the air, made to walk past him. "I just didn't want you to follow me and cause any problems."

Benedict said, "I promise to be a good boy if you can prove this man exists. Isn't this the street you live on? Are you neighbors?"

He was driving slowly alongside her. Suddenly she stopped, as did he and she got in his car.

She said, "I hate you, Benedict Cochrane. No wait, I have decided to change your name. Benedict Cockroach. There, that suits you better."

Benedict said, "So you are happy with being Mrs. Benedict Cockroach? Sophie Belle Cockroach. I like the sound of that."

Then suddenly he turned the car around and went speeding out towards the countryside and the little town of Torrance.

He said, "I am taking you to the pub, Mrs. Cockroach, fancy dinner parties with your betters and candied fruit—not quite your style."

Sophie could feel the excitement build inside her belly and despite her better judgement, said, "Okay, but I feel disloyal towards Mr. Hatter, and don't you towards the insipid Miss MacBride? What a fine mind she appears to possess. Her conversation at dinner was so utterly fascinating."

Benedict said, "No, not in the least and I am sure neither do you, with regard to the handsome and manly Mr. Hatter." He could see the sheer joy on her face—she was happy to be with him. The evening sun cast a magical glow on his lady love's adorable face. There was no one else like her. She never tried to cajole him out of a mood—saw herself as his equal—possibly his better, which she no doubt was—morally, at any rate.

Benedict drove onto a dirt track, not far from the Torrance Inn, and Sophie waited for him to open her door.

Benedict obliged and kissed her gently on her lips. He smiled down at her and as if overcome with a passion he could not contain, kissed her neck and shoulders before returning his lips to hers, with such passion that Sophie's knees felt weak. She stared up at him and he said, "You have bewitched me Sophie Belle Sullivan. I never knew one could feel this way. You make me feel like I will die if I cannot have you. But you are mine, Sophie Belle, aren't you? There is no Mr. Hatter. Then he drew back and said, rather jauntily, "Still, could just be infatuation."

Sophie was never one to spoil the mood of the moment, so she let the last remark pass. He knew it was more than that—as did she. She also refrained from asking her handsome man why he placed her in the center of the dining room table, with Fiona MacBride seated on his right-hand side. She already knew the answer anyway. He took pleasure in winding her up. He set the stage and enjoyed watching her reaction.

A light drizzle started, and Benedict said, "Better close up the roof," as he proceeded to unsuccessfully try to ascertain how the task was done. Usually, he had one of his servants look after the mechanics of the vehicle and he soon realized he had no idea how it closed. By now the rain had picked up its pace and Sophie decided to take over the task. His white tie and tails were becoming soaking wet, and Sophie couldn't help her laughter.

Benedict was not laughing, although he had to begrudgingly say, "Well done," when Sophie had the roof closed within minutes of her attempt at trying. She gave herself a big cheer and then instantly slid on the wet road, in her new boots, and of a sudden, it was Benedict who was laughing, even as Sophie began to cry.

Benedict helped her up, still laughing, although complaining Sophie was making him muddy, and she told him to shut up. "These are my brand-new boots, and they are ruined, and my brand new skirt! Benedict Cochrane, I hate you, and I am glad you have ruined your fancy silk suit and stupid white tie!"

He said, "Oh, plenty more where these came from. You forget I am a wealthy gentleman, due to my esteemed occupation as one of the very finest barristers in Scotland. I will buy you new boots and a new skirt. How's that? Torrance isn't too far now. We will have a whisky and a mutton pie, since you spoiled my venison wellington. Well perhaps a half pint of shandy for you."

Sophie knew she should have insisted Benedict take her home, but somehow, she couldn't bear to leave him. He was behaving as if they were just a normal couple and after all, ring or no ring, they would very soon be married. Sophie was pushing the thought of her impending departure to America to the back of her mind. She knew their little jaunt together changed nothing. She truthfully didn't know this man sitting beside her, his eyes concentrating on the road. She wished she could read his thoughts. His mind seemed to work in the most peculiar manner, and she often had the feeling of holding her breath when he was like this, afraid of him belittling and turning on her once again. Euphemia was right. Sir Alfred was right. Jack was right. She should not be marrying this man of whom she knew practically nothing. Euphemia could fill her in on certain things about him and on their years growing up together, but she told Sophie that there were many nights, weeks even, when he did not come home and gave no explanation to his sister regarding these absences.

Benedict turned and smiled at her. He said, "What a handsome couple we make. I'm sure the Torrance Inn's regulars will all turn to look at us when we go inside. I'm not the type of fellow who would normally frequent such a place."

Benedict's omission regarding Sophie did not go unnoticed. "What about me, Benedict? Am I the usual sort one would expect to find in the Torrance Inn?"

He said, "Oh, so sensitive. Well not really, I suppose, but your brother would fit in well enough. Okay, let's go for it."

The couple walked into the country tavern to the stares of the regulars who for the most part, were men, standing at the bar drinking tankards of ale.

Benedict in his white tie and cutaway that was wet and muddy and Sophie with her muddied skirt, boots and messed up hair, presented quite a spectacle; seldom seen in the Torrance Inn. Immediately the proprietor asked, "Miss, are you okay. Is everything alright?"

Benedict smirked at having been ignored by whom he saw as country bumpkins, but was then totally shocked when Sophie answered, "Oh yes, certainly sir! My husband and I just had a little car trouble and I slipped on the muddy road. I was taking him to the station for a special dinner at the Glasgow City Chambers. He is a barrister you see. I got the mechanism in the gear box stuck and then it started to rain. Fortunately, my husband got us back on the road. However, it seems he will miss his dinner." She laughed and the tavern lightened up as Benedict said, "Mr. Benedict Cochrane, at your service."

The couple sat down to eat but soon the innkeeper's wife appeared and said to Sophie, "Oh dear, you poor love! We cannot have you sitting there in wet clothing! I have a nice room upstairs. Very reasonable and I am sure Mr. Cochrane will be relieved to have his wife, as well as himself, made comfortable. The rain shows no sign of stopping and the wind has picked up terrible. We will be happy to serve your food and wine upstairs in our guest room. This be no place for a lady, and it is obvious Mrs. Cochrane, that you is very much a fine lady."

The woman introduced herself as Mrs. Patter, and she seemed to carry on the complete conversation and plan for the Cochranes spending the night at the Torrance Inn, without any participation from her actual guests.

Benedict Cochrane was highly amused and more than delighted to go along with the landlady's suggestion. Sophie Belle had dug herself into a hole with her tall stories and now she would be spending the night with him, in a tiny bedchamber above a pub, which by this time was alive with gossip about the fashionable couple being shown upstairs.

When Mrs. Patter lit the fire and gas lamps, she said, "There now. I can tell you two be newlyweds. This be a nice cozy room and that's a new mattress on the bedstead. You will be happy together in here.

I will have dinner and wine brought upstairs and brandy for you too, sir." The woman turned to Sophie and led her to a drawer. "A nice cozy nightie for you ma'am. I will have warm water brought up for your convenience, but we also have a fully plumbed bathroom, should you prefer a bath. There is plenty of hot water and no one will disturb you."

When the woman left, Sophie said, "I can't believe you allowed this to happen, sir!"

Benedict said with a wide grin, "Ah excuse me, Sophie Belle, you were the one who said we were already married. A Hatter and a Patter, all in the same evening. How entertaining."

Sophie said, "The bed is very small. However, you cannot sleep on the wooden chair. I certainly will not be sleeping there either. You can lay on top of the covers, and I will lay under them. There, that solves it."

He said, "But won't you worry that I will be cold if you have all the blankets, and I have none Sophie Belle. Isn't that rather cruel?"

He was speaking in jest and well Sophie knew it, as well as she also knew that the thought of a whole night with Benedict Cochrane excited her so. Of course, she knew that it shouldn't, and also that she must act accordingly.

"Okay, there are four blankets. You may sleep under the top blanket. I am going for a bath."

By the time Sophie re-appeared in a flannel nightdress, which was much too big for her, so that she needed to keep hoisting up the shoulders, their food had already been brought up and Benedict had eaten his. There was a decanter of what she assumed to be brandy and not wine, and he was sitting up in the bed with a glass of the amber liquid in his hand. His chest was bare, and Sophie quickly averted her eyes.

She ate her mutton pie and poured herself a glass of brandy. She then walked nervously over to the bed and realized Benedict was fully under the covers.

She said, "That is not what we agreed, sir. You are only allowed the top blanket and must keep to your own side of the bed." Sophie was apprehensive. She was also excited. Benedict Cochrane had the power to make her lose what little sense she felt she still had left. The effect this man had on her. She no more understood it than she wanted to leave the web he seemed to have woven around her.

She said, "Okay, just stay to your side of the bed and don't touch me."

He agreed and she climbed in tugging her oversized nightgown around her. She turned away from him. She knew she had placed herself in such danger. She sat up and said, "I will sleep on the chair."

He sat up too, and turned to her, "Why Sophie Belle? I didn't touch you."

Sophie burst into tears. She realized how much she wanted this man to make love to her and became more afraid of herself than of him.

She made to get up and out of that dangerous bed, but Benedict stopped her. He began kissing her and she could feel her passion for him welling up inside her chest. Her oversized nightgown slipped down. She attempted to pull it back up, in a panic, trying to come to her senses. Her breasts were bare, and she was in a tiny bed with Benedict Cochrane. How had she allowed herself to be placed in such a compromising position? What must this man be thinking of her?

Benedict would not allow her to retrieve the nightgown. He was astounded at how the night was turning out for him. When he planned his nonsensical dinner, he could never have imagined that he would be rewarded in such a manner. Sophie Belle's breasts were even more magnificent than he imagined, when he lay each night in his lonely bed. He cupped her breasts into his hands and bent his head to kiss them, looking up at her with naked desire, before doing so. He was murmuring words of desire and of his hunger for her, and Sophie was in heaven. Soon her bare breasts were pressed against his bare chest. They were kissing one another in such a passion and Sophie was intoxicated by the taste and scent of his skin. She felt unable to resist him, knowing full well that surely her behavior had lost him. He turned her over, and she knew she had to put a stop to this, if it was not already too late to do so. By now her fear was real. What was she doing? This wasn't right. She was not this sort of woman. She started to cry again in earnest, almost sobbing in her shame, and said, "Please no, Benedict."

Benedict abruptly came to his senses. What was he doing? Sophie was looking at him wide-eyed, with fear. She was crying; however, he knew now for certain—how much she desired him. Possibly her desire was as intense as was his. He rejoiced in that knowledge, even as he restrained himself from going any further. He kissed the woman he loved so completely and helped her adjust her nightgown. He said, "I'm sorry Sophie Belle. Please forgive me." Sophie settled down as he kissed her tenderly and they were soon asleep in each other's arms.

Sophie awoke early in the morning before Benedict, and dressed in her clothes, which the landlady must have taken and cleaned, sat and watched him sleep. She realized, more than ever before; how much she loved this man. She would never love another and when she left him, he would surely realize that she was not of his social class—just a shopkeeper's daughter who behaved so wantonly with him. He might decide not to even go through with the wedding and how could she blame him? At least they didn't go all the way; but that was small comfort to Sophie, when she remembered his bare chest pressed against hers; even although the sheer remembrance of it sent chills of pleasure and desire throughout her entire body.

Benedict finally awakened and Sophie loved his black hair all messy and his sleepy countenance.

She stared at him, awaiting his disapproval. He stood up and stretched and she averted her eyes from his bare chest and rather revealing under drawers. She thought he was the most handsome man she had ever seen, and she suddenly felt small and insignificant.

Then he said, "Sophie Belle that is the best night's sleep I have ever had. With you beside me each night, I will be late for Chambers every morning."

Then he noticed her wide-eyed expression, "What Sophie Belle? Were you expecting me to awaken and tell you how much I disapproved of your behavior, of your love for me? Sophie, well let's just say, disapproval is the exact opposite of what I am feeling; gratitude is closer to the mark."

Sophie was still uneasy, and she ventured, "We did not go too far then? I mean we did not go all the way, did we?"

Benedict laughed, "No, Sophie Belle, we did not. I am sorry. I know that I almost lost control in my hunger for you, and I am now grateful to know for certain you feel the same way. Do you suppose I would prefer you to be cold and without passion and affection? Men dream of finding a wife whose desire compares to their own. Most do not get it and they stray. Unless of course, they are like my father and try to win favor with expensive gifts. I am euphoric this morning Sophie Belle, a little impatient, but euphoric. Now I promise to behave myself, until a very special night in the future, when I may finally make you truly mine."

She said, "You mean our wedding night?"

But he did not answer that. He said, "I will take you shopping on Wednesday afternoon. Your new boots are ruined, and I promised you a new skirt too. I will take you to lunch first. Would you like that?"

Sophie was of course immensely excited, and he promised, "I will meet you at noon at Queen Street Station. Now I must take you to Euphemia so she can come up with a story for your brother, although the thought occurs to me in a few days, no explanations nor stories will be necessary, since you will be my wife. I have some errands to run before I can go home and get out of these clothes."

His words both relieved and elated Sophie. He spoke to her so naturally, and for the first time, she considered not boarding that steamer to America which would set sail two weeks from Thursday next.

It appeared once again Sir Alfred had stayed the night. Sophie wondered that he so often did but took hold of Euphemia's hand and poured out a much-abbreviated story, in the privacy of Euphemia's bed chamber.

She said, "Euphemia, I am starting to believe Benedict has become much nicer. He was so wonderful and loving last night. He is taking me shopping and for lunch on Wednesday at noon. Perhaps, I just got him all wrong in my head," and she paused, "Euphemia, I love him so. I don't know why but I do."

Euphemia said, "So are we still sailing for America?"

Sophie thought for a moment. "I suppose that depends on this dreadful wedding he has planned. Possibly, he has been fooling us all along. Perhaps, he is planning something wonderful!"

She ran out the door on her way home, as excited as a schoolgirl and Euphemia returned to Sir Alfred, who was sitting in the garden. "What's going on?" he asked.

Euphemia said, "I fear he may have set our girl up. She is beaming with happiness but once again, it is Sunday. Where is he? I do not trust him one bit—brother or not. He is taking her shopping and to lunch on Wednesday. Let us pray he shows up. He told her he has errands to run today. When did Benedict ever have errands to run? Most especially in a dirty suit."

CHAPTER 7

Wednesday finally came around and Sophie was ten minutes early. Benedict had said noon, so she walked out of the station so she could pretend to arrive five minutes late.

He wasn't there. She thought *he must have been held up in court. He promised. I will wait a while.* Half past twelve and still no sign of him, she thought, *how long should I wait? I will give him fifteen more minutes.* In the end, Sophie sat there until twenty minutes past one.

They called the train to Bishopbriggs, and she boarded it, still looking anxiously out of the window for a miracle. There was no miracle. Benedict Cochrane had once again made a fool out of her, and she stupidly let him. She thought about the night at the Torrance Inn. She remembered what she did—allowed him to do. She thought, *what a mess I have made. I really let myself down, my mother, my father, even Jack. These are awful people—snobs. They have done nothing but make a fool out of me. Even Euphemia and Sir Alfred—they are probably in on it too.*

By the time the train pulled into Bishopbriggs Station, Sophie Sullivan, so ashamed of her past behavior with a man not yet her husband, had made up her mind. The wedding was off, this new friendship with snobs was off. She was finished—finished with all of them.

She walked home to Balmuildy Road and threw herself on her bed crying. Jack came in to see her and she explained.

Jack said, "Sophie, we both have tickets for a new life in America. Try to think upon that and forget about these people. They are the reason we are leaving. Snobs like them, thinking they are better than the rest of us. They are no better than us. Remember that and hold your head high. No matter what has passed between you and that reprobate. It will be his loss and not yours."

Jack's words cheered Sophie somewhat, but not considerably so, and she never emerged out of her room that afternoon nor evening. She was packing her new clothes, grateful that she had brought them home and not left them at the Cochrane's mansion. The only things there were her white dress and new peignoir, neither of which she ever wanted to see again.

~

Benedict Cochrane felt a sense of relief. He had a plan. He had already attempted to rid Carlotta Ramirez from his life, but the woman was relentless. The affair had lasted almost two years, but after he saw Sophie Sullivan for the very first time, he found he could no longer tolerate the woman. He had once seen her as an exotic beauty, a widow close to forty but with the body of a temptress. She had always appealed to the darker side of his nature, and he never had any serious intentions toward her. He had on occasion alluded to it but he never saw her as a wife, or the woman he would walk proudly beside. He never loved her and, for him at least, the relationship was purely physical. He was thirty-two when first he met her at a drunken reunion, which was held in a pub in Edinburgh. He had never been in love as a young man and the simpering debutantes who were paraded before him by his mother, did nothing to stir his ardor.

After his mother passed away, followed quickly by her devoted husband—his father—he took on the responsibility of his spinster sister, and it seemed that neither he, nor she, were destined for love and marriage. He went a bit wild after that. His career as a barrister had taken off. He was rich and the ladies easily fell for his good looks and muscular frame. He looked after himself well too and dressed in the finest apparel. The man about town with a heart as cold as ice. Then one day it happened. It happened because he went to return money to a girl who had saved his sister embarrassment—the day she went to afternoon tea without her purse.

    He had never seen anyone like her. She was spectacular. Her hair so long and full in varying shades of blonde, ranging from flaxen to golden. Her eyes a vivid blue, her sensuous lips, her full breasts, accentuated by such a tiny waist. She wasn't very tall. He stood almost a foot taller, and she led him outside her brother's shop and gave him such a dressing down. No woman had ever done that to him before, and yet he knew. He knew the attraction was mutual and beyond physical. She was not of his social class, yet she spoke better than he. She was a shopkeeper's daughter with the pride and pertinence of a duchess. He didn't want to love her because that would mean he would have to marry her. She was twenty-three, and remarkably had never been kissed. This he could tell. Then he ridiculously invited her for Sunday afternoon tea. He escaped with her that day and kissed her and his fate was sealed. He could turn his back on her and on loving her, but if he did so, he would die a lonely old man, remembering the girl he allowed to sail away to America, and into the arms of another man. Wealthy or not, she would not remain single for long. She was the most enchanting beauty he had ever seen and with dignity and confidence, he would never grow tired of testing.

    Benedict's mind was brought back to Carlotta. He was to marry his dream girl in a few days, then disappear, for a week or so. He would tell Carlotta, he got married to a goddess, and threaten her with some made up legal action, which would have her deported back to Spain—should she choose to interfere with his life. He hadn't seen the woman since the day he met Sophie Belle, but that was only several weeks really. He would have preferred to get rid of her and marry Sophie with a clear conscience but there wasn't time, with that steamer ticket hanging over his head.

He looked at his pocket watch, eleven forty-five; time to make his way to Queen Street Station. It would be delightful to spend an innocent afternoon with Sophie Belle. He knew she was worried about the night they spent together in the Torrance Inn as if she was somewhat tarnished in his eyes. The precise opposite was the case. Although they hadn't quite made love, they came very close to it, and her passion for him so stirred him up, he found it difficult to concentrate on the law. Beauty was one thing, but one would soon tire of beauty, if that was all there was. Sophie Belle's passion excited him beyond anything he could have imagined, because it was born of love, and for the first time in Benedict's thirty-four years, he realized he was in love. No matter how hard he had tried to hold himself back from loving Sophie Belle, he was deeply in love with her.

Benedict Cochrane was smiling to himself as he ran down the steps of the Glasgow High Court. Then he saw Carlotta and his smile disappeared. Carlotta Ramirez had dared to come to Glasgow, dared to approach the Glasgow High Court, despite her unanswered and anguished letters to him, even though, even before Sophie Belle, he had begun to show boredom in their lovemaking, in her body and appearance. Had he never met Sophie Sullivan, he would have still wanted rid of Carlotta.

He had to get her away from the courthouse before she was seen. He led her to a nearby pub, looking at his watch and realizing that once again, he was letting Sophie Belle down. His innocent afternoon had turned into the nightmare of Carlotta Ramirez and of sweet Sophie, waiting at the station for a lover who would not show up.

He thought, *possibly she will wait for me. She may think I was held up in chambers.* However, it took him almost two hours to convince Carlotta to board the train at Glasgow Central Station, bound for Edinburgh, with the promise he would come to her on Sunday next. He didn't say it would be to tell her he got married, nor did he mention his plan to threaten her with deportation. Carlotta Ramirez did not enter the United Kingdom legally. She had come along with her previous lover, whom she abandoned when she met Benedict, and when they began their sordid affair.

Benedict Cochrane ran along to Queen Street Station, but by now it was two o'clock. No woman would wait two hours—not even Sophie Belle.

It was late when he returned home but Euphemia was still up. She asked him how his afternoon went, and he said, "Something came up and I had to stand Sophie up. Well, I did go to meet her, but I was two hours late, and consequently, she had already left."

Euphemia was disgusted. She knew Sophie and her friendship was being severely threatened by the behavior of her brother and she told him so. "I doubt she will marry you now. I think she will have had quite enough of the Cochranes, between that ridiculous dinner party and now this. Where is it you go anyway—these nights you stay out; the Sundays you disappear? Do you have a mistress, Benedict? Are you two-timing and making a fool of Sophie?"

Benedict finally admitted it. "Okay, Euphemia, the truth. Of course, I have had lady-friends, mistresses as you call them, but I have not, nor would I, two-time Sophie Belle. The other truth? I hate this house. However, I keep it up just for you. Not such a bad brother, am I? Also, I suppose it better suits a wife and potential family than the flat I own and prefer to stay at in Kelvinside. I never told you about it, in case you wanted to move there too. Anyway, it is too small, despite the twelve-foot ceilings."

Euphemia was somewhat relieved. She wasn't so fond of the Cochrane mansion either, and would herself prefer a small flat. The house was big and drafty and was situated such that the light barely came in the many windows, except in the late evenings of summer.

She said, "I like it no better than you. I don't think Sophie particularly likes it either. Although she might like it better if you put some effort into making it nice for her. Of course, that is if she is still planning to marry you, after your latest misbehavior."

He said, "You can go and explain what happened I mean about me being late. I will think about all these details, the house, our future lives, after that ship leaves—with her brother on it. Did you know he's got her ticket? At least that's what she told me. There isn't time now and I have matters to take care of. Then you'll see. Things will be different. Your job—make sure she is at the courthouse."

∽

Euphemia went to see Sophie the day after Benedict left her sitting at the station. At first Sophie was withdrawn, and then she spat out that both Euphemia and Sir Alfred were "make-believe" friends, but truly they were snobs, and it was all a set up to humiliate her for paying for lunch that first time she and Euphemia met.

The expression of sheer astonishment on Euphemia's face somehow caused Sophie to burst into laughter and she said, "That is so totally absurd and ridiculous, Euphemia. You and Sir Alfred have been all kindness and benevolence. I am saying all this nonsense to cover up my own stupidity. Most especially the night of the dinner party. Oh, if only there truly was a Mr. Cyrus Hatter!"

Euphemia laughed and took her friend into her arms. "How Sir Alfred enjoyed that. After you left, Benedict basically pulled me off my chair and out into the entrance hall. He was so jealous and angry, and I furthered your cause by saying Mr. Hatter was a dreamboat. Even Sir Alfred joined in and further enunciated his virtues. Anyway, I have found out a few new pieces of information for you."

Sophie said, "He has a mistress. Am I correct?"

Euphemia responded, "Well it wouldn't totally surprise me. However, if so, he is desperately trying to get rid of her. My brother was always the "bad boy" type of man—possibly to be the opposite of our father. That image he has had of himself is slipping away, because whether he knows it or not, he has fallen in love with you. He is having difficulty reconciling himself to the new man he is becoming or trying not to become. When you leave him, he will be in total misery, and we shall then see which Benedict Cochrane wins the battle—the good or the evil one. Beyond that, I know where he disappears to, all the time, and it is not to his mistress. It is to his flat in Kelvinside! He told me he hates our house in Bishopbriggs and that he keeps it on for me. The truth is I would have been happy in a small flat too—oh not with him—God no!"

Sophie was intrigued, "Well he can sell the house after we leave— if he truly wants to—I don't like it much either. It is so dark and depressing. Okay Euphemia, you have convinced me. The wedding is back on, as is our new lives in America. I would very much enjoy seeing Mr. Cochrane in a state of misery. However, I will just have to imagine it, because I will be far away. Euphemia, do you think he might come for me?"

Euphemia said, "It will depend on which side of his nature triumphs. Let's hope for the good. If it is the dark side, then he will be lost forever. You have a little more than a week before the wedding. I think you and I deserve a few days at the seaside. Possibly St. Anne's-on-Sea? My parents used to take us there as children for a summer holiday. I will tell Benedict that I am taking you away to clear your head. I will tell him you are reconsidering your marriage. Allow him to suffer for a few days. We will leave on Saturday and return a couple of days before your wedding. I will keep him away from you until then. What do you think?"

Sophie said, "I think I would love a few days away to clear my head, as you put it. I believe Jack will give me money if I ask him. He is planning to anyway."

Euphemia said, "No, it is my wedding present to you, combined with my apology for ever bringing my brother into your life. I will tell him that I need this time away with you to settle your nerves following his atrocious behavior."

※

Benedict wasn't happy about the plan but went along with it. Euphemia had changed since she met Sophie Belle Sullivan, indeed everything had changed for that matter. It was quite amazing, the effect this shopkeeper's daughter had on the mighty Cochranes. Euphemia no longer seemed to care a whit for what he thought or said, and of course she had Sir Alfred Hicks to champion her cause. He wanted to speak to Sophie Belle, make up some lie about why he again let her down, and regretted sending his sister on the mission instead.

He said, "Well I suppose I won't stop you, but I'm not paying for it. Let her brother do so. I understand he isn't short of a pound or two since selling everything off. I will be glad when he boards that steamer."

He paused, "I will take you both to the train station. I want to see what is in her eyes. Did you ever notice how expressive they are, Euphemia? Every little emotion shows, even when she is putting on airs, as she is so fond of doing. I still blame you for bringing her into my life. She is the type of woman who enjoys tying a man in knots. Possibly I am not the first man to suffer the retribution of Sophie Belle Sullivan. I will be the last however, and we shall see who triumphs then!"

Euphemia couldn't help but laugh at her lovelorn brother, "Fiddlesticks," she said, "all of this drama and pain, you yourself, have created."

Euphemia did indeed keep Sophie away from her brother but really, in his mind, their marriage couldn't honestly begin until after he got rid of Carlotta for good and until after the ship sailed. He was nervous of Carlotta somehow showing up before their day in court, or even on their day in court, as she was still sending him pathetic and somewhat threatening letters—possibly this was best. Besides, he would be able to truly see how much he missed Sophie Belle Sullivan, during her few days at the seaside.

Saturday morning: and the ladies were packed and ready for their seaside sojourn. They would return on Wednesday, so that Sophie had time to prepare for her upcoming nuptials. Of course, she had little to prepare, since she still intended to wear her blue suit. However—just in case—she purchased some beautiful new lace underclothing, petticoats, camisoles, garters and stockings at a lovely little ladies' lingerie shop in St. Anne's. Jack gave her spending money, and for the first time in Sophie's young life she felt like a real lady. She expressed this to Euphemia, who told her, "Sophie, if ever there was a girl destined to be special, it is you. Destiny has much in store for you, this I know, and it will all be good. Also, Sophie, you are very much a young lady, beautiful and kind. You are virtuous too. No matter what my brother would try to have you believe."

Euphemia always made Sophie feel better—special—almost the opposite of what her brother did, and Sophie started to notice the young men, gazing at her and smiling as she and Euphemia went about their day. After all, she wore no ring.

She asked her best friend and soon to be sister, in all of her endearing innocence, "Euphemia, would you consider me a catch? You know, if I were truly single?"

Euphemia said, "Are you changing your mind about my brother? I wouldn't blame you if you were."

Sophie thought about it, "Oh no, never, he absolutely owns my heart. I just wish he thought of me as *a catch*, instead of thinking of himself as one."

Euphemia said, "He already does. He probably regrets having Jack take us to the train station. That was childish, not even evil—just plain childish. He is acting like a big baby!"

Both women joined arms and were laughing as they made their

way down the seaside resort's delightful High Street, and Sophie said, "I wonder who will pick us up at the train station."

∽

The ladies thoroughly enjoyed their few days away, most especially after all the tears and drama of the previous weeks. The August sunshine was warm, and they didn't have a spot of rain. They both bought bathing suits and ran down to paddle in the sea, since neither of them could swim. They enjoyed afternoon tea in their little boarding house, where all the other guests were married couples; one or two of whom appeared to be on honeymoon. This saddened Sophie and again she wondered why she was marrying such a cruel and heartless man. She expressed this sentiment aloud to Euphemia, who said, "Well, you can still call it off. However, tell me Sophie, would you want any of our fellow guests, assuming they were single and available?"

Sophie looked around at the other guests and said, "Goodness no! Benedict Cochrane is the most handsome and manly man in the world. I will miss him so, when I leave him to rot in his flat in Kelvinside."

Euphemia laughed, "Well my brother is well favored—visually at least—but I don't know if I would go that far. However, the thought of him rotting in his secret flat, being kept warm by his bottle of whisky, does indeed please me. For years, I feared his condemnation. I preferred to stay out of his way. Now soon I will be far away from him, although since I have known you, I no longer care about his opinions, and I refuse to follow his orders."

∽

The days went in all too quickly, however, Euphemia was so glad she thought of it. Sophie was rejuvenated and her confidence was shining with her sun kissed cheeks and freckled nose. Both ladies had purchased new summer dresses; Euphemia's a sensible brown with sky blue piping, however even she had blossomed during their days away. She had changed considerably from the lady who forgot her purse that extraordinary day she and Sophie met. Euphemia's bearing, her clarity of speech, and Sophie taught her how to wear her chestnut brown locks to her best advantage.

Sophie had chosen an aqua-marine ensemble, which included a matching top hat, with a veil she pulled over her face when the train arrived at Glasgow Central Station. Both ladies were carrying parasols to match their new ensembles.

Sophie Sullivan's heart skipped a beat when she saw Benedict Cochrane awaiting them. It was another humid August day and surprisingly, he was carrying his topcoat over his shoulder. He wore no tie, and his shirt collar was unbuttoned—his sleeves were rolled up. He was unshaven and he desperately needed a haircut. Euphemia was aghast at her brother's appearance, but all Sophie said was, "Oh my, Euphemia, isn't he the most handsome man in the world! We saw no one who even came close to his good looks and manliness in St. Anne's."

Euphemia simply said, "Too much sun Sophie. What on earth is this supposed to be about? Hopefully, not an attempt to make you feel guilty!"

He approached them and made an exaggerated bow. "The return of the spinsters. No sorry, I believe one of them is getting married on Saturday. You both look well. Looks like you spent a fortune on new attire. Not my money I hope."

Euphemia couldn't help herself, "Benedict, you look an absolute disgrace. Whose benefit is this meant to be for?"

Sophie lifted her veil. She was smiling so happily, and Benedict knew for certain. The love between them had become an unbreakable bond. He wondered if she would disapprove of his mode of apparel—as indeed his sister was voicing loudly. He had never seen her look so magnificent; indeed, like a duchess. Men were tripping over each other to catch a glimpse of her. She didn't show any disapproval of his disheveled appearance—none at all. He could hear his sister talking loudly to the porters and telling him he was the one who should be doing so—still complaining about his hair and untidy appearance. He was ignoring her, and he smiled at Sophie and said, "Sophie Belle, you have freckles on your nose."

Sophie smiled shyly and looked down, his gaze was so intense, she could hardly meet his eyes. Then he lifted her chin and said, "Hello beautiful. I can tell you still love me, no matter what. Your eyes could never hide it."

He then, unceremoniously, handed his coat and hat to his sister and took Sophie into his arms for such a kiss and embrace that Sophie expected to always remember, first thing every morning and last thing every night, for a very long time yet to come.

He finally turned to the porter and told him to load up the Wolseley Tourer. He gave the man a substantial tip for keeping an eye on his car, and the man seemed to know him. He called him, Mr. Cochrane, and Benedict called the man Danny. Sophie noticed none of this. She was in a trance, or so thought Euphemia who wondered; the train to Edinburgh leaves from this station but not to Bishopbriggs. That would be Queen Street Station. Euphemia hoped for the opportunity to investigate her brother a little further before his wedding in two days' time. She had seen several letters arrive from Edinburgh in recent weeks and months, and the handwriting was dissimilar to the usual correspondence he received. His surname was also spelled incorrectly. She wished she had had the courage to steam open at least one of these missives—to ascertain their contents.

Benedict took both ladies to Bookbinder's for an expensive lunch, accompanied by champagne, after which he dropped Euphemia home, and sped off in his car with Sophie, who was holding on to her new hat.

He drove down the road to the country farm track they had stopped at before. He said, "Well you already know how well you look—the sea air, or possibly a few days away from me. What did you do there? Did you meet any men? Did you and Euphemia go to pubs? Did you wear a bathing costume? Were you flirting with other men?"

Sophie started laughing but Benedict said it wasn't funny.

"Okay," she said, "Here goes. The sea air certainly did us both good, although I missed you a lot. We went shopping and swimming—well sort of since neither of us can swim. We did not go to any pubs, although we dined in a couple expensive restaurants. We stayed in a very nice bed and breakfast where all the other guests were couples, some even on their honeymoons—lucky them. I often received admiring glances from gentlemen, both single and not so single. I suppose I looked to be available since I wear no engagement ring. I didn't talk to any of them. I put my nose in the air. Are you happy now?"

"I don't think a young lady should go on holiday without her husband. Are you a young lady, Sophie Belle?"

Sophie said, "I would say I am. I have become, at least at the moment, a lady of leisure, however, I don't believe I have a husband to be concerned about. Why did you come to the train station like that? I like you messed up but Euphemia was aghast!"

He said, "Who cares about Euphemia? Let's spend the night at the Torrance Inn, like we did before?"

Sophie said, "No, please take me home. You are behaving very strangely and when you do this, it scares me. You know it does."

Benedict said, "Perhaps I like to scare you, Sophie Belle. You have avoided me this past week or more, but I have you alone now—in your fancy new dress. What if it got all muddy?"

Sophie began to cry. He was scaring her. Why was he doing this? "You want to destroy my pretty new dress to prove I am just a shopkeeper's daughter. Also, you have thought about my behavior at the Torrance Inn and think I am a wanton. That's what men call ladies who are too, well you know, but it was because, well…. I don't want to talk about it. Okay, point taken. Please take me home now."

Suddenly he changed, his face softened, "Oh God no, Sophie

Belle. I didn't mean that. I was just jealous that being away from me made you look so well. You even have freckles. I love your freckles. As for wanton? Where did you even get that word? Sophie Belle, you are a woman in love, and I am the fortunate man to be the recipient of such love and desire. Tell me I am forgiven, and I will take you straight home."

Sophie calmed down. How could she love a man who so often scared her? He never laid a hand on her. What was it about him? She said, "What about you, Benedict? Are you a man in love?"

He smiled, "Might be, beginning to feel like a probability, unless of course it is still infatuation."

Sophie said, "Oh I give up. Never mind, will you kiss me first? I am not ashamed to say I have missed your kisses. I will even take off my hat so you can mess up my hair."

Somehow her comment brought such a big, happy smile to his face. Sophie couldn't quite understand it. So she removed her hat and they both sat there kissing and cuddling for quite a while, until the intensity began to build up and Benedict suddenly said, "I must get you home, Sophie Belle."

He then sped off without another word, and when they arrived at her house he shouted, "See you at the courthouse, Sophie Sullivan!"

What struck her was his sudden change in mood and he wasn't smiling or even looking remotely happy, when he shouted out to her—as one would assume a very soon-to-be bridegroom would.

When Sophie walked inside the house Jack was packing his suitcases and said, "Are you still coming, Sophie? Are you still going through with this sham of a wedding?"

Sophie said, "Yes, I will still be on that ship, and yes I am still going to marry the slightly unhinged but otherwise magnificent Benedict Cochrane, whom I will be leaving shortly after our wedding day."

Jack said, "I don't know who is crazier—you or him, but as long as you are on that steamer, I will go along with your ridiculous plan."

CHAPTER 8

The wedding day went exactly as expected.

Jack and Euphemia were witnesses, and the judge performed the civil service—against his better judgement. The unhappy couple stood side by side. Neither were dressed for the occasion and Benedict said, "I see you wore that suit again. I am sure your guests will be impressed."

Then it was time for the ring and Sir Alfred couldn't believe his ears when Benedict said, "Damn, I forgot all about that!"

Benedict and Sophie traveled back to the house in silence. Sophie was refusing to look at him and kept her head turned, looking out the car window. She was barely holding back her tears of humiliation. Euphemia and Jack went in Sir Alfred's vehicle, and Sophie was certain they had plenty to say to one another.

When they arrived at the house, Sophie ran upstairs crying, and Jack had to control his temper, as he longed for the day, he would be boarding that train with his sister, away from Norma, away from Cochrane and away from Bishopbriggs.

Sophie was lying across her bed crying but it was Benedict who came up to her.

He said, "I'm sorry about the ring. I am sorry about everything. You deserved better. How about you change into your white dress. You were so stunning in that. Didn't I tell you—I meant to. I will help you."

Sophie stood up and Benedict took off her suit. He left on all her new pretty underclothing—he didn't touch her. Then she realized her stockings were ripped and she started crying again. He found another pair and as he took the ripped stocking off, he told her that her legs were lovely.

He didn't make any advances toward her and when she was changed, he simply said, "I will see you downstairs. Our guests are arriving."

He didn't even kiss her, and her kiss in the courtroom was barely more than a peck on the cheek. Sophie thought of their night at the Torrance Inn. This made no sense. It was too much to bear, and she wished Euphemia would come to her rescue. They probably all thought that he had made love to her. He didn't touch her. He seemed to want her so badly, the night they spent together, and now that she was his, he appeared to have lost interest in it, or in her anyway. She felt sick. How could she go downstairs?

Finally, Euphemia came up to collect her. "Everyone is looking for you," she said. She seemed cheerful until she noticed Sophie's tear-stained face.

She said, "We thought?"

Sophie said, "He helped me into my gown is all. What did you think? Well, whatever you thought, you were wrong. I suppose I must go down. At least for a little while, so his friends can enjoy my humiliation."

Benedict had hired a string quartet and Sophie wondered how he could remember that but not a wedding ring. By the time she went downstairs, folks were dancing and therefore no first dance for the bride. He was drinking with his friends and the ladies pretty much ignored her. After a short while, Jack and Sir Alfred left, disgusted, and Euphemia took Sophie up to the bridal suite. By now, even she knew her brother was drunk, and that the peignoir was a waste. Sophie Cochrane, nee Sullivan, would most definitely be on that ship.

Sophie said, "I want to lock my door. He is down there with several drunk friends, and I am afraid."

Euphemia was reassuring Sophie, when she heard a man's voice shout, "Cochrane, if you don't want her. I would be happy to oblige."

Euphemia locked the door and remained with her sweet friend that night—Sophie's wedding night.

The next morning Sophie realized she was alone. It was Sunday. The morning after Sophie's wedding day. She would be leaving on Wednesday and her cases were packed and with Jack at his house.

There was a knock at her door. It was Benedict—dressed impeccably as he always seemed to be. She sat up, still wearing her pretty new peignoir, which she had decided to leave behind when she left him.

He said, "You look delicious. Positively delightful with your hair tussled, in your pretty little negligée. Euphemia did a splendid job on your room. Do you like it? Anyway, sorry I need to go to Edinburgh today—can't be helped."

Sophie thought *he is talking utter nonsense. Delightful, am I? Delicious even? I am so glad he likes the wedding night boudoir that he neglected to sleep in last night.*

She remained silent. "I will be back on Friday. Big case. I rushed this whole thing didn't I, Sophie Belle? I made a mess of it. It was all that talk of New York, but now that I know your ship is leaving the harbor, and you are not on it, I feel better. I will make everything up to you. Perhaps, take you up North for a week or so. We can be alone together. Also, need to buy you a diamond. I'm truly sorry, Sophie. I don't mean that I married you. You are the loveliest girl on the planet. And I think I might even love you. I was afraid it was just infatuation—that it would pass. Anyway, everyone thinks I put you in the family way, and that was the reason for the rush. That's a laugh, isn't it? I mean you still being a virgin—I think—no that isn't fair. It is obvious you are, to me anyway."

He stopped, waiting for her to speak. She said, "Are you leaving straight away this morning then?"

"Yes," he said, "more's the pity. Seeing you like this and knowing you are my wife, and I could make love to you right now? However, no time. Let's talk when I get back, have a fresh start."

He kissed the top of her head and was gone. *Gone forever,* thought Sophie, *in a way that is a relief. I can take my time. Get ready to be off on my new life. Perhaps if he had thought about all this before? No, he was nervous. He knew he made a fool of himself with that sham of a wedding. Not as big a fool as he will feel upon his return from his important trip to Edinburgh.*

~

Benedict ran downstairs and drove off in his shiny new Wolseley. He felt uneasy somehow, even though he prevented Sophie Sullivan from leaving. He thought, *Sophie Cochrane now. I didn't forget the ring. It is still in my pocket. I wanted to go to her last night but got drunk so I couldn't. All this to keep her off the steamer. Well done, Barrister Cochrane. Now what?* There was no important case in Edinburgh. First, he had to finally end it with Carlotta Ramirez —he had been wanting to do that for some time anyway, and now he could tell her he took a young bride and threaten her with deportation if she gave him any trouble. Then he needed some time to himself. He needed to understand this obsession with a girl, who was in certitude too good for him, and not the other way around as he often so cruelly said to her. Still, she married him. That must mean she saw some good in him. He needed to find the good that he now knew was somewhere inside of him, and throw away forever, the darker side that had engulfed him since his father's death. He pitied his father for loving his cold and unfeeling mother, and in trying so hard to please her. However, Sophie Belle wasn't like his mother. Any doubts about that were laid to rest that night at the Torrance Inn—the night he had been dreaming about ever since.

He parked his car in the lock up and boarded the train. He was soon asleep, after a night of hard drinking. He kept remembering Sophie in her pretty little negligée and wondered what type of man he was. He almost went straight back—almost—but there were matters that needed attended to, before he could return to sweet little Sophie Belle, the shopkeeper's daughter.

CHAPTER 9

Wednesday morning, and there was much laughter and excitement at Glasgow Central Station. Euphemia had done a hat-trick. She was packed and ready to go by Monday night. On Tuesday, Euphemia took care of her financial arrangements, and a telegram was sent to the Carlisles of an additional guest. She didn't want to be there when her brother returned. No one was to leave him a note. The only thing to be left was Sophie's wedding night peignoir, laid out on the marriage bed, the one that never was.

Sir Alfred Hicks promised to go see him. Someone should after all, and why not the judge who married him?

Euphemia Cochrane had a first-class stateroom, but Sophie managed to slip up to see her often enough. Jack was content to remain in his Second-Class cabin and as he put it, "Count his money," since both properties were sold. He had enough to start a new life, and to give a substantial sum to his sister which would allow her to stock up the little gift shop she longed for in New Chestnut.

The voyage was pleasant since it was still summer and soon, they were being met by the Carlisles, who were more than happy to have not one but three Scottish house guests.

Of course, Sophie had to explain. Although when she spoke it aloud it made very little sense. Loretta and David Carlisle resolved to speak to this man's sister as soon as they could get her alone. Also, Jack, why did he allow it?

Loretta said, "So, now my niece is a married woman—sort of—with no chance of making a suitable match in New York, even although, I swear she is the loveliest creature whoever walked the earth! And you Jack, you turn up divorced. In God's name what is going on in Scotland?"

Euphemia asked to speak to the Carlisle's in private, "I may have worked this out on my way to New York, although I could well be wrong. May I be frank with you both?"

Of course, they agreed. "He broke her heart and yet I know he loves her as much as she loves him. I know this because he left for Edinburgh on Sunday morning and I decided finally to have a good rummage through his office, knowing I would not be found out, or at least not until I had left the country."

Euphemia asked for a glass of sherry which David Carlisle gladly provided.

She began, "There was a mistress. Before he met Sophie, but one of long standing, possibly a couple of years. He has been trying to break it off with her, but she will not accept it—begging, pleading and finally threatening. She wrote of exposing him to his high and mighty friends. She accused him of having another mistress and vowed to tell her intimate details of their relationship, if she found this to be the case. I prefer not to say more than that, however, my assumption is this woman has very low morals to have written such graphic detail in a letter. I had to scan over it. Anyway, he has been trying to get rid of her, even before he met Sophie, but now he is determined and also now he is a married man. I believe, of course, he will triumph in the end. Perhaps he will tell her he has taken a young bride. However, possibly too late to win back his sweet Sophie. That is why he never touched her. That is why he married her. He thought it would keep her in Scotland until he got rid of this other woman. Strange way of going about things I know. My brother is brilliant, and brilliant men can be a bit sideways in their way of thinking. Perhaps if he came clean with Sophie, instead of all the nonsense and drama he created? I believe this woman to be much older than him through some of her comments in this regard. Possibly a widow? Also, from her desperate letters, I could tell she was foreign. Her spelling and misuse of words. I do know he has never gone near her since the day he met Sophie, but she has threatened to come to Glasgow. She may have even done so already. There you have it. My brother will be thirty-five in November. One cannot expect him to have been an angel surely. But an angel fell in love with him and he with her. The rest is up to him. My brother is a bit of an odd fish, but Sophie has completely given her heart to him. I hope he comes for her. If he doesn't, he will die a sad and lonely old man."

Loretta said, "My, this could be a novel. If so, I hope it is not a tragedy. Her uncle Carlisle will see that she gets her gift shop. Let's see if that is enough. I somehow doubt it. There is a sadness about her. Do you think he will want to have their marriage annulled? Sophie having left him, quite humiliating I would think. Do you feel Sophie will agree to it, should he suggest such a thing?"

Euphemia said, "Your niece has categorically stated she will not set him free to pursue other women. Of course, that would not rule out a future mistress, but somehow, I don't see it, most especially after his experience with his last one. Call me an optimist, but I see them coming together in the end. I am, of course, unsure when and where that end might be."

It was decided that no more would be spoken about the matter. All five would be traveling together on the train up to New Chestnut and after that, and if Sophie was still in the state of mind, they would have the little gift shop and the apartment well in order shortly after Halloween, which was very popular in New Chestnut.

Euphemia was reassured that the apartment above the shop was not so little. It comprised of four bedrooms, a nice sized kitchen, a well-proportioned parlor, library and dining room. There was also indoor plumbing and a very sweet little garden.

Sophie could barely contain her excitement on the train and

surprisingly, Euphemia was feeling rather enthusiastic too! She didn't particularly like the city and also, she didn't want to leave her little friend up there on her own. Jack said he would probably return to New York City when the apartment and shop were all set up. What could there possibly be for him in such a little backwoods town?

Both Loretta and Euphemia understood Sophie wrote frequent letters to Benedict, none of which she posted, and all of which were locked up in a little wooden box she purchased in Manhattan.

Euphemia and Sophie wrote to Sir Alfred and Sophie wondered if Euphemia was a little in love with him. In her letters, Sophie asked, in what she felt was an indirect manner, what Benedict was doing. Was he angry? Glad? Sorry? Indifferent?

The train arrived and the three Scots fell in love with the small town with its wonderful little main street. The houses all resembled Victorian ladies, with colorful fretwork and many were dressed for Halloween. It was already cold and how Sophie longed for the snowy winters. She thought of Benedict constantly. He was always lurking somewhere in her mind. She was sure he had moved on already. It was almost two months since she left him. She was somewhat surprised that he made no attempt to have their marriage annulled, and she had this information on good authority from Sir Alfred Hicks.

Back in Scotland, Benedict Cochrane boarded the train in Edinburgh with four visible scratches on his left cheek. He thought this would take some explaining. *I have been physically attacked by two women. This last attack disgusted me since it followed her sad and pathetic attempted seduction. Quite frankly, not sure what I ever saw in that woman.* Then he thought about it more, *oh yes, her bedtime antics. Still dear God, I could never go near her again, even if there was no Sophie. Sophie—I will finally make her truly mine. I will spoil her, but I also enjoy arousing that temper of hers. I thoroughly enjoyed her attack upon me.*

I so wanted her after that, and our night at the Torrance Inn has been emblazoned in my mind ever since. He laughed to himself, *she called herself a wanton, so afraid she had gone too far. She might well have done so, but it was without a doubt the most magnificent night I have ever spent with a woman—my woman now. She will likely attack me again, and I am good with that. If she still loves me. I have been a total bastard, cruelly belittling her. I pray she will forgive me. I pray she still hates me because she doesn't. She loves me.* Then he cringed, the ring, her sweet little negligée, getting drunk. Perhaps he had gone too far.

∽

    Benedict Cochrane somehow knew it immediately. The Haberdashery was closed with a sign that read, Under New Ownership—Reopening September 15. He thought, *did Jack really leave his sister behind?* He drove up to the house. Mrs. Thompson, his housekeeper, came out to greet him with a worried look upon her face. No Sophie Belle, no Euphemia. He just stood and waited for her to speak.
    "Oh Mr. Cochrane, sir, they left on Wednesday. Your sister, bride and that brother of hers. Sir Alfred Hicks drove them to the station, but he said to inform you he would be in touch and that he was not traveling to America along with them. The ship sailed on Thursday. We hoped you would be back in time to prevent it, but Mr. Thompson and I had no way of contacting you."
    Benedict said nothing. What could he say? He just proceeded on his way into the now empty house. Sophie clearly lied about the date. She must have intended this all along. Or possibly not? Was it the sham of a wedding that convinced her? A bridegroom who had to be helped upstairs by his cronies, drunk, and beyond all their understanding, with a lovely bride that had been awaiting him? He tried to explain the next morning. She was probably already packed—her mind set on punishing him. Why did she go through with the marriage? She would

still be on the ship, and he had no way of contacting her or any of them, and then he thought, *Hicks! He is in on this. He knows. I will go there.*

Benedict Cochrane washed and changed, but not before he checked his wife's bedroom. Well actually it was just a guest bedroom. She hadn't even been given her own room. He saw her negligée, the one she was wearing the night he didn't go to her. It was laid out on the bed. A touch of drama, no doubt. Also, her white dress was still hanging in the wardrobe. Nothing else was in there—everything was gone—but then she had only been there a couple days. She never really lived there. He realized that she brought nothing else with her on her wedding day. He also remembered that she wasn't overly upset when he left her the next morning.

He went to his sister's room. It was obviously vacated too—just a few older pieces of clothing still hanging in the closet. Her room had been cleaned and freshened by the maids. He realized that Sophie's room was deliberately just as she left it, and he searched for a note, but there was none.

His next stop was his office. Someone had gone through his drawers. Why hadn't he locked them? He remembered; he was hungover. Carlotta's pathetic letters were on his desk and then he saw Euphemia's writing. It was just a short note.

> Benedict,
>
> *I haven't mentioned any of this disgusting correspondence to your bride. However, at least I know where you are. You are with your mistress. Correct? Why would it take you so many days to call a halt to your sordid relationship? Sir Alfred Hicks will be able to keep you updated about our new lives in New York. Sophie and I will keep in touch with him. No one will write to you. No need is there? Nothing to be said.*
>
> *Euphemia*

Benedict already knew Sophie had lied about the date the ship sailed, but what was the name of it? That was negligent of him. He should have checked and not taken her word—and he a renowned barrister? Sophie Sullivan, now Cochrane, was an intelligent girl who certainly got one over on him. He had made the critical mistake of underestimating her intelligence.

He jumped into his car and went on his way to Whitecraigs. It was Friday afternoon and he expected Judge Hicks to be at home.

⁓

He confronted him. "Was I played as the fool here? You knew about their plans, didn't you? Why did she go through with it? To punish me? There will be no millionaire. No anyone. I will not agree to annulment or divorce if that is what she has in mind. And Euphemia, what the hell is in her head? That young woman—I will not call her a lady—has ruined lives and…." He stopped, as if to compose himself, "Sir Alfred, why? Why marry me, only to run away?"

Sir Alfred had been expecting Benedict Cochrane. Their lives had somehow become intertwined. He said, "You know Cochrane, none of this might have occurred had you behaved like a gentleman. Euphemia told me there was a mistress. I am presuming by the scratches on your face, it was a difficult break-up. Regardless, it should have been taken care of before you married Sophie—before you even courted her—but then you really didn't court her, did you, Cochrane?"

Benedict said, "There was no time. I had to keep her off that ship…." He trailed off.

Sir Alfred said, "Well all three of them, the brother too, sailed yesterday, out of Liverpool. They spent Wednesday night with Sophie and Jack's cousin—in Chester, as I recall."

Benedict said, "She never told me she had relatives in England. England, America? You know what, Sir Alfred? I don't know a thing about this woman. All I know is that she has made me into a damned fool. Why? She obviously doesn't care about me—thought of my loving her as a joke. Revenge? I will have the last laugh here! She has not done with me yet. Not until I decide I am done with her."

Sir Alfred sat the younger man down and poured him a drink. He could see he was shattered, almost to the point of tears, so he decided to tell him Sophie's side of the story—at least as he saw it—and to give him some advice.

"There is no doubt the girl is in love with you. However, your behavior toward her was deplorable. That wedding, no ring, getting drunk, all your cronies there drinking. No romantic wedding night? Why Cochrane? She feared you were a monster. She is afraid of you, yet she loves you for some unknown reason. She has gone to lead a quiet life and open her little gift shop. She said you have cured her from men for life. She doesn't want a divorce or annulment. She's a bit complicated. Or is it heart broken. Her uncle in New York is a successful attorney, rather wealthy, as I understand. You surely know her mother was English, married a bit beneath herself, but the family stood by her. The house on Balmuildy Road—they bought that as a wedding gift. Her father already owned the shop and the flat upstairs. Not exactly paupers although you treated her as such. She frankly said as much to Euphemia and I, dirt beneath your feet—something like that anyway."

Benedict said, "Why didn't she tell me any of this. Might have made me feel a bit better. I was worried about her background— somewhat anyway—you know, not being able to dance, working as a shop girl. I might have considered her as a little closer to my equal."

Sir Alfred was astounded, "Good God, Cochrane! You have just lost your wife, sister and been attacked by some low life mistress. She is not only your equal. She is high above you, in every possible way. Anyway, I will keep you informed. They both promised to write to me often. I don't believe they have any intention of writing to you. So, there you have it. I may plan a trip later in the year. I will see how they get on first, of course."

Benedict knew he was being dismissed, and said, "Well if you write back be sure to pass along my good wishes for a successful life in Old Chestnut. I will not be going after her. Let her know that too."

Sir Alfred said, "It is New Chestnut actually, not that it matters to you. I will pass along your good wishes. I am sure Sophie Belle will appreciate them."

Benedict said, "That's what I call her."

Sir Alfred said, "Really? I call her that too. Have an enjoyable weekend, Cochrane. See you at Chambers on Monday."

CHAPTER 10

Sophie loved New Chestnut—from the moment the train drew into the station—and soon Jack was painting and fixing up the shop and the flat above. David Carlisle had hired a couple of local men to help and was footing the bill for the repairs and the inventory required for *Sophie Belle's Fine Ladies Gift Shoppe*, with the understanding that her profits—if indeed there were any—would be used to further stock the little store.

    Sophie's energy in ordering and displaying her new merchandize for the store's grand opening was addictive and she often joked that "Once a shopkeeper's daughter, always a shopkeeper's daughter." Meanwhile Euphemia was busily issuing orders for the decorating and furnishing of the living apartments upstairs. The building was well situated in the center of the town, although not attached to the row of other stores along the little town center. The enthusiasm displayed by their three Scottish guests delighted the Carlisles, who could often be found in New Chestnut themselves, lending a helping hand, most especially Loretta Carlisle, regarding merchandizing the charming little shop. David Carlisle had invested a considerable sum of money in the enterprise, but he too was enjoying the enthusiasm of all three ladies. In recent years his wife had tired of New York society and since they had not been blessed with children, Sophie Belle and Jack were the next best thing. Even Euphemia had won a place in their hearts. Mr. David Carlisle fervently hoped that his niece's man would come to her, most especially when he found out about the opening for a town attorney—not quite the grandiose barrister in the Glasgow High Courts, but sometimes a man could change and possibly he would find he had enough of defending villains and murderers. David decided to write to the mysterious Benedict Cochrane about the position. He was completely fascinated by the man, with whom his sister's child was so very much in love.

∽

Sophie toured the town, checking out each establishment and making lists of what she needed to order to make her shop a success. It was to open mid-November and already all sorts of items were being shipped in. She was grateful for her knowledge of merchandizing as well as Jack's since they had spent all their young lives practically living at the haberdashery. Also, Euphemia had excellent taste in ladies' accessories, as she said, "Well, I have been a lady buying accessories all of my life."

Jack had the little shop sparkling clean and the beautiful mahogany counter was such a centerpiece. Everyone was chipping in what they could, and Jack cleaned up and repaired the dirty old cash register. It was now gleaming shiny brass, and Sophie loved opening and closing the drawer to hear the bell. There was also a bell on the front door and in addition to the usual merchandise of ladies' sundries, Sophie had gone all out on Christmas presents to suit the whole family. There were mechanical toys and train sets with station houses and little towns with tiny painted brass people. Doll babies and doll houses with exquisite miniature furniture, sold separately of course. The shop was delightfully decorated, inside and out, with red ribbon and holly. It was already snowing in Up-State New York and the town looked like a beautiful Christmas card.

The town square was festooned in Christmas finery, and a brass band had been playing in the bandstand every Saturday since

Halloween. It was such a magical little town that Sophie was almost believing in Father Christmas again, or Santa Claus as the Americans called him. She loved to watch the little children's faces as they stood and gazed upon her special children's Christmas display window, which she and Euphemia put together. It was magical, and Sophie remembered seeing pictures in a children's story book, which she used as her inspiration. It was called 'A Visit from Saint Nicholas' and her aunt Loretta sent it to her when she was a small child. Jack had set up the train set, with the Christmas village surrounding it, and there were nutcrackers and elves as well as Mr. and Mrs. Claus who were checking out the long list of names that Euphemia had written out in tiny letters on a scrolling piece of parchment.

They were already making friends, and Euphemia mused they had been invited to more people's homes for dinner in a month, than was usual in a decade! The townsfolk joyfully took them in as if they had always lived there. David and Loretta Carlisle were frequent visitors and often Loretta would stay the week to be collected by her husband the following weekend. The town was only a 2-hour train ride from New York City but might have been a thousand miles away.

Sheriff Sam Spear was a frequent visitor to the gift shop, under the pretext of ensuring that all was as it should be. He told Sophie that as town sheriff, he felt it his duty to keep her safe and the shop secure. The others knew that the sheriff had fallen for Sophie. He assumed her to be a widow, since that was what the town gossips were saying and she was most certainly a woman of mystery, since how could one so lovely, be so sad and lonely. He had suggested giving Sophie riding lessons and she took him up on this providing her brother Jack could also join them, since back in Scotland they had little need to own horses.

This wasn't exactly what Sam had in mind, but he agreed, and Jack was quick to purchase a fine steed for himself and a lovely mare for his sister. Sam and Jack soon became friends and Sam allowed Jack to use his stables. Jack was reticent about discussing his sister. He liked

Sam Spear and wished there was no Benedict Cochrane still filling her head. He hoped one day to find annulment papers in the post, and then Sophie would have no choice but to rid him from her mind. The others, except possibly Euphemia, felt the same way. However, Euphemia knew Sophie the best and even if such paperwork were to arrive, Sophie would never sign it.

One day Euphemia and Loretta cornered Sophie. Euphemia said, "I know he is my brother but Sophie, he hasn't written, and he certainly hasn't come for you. Do you intend to throw away your young life on one so unworthy of your love?" Mr. Spear is such a nice man. He is very much the Cyrus Hatter that you once made up, in order to make my brother jealous."

She turned towards Loretta, "I know it must sound disloyal, talking so of my own brother, however, even I thought he would have done something—anything—to get his wife back, and yet, after three months—not a word."

Loretta agreed wholeheartedly with Euphemia, but Sophie still maintained that although she liked the sheriff, and he was such a good and kind man, she would never stop loving Euphemia's brother.

Again, Sophie didn't refer to him as her husband, but she did in her heart and in her mind and almost every night she re-lived their night in Torrance, almost wishing that they had gone all the way. She longed for Benedict Cochrane. She told both ladies she would never want another man.

Euphemia and Sophie were both writing to Sir Alfred, and he was planning on coming over for Christmas, as he said he was enraptured by their descriptions of the town and their little shop. They hired a photographer to send him some photographs, or rather Sophie did, and although she never said it, all assumed she wanted him to show them to Benedict. She had written dozens of letters to her husband since coming to America, but none were ever posted to him. They were all kept in her little wooden box, which was by now so full she had to squeeze it shut. She ordered pretty wooden boxes for her shop.

They would make delightful Christmas presents and the giver could include sweets or soaps or any variety of trinkets. Later the recipient could keep their private letters or mementoes inside, since all the boxes had a lock and a key with a colorful ribbon attached.

Sophie well knew she had made a life in New Chestnut and could never go back to Glasgow. This was of some concern to her because it meant she would never see Benedict again. She so often dreamed of him making love to her. The longing for him was sometimes simply unbearable. She thought about him every day. Sir Alfred barely mentioned him to her, although possibly he did to Euphemia.

The townsfolk thought Sophie to be a tragic young widow. She never set them straight nor explained it to anyone, and neither did the others tell her secret. There was a sadness about her, that somehow made her even lovelier, and consequently, in addition to the sheriff, she had a few of the single local farmers after her. Regardless, even if there was no Benedict Cochrane, Sophie knew she would never want to be a farmer's wife—up at dawn and feeding the chickens. She loved her little shop, and she loved her new family and Jack never returned to New York City. He had turned to carpentry and was planning his own premises further down the main street with an apartment upstairs. He said, "Away from you women!" But they all knew he was kidding them.

Euphemia was happier than she had ever been in her life, and she was so looking forward to Sir Alfred's visit. Sophie believed that Euphemia was in love with him, but she would no more go back to Glasgow than Sophie would—yet another problem with the women.

The town boasted their very own attorney at law. He was old and about to retire and one night at dinner Euphemia said, "Perhaps I should send the job listing to Benedict. I don't believe Sir Alfred intends to provide his recommendation. He wrote that although my brother is brilliant, he is a little off the beaten track—mentally I mean—and you must have a sound and level head to be a judge. Apparently, you don't need such a thing to be a barrister."

Euphemia confessed to Sophie, "I have written to him. Just a couple times. General sort of things about life in New Chestnut. I didn't mention you particularly, although I wanted to do so. I thought to leave him wondering. Anyway, I entrust that role to Sir Alfred, since you and I both correspond with him. Benedict didn't write me back."

Sophie's heart missed a beat when she heard his name since so seldom was he called by it. No doubt because her dearest family and friends were afraid of upsetting her. She mused, "I don't even know what his handwriting looks like sad, isn't it." She was determined that Euphemia shouldn't ever feel awkward talking about her brother, and besides, Sophie loved it when she mentioned him or when Sir Alfred did.

Then Sophie exclaimed, "You all should know that I will always be in love with Benedict. I intend to become a tragic Desdemona. Perhaps I should start wearing only black and…."

Loretta interrupted her, "My dear, what are you talking about? Why not have your uncle file for divorce on your behalf? It is about time you did. Clearly, he is not coming. He has had more than three months and not a word. You are young and so beautiful. Find another man! That is the first time I have heard you even mention his name. Why now, all the sudden?"

Sophie said, "Oh Aunt Loretta, I always say his name but only in my head or when I am alone. The photographer is coming on Saturday. I want him to take several photographs and one with me standing outside Mr. Magnusson's office with my hands over his name; or better yet, do you think Mr. Magnusson will allow me to affix a piece of paper with 'Benedict Cochrane' above the 'Attorney at Law' sign?"

Euphemia said, "I know Sir Alfred will show the photographs to Benedict so why not? However, Sophie, I can't see him becoming a country lawyer, and you are too afraid to go back to Glasgow and be alone with him. If there is a solution to this dilemma, what could it possibly be?"

Sophie said, "Perhaps when he sees me in the photographs, and when he sees how pretty our town is with the snow and Christmas lights and decorations, he will decide he is fed up with thieves and murderers. I am glad Sir Alfred will not give him his recommendation."

Everyone smiled at her, but none believed that her dream would ever come true—he had been too long in coming, or in even corresponding.

Her aunt said, "Well if he doesn't react to these photographs, it will be time to consider divorce. Euphemia, please insist Sir Alfred shows every photograph to your brother. Sophie, you and your shop and town will be in every one, save one of Euphemia only, for Sir Alfred."

Euphemia blushed and everyone burst into laughter. When this small group of new family and friends were together, there were no formalities nor social restraints.

Sophie said, "Well we shall see. Surely, I can't love this awful man for no reason? Surely there will be an end to the story?"

Loretta said, "Yes, divorce!"

∼

The photographer came to New Chestnut and took several photographs—most of which were of Sophie. Sophie in her shop. Sophie outside her shop. Sophie at the kitchen sink, and the others laughed when she told them her reason. Sophie in the bandstand. Sophie walking down Main Street. Sophie with Jack's snowman. And finally, Sophie holding up Benedict's name on top of the attorney's shingle.

The photographs were ready and at last the package was posted to Sir Alfred. And Sophie waited in vain for a letter or something—anything—from Benedict Cochrane.

Eventually, *anything* came. It was a Christmas card addressed to both Euphemia and Sophie Belle. All he wrote was, Merry Christmas, B.

It was hardly anything. It wasn't even a very nice card. However, he knew their address, and Sophie finally saw his writing. Of course, she grabbed it and kept it in her room, where each night she would trace the letter 'B' with her finger. It had been four months since her wedding day and she was heart sore. Sir Alfred was due to arrive on the 16th but made no mention of Benedict coming with him. Still Sophie hoped that they were keeping it a secret from her. She asked Euphemia who said she hadn't been told he was coming either.

CHAPTER II

Benedict Cochrane was livid when he discovered Sophie had left him, despite the fact he knew he well deserved it. She had outwitted him—lied about the date of her Atlantic Crossing. He had treated her badly—he was aware of that. He never courted nor bought her little gifts. Never told her how much he loved her, even though he did. Would she have stayed with him if he had behaved as he should have done? As a gentleman? A church wedding? A honeymoon? He didn't even provide her with a wedding ring. Benedict was shattered. He wondered why his behavior was so barbaric, but then he knew the reason. All his young life he watched his father pander to a woman who quite obviously married him solely for his money. His mother was beautiful but with a heart of stone, which it seemed she passed along to her son. Benedict studied the law, excelled in it, and played the man-about-town. He knew women fell for his good looks and bad-boy reputation. He knew his reputation as a barrister was unparalleled and he could pick and choose his clients. After a while, he was no longer choosing the cases where he believed his client to be innocent. He didn't much care about that and instead chose the high-profile cases that made the newspapers—cases he knew he would win. He represented the very worst of Glasgow's gangsters, loan sharks, and thugs, and was paid handsomely for his services. He dressed impeccably and walled his sister up in the family mansion, too afraid to cross him—until the day she met Sophie Belle—the young shopkeeper's daughter who turned their lives upside down.

Benedict took some time off to think about his life and his future. He drove north as far as a tank of petrol would take him. It was by then late October and the Highlands were breathtaking that time of year. He had thought of taking Sophie to the Highlands, but it was too late for that. Too late to un-do his deplorable behavior toward her. He was sure he had lost her, and he realized he no longer wanted to defend those who deserved no defense. He suddenly saw himself in the future as an aging lothario. He was thirty-four and he wanted something different. He wanted a wife, a real home, a family and most of all the love of a good woman. He wanted his Sophie Belle back but knew she would never return to Glasgow—not from the bits and pieces Judge Hicks mentioned to him. She never sought an annulment, nor a divorce. He wondered if she still loved him as she once did.

He had finally matured and found the woman of his dreams, or perhaps he had to waste so much time waiting for her to grow up, with eleven years between them. However, he treated her badly. Why? Because he imagined himself finally settling down with a wealthy scatterbrain with preferably a title. Then he met Sophie Belle, the shopkeeper's daughter he soon loved with all his jaded heart. The one that got away.

Upon Benedict's return to the Glasgow High Court, he was asked to dinner by Judge Hicks. Benedict thought the judge was finally going to speak to him about the coveted judicial position—the position he no longer wanted or at least much cared about. The judge poured Benedict a whisky and asked him how he enjoyed his break away. Benedict answered something non-committal. He felt his heart was broken. He was the man who threw his chance of happiness away. Then the judge threw a large brown envelope at him and when Benedict opened it up and went through each ridiculous photograph, with Sophie posing in her shop and all over her little town he suddenly knew it! Sophie Belle was pining for him, as he was for her, and the photograph with the Attorney at Law shingle—the one to which he pretended to take great offense—gave him the answer to his dilemma. A brand-new start. Benedict Cochrane—a country lawyer, with the loveliest bride in the world by his side. A couple of kids, a ramshackle house that would take years to fix up and renovate and a stress-free job, that paid very badly. Benedict Cochrane was truly happy for the first time in his life. He sold the house but kept the flat—just in case—and shipped off his fine clothes. He walked through the Argyle Arcade, which was Glasgow's jewelers' row and there he found it. A huge four carat solitaire. He had it cut to size. He knew her size since he had once found that out from Euphemia, in order to purchase the gold band that he didn't place on his lovely bride's finger. He knew it broke her heart, to be so humiliated. He couldn't quite tell her that he still had his past mistress to get rid of before he felt he had the right to place it there.

Soon he was on his way to New York. He met up with Sophie's uncle who had sent the posting of the position in New Chestnut. It arrived the same day he was given, or rather took, the photographs, leaving only the ones of his sister with the judge.

Benedict said nothing of his plans to Sir Alfred. He was in New York two weeks before the judge arrived and had met with David Carlisle several times. The two men hit it off and as David took care of Benedict's license to practice law in the State of New York, Benedict secured his position as New Chestnut's new attorney at law. The remuneration wasn't as bad as he expected, and Benedict, always the canny Scot, except perhaps on himself, put that down to the Americans' having no clue about the value of a dollar.

New York City was thriving. Christmas shoppers spending a fortune at the brightly decorated famous department stores. Benedict bought himself a full-length raccoon coat, which was the very latest style for rich young men and when David Carlisle berated him, he went back to Macy's and bought Sophie Belle a sable coat and matching fur muff. In all he spent a fortune and when David told him that the folks in New Chestnut were not so much into high fashion, he returned once again to Macy's and purchased two double breasted suits including trousers with turned up cuffs, and a pair of side button boots.

David Carlisle accused the good barrister of being a dandy and Benedict happily agreed. He said, "Well David, I am quite certain that the bumpkins in New Chestnut are all wearing dungarees and plaid shirts, it will be fun to give them something to talk about, but tell me what Sophie Belle is wearing these days, now she is a prominent woman of business. I wonder if she still has her navy-blue suit."

David said, "Yes, I believe she does, other than that, skirts and starched blouses. Never seen her in frills. She might dress a little more girlishly when she gets her man back. Better be quick about it. Sheriff Sam Spear, is teaching her how to ride—Western style."

Benedict said, "Sheriff Sam Spear, really? Nice one Sophie Belle. What is this man like? This officer of the law."

David said, "Popular, easy-going, but he keeps the town safe, along with Deputy Barker. He's a blue-eyed honey blond—like Sophie. He is tall and handsome—and besotted with her."

Benedict for the first time in his life grew concerned—jealous some would say, "And?"

David said, "And, she thinks nothing of him. I never knew a woman more devoted. Insists she pays him, although, I think he finds that a little insulting. When he sees you, he will understand why."

Benedict asked, "What do you mean by that?"

David said, "You are rather unique—a bit of an enigma. I couldn't understand my niece's misguided devotion. I think she finds you thrilling, a challenge. Your good looks are somewhat menacing—a bit of a lady-killer unless I am mistaken, which I very much doubt. The sheriff's looks are kinder, more boyish. My niece is a very beautiful and desirable woman, and very well she knows it. She always has—if you ask me. You have no doubt been witness to her nose in the air. She wanted the unattainable, and she got him. Now Cochrane, go and get your wife back."

Benedict laughed out loud; David Carlisle well understood his niece.

~

The day Sir Alfred Hicks arrived—alone—Sophie broke her heart. She expected that to happen, even though she wore her pretty red Christmas dress. Of course, she greeted him—briefly—and then ran up to her room. There were several customers and Euphemia and Sir Alfred went up to her, leaving Loretta in charge of the shop. Loretta stayed through Christmas and often enjoyed helping with customers. She even earned a meagre wage for so doing. She didn't need it but Sophie enjoyed putting everyone's *weakly* wages in their pay packets. None of them needed the money, not even Sophie, since her brother saw her right, as did her uncle and their merchandize grew nicer and nicer. So much so that their customers started opening small accounts with the store, to pay up their purchases on a weekly basis.

The shop was a huge success, but Sophie's heart was a huge mess.

They knocked on Sophie's bedroom door and she shouted, "Come in," looking at them expectantly.

Sir Alfred started, "Sophie, I don't know how to say this to you. Not when I see how upset you are. I was hoping you had gotten over him."

She shouted, "He has a mistress!"

He said, "No, not that."

Sophie was relieved, however felt she knew what was coming next but still she held the moment off, "The photographs, what did he say? What did he do? Did he take any?"

Sir Alfred responded, "He took most of them, except his sister. Possibly you shouldn't have sent the one with his name on the 'Attorney at Law' sign. That seemed to incense him, and he said, he was going to file for divorce. He spat out the words, "Country lawyer." He said, that was the end of the line, or some such nonsense."

Sophie said, "Well he can't have one. Most especially since the marriage wasn't consummated."

Euphemia blushed but Sophie didn't care.

Sir Alfred said, "Abandonment. I think he believed you would come back eventually. He now knows you won't, and you won't, correct Sophie Belle? You could easily obtain an annulment, but he said he would demand that you submit to a physical examination. That wouldn't be very pleasant for you of course, but possibly better than a divorce—reputation wise."

Sophie said, "I will never submit to that! And he knows it. I won't give him a divorce either! I refuse. I will never sign it! I will drag him through the American courts. Stupid Scotsman! He won't stand a chance against my uncle Carlisle. He will eat him alive. If he wants rid of me, I want every penny he ever earned, and his big house and his bloody car. Also, all his fancy suits and his stupid white wig. Everything. I hate him! I will see him in the poor house!"

Sir Alfred said, "He might just be bluffing because he basically said the same thing about you. The shop, the stock, everything you own. You don't own the shop Sophie, do you?"

She said, "No, but I will soon, and I will see him in hell first. Anyway, big, stupid coward, why doesn't he come and face me like a man, instead of hiding behind his nasty wig and stupid gown. I hate, loathe and despise him."

Then Sir Alfred said the words Sophie was longing to hear, "I believe he is coming. He didn't say when, but he did say he would rather divorce you and would need to ensure an annulment wasn't possible. Sophie, the man is unhinged."

He turned to Euphemia, "Sorry Euphemia, I sometimes forget he is your brother."

She said, "Think nothing of it. I fully agree with you."

Euphemia showed Sir Alfred to the guest room and invited him downstairs for refreshments.

She added, "Is he serious? Why divorce, why not annulment? Why even come here? If he does."

Sir Alfred said, "Euphemia, I do not wish to be indelicate, however…."

Euphemia interrupted, "Alfred, I am not stupid, and it will be over my dead body. If he comes? I think he is bluffing. No mistress you say. Interesting."

Sir Alfred responded, "If he was strange before; he is even more peculiar now. He told me he hates women. Blames that on our Sophie Belle."

"Good," said Euphemia, "Women appear to hate him too! Well, all except Sophie Belle. She has a number of admirers, including the town sheriff. She will be well rid of him!"

They laughed and went downstairs together. The judge had not yet told Euphemia of the position he was offered in New York City. He was considering taking it. That all depended on Euphemia, and for some reason also on Benedict Cochrane and Sophie Belle.

It was Friday evening, the week before Christmas and the shop was busy the entire day. Sophie went back downstairs and, in her anger, made records sales before the store closed, much later than usual at half past seven. Sophie called it "holiday hours," and was giving her male customers a onetime ten percent discount that evening—to encourage them to spend lavishly on their wives—following their day's labor. The town's women loved the idea and held off dinner that night to accommodate the special sale.

Sophie was busy separating the dollar bills and change when Sir Alfred came downstairs. "Sophie, you are flourishing here. You are quite the businesswoman, most especially encouraging the men to shop for their wives at the end of their working day. It is a beautiful little town. It suits you. Why can't you forget that man? He isn't good enough for you—not really husband material."

Sophie ignored his remark and said, "My special sale really worked out well, since most men get paid on Fridays. Poor Euphemia is exhausted with all that gift wrapping. She is the very best at it, so was given the assignment. I remember the first time her brother came into my brother's shop to berate me; he ended up buying a multitude of silly items for his fictional secretary's birthday. I charged him two and sixpence for a sheet of white paper and colored string." She paused, as if enjoying the memory, and then said, "You are in love with my sister Euphemia, aren't you, Sir Alfred. Don't you dare take her away from me."

Sir Alfred said, "So if Sophie Belle isn't happy, no one else is allowed to be? Anyway, I would never do that. I have been offered a fine position in New York City. I won't have to be there every day and could commute. Now, not a word to Euphemia, Sophie Belle. And start thinking this through. Choose a nicer man. One who isn't insane?" He sighed, "I will leave you now to count your money. Please think it over. Sophie. You deserve a better man than Benedict Cochrane."

Sophie's heart leapt at the mention of Benedict's name. It was so seldom said to her.

Sir Alfred could tell that his advice had fallen on deaf ears, and he went back upstairs, to check on Euphemia.

~

Sophie was so busy excitedly counting the day's take, that she forgot to lock the door and everyone else was up seeing to dinner. They had a maid that came in, but she wasn't a very talented cook.

Sophie had her back to the door and heard the bell. She shouted back, "I'm sorry, we are closed! Well perhaps, I can take just one more customer. Please lock the door behind you."

A familiar voice said, "Happily," and Sophie spun around in her amazement!

"But you weren't on the ship? How dare you come into my shop?"

He said, "You invited me in, don't you remember? That is a lot of money there, Sophie Belle. Quite a shame that you are going to lose it all."

Sophie was delirious but determined not to show it. She turned and locked the dollar bills and change in her cash box, but Benedict jumped over the counter and grabbed it from her.

She was fighting him for it. "I know all about your plans and I will see you in hell first! Or the poor house! Give me that box! It doesn't belong to you! You are loathsome and insane, and I absolutely hate you with all of my heart!"

He said, "So you still love me, Sophie Belle. I thought you did and all those silly photographs of you proved it. So, you see the good barrister, defending farmers and cowpokes in the backwater, back of beyond, so he can be with Sophie Belle? Do you really think you are worth it? Because I don't"

Unbeknownst to Sophie, the others, even the maid, Matilda, were listening on the stairs. Benedict assumed they would be doing so, and shouted up, "Judge, I have been in New York for two weeks, consulting with my new attorney. I am now taking my wife into the woods and stealing her cash box. That's a good start, I think, for abandonment."

Euphemia came running down the stairs, "Just leave her alone and get out of here. You are not welcome."

Benedict said, "Long time no see, sister dear. I'm afraid your friend invited me in," and he proceeded to make his way out the door with the woman he loved. Sophie didn't give too much resistance and shrugged her shoulders at Euphemia. She grabbed her coat and then kicked him on the shin before closing the door.

"Now what?" She asked. "Are you going to ravish me in the woods—in the snow? It is snowing or, stupid Scotsman, didn't you notice that. I have much more on you than you have on me, and I will see you in...."

He interrupted her, "Your bedroom, but won't they all be listening?

I intend to be very loud. Your punishment. And then I will divorce you and take your cash box."

Sophie started kicking him again, and he said, "I am not going to make this easy on you. Well perhaps, if you promise to submit and behave yourself."

She screamed, "Submit? It will be a cold day in hell, and everyone in that house will hear me!" She paused, thoughtfully, "Although I'm not sure if I want them to save me. Anyway, it is Friday night and I need to make up my employees' wages with a surprise Christmas bonus, come on," and she led him back inside the shop with her nose in the air, although her heart was singing.

∼

Benedict Cochrane's heart was full. Sophie Belle loved him. That much was obvious, even as she put on a little pair of reading spectacles, to calculate her employees' wages. He was so highly amused. He asked, "May I assist you Store Manager? What do you pay them?"

She said. "Well, Euphemia is my assistant manager and I pay her ten dollars per week, and Aunt Loretta is just a salesperson, so she gets seven dollars—when she is here. This week I am giving out five-dollar bonuses because of Christmas."

He asked, "How much do you pay yourself, Store Manager, Sophie Belle?"

"I am paid fifteen dollars, as store manager."

Benedict exclaimed, "Good Grief, Sophie Belle, those wages are horrific! You need a solicitor to advise you."

She said, "we say attorney here. What is your hourly rate? If you get the position that is."

He said, "For you? Nothing."

"Nothing? Seriously? But you are so greedy?"

"It is not your money I want, Sophie Belle."

She surprised him, "Oh why don't they all go out? Bunny's tavern serves up a decent dinner, and I can smell something burning upstairs, probably the roast beef."

He said, "Aren't you afraid to be alone with the husband you so cruelly left Sophie Belle?"

She laughed, "Let me see, no wedding ring, no wedding night, no honeymoon and a drunken bridegroom. The answer is no! You should be more afraid of me."

"I don't feel afraid. Although, I do feel something, Sophie Belle, might be desire. I suppose that could be it?"

She said, "You owe me a proper wedding night, unless you truly intend to divorce me. Then I will send you to the poor house instead."

He laughed, "You can't. The house is sold. My money is well hidden. You need to stay with me."

She said, "I have so many admirers. Everyone thinks I am a widow."

Benedict grew serious, "You may one day be a widow, but God willing not for a very long time. I'm thinking I might overlook your humble beginnings and occupation and keep you. How does that sound, Sophie Belle?"

Sophie said, "Oh I wish they would go out!"

Benedict said, "Why Sophie Belle? Do you want to seduce me? What is this whole "proper wedding night" you keep mentioning. I seem to remember you mentioning that before. Possibly the night you took me upstairs at the Torrance Inn."

"Benedict! That wasn't my fault! Well, it might have been my fault. Benedict, I love you so. I will never stop loving you. I can't. I tried. Do you love me a little?"

He said, "I'm here, aren't I? I intend to be a low paid country lawyer—sorry—attorney at law, with you standing at the kitchen sink, and making dinner for me and our ten children. Although I'm still not completely certain if it is love? It might just be infatuation. I will tell you later—after I bed you."

Sophie felt her stomach spin at those words and then Euphemia re-appeared, "How nice to see you, Benedict, did I say that? We are all going out. There is burnt beef on the stove and," she paused, "a bottle of wine is in Sophie's room, just in case you are staying the night."

Sophie was glowing and Euphemia saw this. This lovely young girl was besotted with her dreadful brother.

Then the others appeared.

Sir Alfred said, "I thought I was about to enjoy a wonderful Christmas in snowy Upstate New York but look who's here. You might have said, although I knew you were up to something." He turned to the others. "The good barrister has the highest record for *not proven* verdicts in Scotland. We are the only country that permits that. He doesn't care to allow his clients to leave the courtroom with a *not guilty* verdict."

Benedict said, "That's because most of them are guilty. Up to the procurator fiscal to prove it. A poorly paid and incompetent lot."

Sophie realized that introductions were required. She turned to her aunt, "Aunt Loretta, this is my husband, Mr. Benedict Cochrane. The man you have been advising me to divorce."

Loretta said, "I am quite shocked to make your acquaintance, Mr. Cochrane. I now understand my misguided niece's reluctance to divorce you. You are rather good looking. My husband will be here tomorrow—Mr. David Carlisle. He was going to ruin you."

Benedict kissed her hand, "I know him already. I have been in New York for two weeks. I was considering hiring him, but he is too expensive. Besides, it seems there was a conflict of interest, with my estranged wife being his niece. Very shrewd man, intelligent. I was remarkably impressed, most particularly since he is Sophie Belle's uncle. One wouldn't envision Sophie Belle to have such distinguished relatives."

He turned to Sophie and said, "I understand from your uncle that brother Jack is now a carpenter."

Sophie said, "And a very fine one. Two weeks! What have you been up to? This is Matilda. She helps us out upstairs."

Matilda blushed when Benedict kissed her hand and she said, "Charmed, I'm sure. We all believed you to be dead."

～

Everyone left for Bunny's Tavern and Sophie took Benedict's hand and led him upstairs.

"I can't believe you are here. What were you doing in New York? I can't believe my uncle Carlisle didn't tell anyone. There is burnt beef on the stove. You must be hungry. Also, beer in the chiller. No forget that. I need you to be sober. Well, I suppose one bottle won't hurt."

He said, "I was taking care of business. You are different here. It suits you. I suppose once a shopkeeper, always a shopkeeper. I married a shopkeeper's daughter, go ponder upon that one."

Sophie was trying to stay calm. She felt so nervous and shy. She was alone with Benedict Cochrane. She was actually married to him too. She said, "I need to go get ready."

Benedict laughed, "Ready for what, Sophie Belle?"

She said, "Stop it. You know."

He said, "You look ready enough to me. Here, I've brought you something."

She looked at him expectantly and he produced a gold wedding band and placed it on her finger. "I owe you a diamond too, Sophie Belle. I had it in my pocket that day. There was a matter I had to take care of before I could truly be your husband. I thought I kept you off the steamer. Now I am glad I didn't, because you have become quite the woman. A broken heart will do that for a girl. My girl, right Sophie Belle."

Sophie started to cry, and Benedict smiled and said, "Please don't burst into tears when I make love to you. I have waited too long for this. He took her in his arms and kissed her. "Which room is yours?"

She led the way. This was what Sophie was longing for, and now the moment had finally arrived, she suddenly felt incredibly nervous.

She opened her door, and it seemed the ladies had made her bedroom nice. She said, "I'm not sure I am ready now. I mean, I only have flannel nightgowns and I expected to be wearing something beautiful. I am wearing thermal undergarments. Also, I am unsure if this can be considered a proper wedding night, with everyone else out for dinner at Bunny's."

He laughed and drew her to him. "You won't need a nightgown tonight, flannel or otherwise, well not unless it is too big for you and apt to fall down."

Sophie realized that Benedict must have often reminisced about that wonderful night, as did she. She said, "I was so worried you felt disappointed in my behavior. It was just…"

He interrupted her, "Sophie Belle, you have no idea how hard it was for me to hold myself back that night. Yet I knew that I must, I had already taken too much advantage of your love for me. My desire for you was consuming me."

Sophie said, "Well I knew something was very hard anyway, and that's when I came to my senses…sort of…"

He laughed out loud, and Sophie rummaged through her dresser drawers, producing what Benedict thought to be some lacy garment and escaped to their communal bathroom. She eventually returned wearing her modest dressing gown.

Benedict looked at his gold pocket watch and said, "I wonder how long the others will be?" He was seated on the bed, still dressed but with his sleeves rolled up and his collar unbuttoned—the way Sophie loved him best.

She braced herself and took off the dressing gown, "I brought my wedding underwear with me, but I have never worn it since that night. Benedict, you helped me change and I thought I looked so pretty but you didn't touch me. All you said was my legs were lovely. Why Benedict? If you had made love to me that night, I don't believe I would have had the strength to leave you. You got drunk. I was ashamed and humiliated and the next day you went to your mistress. Did you Benedict? Did you go and make love to her instead?"

Sophie was looking at him so expectantly and he decided upon the truth, "I have never touched nor looked at any other woman since that first day I saw you. However, I had to finally finish it off, get rid of her forever, and I did. I had to clear my head afterwards, and I took a few days to do so before returning to find you gone."

Sophie was wide-eyed, "You murdered her?"

Benedict laughed wryly, "No, I just called her nasty and unkind names. I told her I had taken a young, beautiful and chaste wife. I told her you were already carrying my child and that seemed to finally break her. She tried to seduce me, then she attacked me—but not like you—I love when you attack me, you are so little and weak. She threatened me with a knife, and I threatened her with deportation."

He paused for a reaction, but Sophie didn't speak. "So now you know, Sophie Belle, I was not a very nice man when you met me. In fact, I was an utter scoundrel. You changed me, Sophie Belle. I wanted you so much that day, dressed in your pretty lingerie. However, I was unworthy. So, I made sure I got too drunk to even attempt it."

Benedict wondered about this lovely girl's response. She looked so innocent standing there before him, and he half expected her to change her mind about loving him. Then she surprised him. "Okay I am ready now, Benedict."

He smiled happily and stood up. He took her in his arms, kissing her, while deftly removing the garments she had so recently struggled to put on by herself, most especially the corset. She could tell he had done this many times before, but she didn't care. He was murmuring such wonderful words about her beauty and how desirable she was, and they fell onto the bed.

Sophie forgot to be nervous and shy. She was helping Benedict remove his clothing. She forgot every rotten thing this man had ever done or said to her. She loved him with everything she had in her body and soul and of course he was magnificent. Finally, she was truly his.

Finally, she was truly married to this glorious man. Her heart was full of love and joy, but when he laid back contentedly beside her, it suddenly occurred to her, "You still didn't say you love me. Benedict why didn't you say that?"

He smiled sleepily, "I said lots of other things, didn't I? Sophie Belle, you are the only woman I want, and I want you more than I ever wanted any other woman. I'm thirty-five. Time to settle down I suppose or try it out at the very least. Could just be infatuation, however. How does one really know if it is love? It could be I suppose, but what if all we feel is desire?"

Sophie sat up and looked at him wide-eyed, "You really are insane! I thought perhaps it was an act. It isn't, is it? You are absolutely certifiable! What man would say such a thing to his bride? Most especially after four months of longing for her—supposedly."

Benedict laughed, "Shut up and come here. I love your hair—I get lost in it. There I said it."

She laughed too, "My hair? No Benedict Cochrane, you are in love with me, so I will say it for you." And the new woman that Sophie just became, decided to seduce her husband. She found it so natural and effortless in her unbridled love and passion for this man. Soon he was putty in her hands, and it was Sophie's turn to smile—triumphantly.

∽

Sophie woke up. She heard the clock strike 4 a.m. She was alone and she panicked, "Benedict!"

She got up, grabbed her flannel night gown and ran downstairs. Her bedroom was on the third floor as were all the others. The living apartments were on the second floor. She ran into the kitchen, hair wild and barefooted. He was seated in his dressing gown and slippers, drinking coffee with Sir Alfred.

Relieved, she sat down. "I thought you left!"

Benedict said, "I was about to leave. The judge made coffee

however, so I changed my mind. Euphemia is getting married. Who could have imagined such a thing? Alfred here is about to become my brother. He has a better position than me—in the city. Euphemia will be quite well off, so I gave my permission. However, we have to keep it a secret until Christmas Eve—very romantic."

Sophie poured herself a cup and said, "Some men are romantic Benedict Cochrane. I'm going back to bed. Judge, please don't allow him to leave. Although I suppose He would have to come upstairs to fetch his clothes first. Perhaps I should hide them."

She grew thoughtful, "At least you can't pretend to be off to chambers tomorrow, like you used to do. I will show you around the town. Also, the countryside is so lovely in the snow. I will ask Jack to cover the shop for me. I will take the whole day off. Benedict, do you know how to handle horses? I don't mean to ride them, but Jack has a sleigh. The horses are at Sam Spear's. I know! Jack can tether them to the sleigh. Do you know how to lead a team, Benedict?"

Benedict said, "I thought you were going back to bed. Also, how do you think I got around before I had my motor car? On the tramcar? Of course, not much use for a sleigh in Scotland, but I daresay I can manage."

Sophie said, "I always used to take the tramcar. It was far more convenient than the train."

Benedict laughed, "But then; Sophie Belle, that's you."

Sophie stood and lifted her coffee cup, "We can take a packed lunch and a bottle of wine."

Benedict said, "A picnic in the snow. Aren't you afraid your husband catches cold, Sophie Belle?"

She said, "No, and anyway, you have your stupid fur coat. I will wear double layer thermals and bring blankets," and she left, excitedly anticipating the following day, closing the kitchen door behind her. Of course, Sophie intended listening to the conversation within—even if her bare feet felt like icicles. She intended to take her husband to the abandoned cabin she found, when she was out riding with Jack before the snow came down so heavy. She planned that they would picnic by the log fireplace. She would bring plenty of blankets so they could make love in front of the fire. She dreamily imagined how romantic it would be, laying naked under Benedict's raccoon fur coat.

She heard Benedict say, "I am happy for you and Euphemia. You suit each other so very well. Anyway, she seems to have stopped obeying my orders, so what the hell. Perhaps she will obey yours."

Sir Alfred responded, "I have no intention of issuing orders, Cochrane. I sincerely hope your motives and intentions are entirely honorable towards Sophie Belle. I have grown rather fond of her."

Benedict thought he heard a noise, a slight rattle of a cup and saucer. He put a finger to his lips and stood up and approached the door, speaking loudly, "My wife thinks she will be getting her own way from now on. However, she will be in for a big surprise. If I remain in this backwoods town, and that is a big "if", she will need to do as she is told and not the other way around. She might be store manager, but she is not my manager. Might make her give up the shop."

Both men waited and as expected, Sophie marched back into the kitchen and put down her cup and saucer, "How dare you say such things behind my back! You are such a horrendous man. You have no right to come into my shop and tell me what I can and cannot do. As for your "big if? Well, you can just forget about a sleigh ride. Anyway, you probably don't even know how, and…."

Sophie stopped and realized that she had awakened the whole house. She made to run back up to her room, when Benedict grabbed her wrists and said, "You shouldn't be listening through keyholes. If I don't divorce you for abandonment. I might let you keep the shop. However, as your husband I will need to give that some consideration."

By now, it was almost 5 a.m. and Sophie finally realized he was teasing her. Everyone was gathering in the kitchen and laughing at her, and Euphemia was making fresh coffee. Sophie then dipped a little curtsey, grabbed Benedict's hand and led him back upstairs to her bedroom.

Sophie was delirious to have her man at last. She so often worried that she never, ever would. She lay down and attempted to pose seductively on her bed, wishing she had something lacy and alluring to wear. She said, "Okay, big man, I am submitting."

He smiled, "Sophie Belle, doesn't look like submission to me."

Sophie got worried, "It doesn't?"

Benedict was laughing as he threw off his dressing gown.

Sophie was frowning and biting her lip, "Did I do something wrong? You are the only man ever for me, and I would like to get it right. All those experienced women and now me? If I am not alluring, do you think I can be? With some instruction?"

Benedict climbed on the bed and began to kiss her in places he hadn't done previously. "I am tempted to say you need extra instruction, just to watch your bewilderment. Sophie Belle, I am thirty-five, and in all those years there wasn't one woman whom I remotely wanted to spend the rest of my life with; but thinking back, I fell for you that first morning when you walked out of the back shop. You had your cute little nose in the air and took me outside for a dressing down. I was standing thinking I wanted to dress you down, literally. However, I felt the whole thing was ridiculous—still I wanted to see you again. I was hoping to prove to myself that it was totally absurd—ludicrous—and quite impossible."

Sophie said, "Because you thought I was so far beneath you in social standing, and yet, morally at least, I was, and still am, so very far above you. I already knew all about your mistress, I got it out of Euphemia. She was foreign and she couldn't spell. Was she very exotic and skillful?"

Benedict said, "Ah, Euphemia the blabbermouth! Yes, I believe she seemed so for a while, and then it burned itself out. It always did with me, although I suppose with her it took longer."

Sophie pushed him away and stood up and donned her dressing gown. "Such a long line of broken hearts! I hate you Benedict Cochrane. You are an absolute rake. That word was invented for men like you. So when is your ardor for me going to "burn itself out?" And anyway, how long was longer?"

Benedict laid back, stark naked, with his arms folded behind his neck. "Couple years, give or take, although it wasn't an exclusive relationship—for me anyway. Let's forget about all that nasty stuff. I want to talk about us. Anyway, exactly what ardor are you referring to? Mrs. Cockroach? Why don't you come back to bed and seduce me again, and I will let you know how you stack up—against the others, I mean."

He was laughing but Sophie was jealous. Still, how could she be angry? She knew exactly what Benedict Cochrane was like—even when first she knew him—if indeed she did know him. He was confident and self-assured—some might say, completely full of himself. However, she reasoned, he gave up his position as a High Court barrister and sailed across the Atlantic Ocean to get to her. He was now lying on her bed and she knew he belonged there—after all, for all his bad behavior, he married her. Sophie removed her dressing gown, and asked, "So Mr. Cockroach, I expect I am neither exotic nor skillful. So what do I have that is so special?"

He appeared to consider the question and said, "Intelligence."

Sophie shouted, "Intelligence? That's it?"

Benedict said, "Sophie Belle, you already know how you turn men's heads wherever you go. So why state the obvious? Come on, do you realize that this is just our first night together and I am surrounded by your spies?"

She decided to join him on the bed. She desired him so and he laid back enjoying her kisses, caresses and fondling, as she enjoyed hearing him moan and whispering of the pleasure she was giving him. She loved the scent of her man, and watching his muscles ripple, his stormy grey eyes dreamily watching her until he closed them again, his square jaw which was always clean shaven to show off the glorious dimple on his chin. Sophie was swept away in her joy in the pleasure she was giving her man, and she almost didn't hear his words, spoken so quietly.

He turned her over and as she wrapped her legs around him, he whispered, "You are mine forever, Sophie Belle Cochrane, I will never again allow you to get away."

Afterwards, as they lay in each other's arms, Sophie said, "Does this mean you are in love with me, Benedict Cochrane?"

He smiled sleepily and said, "I don't recall saying that. It does mean, you have the loveliest face and the most luscious lips I have ever encountered. Your voluptuous body and sensual womanly scent will always keep me coming back for more. That was the best seduction I have ever experienced, and I would never want you to be experienced. What with other men? You are mine and mine alone and I will need to keep you with me, so no other man can get to you, not even the manly Cyrus Hatter. The last test is this tasty beef wellington you boasted about at my dinner party which you so rudely walked out upon. If it is as delectable as you say it is, I might just tell you I love you."

Sophie sat up, "There you just said it!"

Benedict said, "I was speaking in context."

Sophie hit him with her bed pillow, "Well I know that you do anyway."

The next morning Sophie was up and dressed and opining about Benedict's clothes. She went downstairs to where Jack was complaining and stating that this was a onetime favor, "I have my own work to do, sister dear, and I have had enough years of serving in a shop. The horses and sleigh are outside; however, I doubt your idiot husband knows how to handle them, most especially since it is snowing…yet again."

Sophie kissed his cheek and ran outside, where she raised her head and stuck her tongue out to taste the snow. She was so happy, and everyone could see it. Jack still didn't trust Benedict Cochrane. He was conceited and so very full of his own importance. He had spoken to the others with his concerns and it seemed that they had similar ones.

Finally, Benedict appeared saying, "I can't believe I am doing this in the bloody snow. It has been years since I led a team and even then, it was in a curricle. Where's Sophie Belle? Never mind, there she is, eating snow," and he went out to help her onto the sleigh.

Euphemia saw the love in her brother's eyes. Everyone else wanted to mistrust him, most especially the judge, but she wanted so to believe he had mended his ways and Sophie was finally being given her happy ending.

⁓

Sophie was so excited to be out with Benedict that he felt incredibly guilty. He never formally paid court to her and in retrospect he wondered why she stuck by him.

He found the little town charming, and he enjoyed leading the team of horses through the snowy countryside, until soon they came to an abandoned one room cabin.

He said, "Ah, was this to be our destination. A picnic in a damp and no doubt vermin infested hut?"

Sophie said, "I thought it would be romantic. It looked nicer in October, with the fall foliage. I'm sorry Benedict. We can go home now if you prefer."

Benedict could see the disappointment in Sophie's eyes, but couldn't help but say, "Sophie, that room above the shop is not my home. I need to find alternative accommodation as soon as possible. Everyone watching me—mistrusting my motives."

He led her down from the sleigh but somehow Sophie's day was ruined, where was his sense of adventure?

He said, "I hope it was Jack who brought you here, Sophie Belle, and not the sheriff."

He immediately regretted saying that, when he saw her smile fade. He was thinking of the fine restaurants he used to dine in, and worried about staying in such an out of the way place, however charming. He had an idea, "I will tell you what, Sophie Belle, the day after Christmas I am taking you on honeymoon to New York City. What do you think? A week or maybe two. We can get to know one another and share our love without the overseers back at the shop."

Sophie's face brightened, she exclaimed, "Oh Benedict, a real honeymoon! Oh yes, I would love that! And the shop will be closed the week after Christmas. Can we spend New Year's Eve in New York, too?"

He said, "Yes and I will buy you a new dress for the occasion." Benedict was thinking of the diamond ring and furs he had bought for his wife. Time enough to find or build a house. He could buy the old attorney's place, but it needed a fortune spent on it. He was not about to start living rough at his age.

They ate their lunch and drank the wine in the little cabin, and Benedict lit the fire with considerable difficulty. When the fire began to grow low, he said, "Okay, let's go, Sophie Belle."

It wasn't what Sophie had planned—not in the least, but Sophie's head was already full of Benedict's plans for a honeymoon in New York City.

They returned to the shop much sooner than expected and the others were relieved that at least Sophie was beaming about Benedict's plans for a honeymoon.

Jack was taking back the horses and sleigh and Benedict and Sir Alfred went to Bunny's with David Carlisle, who had just arrived from New York City.

Sophie took her aunt and Euphemia aside, "It was a stupid idea. Benedict isn't really the outdoors type—I suppose anyway—although he seemed to be in Scotland? He was quiet and thoughtful, and I got worried, however, it was just because he was planning our honeymoon in New York City in his head. Oh, Aunt Loretta, isn't he a lot nicer than you expected? Euphemia, he has changed, hasn't he?"

Both women agreed, but when Sophie turned her back, they exchanged concerned glances. The recently reunited couple had been gone less than two hours. They had expected them to be gone most of the day.

The shop was busy until it closed at 7.30 p.m., and everyone headed to Bunny's for dinner.

Benedict seemed to have cheered up somewhat and sat holding Sophie's hand. She could tell he was of considerable interest to the townsfolk. Somehow, even the judge managed to modify his dress and fit in, somewhat at least, but Benedict stood out like a sore thumb. He was wearing one of the suits he purchased in New York City, but these were no less dandified than his black silk suits. Possibly more so, with his side button boots. It was the Saturday before Christmas Eve, and soon the tavern was hopping, and Bunny had brought in some Irish musicians—not knowing the difference really between the Irish and the Scottish persons who had moved in to liven up their little town. Sophie and Jack had taken Irish dance lessons as young children, and when Jack announced this to everyone, they were all trying to persuade him and Sophie to dance to the rhythmic music, which as the night wore on was building to a frenzy, with the considerable amount of ale and whisky that had been consumed during the evening. Sam Spear and a couple of the other guests had joined their table and Sophie began to feel a bit embarrassed with everyone begging her to dance.

Finally, Benedict spoke up. "The first and only time I danced with my wife, she was counting dance steps during the waltz, and as if that wasn't bad enough, she almost pulled me to the floor during the fox trot. I don't think it a good idea for her to attempt Irish dancing. He turned to Sophie, "Remember Sophie Belle, you told me you learned to waltz in school, and you will recollect how that turned out at the City Chambers ball."

He had drunk a little too much, most especially since he and the other men had begun imbibing in the middle of the afternoon. Sophie was humiliated. Never had she felt this way until her husband came into town, just the previous day—enough time to make love to her five times, three times at night, one time in the middle of the night when she was barely awake and again once in the early morning before he fell back asleep.

The others were looking at her sympathetically and she wanted to slap his face. However, Jack angrily jumped up and said, "Back in a minute."

Sophie had an idea of what he was doing or getting and that meant he intended to dance with her and by now she was ready to turn the tables on her charming husband.

Jack returned with the shoes. Both his and hers, both with metal plates on the toes and the heels. Jack spoke to the bandleader, and they immediately started up an Irish reel. Benedict took hold of Sophie's arm saying, "Sophie that was inconsiderate of me. I know it, but please don't make a fool of yourself again on the dance floor. Jack is a bit inebriated, but you are not."

Euphemia was ready to slap her brother's face. She thought, *foolish me, thinking he had changed. If anything, he is worse than before, having already had his way with poor Sophie.* Euphemia looked at the judge and they both grew concerned about his true intentions of even being there. Not quite the good barrister's style, although he did seem to enjoy the young local girls gazing at him with admiration, even naked desire. Before leaving Scotland for America, Benedict had worried about becoming an aging lothario—clearly, he was nowhere near being that.

Then Jack and Sophie took to the floor. Sophie had hitched up her skirt for ease of movement, revealing her lovely legs. Benedict noticed Sam Spear staring at her with desire, or was it love. He decided the sheriff was in love with his wife, Sophie Belle. Sophie was indeed very different here than in Glasgow. He felt he was noticing her sheer loveliness for the very first time. This extraordinary woman whom he had just belittled for no apparent reason, his wife—his beautiful wife. He was the fortunate one and not the other way around. Still, he held his breath as brother and sister stood side by side—their backs ramrod straight, as they immediately broke into the dance with their feet moving so incredibly fast and without a falter that the tavern folks were mesmerized. Soon everyone was clapping their hands and shouting and whistling and both dancers finally finished and took a bow.

Sophie sat down and asked for a glass of shandy. Sam stood up to fetch it for her. Sophie was still livid with her husband and refused to look at him. He clearly understood why. Nevertheless, he followed Sam to the bar and threatened him. He told him to stay away from his wife. Sam sneered, "After that remark you made at the table, and the months you took to come fetch her—she might not be that for much longer. She certainly never spoke of you until you regrettably arrived yesterday."

Benedict was about to swing for the sheriff, however, fortuitously, Jack anticipated such an event and held him back. Sam Spear was staring too openly at Sophie and although she was ignoring him, enraptured, or so it seemed, with her husband, at least until his condescending and unkind remark. No one would have particularly minded if Cochrane spent the night in the town jail, but they were not in the mood for reassuring Sophie Belle for the rest of the night, most particularly, Euphemia.

Shortly thereafter, Sophie's party left, and she was most certainly not speaking to Mr. Benedict Cochrane. Sophie ran up to her room and Loretta made coffee for everyone—black coffee for the men. She then sent Benedict upstairs with a cup for Sophie, whom all assumed would be crying.

Sir Alfred said to Benedict, "That remark was cruel and completely unnecessary, and it turned out she showed us all up. The fox trot is easily learned but one would imagine Irish dancing would be most difficult—all those intricate dance steps. So Cochrane, it seems you haven't much changed after all. Why did you come? Are you still planning a divorce or is it a honeymoon you are planning? I find myself to be somewhat baffled, as I am sure is she."

Benedict said, "None of you know her like I do. All this attention—she is loving it. With all you lot doting on her and now it also seems the town sheriff. I find myself wondering too, why I came that is."

He took the cups provided to him by his sister and went upstairs. Of course, Sophie was crying. It seemed he so easily made her cry. She was kneeling on a chair looking out on the snow and there was a hole in her black stockings. This alone somehow got to him. Sophie Belle was most certainly not high maintenance—at least not yet, but that was his plan for her. And for some unknown reason, she had completely and innocently given him her love and trust, a trust which he had so often broken.

He said, "Sophie Belle, you have a hole in your stockings. Can I help you change them?"

She turned, "No I am going to bed. Why did you say those things about me, Benedict? They were so unnecessary, unless just to humiliate me. I think you hate me because you didn't marry a high-class lady with money. Well, you could have had the plain and pathetic Fiona MacBride, if you wanted. She was certainly eager enough. I didn't make you marry me. You could have chosen a young lady with lots of money. You would have had your pick. You surely should have never married me, the stupid shopkeeper's daughter."

Benedict said, "I suppose I was jealous. I am sorry Sophie Belle, and you really did a splendid job with that Irish dancing. Now, if I tried that, I would surely have fallen on the floor."

Sophie knew he was making up to her, and after all it was only their second night together and she so badly wanted his arms around her.

"Jealous, of what?" she said.

"Not of what, of whom. It seems I truly have a rival now, and not the manly Cyrus Hatter."

Sophie laughed, "So only you are allowed to have girls swooning over you? That's a joke."

Benedict said, "Well, I didn't say he was swooning and anyway, girls can be silly. He must have been shattered when I appeared. So, Sophie Belle, who do you like better? Me or him?"

Sophie knew for sure he was deliberately acting silly. "Well, I have been pining for you since the day you came into Jack's shop, and I decided that I would make you fall in love with me. Benedict, Sam is a nice man, but you and I both know he has nothing on you. You absolutely know how well favored you are."

Benedict said, "There's a nice bed waiting for us. Well, it isn't particularly nice—only when you are in it—same as the Torrance Inn."

Sophie said, "Benedict Cochrane, are you planning on seducing me? After your horrid behavior? I am not sure you deserve it."

Benedict gave her a petted lip and she burst into peals of laughter. "Do you make that face to all the ladies, sir?"

He said, "Now stop talking about "all the ladies," I only want one woman for the rest of my life."

Sophie ventured, "Because you are in love with her?"

And Benedict couldn't help himself, "Well might just be infatuation."

Sophie started punching him again but this time, it very quickly turned into them frantically pulling off each other's clothes and their lovemaking was again magical. They never reappeared downstairs that night, and everyone concluded that all was well again.

~

They made love for most of the night, eventually falling asleep in each other's arms. It felt like moments later when Euphemia shouted in, "Time to get ready for Sunday Service you two, and the children are performing a live Nativity scene."

Benedict shouted, "Oh goody! Go away, Euphemia, Sophie Belle is exhausted. Her husband needs to look after her."

Sophie loved hearing him say husband; the word had been used so little with regard to him. She intended now to call him that in future, since after all, Benedict was such an intimidating sort of name. She snuggled into him, and he pulled the covers over their heads. The snow was falling heavily outside and inside that room there was a pair of young lovers who had finally come together and were basking in their mutual adoration.

Euphemia again shouted, "Sophie, you have your solo to perform this morning. You cannot let them down. My brother can stay in bed, if he is too lazy to get up. The judge and I and the Carlisles are already dressed."

Sophie remembered and she sprang up. "Oh Holy Night," she answered to her husband's unasked question." However, he did say, "So Sophie Belle can sing! Difficult one too, a lot of high notes. Who would have thought that? Why did you never tell me?"

Sophie said, "Well perhaps if you weren't always disappearing, and actually spent some time with me…."

He interrupted her, "Okay, point taken. Well, I am coming along now."

The couple were washed and dressed within fifteen minutes and as usual, Benedict was immaculate in his black silk suit, topped off by his ankle length fur coat, which Sophie supposed must have cost him a fortune. This man did not skimp on himself.

Sophie remembered the pound note he once gave Euphemia for Sophie to buy a gown for the City Chambers annual ball—yet another of Benedict Cochrane's disastrous evenings, and she said—looking down at her plain band of gold and fingering her mother's pearls, "These loose women of yours; did you buy them presents? Jewelry and the like—in order to gain entry to their bedchamber?"

Benedict knew he owed Sophie a number of back payments, as far as baubles and diamonds were concerned, and said, "Oh you know me better than that Sophie Belle. Perhaps an inexpensive bauble here and there."

Sophie said, "Well that is more than you ever gave me! Well, I suppose your gold cuff links, which I stupidly treasured."

He said, "Oh yes, I might want them back. What a strange thing for me to do. Also, you never returned my books. Anyway, you stuck me for one hundred pounds before you left me. I would think that is fair enough. I will buy you a gift in your shop. I think you promised me a ten percent discount."

Sophie huffed out of the room, and said to Euphemia, "Your brother is the most tight-fisted and greedy man who ever walked the earth. I am so happy we never wired him that hundred pounds. Sound advice, sister dear. It seems his stupid books were only on loan to me. I must remember to return them after the service."

Sophie then took Euphemia's arm and whispered, "I think Sir Alfred has something wonderful in mind for you."

Euphemia said, "You mean he intends to declare himself on Christmas Day? I expected that might be the case, or else why is he considering a position in New York City? Of course, I will accept. He is the very best of men."

Sophie said, "Just like my uncle Carlisle! I myself, have the worst of them; however, he is the most well-favored of the lot. Actually on Christmas Eve, Euphemia, and your odious brother gave his permission—no doubt because it will take the responsibility of one of us off his hands! I am so happy for you, Euphemia! You deserve such happiness. You know what's so funny, Sir Alfred is the very best of men and Benedict the very worst. But I wouldn't have him any other way; most especially after last night. Although I expect, it's because he has a lot of experience!"

Sophie laughed at Euphemia's red-faced embarrassment, "Sophie, we are on our way to Sunday service," and Sophie skipped ahead so she could take Benedict's arm.

David and Loretta Carlisle joined Euphemia and Sir Alfred who were now walking arm in arm, and David said, "I can't wait to see my niece's face when she sees that diamond ring. Must be the size of the Rock of Gibraltar!" Then he laughed, "told me the first thing he did was get it insured with Lloyds of London. I'm glad. I wondered the nature of this man, your brother, Euphemia, but is seems our Sophie has finally tamed him—to a certain extent anyway. I expect their marriage to be a tumultuous one."

Euphemia said, "Her love for him never wavered, no matter what he did and no matter how much she said she hated him. As for him, he knew the moment he saw her that she was to put an end to his philandering. It was no longer any fun for him. But oh, how he fought against it! He did every nasty deed in the book of nasty deeds. Still, she loved him and in the end, he gave in. He just wanted a wife, and that wife had to be Sophie Belle."

Euphemia had long since told everyone about the day she forgot her purse and was rescued by the beautiful young woman, destined to steal her brother's heart. She added, "If any of you good people knew him, just one year ago, you wouldn't believe it was the same man!"

Sir Alfred said, "Euphemia, you forget—I knew him well enough—and the man was an arrogant libertine, if ever there was one! Although, I must confess, I did enjoy his courtroom theatricals—saw right through them of course. The problem was the jury seldom did. I wonder how he will enjoy being a country lawyer. I hope for Sophie's sake that he takes to it."

They all went quiet. Sophie Belle was deliriously happy to have her man back. Then Euphemia voiced what they all were thinking, "He better not hurt that sweet girl again."

David Carlisle lightened the mood, "That ring must have cost him a fortune. In fact, I know it did. I can't see Sophie Belle ever wanting to leave New Chestnut and he won't leave without her. I agree that remark he made last night was totally out of line, but then again, so was the way Sam Spear was staring and smiling at her. Let's be jolly. It is Christmastime after all, and let's give the man a chance."

The service was magical with the children posing as a nativity tableau. Joseph was a bit restless, and the congregation tried not to laugh at Mary's admonishing looks toward him throughout the entire service.

Then it was time for Sophie's solo performance of 'O Holy Night' and she walked to the front of the tiny church a little nervously. Benedict had sung in the choir when he attended Glasgow High. There was so much he and his lovely wife had yet to learn about each other, and Benedict looked forward to a lifetime of fun and games with his bride, as their relationship continued to flourish.

Sophie's voice was a lilting soprano—her diction and clarity perfect—and after she sang the first verse and chorus, Benedict walked up to join her. Sophie looked shocked and Euphemia almost dropped her hymnal. He then joined in with his rich baritone and the congregation sat stunned at the newcomers who had come to stay and bring so much entertainment and delight to their small town.

When the hymn was finished, the couple received a standing ovation and Benedict kissed his bride to the complete joy and elation of the congregation.

CHAPTER 12

Monday morning, Sophie and Euphemia took a few hours off to go into their neighboring town, Old Chestnut. It was considerably larger than New Chestnut and they thought to do some Christmas shopping of their own—most particularly for Sir Alfred and Benedict.

Much to everyone's amazement, Benedict volunteered to help Loretta out for a few hours. Both the judge and David Carlisle intended to rest and read the Sunday newspapers.

It seemed the good barrister was determined to outshine his wife's and sister's selling ability. He sold both fur muffs and Loretta Carlisle so enjoyed watching him persuade the shoppers—all women—into purchasing more than they originally intended. He even encouraged several customers to open accounts with the store, so that they could overwhelm and delight the various gift recipients.

By the time Sophie and Euphemia returned on the sleigh from Old Chestnut, he had outdone the previous Saturday's take by fifty percent.

Both women were aghast, and Euphemia said, "Ah, my brother Benedict, ever the fierce competitor, determined to outshine his wife and sister. Sophie, are you intending to pay him for all his hard work?"

Benedict was grinning like a Cheshire cat, until Sophie said, "Well husband dear, would you like to carry on until closing time?"

He said, "Not a chance! I'm off to Bunny's for some edible food and a tankard of ale. But first, I will need to stop by to see Sheriff Sam

Spear, since as New Chestnut's town attorney, I am sure we will be seeing a lot of one another."

Sophie said worriedly, "Benedict, he is a very nice man. Please be kind. You know he taught Jack and me to ride and he let us borrow his horses on Saturday. Also, he allows us to keep our horses in his stables. Well, mine is there anyway because I am unsure how to look after her and Jack won't be building stables until the spring. She is a lovely white mare, and her name is Shandy. Please don't cause any trouble. Benedict?"

Benedict said, "Fine name for the mare that belongs to my wife, who likes to frequent pubs with my sister. Sorry, I believe they are called bars in America. Now Sophie Belle, what makes you worry about me causing any trouble with this lawman? Something to do with his behavior Saturday night? Sophie Belle?"

She said, "Certainly not! I am not like you, and he knows I am a married woman. However, I think he just found that out. No one knew you even existed."

"Don't worry, Mrs. Cochrane, I will be exceedingly congenial when I tell him the jig is up. By the way, the gentlemen are going into the city tomorrow. We need to purchase a few cases of potable wine and Scotch whisky. We will be back on Thursday, in plenty of time for Friday's hoedown. Also, my trunks arrived today so I need to close the deal and pick up the keys of the old Magnusson house, so I can set up shop after the New Year."

Sophie got so excited, "You bought the house! Oh Euphemia, isn't your brother wonderful? I suppose you will also be Christmas shopping in New York too!" Then Sophie noticed both fur muffs were gone, and she assumed Benedict must have purchased one of them, until he told her he sold both to Mrs. Meyers for her daughters.

Benedict said, "Sorry Sophie Belle, no time for Christmas shopping tomorrow."

She said, "Well at least did you buy me something in the shop with your ten percent discount?"

He looked thoughtful, "Oh yes, I believe I might have bought you something this morning. However, I may have instead decided to let you keep all the money I made for you today. As far as Sheriff Sam Spear? I'm not worried about him. I don't want to sound conceited..."

Sophie sighed and thought, *I must be married to the most egotistic man on the planet.* She asked her aunt, "Aunt Loretta, did my stingy husband buy me anything today?"

And Loretta said, "Now Sophie dear, that would be giving away secrets," but inwardly she thought that he might have done a little better, in the selection of the one gift he purchased for his wife.

Sophie huffed off with the presents she had purchased for Benedict that morning and was glad that they consisted only of thermal underwear, dungarees, and two flannel shirts.

~

When the gentlemen left the next morning Sophie decided to snoop through her husband's trunks. She hoped to find something for her, but everything was his. She thought, *my God was there ever a man that had as many fine clothes as my husband?* She then went off to seek out Euphemia and dragged her into her bedroom.

"Seriously, Euphemia? Look at all these suits. Your brother must be the vainest man who ever walked the earth! Everything he has is perfect. Everything he has brought is all for him. Not even a handkerchief or silk scarf for me, and he told me he has no time for Christmas shopping in New York! I swear I hate him and if he doesn't give me something nice for Christmas, I am filing for divorce!"

Euphemia was used to her sister-in-law's idle threats. In addition, she and the others knew about the huge diamond ring he intended to surprise her with. She said, "Sophie, we both know you are not filing for divorce, and we both know the man is a dandy. Perhaps, he got you something very nice already?"

Sophie said, "Do you think that is possible? When he first arrived in New York? He was there for two weeks and had time to do so. Now I wish I got him something nicer than thermals and flannels, but did you see that coat? Must have cost him a fortune! Euphemia, I worry he doesn't like it here and gets bored. I mean, oh I don't know what I mean."

Euphemia said, "Stop worrying about him. My advice, if you care to listen to it, is to continue to give him the run-around, as you did in Scotland. That should keep him on his toes."

Sophie said, "Benedict told me he is calling on Sam Spear. He presumes that he is far more handsome than Sam, which of course he is, however Sam is a nicer person."

Euphemia responded, "I hope we don't have a hoedown brawl, although Sir Alfred would enjoy that. I see my brother and the judge standing all night Friday without taking to the floor even once. Well unless they can persuade the Nelson brothers to play a waltz."

Sophie said, "Oh I hope not! I still have flash backs of the City Chambers ball!" And off she ran to look inside the windows of the Magnusson house. It was extremely old-fashioned from what she could make out. It certainly hadn't seen a lick of paint in years. She ran back to the shop, where Loretta and Euphemia were getting ready to open for the day, and shouted, "Oh my word! I can't possibly live there for months! I hope Mr. Cochrane has plenty of money for paint and plumbing, and all brand-new furniture! Do you think he might not return from New York, with the others?"

∽

Benedict Cochrane was back in New Chestnut in time for the holiday hoedown, although Sophie told him, he needn't have bothered. Sophie wore her blue and white checkered dress and her hair in pigtails tied with blue ribbons. The others said she looked adorable, but Benedict told her that she should change since she looked ridiculous and not becoming for the town attorney's wife.

She thought at first he was kidding her, but when he appeared, as was usual, all dressed in black, she knew he meant it. Her mind was again drawn back to the City Chambers ball, however, on this occasion, he would be the one out of place, and not her.

Sophie walked with Euphemia and Sir Alfred and asked, "What happened in New York? He was so sweet before he left—well sweet for him, I mean. He hasn't taken me in to see the house, which he says he owns and seems distracted. I am so looking forward to our honeymoon in New York, so we can truly be alone together for the very first time. Sir Alfred, do you know if Benedict booked a hotel room when you were in New York City? I am so excited about it!"

Sir Alfred had already told Euphemia that her brother had been contacted by a Glasgow mob king's lawyer, with a very lucrative offer for Benedict to take the case. The charges included money laundering, corruption, and racketeering. He knew Benedict wanted it and was torn. "If he does indeed take it on, he will have to leave next week and will be gone for many months. Also, Sophie is so excited about this honeymoon he promised her. She will be heartbroken—again!"

Euphemia said, "Oh, why did he ever come here in the first place if he is already unsettled after a matter of mere days? Surely, he will not let her down this time. She is so elated to be going away with him. About time too for him to treat his lovely wife!"

Sir Alfred said, "I believe he loves Sophie, but he also loves his old persona, the one that suited him so well in Scotland. It remains to be seen, Euphemia. With your brother there always seems to be a good versus evil battle going on inside him. I thought the good had won out, however one could see his excitement when he read that letter. He has his mail going to David Carlisle's office. I thought that was temporary but possibly not."

The hoedown was in full swing when Sophie's party arrived and she felt that all were watching this new town attorney, dressed totally in black, and hoping for introductions. However, he stood silently closed to any pleasantries or introductions. Sophie stood beside him for a short while and then said, "Go to hell!" And went out to dance and join the others.

She was completely ignoring him, and hoping he could see how popular she was with the young men. The judge and Euphemia danced a few dances, as did her uncle and aunt, and both couples were laughing merrily at the two men's antics on the dance floor. Then the band changed tempo for a slow waltz, and Sophie looked around to find her husband, but there was no sign of him. He had left without her. The day before Christmas Eve, Sophie was crushed, but determined not to show it. Sam Spear took full advantage. He asked her to dance, and Sophie wondered why she didn't fall in love with a man who was kind like him.

By the time Sophie's party left, she was certain many of the townsfolk were talking about her—in the way that small town people do. She felt humiliated, a feeling she had not experienced since she left Glasgow and Scotland behind, or at least until her husband came and had by now caused her to feel that way twice when they were out with company. The next day was Christmas Eve, and the shop would close early, although the morning would be very busy. Sophie decided that perhaps a divorce was inevitable. She couldn't spend her life worrying about whatever mood her husband chose to be in—nervous about whether he would be kind to her or uncaring, or even about to disappear again. She had been invited to go on a midnight sleigh ride by Sam Spear, and Jack would be there too. Sophie determined she was going to go and whispered her intention into Euphemia's ear.

Everyone was quiet when they arrived home, and Sophie pulled out her pigtails. The judge suggested a night cap and as all agreed, Benedict appeared.

He said, "I'm sorry Sophie Belle. Can you forgive me? A lot on my mind, and I am afraid that hoedowns are not very much my style. You appeared not to want for dance partners anyway, so I am sure you didn't much miss me."

Sophie said, "Excuse me," and went upstairs to change and put on warmer clothes. She locked her bedroom door but needn't have bothered since her husband didn't follow her. She reappeared a short time later and announced, "That's me off then. Some of us young people are going on a mid-night sleigh ride." She turned to Benedict. "Don't wait up for me. Jack is coming, and I will be safe enough in Sam's sleigh since he is an excellent horseman. I would invite you all but really everyone going is young like me."

She turned to Euphemia, "Euphemia, your brother will be happier on the sofa tonight—or at least, I will not be sleeping with him. Can you give him a pillow and blanket? One blanket will do."

She then made to leave, and Benedict laughed, "Sure thing Sophie Belle. I am not allowing you to go on your own, without your husband, and I have no intention of tagging along."

Sophie said, "Perhaps you misunderstood, Benedict. You are too old to go anyway, and as far as being allowed. I will do as I choose, and you can go to hell."

Sophie flounced out the door—bravely—but feeling her heart was broken. She thought Benedict would more forcefully stop her, somehow apologize and make everything better. He didn't, and now she was off on a sleigh ride with couples who were all in love—as indeed was she. The only difference was, she was in love with a cruel and uncaring man, who just allowed her to go on a mid-night sleigh ride with another man, without making much fuss about it.

∽

After she left, he spoke to the men, "This case is the case of a lifetime. The money will more than fix up that ramshackle house too. This is what I have dreamed of, however, it will go on for months.

Sophie Belle may never forgive me and find another man. Indeed, she already has." He started drinking heavily and his companions told him to slow down.

Sir Alfred said, "Why not talk to her about it. Possibly ask her to go with you. You know she will be heartbroken. For God's sake man, you told her you were taking her on honeymoon to New York. Is that no longer the case? If not, then why not make it an Atlantic crossing honeymoon and she could remain with you, or at least for a while?"

Benedict almost choked on his drink, "God no! Can you imagine Sophie Belle sitting at the back of the courtroom, giving me little waves? No, I need to go alone. I have my flat in Kelvinside and my car is with Martin. He has a three-car garage, would you believe it? Anyway, I already booked my ticket when we were in Manhattan."

Sir Alfred said, "So your decision has already been made Cochrane, without a care for your promises to your wife. When are you leaving? Surely you are at least spending a week in New York as you promised, to celebrate on New Year's Eve. You could bring her home before you set sail?"

Both men were shocked when he said, "No, not possible. I need to leave the day after Christmas. That's the date I booked my ticket. The courts aren't in session until after the New Year so my timing couldn't be better. I got the last available first-class stateroom, quite fortunate. Sophie Belle will get over it. She always does."

David Carlisle said, "That sounds so callous, Benedict. I thought more of you than that. My niece will be heartbroken. I disapproved of her going out without you tonight, but I find now I am glad she did."

∽

It was almost 2:30 a.m. when Sophie returned home. She felt in her heart her marriage must be over, but she still wanted no other man. She had fun, and the others made so much of her—no insults nor innuendos. They were all respectful and Sophie knew she deserved such respect. She dreaded going home, so Jack accompanied her. All was quiet as she took off her coat and boots and then suddenly Benedict emerged. Clearly, he had been drinking and he began accusing her of what, she didn't quite hear because she ran upstairs in tears. The Judge and her uncle appeared to separate her husband and brother, who were by then rolling around on the kitchen floor.

～

Christmas Eve morning and Sophie's heart was broken. She wished Benedict never came. He had slept on the sofa, without an argument since he was too drunk to care. Sir Alfred took Sophie aside and told her about the job offer—the one Benedict had accepted. The one he was sailing off the day after Christmas to take on.

Sophie was devastated but tried to hide it, as she surprised him. "I am filing for divorce. He came here and got what he wanted—me—and discovered I was nothing special after all. Still not worth a honeymoon, any more than I was in Scotland. I am done with it and with him. I am sorry to say and do this on Christmas Eve, but he has left me no choice. I am still young and there are others who love me. I hereby release him to his old life and mistress. She must have really been something to hold his interest so long."

The judge didn't argue with her, since in truth he felt it was what the man deserved.

CHAPTER 13

Benedict Cochrane emerged, looking rather disheveled and Sophie recalled how she used to love to see him that way, since he was usually so impeccably dressed. However, this was different than on those other occasions back in Scotland—before she was his wife. He asked to speak to Sophie alone. He led her up to her room and Sophie thought, *what now? A parting seduction?*

However, it wasn't that. He told her a little about the case—the chance of a lifetime, and the money he would make. He said, "It will take a fortune to fix up that ramshackle house and it is too small anyway. It would be easier to knock it down and build another. All that takes money. I was offered fifty thousand pounds. Half to start and half when I get him off. Can you even understand how much money that is, Sophie Belle? Do you have enough in your little cash box? No, you have no conception of it, but suffice to say it will build you the finest house in New York, with very many thousands left over. My intention is to come back to you as soon as I've won the case. Then we can truly start our lives together, and I know I owe you a very special honeymoon. Someplace better than New York City. You will be here to supervise the work and Jack will be the foreman. I haven't asked him yet, but he will do anything for his little sister."

Sophie was unconvinced, and said, "And what if you lose. Do they have you killed? These are bad people Benedict. Also, what if there is another enticing case upon this one's conclusion? Will you be staying on? I think you are too greedy. It will be your downfall, and mine—if I let it. I wonder if you miss your Spanish mistress. Possibly I should have asked her for some helpful bedroom hints. Oh, that's right, I had no idea you were two-timing me."

He said, "Sophie Belle, I have never, nor would I ever cheat on you. I married you, didn't I?"

Sophie said, "In a manner of speaking, I suppose, since I was willing to marry a man who ran away from me the very next morning, having deliberately gotten drunk on my wedding night. Sorry the wait turned out to be for nothing much, such a disappointment for you. When are you leaving?"

"I need to leave the day after Christmas. I promise I will be back as soon as I can and you will have the construction of our new home to see to while I am gone."

Sophie was unconvinced, "How am I paying for all of this?"

"Your uncle, and before you ask, I will be providing him with substantial funds."

Sophie said, "Well as you say, it is the chance of a lifetime. What is her name, by the way, your mistress, I mean?"

Benedict looked confused, "Sophie Belle, she is long gone and out of my life forever."

Sophie repeated, "Name please?"

He said, "Carlotta Ramirez, not that it matters."

She said, "It does to me. An exotic beauty, I am sure. She will be so pleased to see you back in town. I am going downstairs."

He said, "Wait, I bought you something," and produced the huge diamond from his pocket, placing the ring on her finger."

She said, "Is it real? An awfully fine thing for a shopkeeper's daughter? My insurance I suppose. It must be worth a fortune. No, I don't believe it to be real. You would never purchase such a beautiful, expensive item—for me? This must surely have cost more than the one pound note you once gave your sister for a ballgown—for a ball to which you regretted taking me. It turned out that I was indeed an embarrassment after all, as I recall."

Benedict said, "Sophie, why do you love me if you think so little of me?"

Sophie responded easily, "I can turn that question around to you. Again, sorry I was a disappointment—in the end."

Benedict appeared to get angry, "If you are a disappointment, it is because you willfully choose to misunderstand me and take everyone else's point of view. Sophie, you knew who and what I was when you agreed to marry me. No one forced you into it. Remember you left me, not the other way around. I had plans to take you up to the Highlands and truly begin our life together."

Sophie noticed that Benedict had dropped the "Belle" from her name. She was sad and despondent—on Christmas Eve—even with a diamond ring on her finger. She said, "Well we shall see what the future brings to us both. I feel I have heard that line several times before, how at some point in the future we can begin to build our lives together. However, that time never seems to come around, does it Benedict?" And she walked out of the room, leaving him standing there. She thought, piece *by piece and bit by bit, he is destroying what we had that was so special. Perhaps I bore him. A few nights with me and he is desperate to leave.*

∽

As he did, the day after Christmas—once again impeccably dressed and wearing his expensive beaver fur coat. It was the Christmas that Sophie was so excited about. He destroyed it and when he made love to her that night, she forced herself not to respond. He seemed confused, hurt even, but that didn't stop him leaving, and Euphemia and all the others felt they could never forgive him.

Sophie made it through Christmas and New Year and then the sickness began. She knew she was with child—Benedict's child—and she spoke very little about it. She was sick every morning and the sickness continued. It continued into April, when she was bridesmaid at Sir Alfred and Euphemia's wedding.

Sir Alfred was building a fine home for his bride, and Sophie dreaded being left alone in the flat above the shop. He had his solicitor see to the sale of his home and furniture back in Scotland and said there was nothing worth bringing to America. "Dusty old things," according to him.

Sometimes Sophie's aunt and uncle Carlisle came to stay but those first three months of the year were bitterly cold and oftentimes the train tracks were impassable. Still, this caused a delay on the construction on both houses, and for that at least, Sophie was glad.

The construction began to pick up again in late April and Sophie asked Euphemia, "Why am I not glowing and happy? I am past four months and I feel tired and gloomy all the time. I wish he never came at all because I fear that something is wrong with me. I fear my baby is evil, like his father. I find I fear everything and wonder if he is fixing up his fine home in New Chestnut so he can sell it. I should be buying the sort of items, I should have been given as wedding presents—fine bone china, crystal glasses, and silver candelabras. Of course, I wasn't even given a wedding ring at the time, let alone fine tableware. I wonder if your brother auctioned all that stuff off when he sold the house. Surely, he should have given you a say in the matter?" She stopped, "You know something Euphemia? I had more possessions in Bishopbriggs, and I had very little there. Still at least I now have a wedding and diamond engagement ring to pawn if need be."

Euphemia reassured Sophie that she and Loretta would take care of her, and not to worry about such trivial matters. She should be concentrating on her baby now.

Sophie said, "You are correct, I have those who love me and I know will see me right. Unfortunately, my husband is not one of them. Anyway, be that as it may, I have decided to snap out of this malaise. The gift shop is going to become a miniature department store. When we move out, we will have Jack fix up the second floor and incorporate ladies' lingerie and children's clothing. Possibly men's sundries and novelties. Also, the kitchen and dining room can be turned into a beautifully appointed tearoom—like the Willow Tea Rooms in Glasgow. The ladies of New Chestnut will be so appreciative, since all they currently have to choose from is Bunny's Tavern and The Empire Diner. They can dress up and take tea, just like we did in happier times in Glasgow. Of course, we will need a talented cook and we must advertise when the time is right. What do you think, Euphemia? Jack is doing a fine job with all the construction going on and my uncle Carlisle has been generous, providing the funds for such an undertaking on both my house and our shop."

Euphemia was heartened by Sophie finally making plans, since she wasn't exaggerating when she had called herself gloomy. However, what concerned her was the comment about her baby being evil.

"Sophie, I think your plan for a tearoom is a capital idea. This town could certainly do with one. Also, the ladies may well make a few purchases on their way upstairs to take tea! When first we arrived in New Chestnut, I had little conception that we would soon become business partners in such a successful undertaking. We can plan together, with Loretta's kind assistance, how to replicate our favorite Glasgow tearooms. However, Sophie dearest, babies are never evil, not even my brother's and he isn't evil either, even although I have called him so in the past. He is selfish and greedy, thoughtless, and it seems his ambition is the driving force of his life. If you two never come together, you will have your very own baby who will love you as no other—not to mention a successful and lucrative business with your sister."

Sophie asked, "Do you ever intend to tell Sir Alfred that we are equal business partners in this endeavor?"

Euphemia said, "Oh I will when the time is right. I have had too many years of being told what to do by my brother, and although my husband is remarkably different from him—thank goodness—I am enjoying my small bit of independence and privacy regarding the matter. After all, he has made no investment into our little enterprise, and thankfully neither has Benedict, so in reality, it is none of their business."

The conversation cheered Sophie, although she confessed, "Euphemia, on Christmas night—the night before Benedict left—I acted cold and lifeless when he came to me. I knew he was hurt and confused, and I was glad. That is the last memory he has of me. I suppose I should have written back to the one letter he sent, but I didn't. I am certain now that he has moved on to another woman."

Euphemia said, "So it seems after everything, you still love him. I wish you didn't, but I doubt he has taken a mistress. I will not add adultery to his many lists of crimes. He likely sits in his flat each night drinking whisky and counting his money."

This made Sophie smile a little sadly, "I wish I went with him, and then I remember he didn't want me. He didn't ask me for fear of me waving at him in the courtroom."

Sophie dressed for dinner that night and fixed her hair. The first time since her husband left that such care was taken with her appearance. She announced, "I have decided to stop pining for Benedict Cochrane. Instead, I will concentrate on remodeling the shop and the house and when my time finally comes, I will employ a nanny. If the baby is a boy and he looks like his father, I will send him over to Scotland to live with him. That way he can be taught to be cruel and selfish, nothing like his grandfather Cochrane, whom I am told was loving and kind. Can we toast on that?"

Sir Alfred said, "Sophie Belle, you will do no such thing. Well, all that renovation, of course, but you will love your baby and will not send him away to be like his father. Besides, your husband should be home long before that. The baby is due in September and that trial will end before summer. I am sure of it."

He was being upbeat, but then Sophie responded, "Alfred, he is already "home" in Scotland. He wasn't here long enough to call

New Chestnut "home." In any case, I might die in childbirth. Lots of women do. What then? Well unless the baby dies too and that will be the end of Benedict Cochrane's troubles."

The judge and Euphemia were very concerned to hear Sophie speak this way. It was so unlike the loving and kind girl who sent all the photographs to her husband in anticipation of him coming to her. She no longer expected him to come. She was still writing to him but was not posting her letters. She had started filling another wooden box—the one Benedict bought with his ten percent discount. He gave it to her empty—no candy nor soaps inside, as she often suggested to her customers. Also, for reasons known only to himself, he had left the fur coat and muff at the Carlisle's house when they returned from New York the day before the ill-fated holiday hoedown. The Carlisle's mutually decided to bring these items down to Sophie and both were wrapped with red ribbon. No one understood why Benedict didn't give the furs to his wife for Christmas, as had been his intent, but then that cursed letter offering him the McNulty gangland case seemed to completely turn his head and change his intentions.

Sophie's fur coat and muff were often admired by others—they were beautiful and of the finest quality, and Sophie said they were gifts from her aunt and uncle, even although she knew they truly came from her unkind husband, who had chosen not to give them to her at Christmas. She often wondered why he gave her such an expensive ring, but decided that at the time he bought it, her husband's good side was winning over the evil side—the side that eventually won the war within his heart.

∽

July 1, 1911, and Sophie came down with influenza. Both houses were nearing completion and David Carlisle was enormously proud of his nephew, who had hired men for the two projects as well as the newly expanded *Sophie Belle's Gift Shoppe*. The store was closed for the month of July and was to reopen in late August with a new moniker, *Sophie Belle's,* since the merchandise was being greatly expanded upon, and the refurbished tearoom was a delight. They employed a cook and three part-time waitresses. Sophie and Euphemia were spending the money they took in over the holiday season on the newly refurbished shop. In addition to that, Euphemia had her own inheritance to play with, and Jack had given Sophie a substantial sum of money. David Carlisle took care of the legal aspect of the women's new partnership and of course was keeping the matter under his hat.

Sophie believed her uncle Carlisle was paying the greater part of the considerable expenses she was accumulating for her new home, and at least at the present time, he did not correct her. He was unsure about Benedict Cochrane's intentions. He certainly sent considerable funds for the construction and furnishing of his fine house but made no mention of when he intended to return to it, or more importantly to his wife.

No one was to tell Benedict of his wife's confinement and by the time she came down with influenza, she was saying it was none of his business. However, when Doctor Kauffman took the Carlisles and Hickses aside, along with Jack Sullivan—he pulled no punches.

"Mrs. Cochrane is very weak. I must confine her to complete bed rest, or I fear she will not have the strength to get well and to deliver this baby. She must be made to eat good nourishing foods. Fruits and vegetables are in abundance this time of year. The weather is still fine and she may sit in the garden on a warm afternoon, but no more. Where is this husband of hers?"

Following this lecture, the others felt exceedingly guilty. Benedict had been gone for over six months and Sophie and her child were in great peril, according to the doctor, at any rate. Sophie argued that she had too much to do, and therefore Loretta settled in for the summer to take care of matters. Euphemia was always by Sophie's side, in addition to seeing to the baby's furniture and clothing, since Sophie had done little in this regard. It was decided the ladies were too angry and full of accusations to write to Benedict, most especially his sister, and therefore, it was Sir Alfred and David Carlisle who were given the assignment to let Benedict have it—straight! First the judge.

> July 11, 1911
>
> Benedict,
>
> I know not how your case is coming along, however, your wife and unborn child are in great peril. Dr. Kauffman is extremely concerned and has cautioned us. Sophie Belle is confined to absolute bed rest and your sister and the rest of us are in daily trepidation of what the next day will bring.
> There you have it. I cannot particularly wish you success in your endeavors, unless the loss of your lovely wife and unborn child are worth it to you—a fitting sacrifice for your resounding success as Scotland's most prestigious barrister.
> Should you hear from me again, it will be of their passing, in which case I will damn you to hell.
>
> I remain,
> Sir Alfred Hicks

This was angrier than intended, but Sir Alfred Hicks knew Benedict Cochrane the best, apart from his sister. Within his heart, he felt Sophie would pull through this. The young woman was a determined little thing; however, this man had so broken her heart and spirit, and she who was always so lively and cheerful was now so sad and subdued. This was not Sophie Belle's true nature, and Sir Alfred loved her so very much. Had he been younger, he might have truly been a rival to Benedict Cochrane. Sir Alfred loved his wife, Euphemia, but Sophie Belle was so very special to him—ever since

Cochrane left her standing alone, humiliated, in the Corn Exchange public house in Glasgow—not so very long ago. She looked like a princess in a fairytale, Cinderella possibly, since her clothes were quite inexpensive compared to the Cochranes, who left her there to pay the bill. Sir Alfred never forgot that night. He sometimes felt that Euphemia should have been stronger. However, Euphemia had been a loving sister to her ever since.

In the case of David Carlisle, Sophie and Jack were fast becoming the children he and Loretta were never blessed to be given. Sophie had spent her youth caring for her mother—David Carlisle's only sister— and then her father, until both of their demise. He was angry. He had been the only one in communication with Benedict Cochrane and Benedict was still wiring over funds as promised. However, enough was enough. Sophie was a changed girl, and now it seemed Dr. Kauffman felt her and her baby's lives were in jeopardy. His letter was a little kinder than Sir Alfred's.

July 11, 1911

Benedict,

Things are not well in New Chestnut. My niece is carrying your child, due in September, and according to her physician, all is not as it should be. Therefore, Sophie has been prescribed complete bed rest. She is not adhering to this and I worry about the lives of her and her unborn child.

I know you have made a great deal of money on this case. What I am unsure about is your plans and intentions for the future. My niece is not as you remember her. She is solemn and sad and doesn't seem to care about her life nor indeed her unborn baby's. If you are not planning to return you must inform me of such, so my wife and I may endeavor to guide Sophie on her new path that lies ahead. As you are aware, there is a man here who loves her. Sam Spear is ever at her side. It seems to matter not to him that she is carrying your child. Perhaps you are fine with this? Nevertheless, it is time that you made your intentions clear, at least to me.

Possibly you are already planning your return. However, for Pity's sake man, if you are not coming back, let me know so that suitable arrangements and accommodations may be made. Benedict, I have no idea if you still love her or not. She loves you—this I can tell despite her words, but in so doing, it may well be the destruction of her and of your child.

There I have given it to you straight—without recriminations and accusations—no matter what I feel inside.

One final note. If you no longer love her or have fallen for another, please stay away. I will see that everything is fairly and properly divided in the event of divorce. She has a family. Of course, should the baby survive, even if, God forbid, Sophie does not, you will be responsible for child support.

Your obedient servant,
David Carlisle

Benedict Cochrane had sailed to England with a heavy heart. He spent New Year's Eve aboard ship and felt like a total bounder.

The train ride up to Glasgow was no better. Sophie Belle had just laid there, that last night. She showed no emotion, no love nor passion. He had disappointed her, and forgetting to bring her furs didn't help, despite him giving her that expensive diamond.

Of course, she didn't understand. How could she? One works all one's life for a case like this and at such a hefty fee, he was surprised they didn't balk at it. It only proved the reputation he left behind him in Scotland and moreover, he needed that money in order to build his house in upstate New York and live his life in the manner to which he had been accustomed. Sophie Belle was content with so little, but Benedict thought he knew enough about women for all that to change. Again, he asked himself, "Is Sophie Belle worth giving up the life I have enjoyed living for thirty-five years?"

He had believed that she was, when first he set sail, and was settling in nicely with his new wife, until he received that letter and proposal—too lucrative and important a case to pass along to another lesser barrister.

He was paid his retainer, twenty-five thousand pounds, and wired the greater portion of it to David Carlisle. He had plenty to get by on and his beaver fur coat earned him the reputation of being stinking rich—although he wasn't quite that. He also took on two smaller, less sensational cases in-between and was soon busy day and night.

He wrote once to Sophie Belle, but she didn't write back. Proof enough that she was happy with her new life, and possibly with the town sheriff, Sam Spear, who dangled after her the night of the hoedown. She had gone out with him on a sleigh ride until after two in the morning. Of course, Benedict should have prevented it, but by then he had already booked his passage back to Scotland. He had made up his mind to take the case and leave the day after Christmas, thereby breaking his promise to take his wife on honeymoon. Sophie was so excited about their honeymoon in New York and once again he let her down.

And what a jolly Christmas it was. Sophie gave him some ridiculous cowpoke clothes. It was as if she forgot who she had married, and he was not a man who wore flannel shirts and dungarees—not even in New Chestnut. Still, he fully intended to return by April or May at the latest, in the beginning anyway.

When he met with his client, he was confident that he could get him off. However, he didn't want off completely. He wanted to serve some time—but Benedict was warned, no more than six months. He was told this would add to McNulty's notoriety, and the man laughed when Benedict told him, he could think of no one more notorious in the whole of Scotland. McNulty also added that there was a man in Barlinnie prison with whom he would like to reacquaint himself. Benedict Cochrane knew exactly what he meant by this, and it was certainly not, "for old times' sake," as his client had added to his comment.

Then the threats from McNulty's henchmen began. The case was more complex than Benedict imagined, and he demanded a larger fee to continue as their boss's barrister. McNulty was already in jail, having been denied bail and since he didn't want to lose the best barrister in Glasgow, especially one without a moral compass, he paid the additional legal fees. In total, Benedict was to be paid sixty thousand pounds. He was also aware if he failed in his endeavor, his body would be later washed up in the River Clyde.

Benedict Cochrane had never taken on such a case for a man so clearly guilty of the crimes of which he was accused, and his wouldn't be the first body to be found in the river—curtesy of McNulty's gang of thugs—should matters turn out for the worst.

For these reasons, and his guilt about his innocent wife, Benedict Cochrane did not pursue any further correspondence. If things went badly, Sophie Belle would have her shop and a lovely home and would not need another man to support her. She was pure of heart; how could he ever tell her about this case upon his return? However, McNulty was famous in Glasgow, or at least his name was infamous. Jack may have spoken to Sophie about the man, and she would surely then have pondered about the nature of the man she had married, to take on such a client. She also believed her uncle was bankrolling the house. This he wanted, in case things went badly for him and she found herself in some sort of moral dilemma.

Benedict wondered that Sophie Belle had not conceived, but it was probably just as well. At least that was what he told himself, because deep down inside, he wanted a son. That was the good in him, this longing for a real family—a family he would only ever want with Sophie Belle. He had remained faithful to her. Opportunities were always abundant for the good barrister; however, he was never even tempted and was grateful that Carlotta Ramirez had taken on a new lover—or so he had heard from Nicholson.

One fine spring day Benedict Cochrane took a drive out to his old house in Bishopbriggs. The new owners had worked wonders. They had cut back the old hedgerow and the house appeared more open to the street below. He spotted the mistress of the house. She was sitting outside on a bench with a small child on her knee. Then he saw her husband coming out to join them, kissing his wife's cheek, and his baby's chubby hands. A maid brought out tea. Benedict thought, *happy family—that could have been me— in that very same house.* Somehow, it didn't seem as foreboding as when he lived there with Euphemia. Perhaps, it was they who made it foreboding, and the thought occurred to Benedict that he was married from that house, yet never made love to his wife in it—not even on his wedding night. He said aloud, "Bloody sad blighter, Cochrane," and went on his way.

However, each morning, his dark side appeared in court to spout forth a quantity of lies and basically rip the procurator fiscal's solid case apart. Barrister Cochrane laughed out loud at the lack of any evidence. He postured and pontificated and each day, several young girls would appear at the back of the court room, just to swoon over his antics. McNulty, in the accused dock, appeared to be watching all of this with some amusement, and Benedict deliberately steered his eyes away from him, until it was time for McNulty to take the stand. By now, Benedict knew the major charges would be dropped and besides, the jury would be reluctant to find the man guilty. Benedict's job was to *catch* McNulty out on some insignificant charge. This he did, and when the jury came out with several not guilty verdicts, Mr. McNulty was taken to Barlinnie prison for a sentence of three to six months on the one remaining charge of petty larceny.

Benedict Cochrane shook hands with his client, who gave him a wink and said there would be a little extra for him, most especially since he was a little doubtful that his barrister could pull off the small sentence he wanted, and for such a ridiculously nonsensical crime.

In total the case brought barrister Cochrane the unheard-of sum of seventy thousand pounds—a fortune. He wired most of it to David Carlisle, who managed his investments in New York, and then took himself off to his favorite spot in the Highlands of Scotland. He sailed from Mallaig to the Isle of Skye. There were a few tourists but not many, and he booked a week in a small bed and breakfast in Portree. Benedict spent his days hiking in the types of clothing he never would have considered wearing—hiking boots, duffle bag, waterproof anorak and warm wool trousers tucked into his boots. His landlady packed him a tasty lunch every day, and he always carried a hip flask of malt whisky.

To Benedict, it felt like a re-birth. He was a man of considerable means, with a beautiful wife pining for him in Upstate New York, or at least he hoped she was. He had a house there, in New Chestnut and wondered if Sophie Belle had any taste in decorating. Still, he could make changes upon his return.

Benedict Cochrane booked another week at the small inn, since the weather turned unusually warm, and he went swimming in the still frigid cold North Atlantic Ocean. He had never done such a thing since his summer breaks from Glasgow University, and it suddenly hit him—he was no longer the twenty something man about town—he was a thirty-five-year-old man with a young and enchanting wife. Sophie Belle wasn't afraid of hard work, as were many of the women in his past acquaintance. Amazingly, neither was his sister, Euphemia—a fact that genuinely surprised him.

 He cut short his second week with the excuse of missing his wife in America. He showed his landlady, Mrs. Myrtle, the photographs Sophie sent him the previous year, and Mrs. Myrtle asked him what he was doing in Scotland, with such a beauty awaiting him so far away.

        ~

 Benedict packed up his gear, including his black suits that he hadn't worn on his Highland excursion. He laughed at himself sitting in the first-class compartment of the train. His boots muddy, badly in need of a shave and a haircut—his clothes, warm and sensible and thoroughly unfashionable. There was a man sitting across from him in the train. He kept looking at Benedict and eventually Benedict introduced himself, expecting the usual accolade he was so freely given in his native Scotland. However, the man simply said, "I know who you are, the good barrister who sets the guilty free."

 Benedict laughed and said, "No, no longer him. The man leaving all of that behind to join his bride and begin his new life in America."

 They struck up a conversation, which passed the time until both men fell asleep to be awakened when the train finally arrived at Glasgow Central Station.

 Benedict bid the man farewell and then took the subway to his flat in Kelvinside. He thought, *I will need to go through my stack of mail and then start packing for New York. I will book passage on the first ship that has a first-class ticket available.*

 Benedict poured himself a whisky—the only potable drink in his flat. There was no food and that was another thing he would have to take care of in the morning. His charwoman was supposed to keep the flat clean, and since she had done a very poor job of it—he would have no qualms in paying her off when the time came, hopefully within the next month or so.

His attention was immediately caught by two letters from America. One from David Carlisle—not totally unexpected, given their business dealings, but also one from Sir Alfred Hicks—who was by now his brother-in-law, although unfortunately, he could not be there to give away his sister, the bride.

He read the judge's first. He started and then had to sit down to take it in—and then looked at the date stamp which was several weeks ago.

He picked up David Carlisle's and tore it open. The letter was less vindictive but just as straight forward. Again, written several weeks ago. What did they all think? That he just ignored the fact that his wife's, his Sophie Belle's and his unborn child's lives were in jeopardy? The baby due in September? It was already August, and he wasn't even booked on a ship!

Change of plans. Benedict found a ship sailing in two weeks. That would be the end of August before he even got there. He was going second class, as it was all that was available, and he didn't care at any rate. He would have gone over in steerage if that was all they had.

He took himself to the post office first thing in the morning. Three telegrams to send.

The first to Sophie Belle:

> **I am coming home. I love you. I have always loved you. Please look after yourself and our baby. I can't face life without my Sophie Belle.**

Then his sister:

> **You should have written sooner. Don't let her die. I am on my way.**

Finally, David Carlisle:

How could I know? I am on my way. Keep her safe. There is no one else.

Benedict Cochrane did not respond to his new brother-in-law. He felt the vindictiveness of his short note, proved what he had always believed. Alfred Hicks was very fond of his wife, Euphemia—loved her in his way—but he was in love with Sophie Belle. His letter was way over the top, for a man who was only related through marriage, a man who had known her less than two years. This was about as long as Benedict had known Sophie Belle too, however, he was her husband, and he was also the man she was in love with—at least he hoped that was still the case.

That was the longest two weeks ever for Benedict Cochrane. He spent much of it buying pretty things for his wife, lacy lingerie, and a gold locket that would hang all the way to her waist. He even purchased two pretty gowns from Copeland and Lye department store. She wouldn't fit them now, but they had her size on file, and they would fit her in the autumn. He thought about buying a gift for his baby, but decided that might be bad luck—besides, it occurred to him that he knew absolutely nothing about babies and children.

Finally, it was time to board ship and unlike the last time Benedict made the Atlantic crossing, he took no pleasure in the voyage. He spent most of his time in his cabin, writing letters to Sophie. He was hoping she had been doing the same, and he intended to ask her if he could have all the letters, she had written to him while they were apart, so he could get to know and understand her better. Something had changed inside of him. He realized that the good had finally won over the dark side, and he fervently hoped that it wasn't too late to tell Sophie how much he loved her since the moment he first laid eyes on her—even when he fought so hard against it.

CHAPTER 14

Each person received their telegrams on the same day and in the case of Sophie, a complete transformation took place.

This girl they were all so worried about, who was wan and sickly, pale and weak, suddenly sprang to life. She was so heavily pregnant by then that she couldn't run around getting everything ready for the baby, but she did her very best, and could no longer be kept in bed.

She shouted, "He is coming, and he loves me. He actually wrote that or rather the telegram said that, but it was his words!"

Then she received a second telegram, then a third, so that by the time Benedict set sail, he had sent her a total of six telegrams and each one said, "Wait *for me, I am on my way. I love you!*"

Sophie carried them in her pocket, and slept with them under her pillow, along with the one photograph she had of Benedict and the Christmas card signed, B.

Everyone was much relieved and the men who had worried about the lack of response to the letters sent so very many weeks ago, presumed Benedict just received, or at the very least just read them, the day he sent the telegrams off.

When Euphemia read hers to her husband, he worried that possibly his letter was a bit strong. However, she said, "Well, he is coming, isn't he? And God knows what a relief that is for us all, the way our girl has sprang to life."

It was September 1, and the baby was due in three weeks. Sophie was so huge she worried that Benedict would change his mind about loving her when he finally arrived and saw the shape she was in. She told Euphemia and her aunt, "He needs to tell me in person—that he loves me, I mean, and who could love a big fat watermelon?"

The women were not surprised about Sophie's reference to watermelons. She had never even heard of them in Scotland but had been eating more than her fair share all summer long, in fact they were her primary source of food, no matter how the others encouraged her to eat more sensibly. However, although Loretta was surprised that Benedict had never actually told Sophie he loved her, Euphemia was not, and called it his little 'Hard to get' game.

~

Sophie was sitting in the garden. It was still warm, and Jack had fashioned an outdoor recliner for her, with soft pillows. She had fallen asleep, and Euphemia was on her way outside to cover her up in a soft brushed cotton blanket, when finally, she saw her brother approach. Never had she been so happy to see him, and as he put his finger to his lips for her to remain silent, he dropped his suitcase and took the blanket.

Euphemia walked back inside and alerted the others who were all watching from the window.

Benedict quietly approached his heavily pregnant sleeping wife, and as he placed the blanket around her, he gently kissed her lips and whispered, "I love you, Sophie Belle Cockroach, and I love our baby too."

Sophie immediately opened her eyes and said, "Benedict?" And then burst into tears.

Benedict said, "Do you remember that Sunday afternoon tea, when I took you away in my car? I pulled over to the side of the road and kissed you, and you burst into tears. Must have been something scary about me. However, I am not so scary now, and I have decided that I will need to personally deliver our baby. Can't trust these American doctors, nor God forbid, my sister."

Sophie's heart was singing, but she said, "Oh Benedict, why did you never tell me you loved me before? You knew I wanted you to say it so badly, and now I look like a giant watermelon."

Benedict said, "Sophie Belle, I fell in love with you that first day, when you were giving me a telling off outside your brother's shop. I have never tasted watermelon, an American fruit, as I understand. So, is that a baby you have in there? Or a watermelon?"

Just then the baby started kicking, almost as if in response to his father's voice, and Sophie took her husband's hand and placed it on her belly. He started laughing and then there were tears in his eyes. He said, "I am so sorry Sophie Belle, for all the rotten things I said and did. I wasn't scary, I was scared, scared to love someone as much as I love you, but what the deuce? I can't fight against it any longer. It takes up too much energy and I'm getting too old for that."

Sophie said, "But you always said I wasn't good enough for you. The shopkeeper's daughter and all that sort of thing."

He said, "It was the other way around. Still is. I just made us a fortune, sending a very guilty man to Barlinnie prison for three to six months, per his instructions. I am done with all that, I am ready to put on those awful clothes you gave me for Christmas and then I'm going to give Sheriff Sam Spear a proper doing—as we say in Glasgow."

Sophie said, "Who?"

Benedict said, "Your boyfriend. Remember the sleigh ride? Your uncle told me Spear's in love with you and has been hanging around."

Sophie was laughing, "Stupid Scotsman, I went out with Jack that night too. I was hoping you would be jealous and come after me. But you were too evil at the time. Why aren't you evil anymore?"

Benedict said, "Got fed up with it. Too much effort. Now can you walk? I mean to show me the mess you made of our house, spending all my money."

Sophie sat up, "Of course I can walk, or rather waddle but I thought it was my uncle's money?"

Benedict laughed, "He might be a generous man, but not that generous. Seriously Sophie, I needed the money, I want your home, indeed your life to be perfect. Now, let's go see how bad the place looks."

Benedict helped his wife up and they walked across the road, hand in hand, to the house where several men were painting and hammering, and Jack appeared. "Oh, you came back? About time, isn't it?"

Benedict said, "I thought I should check on how Sophie Belle was spending my money. Looks like I will be busy Sullivan, making this place habitable."

Jack scoffed and Benedict turned to Sophie, "Not bad. Let me see the bedroom."

Sophie turned Scarlet, "Benedict!"

He of course understood, but said, "Isn't that where you are going to have this baby? Also, I've changed, but not that much. We will need to employ a housekeeper, maid and a nanny. Oh, and a gardener, handyman sort of person."

Sophie just said, "I'm tired, you can talk to the others about that stuff, but not yet, I want you to lie down with me first, just until I fall asleep. The bedroom is all done, except for the bed. I was too sad to order a new bed."

Benedict said, "No matter, back we go to the flat above the shop. Leave everything to me now. You just need to rest and take care of our baby."

∽

Benedict dozed off before Sophie. She watched him in wonder. He seemed different somehow, kind and concerned. He had been gone for more than eight months, her whole pregnancy really, and she wondered what had truly occurred to cause this transformation. Of course, it could just be very temporary, and she worried that it would be some time before he could make love to her again. Did he realize this? Would she need to explain it? Then she looked down at her belly and thought, *who would even want to attempt that with me? Certainly not my husband.*

Benedict must have sensed her watching him and he opened his eyes, "What's wrong, Sophie Belle? Are you sorry I came back?"

She replied passionately, "Oh no, Benedict, I am beyond happy about that. However, I am not the way I was when you left, if you know what I mean."

Benedict was confused, "In what way Sophie Belle? Your feelings for me? Did I take too long? Do you love another?"

Sophie re-assured him, "No never! You are the most handsome and well-favored man in the whole world. The problem is me."

Benedict said, "Sophie, you are worrying me. Why are you the problem? Most especially if I am the handsomest and most well-favored man in the whole world?"

Sophie started to cry, not an occurrence Benedict was unfamiliar with—her sudden tears, and he said, "Sophie, are you going to tell me why you are the problem?"

Sophie said, "Well—and this is embarrassing—I look a lot different than when you left. I was beautiful and desirable then and well I knew it, but even so, you still left me. Now I am a God-awful sight, and I am not sure if you know—well I doubt you even care—but certain things are not possible at the present time."

Relieved, Benedict burst into laughter, but could tell that Sophie was truly worried. He was reminded of how awful his past behavior was toward her. However, she loved him for all his faults and bad behavior, and in a way he never deserved to be loved.

He said, "Sophie Belle, are you referring to our lovemaking, or should I say, the sheer lack of it since we came together."

Sophie said, "Well that last time I was still pretty, and I pretended to be dead because I was so hurt and angry at you and we have been married for more than a year and were only intimate—so to speak—for one week of that time. I honestly believe you have been true to me—I think—however, as much as I would like to please you, it just isn't possible—for quite a while."

She sat up with a considerable effort and stared at him wide eyed. "I mean, you are such a manly sort of man and—Benedict, please say something and stop grinning at me."

He finally put her out of her misery, "Well I am glad to hear that you find me manly, just like Cyrus Hatter. You never called me that before. Sophie, I am not a total imbecile. Now, and for the months ahead, my job is to care for you and if God is good, our baby, and that is more than enough for me. Also, for what it is worth, you are still the loveliest girl—woman—I ever laid my eyes upon."

Sophie was still not convinced, "Truly, Benedict? I mean you aren't going to suddenly change your mind and take off again."

He said, "Scout's honor," and made a salute. "You didn't know I was once a boy scout. I also sang in the Glasgow High school choir and was on the swimming team. I even won awards for diving. French was my least favorite subject, and I was beyond impressed by yours during that lunch when you walked out on me. However, I can write equally well with both my right and left hands because I was naturally left-handed as a child. I had a very cruel master in grammar school who used to rap my knuckles unless I used my right hand. I'm rather glad now that he did. In other words, you and I have so much to talk about and learn about one another. That is how we shall pass the time until the happy day that I once again make love to my beautiful wife, even more beautiful now than ever, with my child growing inside her. And Sophie, no more time apart and I promise you, as God is my witness, you will have your honeymoon—not right now of course—but it will be something wonderful, and worth the length of time you have looked forward to it."

He had been kissing her gently and playing with her hair while he spoke, and Sophie was entranced. Never had she known him to be so loving and kind. She was almost afraid to speak and break the spell.

He said, "Sophie Belle, I don't believe I have ever known you to be so silent," and he was smiling so kindly at her, that as was her usual, she burst into tears, just as Euphemia was walking past their chamber.

Euphemia knocked softly on the door, and in a loud whisper, asked if Sophie was alright.

Benedict shouted, "Come in," and she opened the door.

She too could see the tenderness in her brother's countenance, as he sat up and said, "I need to thank you Euphemia, for taking such good care of my wife." He spoke kindly and both he and Euphemia turned towards Sophie, when she again began crying.

Euphemia sat down on the bed and took Sophie's hand, "Sophie, are they tears of happiness?"

Sophie said, "Not really, I am worried about Benedict turning evil again because he has been so kind since he arrived. Of course, that was only a few hours ago."

Euphemia smiled, and turned to her brother, "So Benedict, how are you going to reassure your wife. I can't say I don't understand her apprehension, given your past conduct."

Then she turned back to Sophie and said, "I think we should at least give him the chance to rectify his past behavior. He was coming back to you anyway. The news of the baby just hastened his departure. Also, that was all his money, used to fix up the house, your house Sophie, where you and your husband will live long and happy lives, raising a family together."

Sophie seemed comforted by Euphemia's words, and as Euphemia stood to leave the reunited couple alone together, her brother delayed her. "Euphemia, is all arranged, I mean the doctor, the boiling water, the nanny, a bed? I hope you have seen to everything, women's things as well, I mean."

Euphemia said, "Boiling water? Oh dear, Sophie Belle, how have we managed without my brother all these months. Benedict, we are very well prepared, and Sophie's bed is coming this week along with other furniture and furnishings. Many things are stored in my home and Alfred is anxiously awaiting the final preparations and renovations to be completed so we can move our girl into your new home, and I can move into mine."

Benedict said, "I need to interview the nanny and other servants. Also, who selected the furniture? I probably need to replace it."

Sophie cheered, "Mostly it was me, Benedict, except the bed!"

He responded, "Okay, will most definitely need to replace it."

Sophie hit him with a pillow and Euphemia left them to it saying, "Just don't chase off our prospective nanny, Mary Beth. She is a lovely person, Benedict."

Benedict was true to his word and was soon supervising a much-reduced workforce since several of Jack's laborers and tradesmen had left Mr. Cochrane's employment. Jack had stated more than once, if it wasn't for his sister, it might have been better if the good barrister stayed in Glasgow, where he belonged, alongside the thugs he preferred to represent.

Benedict told him to prepare an itemized bill for services rendered. He said, "I don't work for free, and don't expect another man to do so—even if he is my brother."

This heartened Jack, somewhat anyway.

Both the Hickses and the Cochranes had moved into their new abodes. It was just days before Sophie's rapidly approaching time but between them all they had managed it. The third-floor apartments above the shop were abandoned at the present time, pending a decision to be made at some point in the future with regard to what to do about them. It had been decided that Sophie's aunt and uncle would stay with her and Benedict during future visits and he showed no objection to the plan. The Hickses, Carlisles, Cochranes and Jack Sullivan had grown into a very close family unit, with so many months living in such close quarters above the shop, and they often dined at each other's houses.

Of course, Benedict was the only man in the legal profession making his living in New Chestnut, since Sir Alfred spent considerable time in New York City and David and Loretta Carlisle's permanent home was in Manhattan. Both couples wondered how Benedict would adapt, although, at least at present, he didn't seem to much care and was certainly behaving like an excited and nervous father to be, which somewhat surprised the others.

They were all seated around the dinner table eating burnt beef and corn on the cob, since Sophie didn't have the heart to let Matilda go. However, Benedict was re-assigning her duties to housemaid and looking to hire a cook.

Sir Alfred asked, "Cochrane, you have already employed a housekeeper, nanny, parlor maid, gardener, and stable lad, in addition to Matilda. This is certainly more staff than Euphemia and I require, are you sure you can afford it on a country attorney's fees?"

Benedict said, "Judge, I probably have more money than you, following my last big case. I have invested well too. However, should I find myself in need of another windfall, I can easily take myself back to Glasgow if something juicy were to come along. McNulty already indicated that he may need my services again in the future."

Sophie gasped in horror at the very idea, but he reassured her, "Next time I will take my wife and sister with me so they can both wave at me from the back of the courtroom."

He was smiling when he said it, and no one knew if he was in earnest. However, all were feeling jolly and Sir Alfred asked, "So brother Cochrane, did you have your usual contingent of swooning lassies in the courtroom as you playacted for their benefit?"

Benedict said, "Not so much for their benefit, more out of fear of being found in the River Clyde. Still, missed Judge Hicks, looking down his long English nose at me."

Suddenly Sophie gasped, and Benedict said, "I didn't look at any of these lassies, honestly, Sophie Belle. I didn't." But then they all abruptly realized.

Sophie stood up and said, "I think my baby is coming!"

Dinner was quickly abandoned—it was practically inedible anyway—and everyone sprang into action with their appointed tasks.

Benedict led his wife slowly up the stairs, having unsuccessfully tried to carry her up. Jack ran for the doctor and the women were bustling around the room, preparing the bed and hot water and towels. Neither woman had assisted in a birthing before, but had been well prepared by Dr. Kauffman, who would be bringing along a midwife, and the judge's, Jack's and David's jobs were to keep Benedict downstairs, forcibly, if necessary. Benedict had tried to persuade Dr. Kauffman to allow him to attend the birth but was quite emphatically turned down.

Benedict, who had kept insisting that Sophie Belle needed him upstairs finally settled down to his fate once he heard her screaming and cursing him with all she had in her little body.

He said, "I don't know why I am getting cursed. It isn't all my fault."

And the other three men looked at him, in exasperation.

The labor went on for hours, and just as Benedict announced he couldn't take it any longer, they heard a baby cry.

All four men ran upstairs and waited. By now Benedict was terrified. They all were—and the men stood silently outside the door awaiting news. It was a good half hour or so, before the women and doctor appeared, and Dr. Kauffman said to Benedict, "You have a fine healthy son. Nine pounds ten ounces and your wife has survived her ordeal. She wants to see you first, Mr. Cochrane."

Relief washed over all, most especially Benedict who had in truth, been petrified throughout—his Sophie Belle in so much pain. He knew with certainty that his life would be over if he lost her.

He opened the door quietly and there she sat, the love of his life, holding his newborn son. It was an image Benedict wanted to remain in his mind for the rest of his days. Benedict Cochrane had become a family man. No more the rake nor the scoundrel. Everything he needed in life was in their brand new bed, which had just been delivered a few days previously.

Sophie looked tired but happy and she asked him if he wanted to hold his son.

Benedict was too afraid to do so and said he would prefer just to lay beside them for a while. He was soon counting fingers and toes. He also had a look down his tiny baby's napkin and Sophie laughed at him.

Soon everyone had gathered in Sophie's room and was cooing over the newborn baby and Euphemia lifted her brand-new baby nephew into her arms, with a wistful look in her eye.

Benedict proudly declared, "Handsome chap, isn't he? His father's very image. I feel I did an excellent job in his creation and should be heartily congratulated. I am willing to disregard Sophie Belle's bad language which we all heard from downstairs—given the circumstances."

The others scoffed, as Sophie rolled her eyes and said, "Yes husband dear, my role in his creation, as you put it, was so very small carrying him around for nine months and all of those hours of torture—a trifle compared to the part you played."

Benedict Cochrane was beaming, and Sophie felt so proud to have made him so happy, her once so cynical husband, with all of his cynicism apparently washed away by the sight of his brand-new baby boy. The transformation was as unexpected as it was amazing, and Sophie made a sudden decision.

She said, "We need to give him a very special name. I have been thinking and thinking for so many months and keep changing my mind. We could call him after my father?"

Benedict said in jest, "What, Sophie Belle? Old Sullivan?"

She said, "Shut up stupid Scotsman. His name was Henry. Anyway, I have changed my mind. I have decided to call him Benedict Junior, only he will be Benny for short."

Benedict said, "I thought you hated my name?"

Sophie said, "Not anymore, I suppose because you love me now, and it is nice to call a son after his father."

Benedict was doing his best to hold back the tears he felt welling up in his eyes. He didn't expect to feel so emotional, the feeling was quite overwhelming, his frozen heart was rich with the love and protectiveness he felt toward his brand-new baby son and his adored wife, who had made him a father. Everyone could see it—this transformation— most especially Euphemia. She had never seen her brother so deeply moved and soon she realized that she was crying too. She carefully gave her brother his newborn son, and in so doing, kissed his cheek and congratulated him. Benedict smiled at his sister in a way she never quite remembered him ever doing, and she could feel her heart melt for the brother she once thought she hated, but through it all now realized that she loved. The others were watching the exchange between brother and sister, most especially Sir Alfred and Sophie, and they too smiled at one another.

Soon the midwife reappeared to show Sophie how to feed her baby and everyone was told to leave. Of course, Benedict was allowed to remain with his wife and child. He was a father! He may have missed the entire pregnancy, but nevertheless, there it was, and the other three men who had waited with him down below were not. Of course, Jack still stood a fighting chance, if he could find a woman to marry him, and there might still be hope for Euphemia and the judge.

Baby Benedict, Benny, was three months old and once again, Christmas was almost upon them. Sophie was an attentive mother, despite having a live-in nanny and housekeeper and two part-time maids who lived nearby in Little Chestnut. Her husband had provided her with the life she once dreamed of having—not so very long ago—in her little bedroom in the tiny bungalow on Balmuildy Road—but never truly thought would be hers. She was mistress of a fine home and wife to the town attorney at law who was also considering running for mayor—much to the chagrin of his brother-in-law, Sir Alfred Hicks. Sophie was living the life of a fine lady, even although Benedict still, on occasion, referred to her as the shopkeeper's daughter. Sophie would retort that she was now the shopkeeper as was his sister which made him, not only a shopkeeper's husband but a shopkeeper's brother as well. Euphemia had finally confessed to her brother and husband that she and Sophie were equal owners and partners, since Euphemia had provided the funds for her half of the enterprise.

Sir Alfred was, perhaps, more shocked than Benedict, who laughed out loud when the ladies finally revealed this to their husbands. Sir Alfred said, "This being the case, Euphemia, why do you call yourself the assistant store manager?"

She answered, "I do so because, if it wasn't for store manager, Sophie Belle Cochrane, I would still be unmarried and at my embroidery in Bishopbriggs. She changed all four of our lives, not just mine but yours and Benedict's as well."

Sir Alfred said, "No it was Cochrane who changed my life. What if he hadn't left Sophie Belle in the Corn Exchange to pay for your dinner when he gallantly made you leave her behind?"

Euphemia said, "Fiddlesticks! What if Sophie Belle didn't rescue your forgetful wife, one Monday afternoon, when they both took tea in the Willow Tea Rooms?"

Benedict said, "No, you all have it wrong. I am the one to be congratulated for inviting the most impolite shopkeeper's daughter to Sunday afternoon tea—against my better judgement."

Sophie sat beaming in her happiness and in all who loved her. She could never have imagined that her life would turn out so well.

~

Sophie Belle's was a resounding success and the women found it necessary to hire several girls to serve in the shop, in addition to the staff they employed for the busy upstairs tearoom. Neither Euphemia nor Sophie could spare the time to wait on customers every day, as they had done the previous year, due to marital commitments, and their husbands' displeasure in them so doing. However, the success of their mutual enterprise quite astounded their husbands and David Carlisle, who all opined they should possibly give up the law and go into trade as the women had done. Even Loretta was more fully involved, since she oversaw the menus and restaurant staff.

Be that as it may, the Cochrane's marriage was currently not quite the same resounding success, due mainly to Benedict Cochrane, who was unsure as to how these things worked.

Sophie Belle had certainly regained her figure and was wearing the dresses he bought her in Glasgow. She was radiant in her happy life and he so desired her. He was still sleeping in his dressing room. It had been a year since they made love and that last night, Christmas night, had been a disaster.

Sophie was in a similar frame of mind and braced herself to call upon Euphemia. "This is awkward, Euphemia, but here goes. Benny is three months and Dr. Kauffman tells me I am perfectly healthy, however…." She broke off and Euphemia broke into peals of laughter.

"Benedict came to see Alfred a week or so ago, and Alfred told him at least a year. He was laughing when he said it. Surely to God, Benedict didn't believe him? Why doesn't he ask you, his wife, or even Doctor Kauffman?"

Sophie said, "Well, I suppose, he isn't as smart as he thinks he is. I will need to seduce him tonight, I think. He needs to stop sleeping in his dressing room. I think it is time for me to make my delicious beef wellington. I must run to the butcher's shop."

Sophie ran off and Euphemia had long since ceased to be embarrassed by Sophie's oftentimes overly frank conversation. She smiled to herself, remembering how her brother used to be. It was quite remarkable how life in New Chestnut had changed him, indeed changed all of them, for the better too.

Benedict had been in Old Chestnut visiting a client, whom he was overcharging to solve an argument about the boundary line between his and his neighbor's land. It seemed they hated one another, and the main cause of concern was a stream that ran straight through the boundary and neither man would believe this to be the truth of the matter. This, of course, was very different from what Benedict was once used to in Glasgow, but it paid well enough. It was certainly less stressful and often very entertaining. He would enjoy telling his wife about his day over dinner and she would laugh happily at his tales. Benedict had surprised everyone by being a hands-on father and would often even bathe his son at night, once he got the hang of doing so. Sophie loved this about her husband and all the wonderful things they were learning about each other. However, recently he was again behaving quite badly and Sophie knew the reason for his often sour demeanor, most especially since she was feeling very similar.

It was the night before the annual Holiday hoedown and Benedict had promised Sophie Belle to behave. However, he felt frustrated and especially irritable on that snowy evening.

Sophie was already in her dressing gown and slippers when he finally brushed the snow off his boots and walked inside. He said, "That damn truck broke down twice today. I'm buying a team and a sleigh. This weather is not good for driving. Why are you ready for bed, Sophie Belle? It is just six o'clock. I'm hungry."

Sophie said, "My, such a loving greeting from my husband. Can I talk to you upstairs? It's important."

He said, "Can't I at least eat first? What's that I smell? It smells good."

Sophie said, "It can wait. I need to talk to you now."

Benedict moodily followed his wife upstairs and she said, "I swear, sometimes I wonder what I ever saw in you. You are an incredibly horrible man, when you choose to be so."

He said, "Is that why I am being dragged upstairs? For a lecture?"

Sophie opened their bedroom door and there was her very own beef wellington set out with all the trimmings and a nice bottle of red wine. There were candles on the table and all around the room and after she closed the door, she removed her dressing gown to reveal her most alluring negligée—one that Benedict had purchased for her in Glasgow.

He just stood there with his mouth open, "Are you sure it's okay?"

She said, "Of course it's okay. Unless you don't feel as yet ready."

Benedict smiled broadly and said, "I prefer my dinner cold," as he took his Sophie Belle into his arms, while at the same time she was removing his clothes. They fell onto the bed and joyously made love, before sitting down to their romantic dinner, after which they made love again.

Eventually Benedict asked, "Don't we have a baby?"

And as if right on cue, they could hear him crying for his next feed. Sophie donned her dressing gown to go fetch him, so as not to embarrass their nanny, Mary Beth, and Benedict asked, "How long does this go on?"

Sophie said, "I think six months is long enough,"

And Benedict said, "Christ, March?"

~

The next morning the couple awakened entwined in each other's arms. Benedict said, "I promise to be a good boy tonight at the hoedown; however, I am not dancing until the slow ones at the end.

Did you ever learn, Sophie Belle? I mean to waltz or really anything normal like that?"

Sophie said, "Well I only ever had one dance partner and he abandoned me after one dance."

Benedict was happy with his new life, most especially now that intimacy was back, and Sophie Belle was as passionate as ever. He said, "Okay, we can count steps together, I suppose." But he was laughing, as was she.

CHAPTER 15

That holiday season was a great success, as indeed was the holiday hoedown, so different from that terrible first year in New Chestnut.

Sophie at first worried that history might repeat itself, and her husband would be offered another *chance of a lifetime* back in Glasgow.

Benedict was aware of this and decided to make the most of his advantage in this regard. He came downstairs on the night of the hoedown, dressed in the dungarees and flannel shirt that he had been given by his wife the previous Christmas.

Sophie, once again with her hair in pigtails, dressed in her blue and white checkered dress, couldn't help but laugh at his sullen expression. She said, "My dear husband, are you happy dressed in those clothes?"

He answered peevishly, "I feel like a total idiot. Thank God Martin and Nicholson aren't here to witness this humiliation."

Sophie conceded that this mode of apparel really did not suit the man she so adored. Benedict Cochrane was most definitely a dandy—he always had been—and his wardrobe was considerably larger than hers. He was indisputably a black suited, stiff collared, immaculately attired sort of man, clean shaven to show off his dimple and handsome face. She had long since learned that the slightly messy hair was quite deliberate. It had the effect of making women want to tidy it for him.

She said, "I really don't think I like you dressed like that. You look rather silly. Although I think, by the way you are standing, you are trying to look silly."

He said, "I'll just be a minute," as he ran upstairs and came back down again, clad in his usual black attire.

Sophie giggled, and as she straightened his hair, said, "There, that's better."

True to his word, Benedict stood and watched the dancing, this time accompanied by the judge who said, "Well last year, I was intending a proposal of marriage to your sister. We have been married these eight months now, so no need to be making a fool of myself tonight. David Carlisle can do what he likes, I think he has been in America too long. He has forsaken his British reserve."

Finally, the music slowed down and Benedict braced himself, "Here goes," he said with an air of resignation.

He retrieved his beautiful wife, even dressed as she was, like a country bumpkin, and said, "I wish Sheriff Spear would find himself a wife, preferably not mine."

Sophie said, "I like it when you are jealous. You are such a vain man and I like it when the tables are turned. I have decided to allow you to accompany me on the midnight sleigh ride. Even although you are a little old for it."

Benedict sneered, "I am sorry my dear, but I do not currently own a sleigh and you are not going out with Sam Spear again, whether Jack goes with you or not."

Sophie said, "Dearest one, I have a surprise for you. Jack has it hidden in his stables. He is saddling our very own horses to it too. Merry Christmas, Barrister Cochrane!"

Benedict laughed, "Never thought to receive a sleigh for Christmas. I was expecting more cowpoke clothing."

Sophie kidded, "Well I did buy you thermal underwear, although I decided to forgo the flannel shirts."

He said, "Okay, let's get this embarrassment over with," as he led her onto the dance floor.

And Sophie smiled remembering his dreadful behavior at the Glasgow City Chambers annual ball in 1910. It was not so long ago really, less than two years, but so many incredible things had happened since then and her wonderful husband, the much-maligned Benedict Cochrane, was responsible for every happiness she now experienced every day. She enjoyed his cynicism. She loved his magnificent lovemaking, which she mused was brought about not only by his love for her, but also his considerable experience.

As they walked onto the dance floor, she recalled Euphemia's sound advice about giving him the "runaround," and she said, "I don't want to waltz. No one here knows the difference anyway. I prefer the fox trot."

Benedict said, "Not a chance in hell," as he made to lead her into a waltz.

Sophie said, "Do I need to lead? I demand to dance the fox trot."

Benedict braced himself. After all, he had promised to behave, and as he nervously led her into the dance, she positively amazed him. She was graceful and her body flowed along with his, quite effortlessly, or so it seemed to him. He noticed the others were laughing and he said, "Who taught you? And don't say Sam Spear."

Sophie said, "Benedict, if one can excel at Irish dancing, the fox trot is a walk in the park. Had you taken the time to dance another couple dances with me, instead of heading to the gaming bar, I would have been proficient by the end of the night. As it is, I had to rely upon Euphemia, Alfred and my uncle Carlisle."

Benedict laughed, "I am glad I deserted you that night. I enjoyed the sound thrashing you gave me afterwards."

Sophie said, "Followed by the worst marriage proposal in the history of time! I knew I wanted to marry you more than anything in the world. I also knew I would be on that steamer to America shortly afterwards."

Benedict finally asked, "Why did you marry me if you intended to leave me? I never really quite understood that. I still don't"

Sophie said, "That is because you are a stupid Scotsman. I was determined that no other woman could have you. Well even if they did have you, so to speak, you couldn't marry any of them. Not even a rich and titled lady, of whom you so aspired to wed. I also knew, somewhere deep inside of myself, that eventually you would come for me—and eventually you did. You were such a challenge, but I determined that I would make you fall in love with me, that very first morning when you came to my brother's shop to insult me. You can ask Jack, because I said it aloud to both him and Norma," she paused, "I wonder what became of her anyway?"

Benedict said, "Who cares. You little minx. And that night at the Torrance Inn. The night that tormented me for so long? Was that planned too?"

Sophie laughed, "Oh no, I just took advantage of the opportunity given me. There may well have been a smaller nightgown in the armoire. I didn't really look any further when I found the enormous one. However, I didn't expect to get so carried away. I wanted you so badly! It was torture, to finally behave myself."

Benedict was smiling happily, "Do you think we might fit in some of that torture before going out on the midnight sleigh ride?"

Sophie said, "As you well know, we have no need to stay here to the end. You didn't last year. Let's go!"

The Cochranes finished their dance and then grabbed their coats and snow boots and left.

Loretta and David Carlisle approached the judge and Euphemia and Loretta said, "I think we can stop worrying about our girl now."

And Euphemia responded, "Yes, I agree, Sophie Belle won in the end." She paused, thoughtfully, "well hopefully so?" And they all chuckled.

CHAPTER 16

August, 1912–the Cochranes had been married two years and Sophie's adoration of her husband had never lessened. Benedict Cochrane's mysterious and cynical nature was still evident, often enough, but Sophie knew he was devoted to her and their baby, and besides, she was well accustomed to his caustic remarks, infrequent as they now had become—for that at least she was grateful. Almost a year had passed since he came back from Glasgow and he seemed to show little regret regarding the matter, outwardly at the very least.

Baby Benny was soon to celebrate his first birthday and Sophie was already starting to make plans for a garden party in September. Her garden was delightful. She had a gardener, John Connelly, who kept it so beautifully that she and Euphemia often took tea there amid the many fragrant rose bushes. Sophie was living the life of a fine lady. The fine lady she so aspired to be all of her young life as she studied so many books on etiquette and spent such a considerable portion of her wages on elocution lessons and deportment.

She had expected her outlay to be a sound investment for America. However, she was given the opportunity to have much more urgent use of her recently acquired skills—the day Benedict Cochrane came into her life. There were always more downs than ups in their relationship, and she was still awaiting that honeymoon. Nevertheless, she understood that her baby was probably too young to leave for any length of time. She also understood that her honeymoon should have been taken at the time of her marriage and not years afterwards. She knew the reason for all of Benedict's odd behavior at the time. His idea of keeping her off the steamer ship, while at the same time leaving her to finally finish matters off with his old mistress. She understood all of this, or at least she thought she did, until one day when Mr. Falconer brought the morning post. She casually flipped through the letters on her way in to place them on her husband's desk, when she noticed one from South Carolina—one with his name spelled incorrectly and writing that looked feminine in its appearance.

Shortly thereafter on an especially fine afternoon, Sophie was sitting drinking tea with her sister-in-law and aunt in her beautiful garden, when she suddenly remarked. "I really don't see the point of a honeymoon after two years of marriage. Even though we have only been together a year. I believe I will be past forty by the time Benedict gets around to arranging one, and of course, he would never leave Benny. One cannot go on honeymoon with a one-year-old in tow."

The two other women looked at each other and Euphemia said, "Meaning?"

"Well, you have all been on summer holidays this year. Aunt Loretta to Europe and Euphemia, Miami. Such generous husbands. I have decided that I will go on honeymoon on my own. I will be going to Florida. There is a train straight through to Miami and it will still be nice and warm in October. I will go after Benny's birthday. Benny has a nanny, an aunt and a great-aunt—not to mention a father. Euphemia, the only holiday I have ever had, was those few days in St. Anne's-on-Sea. You both may recall that the previous seven years, I spent being nursemaid to my parents. I remember my husband told me once—while we were enjoying our lunch in a fine French restaurant in Glasgow, the sacrifice of my youth made me into a sad little thing. He said I probably shouldn't have told him. That was the day I walked out on him and allowed him to finish his lunch on his own."

Euphemia said, "Sophie, I agree with you on many points you have made, but why not suggest that Benedict take you on this trip to Florida. Perhaps he thinks you wouldn't want to leave Benny. Of course Loretta and I will be here to take care of him—Mary Beth too."

Loretta was less sympathetic towards Benedict Cochrane. She had never truly warmed up to him, as indeed her husband had very much done. "Euphemia, surely your brother should be the one to arrange and come up with such a plan. I certainly have never had to ask such a thing of Mr. Carlisle."

Euphemia considered, "Of course, you are correct Loretta, but Sophie, what has brought this on? You seem a bit angry, or is it depressed."

Sophie confessed what she had found. "Call me what you will, but I saw that a letter came from South Carolina, addressed to him. The writing was feminine, different from his usual correspondence and his last name was spelled incorrectly, with a 'k' instead of an 'h', in Cochrane—perhaps that was a deliberate mistake. Anyway, I had a strange feeling about it and decided to carefully steam it open and re-seal it. It seems an old friend of his has tracked him down, possibly through one of his Scottish cronies, and she now resides in South Carolina. Kind of her to invite him down to see her."

Euphemia exclaimed, "Surely not, Sophie, Carlotta Ramirez? When did this arrive?"

"One week ago, and he has been a bit moody ever since. I was so ashamed to tell you both—most especially since he never mentioned it to me. Possibly, he is planning his own holiday—to South Carolina."

Loretta asked, "What exactly did it say, Sophie? And why didn't you rip it up and throw it away?"

Sophie said, "A couple of reasons, the main one being, I could tell it wasn't the first letter he received. She begged him to go see her. She said she regretted how they parted company after two such wonderful years. She said she blamed herself, since she should have understood that of course, he needed a young wife, who could provide him with children. Then something along the lines of her anxiously awaiting his response. Oh, she also mentioned that she still had…" Sophie paused and with great difficulty, said the words, "his gold cuff links."

Both women sat stunned, and Euphemia felt sick to her stomach, since she knew about the pair Benedict had given to Sophie, and how she treasured them these past two years, often wearing them with the starched striped blouses that she usually dressed in. Sophie Belle was never the sort of girl who wore frills.

Loretta asked, "So what now, Sophie? Will you confront him?"

Sophie said, "Yes, and I am sorry ladies, but I need moral support. I will bring the matter up after I tell him about my holiday to Florida. The train conveniently stops in South Carolina. Possibly he could disembark there, as I carry on to Miami."

Sophie added, "Please not a word to your husbands. We are all dining together tonight—perfect timing. I believe that a week was long enough to tell me about this. Well, I suppose why would he? He certainly didn't mention the other letter he received."

Euphemia was disgusted, as she knew both Alfred and David Carlisle would surely be. "Do you know if he kept the letters, Sophie, dearest?"

Sophie said, "Well if he did, they are well and truly hidden. I did a thorough search of his office, and he has a tendency not to lock his drawers. Of course, they could well be in his safe, I don't know the combination of the lock. Anyway, Aunt Loretta, I am so grateful for those beautiful dresses you purchased for me. I intend to wear sapphire blue this evening. It should go very nicely with the sapphire earrings my husband so generously gave me last Christmas. I was hoping for a matching necklace for my birthday, however, since he forgot it was my birthday, I made do with the money he gave me instead. Now I am glad of it, since I will need it in Miami. I will ask my uncle Carlisle to see to my ticket and hotel. He is rather good at that sort of thing. I will buy myself a new set of cuff links from the shop. There is a rather sweet sterling silver set—yes, I shall buy them at cost. I will, of course, return Mr. Cochrane's cuff links. He may have need of them for another clueless young woman." Sophie paused thoughtfully, and laughed, "Or perhaps a clueless old woman. It makes no difference to him either way."

Sophie flounced off with her nose in the air, and Euphemia said to Loretta, "I could kill him. Such stupidity. If only she hadn't seen that letter. I believe it was the cuff links that broke her heart—even more than the fact this woman appears to have followed him to America. Sophie treasured hers so. Well, I will go see to the table. Tonight, should be interesting. Perhaps I should decorate it with candied fruit."

Loretta didn't understand the reference to candied fruit but just as she was about to follow her niece upstairs, her husband appeared, a little earlier than expected. She said nothing to him. That was Sophie's decision, regarding how to handle the matter, and instead led him into the parlor for a glass of brandy and a cigar.

∼

David Carlisle and Sir Alfred Hicks were on the 4 o'clock train from Manhattan to New Chestnut. Dinner was at the Hicks's house that night.

Both men knew of the letters, in addition, both men knew about the letter received from Mr. McNulty's lawyer, strongly calling for Benedict Cochrane to return to Glasgow to represent his client who had been "wrongly" accused of a double murder.

David said, "I think he should go. Although not sure how Sophie Belle will take this news. As for the old mistress appearing on the scene again? Benedict certainly has some problems to sort out. It might be easier to get McNulty off than to prevent this woman coming to New Chestnut. Poor fellow, there is much to be said for a quiet life. It seems his past has come back to haunt him."

Sir Alfred responded thoughtfully, "Cochrane was always somewhat of a scoundrel, lived life on the edge—so to speak. He was settling down nicely with our Sophie Belle too. He will have to decide upon this case in Scotland, the money offered him is outrageous, however that is only if he can set this man free. I sensed somewhat of a veiled threat in the wording of the letter—McNulty's "expectation" of seeing the good barrister in Scotland next month. He will miss his son's birthday and depending on the complexity of the case, possibly Christmas besides. I wonder if he will mention it tonight at dinner. As for that Spanish woman, best ignore her—in my opinion anyway."

∽

    Benedict Cochrane was later than his normal time. He had stopped at a bar in nearby Dolington. He had a client there—a widow, whose deceased husband's children from a previous marriage were trying to take her house, and all that she had, away from her. The law was on the woman's side and Benedict intended to make these adult children, who were already well placed, pay for such unkindness. The woman had nursed her late husband through a long and lingering illness, when none of his offspring came near.
    Benedict thought of his Sophie Belle, doing the same for her parents, and the unkind words he spoke to her that day at lunch. No wonder she walked out on him. Jack was a good man, for all of Benedict's snide remarks. He was good to his sister, however, had it not been so, and had there been no aunt and uncle Carlisle, Sophie could have indeed ended up standing at the kitchen sink with a husband of very limited means. Regardless, she saved Euphemia in the Willow Tearooms. Her kindness brought them together. However, what if there was no urgency? What if there was no trans-Atlantic ticket? Would he still have been so desperate to marry her? A penniless girl? For all her airs and graces? He would like to believe that he would have been so, but now, he had not only the case in Scotland—which he knew he would take on—to deal with. He also had the wretched Carlotta Ramirez, reappearing in his world again.

By the time he got home, his wife and the Carlisles were already dressed for dinner, and in the case of his wife—most inappropriately.

Benedict said, "Loretta, I appreciate your kindness, but my wife doesn't dress like that. Simple starched blouses and cuff links are more her style. Besides, it's somewhat indecent—too small up top."

His reference to cuff links caused Loretta to look anxiously over at Sophie, a look that Benedict caught and wondered about, even as he said, "Sophie Belle, go and change, you are embarrassing your uncle and frankly me. Loretta, has Sam Spear been invited this evening? That could explain the dress."

Sophie Cochrane did not take the bait, neither did she change. She merely grabbed her wrap and flounced out the door saying, "Go to hell, Benedict Cochrane."

Benedict turned to the others and David just shrugged his shoulders, as his wife announced, "I am going now too. I am interested to see this candied fruit that Euphemia was referring to earlier. What a splendid idea! Euphemia is so creative. A most unusual effect, I am sure."

Benedict recognized almost the exact words; his Sophie Belle had spoken at his ridiculous dinner in Bishopbriggs—arranged just two weeks before his disastrous wedding. He remembered how in love he was and the night that followed at the Torrance Inn. He felt like a total cad—speaking to his lovely wife that way—and in front of others. He knew the reason why, the letters, the McNulty case. He felt as if he was drowning in anxiety.

He said, "You go David, I need to run up and get changed."

Benedict immediately noticed Sophie Belle's cuff links, thrown in among his many others. They were the ones he gave her on that magical day, when she sat in his motor car, in an old careworn dress. He gave them to her, and she treasured them. He thought, *God knows, I gave her little else in the way of trinkets. But why is she returning them, and why now? That ghastly woman mentioned cuff links in her letter, the ones she took from me, and I left them with her in my hurry to leave her* flat that morning, so long ago. That was so very different. I destroyed her letters, but the last one mentioned these cuff links. Is this some strange coincidence? The letter was unopened when I came upon it. What is this all about?

∽

When Sir Alfred commented upon the candied fruit that his wife was having set out on the dinner table, along with her usual flower arrangements, she couldn't help herself, "Did you know about these letters? Did you know that woman is in South Carolina?"

Euphemia told him about the cuff links and Sir Alfred remarked, "This is most unfortunate. Of course, steaming open a husband's correspondence is quite reprehensible—even for Sophie Belle. However, Euphemia, this is not the worst of it."

Euphemia sat down, bracing herself, a shocked look upon her countenance, "What do you mean, Alfred? He has met with this woman. Oh God I am disgusted with him."

Alfred said, "No, not that. He has no interest in her—none at all. He is going to have to go back to Glasgow—within the next week or so. McNulty expects him to return to defend him in a double murder trial. Your brother has little choice. I read the letter, somewhat veiled threats, should he not take it on. The money is outrageous. One hundred thousand pounds, but only if he gets him off or rather, a 'not proven' verdict is the one this thug wants. He wants his guilt to be apparent to his enemies, as he walks the streets a free man."

Euphemia wasn't sure how to feel. It was all such an unexpected mess. Both she and her husband agreed to say nothing until the Cochranes brought up either subject and they were heart sorry for Sophie Belle, who had just arrived at their home, accompanied by the Carlisles.

Sophie was too jolly—given the circumstances—and everyone could see right through her act, even as she exclaimed, "Oh Euphemia, candied fruit! My husband's favorite. He is changing and will be here shortly. I left him to it."

Benedict arrived soon thereafter and when all were called into dinner, he said, "Sophie Belle, candied fruit—remember that night? Cyrus Hatter and the Torrance Inn? Why did you return my cuff links? I thought you treasured them. You said so often enough."

Sophie didn't quite expect her opening so soon. In fact, she was surprised he brought the matter up at all. She said, "I have no further use of them. I am changing my style. At any rate, I find I have quite gone off them. They are nothing special after all. I have a set in the shop, sterling silver with a blue topaz stone in each. Quite expensive for Sophie Belle's, but of course I will buy them at cost. You may have another use for your old cuff links, since I indeed do not."

She turned to her uncle, "Uncle Carlisle, I must ask a favor of you and hope you will oblige or at the very least advise me on how to go about such an undertaking. I am planning to go to Miami in October. The train goes all the way there, although it stops in South Carolina." She added that deliberately, and well most of the others knew it.

"Anyway, my Aunt Loretta and sister Euphemia have volunteered to assist Mary Beth with her duties, and besides, Benny's father will be here, at least in the evenings. I feel the need to get away. You have all been on holiday this summer, and my husband has visited the Highlands of Scotland many times—on his own of course. I have only ever had one holiday in my life. I find I need another one, surely that is not selfish of me."

Benedict turned, "Sophie Belle, what are you talking about? You are not going anywhere without your husband. I may take you to Miami—if that is what you want—but not this year, perhaps in the spring. I know I still owe you a honeymoon. I am aware of that; however, it is not my fault that you conceived so quickly, and Benny is not yet one. As far as the cuff links are concerned, it is quite hurtful. You've gone off them? Or is it me you have gone off? At any rate, I will be in Glasgow, another reason you can't go to Miami, even if I was inclined to allow you. I will be leaving next week."

For a moment Sophie sat there dumbfounded. His comment about her conceiving so soon—such cruelty—and he loved his son, this she knew for sure. Everyone was quiet. Did that mean they already knew? They knew about Carlotta Ramirez. About Benedict's plans to take her to Glasgow? She felt her heart had been ripped out of her chest, even as her husband continued eating and the others were staring at her with mixed emotions.

She arose and said, "Snobs! I hate all of you! You ladies allowed me to pour out my heart this afternoon, when all along, you knew!" Sophie felt she had to get away from all of them, and she ran out of the room shouting, "Have fun in Glasgow, Mr. Cochrane. I hope your slattern of a girlfriend enjoys herself too and at least she's too old to conceive! Most especially "so soon!" I promise you will never see your son again! Never, ever again!"

After she left, Euphemia stood up, "Benedict, she read the letters, well one of them. The one that mentioned your cuff links. She knows nothing about the McNulty case and now assumes you are leaving with that awful woman! Also, why would you say such a terrible thing to the mother of your beloved son?"

Benedict said, "I suppose I shouldn't have said that, however, it is the truth. As far as the letters? I destroyed that woman's pathetic letters. I found each unopened. There were two of them and I wrote back and told her, if she came anywhere near me or my family, I would have her arrested. Also, I didn't give her the cuff links, she took them. I couldn't find them one morning and, in my desperation, to get away, left them there. Why in hell's name would Sophie assume that I was taking this woman to Glasgow? Euphemia?"

Euphemia said, "Well you, yourself, just told her you were going there, and since she has no knowledge of your new assignment, she made that assumption. My God Benedict. I am disgusted with you.

You haven't changed, have you? You are as deplorable as ever you were."

Euphemia and Loretta arose from the table, and Loretta said, "Euphemia, let us away and leave these men to it! They have tarnished us with their lying and secretive behavior."

Sir Alfred said, "Good God man, aren't you going after your wife, to set her mind straight? Now we are all being brought into something which has nothing to do with us!"

Benedict didn't really surprise the other men, when he said, "First of all, she shouldn't have been reading my correspondence. My assumption is she steamed it open? Unacceptable behavior. Anyway, regardless, I am sure she has thrown herself onto our bed crying and waiting for me to go make nice—which, of course, I will do—after I have finished my delicious dinner."

David ventured, "Benedict, she thinks you are taking off to Glasgow with this old mistress of yours. Don't you feel you should go and explain?"

Benedict said, "Again, she has no business steaming open my correspondence. I don't like that at all—wife or not. Then having done that, she chose to confront me in front of your wives, causing me to have to admit to spending the night with a whore."

Sir Alfred, disgustedly said, "Whore? I thought she was your mistress."

Benedict finally stood up and threw down his napkin, "Same thing really. Anyway, time to go make nice. Although she will not be pleased to hear my true reason for going to Glasgow. Nevertheless, she will get over it. Oh, and David, no train tickets to Miami. The last thing I need, Sophie Belle wondering around Miami on her own."

After he left the other men to their port and cigars, the judge opined, "Sophie Belle is so very lovely. She could have had any man. I am sure of it. Why Benedict Cochrane?"

And David Carlisle said, "Because he is the man she chose. She wanted the bad boy, the unattainable. She got him and all will be well in the end. It always is and he knows it. She will always forgive him and he loves her just as much. Well matched, I would say."

The judge said, "Shame he got to her first."

And David Carlisle looked at him, a little quizzically, but said nothing.

∽

Benedict walked home at a leisurely pace, practicing how to console his wife regarding his upcoming trip to Glasgow. He also had to explain away the cuff links and thought, *damn Carlotta, what is she doing in America? And damn my wife for steaming open my mail.*

He was again back in everyone's bad books, but how could Sophie Belle even begin to think he was taking that woman to Glasgow? He had given his wife everything she never had growing up—in addition to all of his love. He was more angry than contrite, although he regretted the remark about her conceiving so soon. That was nasty—deplorable even—as Euphemia had called him. When he arrived home, he went straight up to his wife's bedroom, expecting to find her laying crying on the bed.

She wasn't there, so he tried the nursery. His beloved son was asleep, and he wanted to take him into his arms, most especially in his guilt and regret about his disgusting remark, but Mary Beth, begged him not to wake him.

He went back downstairs to ask his housekeeper, Mrs. McGowan, if her mistress had returned home, but it seemed she had not.

Again, he grew angry. What game was this? He tried the shop, but it was all locked up with no sign of life. He thought, *Sullivan, she wouldn't go to Sam Spear's place, or at least she better not have done so.*

He saw Jack's horse outside of Bunny's. Spear's horse was there too. Benedict walked into the tavern expecting to find Sophie Belle seated with them, but she wasn't there. He asked if they had seen her, but it seemed that they hadn't done so and finally Benedict began to panic.

He tried to make little of it and left both men to their ale, but they followed him outside.

Jack asked, "Cochrane, what happened? Where is she?"

Benedict said, "Well if I knew the answer to that, I wouldn't have asked you, Sullivan. It seems her feelings are hurt. You know how she is. She probably went back to the Hicks's."

Benedict spoke calmly but he felt deep inside that she wouldn't be there. His anger turned to worry, although he was furious that she would do such an irresponsible thing.

Of course, she wasn't at the Hicks's house and all five men mounted their horses and went out to search for her.

Again, Jack asked, "What did you do, Cochrane?"

Benedict responded, "Absolutely nothing, but we all know you Sullivans are a bit touched in the head."

The two men were about to come to blows, not for the first time, but David Carlisle, expressed the urgency of the situation and if the men wanted to fight—they could do so after they knew that Sophie Belle was safe. She hadn't taken her horse, so a fall wasn't possible. Was she hiding?

At first, in his anger and worry, Benedict believed this to be the case, and vowed that he would sternly berate her, once she decided to show herself. However, the light began to fade, and two hours had passed and by now everyone was worried sick.

The men took turns to check back at the house and at the Hicks's, but she had not returned. Benedict knew she was afraid of the dark. They all knew this and finally it seemed that she had met with an accident—or perhaps she was simply lost. They prayed that nothing worse had befallen her.

Soon it was dark, and in the countryside, the night was black. Sam and Jack had flashlights, but Sophie would have only a crescent moon to guide her. The others suggested starting again at dawn, and

Benedict stared at them in disbelief. "You all go if you choose to do so. There are wild animals out here and God knows what else. I will not go home until I find her, and shame on the rest of you for doing so."

Sam Spear said, "I will not be going home, until I know she is safe."

Jack agreed and said, "Whatever has happened to my sister, Cochrane, I know you are the cause of such foolhardiness on her behalf."

Again, the three younger men seemed more inclined to fight, rather than search for Sophie and both David and Alfred decided they had better stick with it.

∽

Sophie felt that finally her life of joy and contentment, comfort and love had come to an end. She could again see her future, working every day in the shop. She could never stay with Benedict Cochrane now. She had been lied to and treated like a fool—easily done by a man such as him. For all her airs and graces, she was still just a simple Scottish lass, born to a life of toil and the care of others. She was different from every other person seated at dinner that evening—and well they all knew it.

She felt foolish. She felt stupid and naïve, nothing like the cultured and sophisticated family that she spent her days with. She was more Matilda than Euphemia. She laughed cynically at herself—*airs and graces indeed*. She had been running, but by now was out of breath and she slowed down her pace. She had been crying and hardly noticed her surroundings, but the woods had grown darker with the evening sun hardly making its kind and comforting way beneath the towering trees which were still rich with summer foliage. In another month or so, the leaves would turn to shades of amber and orange—purple and red—before finally turning brown and falling to form a thick blanket on the forest floor. She recalled the first year in New Chestnut, when they had just arrived. How she had laid happily among the leaves rolling around in her joy of a new beginning, while at the same time blissfully anticipating her husband coming to find her. She had been certain that he would eventually do so—and he did—at least for a short while.

Sophie berated herself. Real life was different, and happy endings were only where unhappy beginnings began. She soon realized that she had walked too far and was well and truly lost. She had been walking in circles, coming across the same felled tree again and again. Her new dress was dirtied and torn at the shoulders. It really was rather tight and revealing and Sophie cursed her bosoms laughingly.

She was still unafraid, feeling quite certain that she would soon hear Jack's voice calling for her. Jack had always taken good care of her. He was the only one fully aware of what she had gone through, those years of being nursemaid to her parents. She often resented it so and when she cried in her unhappiness, Jack would comfort her. Then the letter arrived from her aunt and uncle Carlisle, and she believed her time had finally come. She always referred to her parents as her mother and father—in her mind and to the others who were now in her life. However, growing up they were Ma and Pa—her secret which was well kept by Jack. Sam Spear knew much of this— her true childhood. They had confided much to one another during the months of her confinement. The months her husband spent in Scotland. Sam had been raised on a farm. He had two older brothers and similarly to her, he had to find a new living, since the farm was not profitable enough to support him in his future. He became the sheriff in New Chestnut and had a fine reputation. His only mistake was in falling for a stupid girl, who had married a bonafide snob, who cared so little for her. Everyone could see this—everyone but the stupid girl—Sophie Sullivan.

Sophie thought she heard shouting in the distance—men's voices, Scottish and American accents. She shouted back but her voice got lost in the thick wood that surrounded her. She endeavored to run in the direction of the voices, since she was beginning to become afraid in the darkness that was now enveloping her. She started to cry and as the tears clouded her vision, she stumbled and suddenly felt herself falling. The ravine—she knew about it but had never approached it in fear of somehow falling into it. She was afraid of the dark and she was afraid of the ravine and as she began her descent, she banged her head on a tree limb which was somehow sticking out of the side of the steep slope. She grabbed hold of it and sat down and braced herself. The ravine was deep, but she wasn't terribly far from the bottom. She gently slid down the rest of the way until she was safely seated far below the forest floor. She had hurt her ankle and her hands, elbows, and face were bleeding. Also, her head hurt from when she first hit the tree, and she could feel a large lump on the side of her head. There was a stream at the bottom, and she drank a little water and washed her face and arms, and the water stung her wounds. She thought, *Jack will never find me here in the darkness—unless of course, he is with Sam, who knows these woods like the back of his hands.*

The summer night was still warm and Sophie's head and whole body was hurting. She braced herself to wait until early light to figure out how to get out of the mess she had put herself in. She remembered Benedict's words. He was taking Carlotta Ramirez to Scotland, and she cried herself to sleep in her misery.

~

Jack and Sam led the way followed by a much-dejected Benedict Cochrane. They sent the two older men back to their wives and were beginning to think that possibly they would have to wait until first light. The batteries in their flashlights were starting to die and they had begun alternating one at a time. Benedict had no flashlight. He also knew he was the cause of whatever misfortune had befallen his wife—his sweet Sophie Belle—the woman he took so much for granted in her obvious adoration of him. He knew he was undeserving of such adulation but accepted it as his right. Sam had mentioned the ravine and they were on their worried way towards it. What if she had fallen to her death?

They finally came upon it and looked down into its depths. There was enough life left in one of their batteries that they could see the outline of a woman lying motionless at the bottom.

All three men stood for a brief moment bracing themselves, terror within their hearts. Benedict knew that if his wife was dead, it was his fault, and he couldn't even meet the eyes of the other two men standing there. Beyond that, his life would be over. He had as good as murdered his beautiful wife. He loved her with every inch of his jaded heart. He just wasn't adept at showing it—opening himself up to ridicule, the way his father had done. Benedict's mother despised her husband, even despite his unswerving devotion—his constancy of affection towards her, undeterred by her obvious disdain of him. Benedict often wondered if she was different in the beginning. Surely, she must have at least appeared so, in order for him to offer her his hand in marriage.

Sophie Belle was not his mother. He had given her so few tokens of his affection. He even forgot her birthday—he gave her money, so she could purchase her own gift. The woman who had given him his beloved son. Most men rewarded their wives with some bauble for all she had been through—the agony of childbirth. The thought never even occurred to him.

Sophie Belle dressed in simple skirts and blouses. She was so utterly enchanting, her face, her hair, her magnificent body. She looked like a siren in the dress her aunt had purchased for her, yet instead of pride he felt some sort of strange jealousy—embarrassment even—for other men to see her thus. He knew the reason. It had been told to him often enough. Sophie Belle could have had any man. She should have a man who placed her on a pedestal; but instead, she chose an underserving blackguard—Benedict Cochrane.

Benedict was aware of the other men shouting down, even as he stood frozen in his fear. Then quite miraculously, he heard a small voice from below, "I fell down." That was all she said and without a thought of the others, he went running down, sliding most of the way, due to the steepness of the slope. Jack and Sam had run around to the other side, which allowed an easier descent to the woman feebly shouting from below.

Benedict reached her first, but she was pushing him away, and when Jack and Sam reached them she was shouting, "He is going to Scotland with his Spanish mistress! Jack, please take me home. I need to fetch Benny." Then she passed out.

Jack said, "Well Cochrane, I have no idea why she would think such a thing. Even I know that is nonsense, maybe you can explain it later. We need to try to get her home first."

Sam was examining her limbs, and said in relief, "Nothing broken, although she is banged up quite a bit. Her ankle looks sprained. This won't be easy. We will need to somehow carry her to the top and then get her onto a horse."

Benedict came to his senses; Sophie Belle was going to be just fine. He had some explaining to do, but at least now, it could wait.

The men somehow, with great effort, managed to get her to the top of the ravine and they were grateful she was such a little thing.

Sam said, "Thank God, she's as light as a feather."

Jack said, "Aye," and looked at his brother-in-law with somewhat of a smirk.

Benedict understood the smirk and said, "She had a ten-pound baby in her belly at the time!"

Jack laughed and explained it to Sam, and when they reached the top, Benedict said, "My horse. Hand her up to me."

Sophie Belle awakened and asked, "What happened?" And then, even as she held fast to her husband, she murmured, "I hate you," and lost consciousness again.

Soon the household staff were scurrying around as Benedict shouted orders. Sam left—reluctantly—but Jack hung about as the

Hickses and Carlisles soon appeared, and Benedict was telling his sister off for putting stupid ideas in Sophie's head.

Sir Alfred said, "Now just wait a minute Cochrane. Don't blame your sister for your own stupidity."

Sophie was semi-awake. Dr. Kauffman had given her a spoonful of laudanum and declared her injuries to be minor, even as he bandaged her right ankle and dressed the wounds on her face and arms."

He left them to it and smiled to himself as he could hear the grand Cochranes and Hickses arguing with one another.

Euphemia said, "No brother dear, this is your usual insanity. She truly believed you were taking your old mistress off to Scotland! And what did you do? You sat and finished your dinner. By George, I would love to throw that candied fruit straight at your face! I wish I had done so!"

They all turned as they heard Sophie laughing quietly, she said, "Oh it hurts to laugh, but you are all so funny. Benedict, why don't you take the candied fruit to your desperate old girlfriend?"

Benedict began to try to explain, trying to maintain his composure. However, Sophie had fallen asleep again and he ushered everyone out of her bedroom.

Jack said, "Someone needs to stay with her. Someone she trusts. I'll stay. It's the laudanum. What if she wakes up and finds lover boy, sitting sleeping on her chair."

Benedict said, "I am going to let that remark pass, since I could never refer to you as such, most especially as I recall your ex-wife. I will be on the bed watching her. The rest of you leave. The servants will surely alert you if they hear screaming."

Jack was reluctant to leave, so were Euphemia and Loretta, however, Benedict was her husband and he had had quite a night of it between worry followed by ridicule. Sir Alfred and David Carlisle ushered them all out.

Benedict saw them out the door and returned to his wife's bedroom. He took off his outer garments. His dinner suit was ruined, as were his shoes, since he didn't take the time to change into his riding boots. He put on his dressing gown and laid down on the bed. He was leaning upon one arm and was watching his Sophie Belle sleep. He thought *it will be difficult to leave her. The case will be over by Christmas, or at least I hope it is, or she will never forgive me, and it will be my son's first real Christmas. I could tell her that I will take them both to Scotland—the Highlands—in the spring, but that is not exactly a honeymoon. Bit late for that sort of thing anyway, and if this case drags on through Christmas, how will I spend my time when the courts are closed? I will probably be invited to the Martins or Nicholsons, and of course they will also invite Fiona MacBride, who has yet to find a husband.*

He then sat up, inspired, *Sophie Belle can come with me, Benny too and the nanny—possibly Euphemia, at least for a while? But we can't all fit in my tiny flat. If only I hadn't sold the house.* All this conjecture made him grow weary, and as he started to nod off beside his wife, he was suddenly awakened. Sophie was trying to push him out of the bed. She was crying and he tried to calm her down. He tried to explain about the McNulty case, the cuff links, Carlotta, but soon Sophie was back asleep, and he dreaded what accusations and recriminations he would face in the morning.

CHAPTER 17

Sophie soon recovered, but she was no longer looking at her husband with adoration. She was no longer looking at him at all. There were no accusations nor recriminations because she didn't speak to him. The week passed quickly and soon he was to be off again. Their relationship was strained, and she couldn't bring herself to fully forgive him. She felt there was too much to forgive. She felt like Benedict Cochrane's doormat.

She had told him it was best he slept in his dressing room, since she was so sore after her fall, and he agreed to do so. Then the morning he was leaving, she finally spoke to him, "Benedict, I thought our love was so special, but the only thing special was my love for you. You have never spoiled me with trinkets, taken me away for a few days, even somewhere nearby. I am no longer sure if this is enough for me in a marriage. I might need more. Euphemia is spoiled. My aunt Loretta is spoiled. I am married to a man who forgot my birthday. I feel you have grown tired of this shop girl. Finally, you are weary of her. That is just the type of man you are. A man without depth of character."

Benedict tried to intervene, to reassure his lovely wife because none of this was true. He had just made the mistake of taking her love for him for granted—her absolute devotion to him. Had it finally run its course?

He asked her this question and she simply said, "Benedict, I am not the one who is always leaving, hiding letters and God knows what else. I am sending you off to your homeland with an open heart. You will not always be in the courtroom. You will have time to think and consider whether you prefer to stay in Scotland or come home to me, and to your son, with a full heart. If you can't do that. It is probably best you stay away."

Then Benedict surprised her, "Sophie, those letters you used to write to me—can I take them with me?"

Sophie said, "There's an awful lot of them. Well, I suppose they were written to you. Will they fit in your suitcase? With all your fine silk suits?"

Benedict said, "I'll make them fit," which he did, by removing one of his black suits and a couple of his shirts.

He left, making his way towards the train station and Sophie watched after him. She suddenly realized, *what am I doing? Again, sending my man off like this? Sophie, you knew who he was, and you married him anyway because no other man could ever take his place. It was not his choice to move to America. It was yours.*

Sophie shouted and ran after him. He turned, surprised, and as she ran into his arms, he kissed her and twirled her around. He seemed relieved that she was giving him full permission to go and to take her everlasting love along with him.

Sophie walked with him, arm in arm, and said, "Benedict, do you think when you return, we will be able to start our lives together?"

At first, he looked confused and then laughed out loud, "Yes, I believe I have said that to you a number of times, same thing honeymoon."

Sophie said, "Benedict, it finally occurs to me that we started our lives together, the day you came to my brother's shop. The Hickses have their lives, the Carlisles, theirs, and this is ours. I wouldn't have it any other way."

Sophie waited with her husband until the train finally came into the station and said, "Benedict, go with my blessing and may God keep you safe and well. I will be here waiting for your return—whenever that is."

～

Benedict Cochrane was smiling broadly as the train left the station and he waved until his beautiful wife was just a dot on the horizon. Such a difference from the last time he left.

Benedict wondered what came over his sweet Sophie Belle. She appeared to hate him since the night she fell, and who could blame her? However, something happened within her heart as she watched him walk away. She finally understood. He loved her beyond measure as he did his incredible son. He even loved his life in New Chestnut. However, the excitement of anticipation, when he donned his wig and gown and walked into the courtroom, with the packed gallery, entirely due to the acclaim he had earned as the most sought after and elusive barrister in Scotland, was unparalleled. The challenge of taking the procurator Fiscal's airtight case against the accused, and ripping it apart, captivated and consumed him.

Benedict Cochrane now understood, even if others did not, that he was both of these men, and both of these men were in love with Sophie Belle Cochrane. He was grateful she finally understood this about him, and he spent his journey to Scotland reading her many letters to him. Some were loving, others accusatory, some sad, some hopeful, but in every single letter, whether she professed to love or to hate him, her love for him was fully evident and constant. He thanked God for this.

Benedict Cochrane, met with his client, James McNulty who was out on bail, accused of the murder of two men, neither of whom Glasgow would be the worse for their demise.

Mr. McNulty apologized for taking him away from his lovely wife and Benedict asked in jest, "What makes you think she is lovely?"

McNulty said, "Oh, I know many things Cochrane—many, many things."

Benedict let the comment pass without further thought or analysis as he set about building the defense for his client. This case was easier than the last one, even though the charges were more serious. The prosecution had evidence that was easily contradicted. Benedict told his client he felt confident he could obtain a 'not guilty' verdict, but McNulty insisted upon 'not proven.'

It was late October, and this time his wife and he were exchanging letters. He read about his son's first words, which included "dada" and the fact that he was walking and getting into mischief. Benedict was certain he would be home long before Christmas but hesitated in promising Sophie Belle this, lest he let her down—again. Still, he was anxious to hold her in his arms and tell her of his love. A combination of the many letters he received and those from the past. He was truly ready to finally begin his life anew with his Sophie Belle.

~

Shortly after her son's birthday, Sophie called a family meeting to inform them of her plans.

"I have decided that I am going to Scotland. I am going to watch my husband, possibly for the last time, weave his magic in the courtroom. Clearly, I cannot take Benny, but Aunt Loretta, will you stay to keep order in my home? Mary Beth is more than competent regarding his care, and Uncle Carlisle, you could stay here much of the time. I will be gone about a month, considering it takes six days each way to sail over there and back."

Sophie waited for a comment but there was as yet none, and she continued, "Jack, I am putting you in charge of *Sophie Belle's*. Our staff are well trained and very efficient, and besides, I know you fancy Lizzie Wilkins, my newest sales assistant. You will be able to train her on stocktaking in the back shop."

Finally, Euphemia said, "What about Alfred and I? Do we have a part to play in these well laid out plans?"

Sophie said, "Oh, I thought I mentioned. You are both coming with me. I cannot travel on my own. I might get lost, and Benedict can't be nasty to his sister and wife, in Sir Alfred's presence."

Sophie had her fingers crossed behind her back. She so wanted to do this. She so wanted this one last trip to Scotland and to surprise her husband. His letters were so loving, and she read them over and over again in wonder. Benedict Cochrane certainly had a way with words and Sophie thought, *no wonder he so easily mesmerizes the jury,* and she laughed when she imagined how his 'wee lassies' in the gallery would envy her—his wife—when word got out, as it surely would.

Still there was silence and Sophie pleaded, "Oh please! When do I ever ask for anything?"

Jack was soon accompanied by the others when he said, "Actually, all the time, sister dear."

Miraculously, everyone approved of her plan. Benny was a good baby and Mary Beth was well and truly capable of handling him, with Aunt Loretta's kind supervision. Jack would have a chance to work side by side with Lizzie Wilkins—such a pretty, young girl, who had caught his eye, and the Hickses were excited to take a trip home and even to have the opportunity to watch Barrister Cochrane perform in court.

David Carlisle said, "Well I too am all for it. I will stay behind and keep an eye on all who are left behind, including you, Jack. No doubt there will be a few surprises for you all in Glasgow. However, we must make haste. That trial will not last very much longer."

Judge Hicks agreed, and he too was excited to walk through the imposing doors of the Glasgow High Court again, after almost two years away.

Sophie couldn't quite believe that was so effortlessly done. Everyone so easily persuaded! Of course, she would miss baby Benny but would be back long before Christmastime and would fully make it up to him. Sophie felt the need to somehow prioritize Benedict and her marriage. He had given her so much. The plan was for Benedict and her to go off on their own and then meet up with the judge and Euphemia the day before the ship was set to sail back to New York. This would allow them to truly be alone together for the very first time since their marriage.

Within two weeks the threesome were boarding the Olympic. The tragedy of the Titanic was still in everyone's minds and conversations. It had sunk earlier that year, in April 1912, but most trans-Atlantic voyagers were of the opinion that such a disaster and tragedy was unlikely to occur ever again, since many improvements had been made to reassure the public. These included sufficient lifeboats as mandatory on all ocean liners and the establishment of the International Ice Control which kept twenty-four-hour radio watch on foreign-going passenger ships.

On this occasion, Sophie had her own first-class stateroom, and she could hardly believe that she, Sophie Sullivan had become a fine lady of such consequence, that her uncle wouldn't even consider a second-class ticket, even although she insisted it would be good enough for her.

The other first-class passengers were elegantly decked out for dinner, and Sophie was grateful for her Aunt Loretta's good taste and generosity. A few days before the travelers were to be on their way, her aunt arrived in New Chestnut, laden not only with her own luggage, since she would be staying at the Cochranes for the next month or more, but also several new skirts and blouses, dresses and lingerie for Sophie.

When Sophie exclaimed about the expense of all these beautiful new items of clothing, Loretta said, "Don't worry child, I will be charging everything back to your husband. I wonder how many new suits he will be returning with this time around."

Sophie and the Hickses were invited to dine at the captain's table twice, and Sophie felt like a princess.

Finally, they arrived in Liverpool and Sophie's heart was so full, in her impatience to be reunited with her husband. It was late morning by the time the train arrived at Glasgow Central Station, and after the small party freshened up in their rooms in the Central Station Hotel, and ate a very light lunch, they were quickly on their way to Glasgow High Court.

CHAPTER 18

The small party had arrived in Scotland just in time for Barrister Cochrane's closing argument. A court warden, Mr. MacTavish, immediately recognized and warmly welcomed Judge Hicks, who shook his hand.

He said, "Sir Alfred, it is a fine day indeed to see you again within these walls. The Glasgow High Court has missed your esteemed presence."

He then looked towards the ladies as if awaiting an introduction, "Sir, the gallery has been packed almost every day, and if possible, even more so today with Barrister Cochrane's closing argument. The procurator fiscal's was yesterday, so it wasn't quite as overcrowded. Today, I had to turn some of Barrister Cochrane's wee lassies away. On several occasions Judge Randall threatened to have them all removed, and the accused keeps turning and winking at them. Mr. Cochrane ignores them. Sir, you know what he is like, in a league of his own, and so entertaining to watch. But Sir, didn't you also take a position in New York? Are you back for good?"

Finally, Sir Alfred managed to get a word in. "It is grand to see you looking so well MacTavish. May I introduce my wife, Lady Euphemia Hicks, and my sister-in-law, Mrs. Benedict Cochrane. My wife is the good barrister's only sister and she and Mrs. Cochrane are anxious to watch his closing argument. Is there room for us in the gallery?"

Mr. MacTavish went red in the face and was staring at Sophie in awe. He said, "Aye sir, I will see to it." And as if he couldn't help himself, "Mrs. Cochrane, the entire court, judges and lawyers alike, have wondered about Mr. Cochrane's wife. So many rumors, since he says not a word of clarification. I am not sure how to address you ma'am, since it is said you are a foreign princess."

The poor man bowed to Sophie and Euphemia had to hide her amusement behind her gloved hand.

Sophie could hardly believe such a rumor existed about her, a shopkeeper's daughter. She was immensely diverted and shook the poor man's hand, and said, "Well Mr. MacTavish, I will leave it to you to tell any tall story that you prefer to tell the others, however, I am proud to call myself a Glasgow lass, as I am proud to call myself the good barrister's wife."

The man broke out in a broad grin and said, "Aye, Mrs. Cochrane, I believe I will confirm to the others, the truth of it. You are a foreign princess. Indeed, you are."

As the man excused himself, to eject several of Benedict's 'wee lassies' from the courtroom, in order to clear some space, Sophie said, "Good enough, Mr. MacTavish, just don't say from Spain."

Mr. MacTavish agreed and had no idea why the fine lady's comment created laughter from the judge and his lady wife.

~

The judge and ladies took their seats on the newly vacated bench at the very back of the gallery. Judge Hicks had requested that bench so as not to distract Barrister Cochrane.

Soon Benedict and the other lawyers entered the courtroom, donning their black gowns and white wigs, and they made their way to their respective benches. Sophie was transfixed. She was reminded of the time he invited her there, not so very long ago and how she dreamed that one day he would belong only to her. He didn't look up at the gallery, and Sophie heard a few of the girls in front of them, dreamily wishing that he would.

Benedict was shuffling papers around. He looked very serious and deep in thought, until next his client, the accused, was brought out dressed immaculately in a dapper navy-blue suit. Sophie, wide-eyed, put her hand to her mouth to try to stifle her sharp intake of breath. She didn't quite manage to do so however, and since the courtroom had gone quiet, her gasp could be heard beyond the bar. Sophie hid her face behind the person in the next bench and at Euphemia and Alfred's questioning looks, explained, "His name isn't McNulty—or at least I don't believe it is? It's James McGuigan. He is my godfather, my uncle Jimmy. Not really my uncle but he was my father's best friend and he used to visit often when my father was sick. He always gave me sweeties and a half-crown. He called me Sophie Belle and was responsible for choosing my middle name. I thought he was dead because…oh Benedict must get him off! There is no way my uncle Jimmy is guilty. He is the very best of men!"

Sophie braced herself to look toward the bench where both men were seated and both men were turning toward her, Sophie's husband and godfather—the former with a shocked expression and the latter with a smile and a wink. The men turned away and entered into a hushed discussion, until finally all were told to stand for Judge Randall.

The Hickses sat in amazement at this totally unexpected and bizarre development. The much-feared McNulty was Sophie Belle's godfather? What next?

Of course, Barrister Cochrane's closing argument was brilliant, and Sophie was as enraptured by her husband as Euphemia was proud of her brother. The accused was led away, and he smiled back at Sophie, who couldn't help but give him a little wave. The jury were given their instructions by the judge, and again all stood as the judge exited the courtroom.

Judge Hicks went down to see Benedict and they both walked back to Chambers. He had told the ladies to make their way to Bookbinders and he and Benedict would meet them there.

∽

The men eventually appeared at the restaurant and Sophie looked up expectantly at her husband, who was wearing a very expensive black leather coat with a fur collar. She was nervous he would be annoyed that she came and left Benny in the care of the others.

He wasn't annoyed. Benedict beamed a great big smile and said, "Well, my dearest wife, what can I say? I couldn't be more surprised if someone hit me on the head with a sledgehammer."

The judge and Euphemia burst into laughter and Benedict bent and kissed his wife, with a look that was unmistakably desire, and sat down. He said, "The jury won't be out for long. Open and shut case… not guilty. When 'Uncle Jimmy' saw his goddaughter, he changed his mind. He decided against 'not proven,' much to my relief. It made my whole argument a lot easier."

Sophie said, "So you are confident that he is innocent, Benedict? Can I meet with him? Can we have dinner with him? I have so much to tell him!"

Benedict said, "I didn't say he is innocent. I said I am confident he will be found not guilty. There is a difference. Also, Sophie Belle, it turns out he knows all about you. Well, most of it anyway."

Sophie and Euphemia looked confused, and he continued, "It seems your uncle Carlisle, otherwise known as Davy Carlisle, is a longtime acquaintance. They conspired to send you to New York, upon your father's demise, and to marry you off to a millionaire. Uncle Jimmy's men saw to it that the local lads stayed clear of you, most especially after the disappointment of brother Jack marrying Norma.

Even with that little nose of yours always in the air, I must admit I was somewhat surprised that you were so completely innocent at age twenty-three. I wondered what was wrong with Bishopbriggs's young bucks, even although I was glad of it."

The ladies sat rapt at Benedict's explanation, which Sir Alfred had already just heard. Benedict continued, "I too was almost warned off—not that I'd have listened—but it seemed Uncle Jimmy was highly amused by our whirlwind romance. I daresay, he probably thought I might come in useful one day as well. So anyway, they left us to it. It seems Mr. David Carlisle is masterful at keeping secrets, even from his wife, who wouldn't dare open his correspondence—unlike my wife. He has kept an eye on you from afar and both he and McNulty, McGuigan, whomever, were greatly touched by your sacrifice and care of your parents; one after the other." Benedict added, "I once made a very cruel remark to you about that, Sophie Belle. Can you ever forgive me? I didn't mean it. You had such a stranglehold on my heart and that made me very nervous. You made me nervous. You still do. Most especially now that I know your godfather. He did say one thing. He thanked me for loving you and giving you the life, you deserved. He also added, there was never a chance of me ending up in the River Clyde; although the fear of it was an excellent incentive to succeed in my endeavors."

Sophie had taken hold of her husband's hand and was kissing it tenderly as he spoke. Benedict added, "Somewhat explains his generosity. I might even treat my wife to a new striped blouse or perhaps a blue suit."

The men were about to order an early dinner, when Benedict was called back to court. A court warden came to fetch him. The Jury had reached a verdict.

They quickly settled up and left the restaurant. Sophie sat nervously as if she were the one awaiting judgement and then she heard the jury foreman say, "Not Guilty on all counts."

She ran down to embrace her uncle and laughed merrily at the "wee lassies," rushing down for Barrister Cochrane's autograph. Benedict rewarded them with a smile and signed a few before saying, "I best be careful, that's my wife embracing my client."

The courtroom was cleared, and James McNulty was a free man. Dinner was arranged for the following evening, in a private room in La Bonne Auberge. It was clear there was a genuine affection between this hard man and his innocent goddaughter. Benedict and the others stood a little apart as the man spoke quietly to Sophie, while holding both of her hands in his. Sophie again embraced the man and as she happily made her way back to them, Euphemia remarked, "Never again allow me to pass judgement or even have opinions on the nature of a man. Clearly, I was as wrong about Mr. McNulty as I was about you, brother dear."

Sir Alfred said "No, my dear, you were correct in your character assessments. Sophie Belle just has a way of turning and twisting a man's head so that one day he awakens to find himself a hero."

Euphemia thoughtfully considered this and of course her husband had stated it perfectly. She knew he loved Sophie Belle, as did she. Their lives were all so much the better for her being a part of them.

∽

The two couples dined at the Central Hotel and further discussed the revelations of the day, although Benedict was anxious to get his Sophie Belle alone, and sat yawning and remarking on such a long and exhausting day.

He suggested that he and Sophie stay the night at the Central Hotel and that he would gather his belongings the following day. "I need to pack for our jaunt up north and also have everything ready to just pick up for our journey back home." He added, rather tentatively, "I have been invited to dinner at Harvey Martin's this Saturday. I can cancel or tell him to expect three additional guests."

Sir Alfred said, "I can't imagine Sophie Belle having any interest in dining with the Martins, Benedict."

But Sophie responded, "Oh no, you are wrong Alfred. We are absolutely going! And Benedict, I am coming with you to your flat tomorrow. I intend staying there until we begin our travels—unless of course you have something to hide."

Benedict looked slightly uncomfortable, "The place is a bit of a mess actually, Sophie Belle, somewhat embarrassing. Why don't I go and tidy up first?"

Sophie narrowed her eyes and stared at him. Benedict sensed this was her response and said, "Okay, we will go together. I have nothing to hide," as he secretly berated himself for sacking his charwoman.

⁓

Sophie burst into peals of laughter, "Oh my Lord, Benedict, this place is a disgrace!"

Benedict said, "Don't say I didn't warn you. I have been rather busy—getting Uncle Jimmy away with murder." He spoke while lifting shirts and ties, papers and books from the floor of his flat, and Sophie could hardly believe that her fastidious husband had been living in such a hovel.

She was watching him clear various items off the floor. He looked embarrassed, to say the least, and Sophie was deliriously happy. They had made love for much of the previous night, and she indeed felt as if she was finally on her honeymoon. She said, "I want to see your bedroom."

Benedict said, "It's a mess, perhaps I should at least make the bed first?"

However, it was easily located in such a small one-bedroom flat, and Sophie was already opening the door, with the intention of having a thorough search. However, before she even noticed the unmade bed, she saw all of her photographs pinned onto the walls. Her letters were on the floor and on the bedside table. Benedict appeared at the doorway and said, "I know, bloody sad blighter."

Sophie never loved her man more than she did in that moment. She was everywhere in his private place, her photos, her letters, and a door to one of his wardrobes was laying open and she spotted her white dress, the one she left behind.

He said, "I kept your peignoir as well. Tears of regret on that particular item of clothing."

Sophie pulled him to her and onto the bed, then she laughed and said, "Benedict, when is the last time you changed your sheets?"

He said, "I sacked my charwoman. The place was dirty when I arrived, and I had been paying her to keep it clean."

He was trying to speak between Sophie's joyful kisses, "Bit embarrassing, actually."

Sophie said, "Right, this is my new dress my aunt Loretta bought for me, although she will be billing you for it. I need to take it off before I get to work on this flat. Do you at least have clean bed linen, a sweeper, disinfectant, beeswax?"

Benedict was bemused, "Aye, in the kitchen, but you can't…"

Sophie said, "Shut up stupid Scotsman! You just sit down and rest. You have been working hard and I haven't cleaned since the apartment above the shop. I need the exercise."

Benedict said, "Okay, I will make you a cup of tea first."

Sophie soon had the flat spic and span and Benedict was enjoying watching her and as he lay with is feet up on the sofa, he mused, "I never could have imagined such a thing. Me, laying here, while a beautiful woman cleaned my flat, dressed only in her knickers and camisole. I could get used to this."

Sophie finally threw herself down on top of him and said, "Wait till you get the bill. I need a bath!" Then she remembered, "Mr. Cochrane, do you still charge for hot water?"

He laughed. They were both so happy and he said, "This is the first time we have been alone together. I mean as husband and wife. I daresay that is what has been wrong between us."

He jumped up. "Okay, Mrs. Cockroach. I will run you a bath. Hot water free of charge. When we return home, I shall sack all the maids. I much prefer watching you clean up…in your lacy undergarments, of course."

Sophie loved Benedict's flat. She had the feeling of never wanting to leave. Nevertheless, dinner with Uncle Jimmy in a private room was that night, and they were laughing as they bumped into one another trying to get dressed in the tiny bedroom.

CHAPTER 19

Dinner with Mr. McNulty went exceptionally well. He was clearly on his best behavior and shared stories of Sophie's father as a young man. Mr. McNulty told Sophie that her father once saved his life. He said, "I was carried away by a strong current in Loch Lomond. We young lads were roughhousing, and I would have surely drowned, had Henry Sullivan—a right powerful swimmer—not been there to pull me out of the water, thereby saving my life. I never forgot that, nor the great debt I owed to him." He smiled warmly at Sophie and continued, "I promised your pa that I'd ensure between me and Davy Carlisle you would never want for a thing. We watched how you strived toward self-improvement all on your own and knew that you were a very special wee lassie. Beauty is one thing, but you have much more than that—brains and determination."

Sophie asked her godfather why she was led to believe his surname was McGuigan, but the man just winked at her and said, "Never you mind Sophie Belle."

Sophie was tearful when her godfather got up to leave, but he reassured her that his days of flaunting the law were behind him, and he would soon be immigrating to New York. "I am embarking on a new chapter in my life and I will be expecting an invitation to your fine home for dinner, Sophie Belle Cochrane, just as soon as I am settled."

Sophie was excited to hear this news and said she couldn't wait to tell Jack. She then produced the signet ring that she had kept these past years with her father's 'secret stash,' and said "I think you should have this Uncle Jimmy as it is all I have to give you that belonged to pa."

The man kissed it and placed it on his right hand as he stood to take his leave. He embraced his goddaughter and with tears in his eyes asked, "Did you ever spend his wee stash, bonnie lassie?"

Sophie said, "Oh no, Uncle Jimmy, and I will pass it down to my son."

He laughed and embraced her again and after he left, her husband said, "Pa?"

And both Euphemia and Sir Alfred smiled lovingly when she cried in her husband's arms, "Yes, she said, he was pa and my mother was ma."

It was such an emotional evening and when Sophie and Benedict returned to his flat, she showed him her secret stash. Benedict had to hold back the tears for his beautiful bride, worth a thousand times more than any other woman who had ever crossed his path. He kissed her and said, "Yes, you keep that safe for Benny, a gift from his grandpa Sullivan."

Sir Alfred and Euphemia were emotional when they traveled back to their hotel, and Euphemia said, "We witnessed something so very special this evening, such depth of feeling, and I know my brother felt it too. God bless our dearest girl and her secret stash. Alfred, how can we bear such sweetness?"

Sir Alfred agreed with his wife but remarked, "Well tomorrow night at the Martin's will be an entirely different affair. Of that I am certain."

Sophie was immensely excited—she was staying in her husband's secret flat! She made a cup of tea and allowed him to get washed in the bathroom. This was a more intimate setting than she had ever been in with her husband. She was completely alone with Benedict Cochrane, and she found the thought of it thrilling.

Benedict emerged from the bathroom in his dressing gown and slippers. He seemed a little nervous, and Sophie tried to hide her amusement. She offered him tea, but he poured himself a whisky instead. He said, "I will be in the bedroom. The bathroom is all yours."

Sophie said, "Well considering your flat consists of a living room, kitchenette, one bedroom and a bathroom, I daresay, I will be able to find you."

She rummaged through her suitcase, and Benedict noticed something black and lacy in his wife's hands as she made her way to the bathroom.

Benedict shouted, "And a hallway," as he gulped down his whisky. He knew Sophie Belle was up to something. He had never seen her in black lace. So completely naked, he jumped into bed and waited—and waited.

Sophie stood regarding herself in the bathroom's full-length mirror. She smiled thinking, *what other man would have so many mirrors in his tiny flat?* She felt spectacular in her indecent black negligee. She tussled her long blonde hair, dabbed some Narcisse Noir—another Aunt Loretta purchase—behind each ear and walked out barefoot to the kitchen.

Benedict called out to her and asked what she was doing, and she shouted back, "I can't seem to reach the matches on the kitchen top shelf. Can you help me, Benedict?"

Benedict threw on his dressing gown and got out of bed saying, "Sophie Belle, have you taken up smoking? Why do you need...." His voice trailed off. Sophie was stretching as if trying to retrieve the matches, but then turned toward him with such a seductive expression—Benedict's jaw dropped. She was sensational—a man's secret fantasy, and he immediately felt his whole body respond as he approached her.

She knocked the matches off the shelf—quite deliberately, or so it seemed to him, and knelt as if to retrieve them, but she didn't do that. She looked up at him with naked hunger and Benedict threw off his dressing gown, somewhat in a state of incredulity. Sophie Belle set about pleasing her husband until eventually he pulled her up and turned her around. They were still in the tiny kitchenette and several items were knocked off the kitchen sink, before Benedict lifted his wife and threw her on the bed, in the bedroom with her photographs everywhere on his walls.

Something wonderful happened between them that night, and Benedict whispered, "Mrs. Cockroach, I think you just had your proper wedding night, or perhaps, it was me who had mine."

Sophie laughed in her happiness, "Mr. Cockroach, do you still feel it might just be infatuation?"

He said, "Absolutely, although it would seem I am also completely besotted with you—might have to think about the love part."

Sophie snuggled into her husband and said, "I feel I never want to leave your flat. Can't we just do day trips?"

Benedict said, "What about your honeymoon? I was intending to take you up North. The scenery is magnificent."

Sophie said, "But Benedict, it is November. Anyway, if we sleep here every night, I can tell the others you were too stingy to pay for a hotel. Won't that be fun? Also, I can make you dinner and look after you just like a real wife."

Benedict said, "I seem to recall you telling me—right from the start you absolutely didn't want that, Sophie Belle. You wanted to be a fine lady and I made you my fine lady."

Sophie was quiet, she wondered if her husband thought perhaps, she was showing her true colors—the shopkeeper's daughter—but it was only for two weeks?

She said, "Okay, stupid idea. Sorry Benedict. I just thought it would be fun. Forget I said it."

He said, "Are you sure, Sophie Belle? To tell the truth, these past months have been grueling, most especially since I didn't know at the time that McNulty was your uncle Jimmy. I promised you a proper honeymoon and now we can go traveling. However, I would love what you just described, and yes indeed, we can take little day trips together."

Sophie said, "Benedict, this is a proper honeymoon to me, because I will have you all to myself and that's all I want, Mr. and Mrs. Cockroach, for a whole two weeks."

Benedict said, "What about this dinner tomorrow night?"

Sophie said, "I am going to dress up and look magnificent, and you are going to fawn all over me, the entire night—most especially if the insipid Miss MacBride is in attendance. Are you agreeable to that, sir?"

Benedict laughed and said, "I think I can manage it, Sophie Belle Cockroach, on condition I may look forward to your special treat afterwards." He then reached under his pillow and produced a red box. "It was supposed to be for Christmas but thought you might want to wear it tomorrow."

Sophie quickly opened the box, and exclaimed, "Is it real! Oh, Benedict, it's beautiful! Are they real sapphires and diamonds? I will wear it tomorrow night with my sapphire earrings! I don't care if they are real or not, it is beautiful!"

Benedict said, "Sophie Belle, what does it say inside the box?"

She read it, "Cartier?"

He said, "And what is Cartier?"

She said, "A jeweler?"

Benedict said, "I married a shopkeeper's daughter. Yes Sophie Belle, it is a jeweler. And will you forever ask if the jewelry your husband gives you is real? Suffice to say, yes, wife, all real." Why don't you wear the white gown tomorrow night? You were so stunning in that."

Sophie said, "Benedict, is that your way of making sure I do not buy another? Everyone will recognize it—well the women will anyway, and I need to get my hair done up? Benedict, I *must* look sensational tomorrow night, most especially since the old hags made fun of my clothes at your horrid dinner party."

Benedict said, "Let me see what you brought with you."

Surprised at her husband's interest in her apparel, as opposed to his own, she pulled out her second-best gown, since she wore the sapphire blue already that night for dinner with Mr. McNulty.

Benedict took it from her and said, "No, I want you in white. Tomorrow, I will take you shopping, and you will need to get your hair done up. There is a place on Byer's Road, his and hers sort of place. I need a haircut and a shave too."

Sophie again snuggled into her husband, and soon they were both asleep. She anticipated the next day shopping with him. What a special treat!

∽

Once again, the Cochrane's were laughing when they each attempted to get dressed in Benedict's tiny bedroom.

Benedict chose Sophie's dress. It was cut daringly low, and the style was very form fitting. He, of course, also picked up a few new white shirts for himself. However what surprised Sophie was him telling her to pick out some black lacy pieces, which she did with some embarrassment, most especially with her handsome husband standing rendering his opinion—and as was usual—to the admiration of the sales assistants."

The couple ate lunch in the Corn Exchange, and if Benedict recalled that terrible last occasion when he totally humiliated Sophie, he didn't mention it, and neither did she.

Sophie was glad she brought her sable as she again pondered the cost of Benedict's newest acquisition; the fur-collar black leather coat.

They were picking up the Hickses at the Central Hotel and as Sophie got out of the car in order to sit in the back with Euphemia, she said, "Sophie, is that a new gown? And a sapphire and diamond necklace too? What on earth has come over my brother?"

Sophie smiled shyly as she caught Benedict looking back at her in his rear-view mirror, and said, "Well, we made a deal, of a personal nature. Also, Benedict will be saving money on hotels since we are doing day trips and staying in his flat. He sacked his charwoman, so I am in charge of the cooking and cleaning too."

Euphemia could see her sister-in-law was beaming with happiness, so she chose not to berate her brother about these arrangements, even though Sir Alfred said, "Cochrane, you never change. Didn't you just make one hundred thousand pounds?"

Benedict responded, "I find it unlikely that I will be defending any future clients in Glasgow, so economies must be made. Might have to let go some of my staff and have Sophie Belle chip in with some of the chores."

They all realized—or at least hoped—Benedict was kidding and there was much lighthearted banter and laughter on the way to Whitecraigs, and the Martin's home.

There were several motor cars and carriages outside the residence, which was all lit up, and finely dressed ladies and gentlemen were being welcomed by uniformed footmen. Sir Alfred said, "Full house. I expect their noses are bothering them. They want to see if our Sophie Belle's behavior has improved any since the last time, we all almost dined together. Do you think Martin hired the footmen for the night?"

As Benedict helped Sophie out of his car, and threw the keys to the valet, he said, "Yes, I charge thrice more than he for services rendered, and I never employed footmen."

Sophie said, "Is that what you did that night for your awful dinner, Benedict?"

He said, "Absolutely, all for your benefit too. Only for you to walk out on it," and he whispered, "of course, I was glad that you did," as he kissed her brow.

Euphemia took Sophie's hand, "Sophie, remember your airs and graces. You look terrified. You will be the loveliest young lady in attendance."

Sophie laughed, "You mean like at the City Chambers ball?"

Benedict said, "No worries, I've got Sophie Belle covered. Different occasion this time, besides, Sophie and I have made a deal. I need to be a good boy tonight."

Sir Alfred said to Euphemia, "I hope he means it."

And Euphemia smiled, "Oh I am sure he does, husband. Did you not see that smile?"

∽

On this occasion, Benedict Cochrane helped his wife remove her sable. He then led her into the drawing room where already most of the guests were assembled.

Harvey Martin approached the foursome to welcome them to his home and said, "So you have finally made an honest man out of Barrister Cochrane, Mrs. Cochrane. We all had bets on it that you would. My good friend is no fool. If I may say so, you are a delight to behold at my humble gathering. Come, allow me to introduce you."

Sophie took Harvey's arm, while looking around at her husband, who was smiling proudly at her.

She said, "Thank you Mr. Martin. I always thought you were the very best of Benedict's friends."

He said, please it is Harvey, Mrs. Cochrane, or may I call you Sophie Belle. I understand from our court warden that you are a foreign princess. You certainly look the part tonight."

Sophie received a lukewarm welcome from many of the ladies— too many names to remember—and a very kind greeting from the gentlemen. Sophie noticed that Euphemia was being introduced by Marsha Martin, and since Harvey had an amusing comment about many of the attendees, Sophie knew that she was the more fortunate of them both.

Benedict was standing with Sir Alfred, and Sophie was astounded when she saw Fiona MacBride approach the men, most particularly her husband, and soon she heard that annoying giggle, she remembered so well.

Eventually Harvey brought Sophie back to her husband and Sir Alfred, and Euphemia was returned to them too.

Benedict was grinning ear to ear and said, "Sophie Belle, the gentlemen seem very impressed with you this evening, although not particularly the ladies—jealousy of course. Miss MacBride, doesn't my wife look well this evening?"

Fiona MacBride's face turned red as she muttered some remark and walked away.

Sophie said, "Mr. Cochrane, are there any other broken hearts in the room I should be mindful of? There seems to be several unattached ladies in attendance. I wonder, is Mrs. Martin hoping that one of them catches your eye?"

Benedict laughed out loud, and Sir Alfred said to Euphemia, as they walked into dinner, "I am hoping for a civilized evening, tonight."

Euphemia remarked, "Hardly likely. Marsha Martin has placed Fiona MacBride on the other side of Benedict—ridiculous woman!"

Oysters on the half shell were served, followed by fois gras, vichyssoise, poached salmon, roasted pigeon and lamb. Sophie knew to eat just a little of each course, daintily and without dropping anything on the white linen tablecloth. She felt as if those surrounding her were watching her table manners, although as she began to relax, she decided it was just her own nerves causing her to feel that way. Sophie did notice Fiona MacBride's wine glass being freshened several times during the course of dinner. This worried Sophie a little, as soon

Miss MacBride was attempting to flirt with Benedict, without a care for his wife, seated on the other side of him.

Benedict was beginning to look irritated, and everyone stopped talking when he said, "Fiona, do you think you might turn your attention to Mr. Nicholson, who is seated on your other side? You are such a total bore and I am trying to enjoy my dinner. Also, I don't suppose my wife appreciates your attentions toward me."

Fiona MacBride went red in the face. She said, "So Mrs. Cochrane, I hear you are putting it about that you are some foreign princess. Well, we all know the truth of that. We also know that you trapped Mr. Cochrane into marriage—everyone knows that! So don't think that your background is a secret. I believe they call women like you an adventuress!"

Even the hostess, Mrs. Martin, was shocked by her friend's outrageous behavior. Clearly, she had partaken in too much wine—not for the first time, and Mrs. Martin was about to call the ladies to withdraw when Sophie finally spoke up."

"My my, Miss MacBride, you really must try to control your consumption of alcohol—not very attractive in a young woman—in any woman. So, I see you are still after my husband, and once again I must intervene. As we adventuresses know, getting inebriated and making a fool of oneself is not the way to a man's heart. I think you should try to behave yourself."

This remark angered Fiona MacBride who had long unsuccessfully set her cap at Benedict Cochrane. She spat out, "You don't even know how to dance. You are nothing but a low-class shopkeeper's daughter—a nobody—and everyone knows how you got your husband!"

Sophie said she wanted to leave, "Enough is enough, Benedict. Please let us…"

Benedict exploded, "How dare you insult my wife! And Fiona, if you were the last woman on earth, I still couldn't touch you. Harvey, is this woman leaving or am I, along with my lovely wife, sister and the esteemed Judge Hicks."

Harvey Martin motioned to his wife, and even she was aghast at such behavior. Harvey then took Fiona's arm and led her to the footmen outside. The young woman was still ranting about Sophie. Sophie had had enough. She said, "Excuse me, Mrs. Martin, I think I too should leave. I thank you for your kind invitation however."

Euphemia and Sir Alfred, were also standing up when Marsha Martin said, "Please don't go, Sophie, may I call you that? I could never have dreamt that Miss MacBride would behave in such a manner. Harvey has brought in a ragtime band for a grand night of entertainment."

And indeed, the evening greatly improved with the departure of Miss MacBride. Sophie was almost glad that the young woman made such a fool of herself, since her rude remarks made toward Sophie seemed to have the effect of making the other ladies much nicer and more considerate toward her.

It was late by the time the dinner party began to wind down, and after dropping off the Hickses at the Glasgow Central Hotel, Sophie said, "This is the official start of our honeymoon," and before Benedict could respond, she was fast asleep.

~

Sophie awakened and realized she did not keep her end of the bargain. Benedict had gently helped her into bed, and she was asleep before she even knew it.

Breakfast, she thought. They had called into the butcher shop the previous afternoon and purchased Ayrshire bacon, pork sausages, eggs and potato scones.

Sophie silently got up and made breakfast for her husband. She had donned her black lacy negligee, but then worried, *what if he thinks this is not the behavior of a fine lady?* She felt confused. She still didn't understand in which world she belonged. It was straightforward for Euphemia and her aunt Loretta. Somehow it was even mostly straightforward in New Chestnut, but she was back in Glasgow, where the old rules she grew up with still applied. Also, she had, within two days of being in Glasgow, cleaned and cooked for the good barrister. Why did he keep this flat? Did he bring other women here? Fiona MacBride?

Sophie carried her husband's breakfast on a tray and laid it on the bed beside him. He sat up and said, "I have been smelling this cooking this past half hour. I thought perhaps you ate it all yourself."

Relieved, Sophie jumped back into bed. Soon they were feeding one another, and Benedict said, in jest, "Much to be said for marrying a working-class lass."

It was like a slap in the face, yet he didn't realize it—at least not until she got up and said, "I'm sorry Benedict, this was a stupid idea. Our whole marriage was a stupid idea. I will aways be some lesser being to you. I see that now."

Benedict said, "Sophie Belle, stop being ridiculous and come back to bed. I'm sorry, I meant it as a joke."

She said, "You mean I'm a joke. All my airs and graces. I wonder what those people really thought of me last night. Also, why is Fiona MacBride so horrid? Did I just clean up the flat where you bring your mistresses?"

Benedict scratched his head in confusion, then reached out his hand toward his beloved wife. "Sophie Belle, look around, what do you see?"

She said, "My photographs. But what if you just put them there because I was coming?"

He said, "Sophie, I had no idea you were coming, don't you remember? You surprised me and no doubt were planning a thorough inspection of my flat. Go ahead. Go rummage through everything. See if you find anything other than legal paperwork and your letters. I am sorry I made the working-class comment, but would you choose to be someone else, because if you were someone else—other than Sophie Belle Sullivan, with her little nose in the air. I don't believe I would be in love with you."

Sophie lightened up, "And you promise you never brought other women here?"

Benedict said, "I promise. No wait, that's a lie. The charwoman before I gave her the sack."

Sophie was reassured, all this self-doubt she felt was inside her, the feeling of being lesser. Her husband just kidded her about it. Their start to life may have been very different but he always knew that and married her anyway. "Okay, last question, am I prettier than Carlotta Ramirez. I rather think I am prettier than Fiona MacBride—my arch-rival."

Benedict laughed, "Sophie Belle, you are prettier than everyone, and well you know it. You are a successful businesswoman, a wonderful mother, and you snagged Glasgow's most eligible bachelor."

Sophie was laughing now too, "Well I suppose you were extremely eligible. Of course, you might not have been if any of your 'wee lassies' saw your flat. I brought my birthday money. I am buying new sheets. These are rather careworn—surprising for a man who is so fastidious about his mode of apparel."

He recollected, "Sophie Belle, do you still have that flowery frock?"

She said, "Yes, but I didn't bring it with me."

He said, "A bit small up top."

Sophie said, "Do you wish my bosoms were smaller?"

Benedict said, "Ridiculous question, Sophie Belle, to ask any man, most especially such a well-favored manly man. By the way, remember we made a deal?"

Sophie said, "But it's daylight," and she was laughing.

He said, "So what? I was a good boy last night. I even put you to bed, after all that dancing with other men."

Sophie smiled seductively, "But I am too shy."

And Benedict said, "No you're not."

※

Sophie Cochrane spent the next few days cooking and looking after her husband's tiny flat, and after her husband's every want and desire.

On the fifth day she said, "Okay, you can take me to the Highlands now," which he did, and on the boat to Skye, he sang the Skye Boat Song to her, with his rich baritone voice and Sophie felt so in love with her wonderful man. She expected his caustic comments to recommence upon their return to everyday life back in New Chestnut, however other than his one reference to his "working-class lass," and a couple of funny remarks about the shock of finding out Mr. McNulty was her loving godfather, Benedict Cochrane was indeed a very good boy. Sophie felt this had much to do with her newly acquired skill in the bedroom, however, never had she known him to be so generous; buying her trinkets and really anything that caught her eye.

They returned to the flat in Kelvinside a few days before they were to meet the Hickses in Glasgow Central Station to begin their journey back to New York. They were both missing baby Benny and were buying him little gifts for under the Christmas tree, which Benedict would be felling shortly after their return home. Sophie also bought Shetland wool sweaters for Jack and her uncle Carlisle and much to Benedict's disapproval, Sam Spear. She purchased a lambswool shawl for her aunt Loretta and woolen scarves and gloves for both the household staff and the girls in the shop. Sophie never called those who worked in her home servants, but Benedict did, and she chided him on being a snob.

The Cochrane's were happy in each other's company and Benedict didn't even complain about reaching into his pocket for all these Scottish woolen gifts. Of course, since it would be cold in New

Chestnut, he picked up a couple made to measure black woolen suits for himself and full Clan Cochrane highland regalia including a tartan kilt and a deerskin and horsehair sporran. He also bought a Cochrane tartan skirt and waistcoat for his wife and planned for them to wear these new acquisitions to the Holiday Hoedown—Benedict having expressed the desire for his Sophie Belle not to don the blue and white checkered dress—yet again.

Sophie's long-awaited honeymoon was drawing to a close. She felt a little sad, although she longed to take baby Benny back in her arms.

Benedict had gone out for wine and malt whisky and Sophie was making beef wellington in the tiny kitchenette, when the doorbell rang.

She wondered if Benedict had forgotten his key since they had had no visitors—since she arrived at any rate. Sophie opened the door a little cautiously and there stood a woman. Sophie knew right away who she was, her Spanish dark good looks were quite a giveaway.

Sophie wordlessly opened the door wider, and the woman walked inside. She thought, *my God, this woman has followed my husband around the world. Why?*

Carlotta Ramirez was, by Sophie's reckoning, in her early forties. She was also very beautiful—as dark as Sophie was fair—full figured and finely dressed. She was tall, considerably taller than Sophie. She almost appeared regal, dressed as she was in expensive furs. Sophie was wearing a plain skirt and pinstriped blouse. She had intended to change into something nicer for Benedict, once she got dinner in the oven. Sophie had imagined this woman to be old and long past her prime—she wasn't—she was beautiful. She felt such a stab of jealousy, standing in her ordinary apparel—once again lesser and insignificant, trying hard not to imagine this Spanish beauty and her husband together—making love, as they must have done so many times.

Sophie said, "I know who you are but what do you want? If your answer is Benedict, well you can't have him. He is my husband and the father of my child. I know all about you. I know about your letters. I even read one that you sent him from South Carolina."

Finally, Carlotta spoke. "So, you are the little schemer who caught Benedict Cochrane out. South Carolina? Oh yes, I had a very brief marriage to Mr. John Dixon of Edinburgh. The marriage took me to the backwoods of South Carolina. However, he became sick on the voyage to America and never fully recovered. He died and we were married less than six months. However, he left me well enough placed—more than can be said about your so-called husband. I am on my way back to Edinburgh. I may be Spanish, but I hate the heat, and I hated South Carolina."

Sophie heard herself offering her unexpected visitor tea, but the woman said she preferred something stronger, and Sophie poured them both a glass of sherry.

Sophie said, "He will be home soon. What is it that you want? Your affair is long over, and he belongs to me now. He doesn't love you. He loves me. Perhaps you should have held out for a wedding band." Sophie recalled that Benedict didn't give her one either until four months after they were married. However, she had the marriage certificate.

Carlotta said, "You look so young and sweet. However, you are not so sweet, are you Mrs. Cochrane?"

She practically spat out the words, "Mrs. Cochrane," and Sophie responded, "Not when it comes to women chasing my husband. I think possibly you should leave before Benedict finds you here. I can't even imagine his reaction when he discovers I allowed you across the doorway."

Carlotta said, "It was sheer chance. I saw you both on Buchanan Street. He was carrying shopping bags with a silly smile on his face. I hardly recognized him. I wondered; has he lost his edge? I always loved his frown. Well actually I loved more than that."

Sophie said, "That's enough. I want you to leave."

Carlotta said, "He promised me marriage. We were to be married.

Then one day he came to my flat in Edinburgh and told me he had married another, that you were carrying his child. So, you managed to entrap the good barrister—but you weren't, were you? Not at that time. You made it up and yet he married you."

Sophie was remembering Benedict's past words. He had mentioned casually what he said to this woman, that his bride was with child. He even joked about it the morning after their wedding, as she sat there in the marriage bed that she had slept in alone, on her wedding night. Is that what he told everyone? Did they all believe that? All those people at the Martin's home? Fiona MacBride? She wondered if he had some sort of background with the insipid Miss MacBride—after all, her behavior at the Martin's dinner party was over the top—outrageous.

Sophie stood up and said, "Believe what you like—if it makes you feel better. You allowed yourself to be used by a man. I am sure you are not the first he abandoned. I have no illusions about my husband. I also know that he is my husband. He will never be yours. Please, enough said, please leave before he finds you here."

However, no sooner were the words out of her mouth, than she heard the door to the flat opening and Benedict shouting, "I'm back, Sophie Belle. I bought you…"

He stopped when he walked in and saw Carlotta seated on his living room sofa. Sophie thanked him for the flowers he was carrying in his hand and took them from him. She simply said, "They are lovely. I will place them in water," and she walked into the tiny kitchenette where she could hear every word spoken in the adjoining living room.

He said, "Why are you here, Carlotta. I thought I made it quite plain that you were to keep away from my wife and family."

Carlotta said, "Oh I see, you still have that steely eyed frown. You must save it for the courtroom and your mistresses. I saw you and your young wife, sheer chance really, and I must admit that I was shocked to see you carrying shopping bags with a great big smile on your face. I wondered, did my man really change so much?"

Sophie had to hold herself back from rejoining them and severely berating this bitter woman, who no longer appeared so beautiful to her. However, she knew better, and to allow Benedict to handle the situation. Sophie always put the thought of her husband's past lovers out of her head—but to come face to face with the woman he was breaking up with, when first she met him? She felt sick, yet the pastry for her beef wellington would spoil, if she didn't quickly finish rolling up the beef inside of it, and place it in the oven, so she set about her task, miserably listening to them speaking in the other room.

Benedict said, "First off, I am not your man, and beyond that, why do I find you in my flat, no doubt talking nonsense to my wife? Carlotta, I don't care why you are here. I just need you to leave. I have nothing to say to you and you have nothing that interests me. Allow me to show you to the door."

Carlotta said, "Don't you feel a bit stupid Benedict? There was no child. I have been making enquiries. Your son is barely past one. She tricked you into marriage, didn't she? You knew I was unable to provide you with what you wanted, a son. Well, I suppose she did—eventually."

Sophie had enough. All these lies being told about her in the next room, as she meekly prepared dinner like a good little wife in the tiny adjoining kitchen. She marched back out into the living room.

"You are still here? Benedict, this is insufferable. I am sorry I invited this awful woman in."

Sophie turned towards Carlotta, "You might be dressed as a fine lady in your furs, but we both know what you are."

Benedict said, "Sophie, please allow me to handle this." He took a hold of Carlotta's arm and led her out of the flat, closing the door behind them—the door he had just walked in, carrying flowers for Sophie.

Sophie sat down. She was trying to wrap her head around what had just happened. He was outside talking to this woman. He had closed the door upon Sophie—no doubt seeking privacy for whatever he had to say to her. He was with Carlotta Ramirez more than two years—technically longer than he had been with Sophie since they had spent so much time apart. Time, he spent alone in his flat in Glasgow, three thousand miles away from his wife.

Sophie thought of the photographs and her letters. It seemed that possibly, Sophie had won in the end—whatever inner struggle he had going on. Euphemia had called it good versus evil. Perhaps that was not the case at all. Perhaps it was Carlotta versus Sophie. A young woman to give him children versus a beautiful mistress who couldn't. He left Sophie the morning after their wedding, and he didn't return for days. What was really the truth? And why did everyone believe this about her. Then she supposed *they believed it, because he led them to believe it.*

Sophie looked out the window, and they were in earnest conversation. Carlotta Ramirez and Benedict Cochrane. Sophie walked away and sat down again. She wondered about many things. Was her whole life a lie? A lie built around Benedict Cochrane's vanity. All his fine suits and fur coats. However, he needed a woman—a wife—to provide him with a son, and Sophie graciously obliged with one who looked just like him. She recalled in that half hour she waited for him to return—the comment about her conceiving so soon, the excuse for not taking her on a honeymoon. The sad little thing, whose father turned out to be so dear to James McNulty that he overpaid for the good barrister's services.

Benedict Cochrane didn't invite her to Glasgow. She arranged the whole thing herself, and with amazing luck, just in time for her to witness him again in the courtroom defending James McNulty—Sophie's Uncle Jimmy McGuigan. Sophie felt sick. Who was this man whom she so impetuously married and to whom she so carelessly gave her whole heart.

She heard the door open. Benedict said, "I put her in a Hansom cab. That should be the end of her treachery."

Sophie thought, *what a peculiar thing to say? Benedict the innocent.*

She said, "Dinner won't be ready for a while. I am going into the bedroom to pack. We have two more nights. I will spend it at the Central Hotel. Benedict, this thing we call a marriage—it is over. You dishonored my good name. You did so to explain why you were marrying a shopkeeper's daughter. The girl who sold ribbons in the haberdashery. You lied about me. You led your friends and mistress to believe that I was knocked up, and you, such a gentleman as to marry me. Benedict, I feel sick. Please go away. This is your secret flat. I should be the one to leave."

Sophie couldn't even look at the man she had so loved—who was he anyway? She started packing up her things—her baby's gifts, the gifts for her aunt and uncle, Sam and Jack. She stopped. "Our wedding night—you got drunk. I received no wedding ring. Of course, everyone believed that about me. You set me up. Stupid me—I was too innocent to imagine such a thing. In fact, thinking back, what was in my head? Benedict how could you be so cruel? Even now, our wonderful fortnight. You didn't invite me to come. I invited myself."

Sophie turned, "I have a lot of luggage with all the Christmas presents we bought. Would you mind at least helping me down the stairs? Then I will be out of your life forever."

Benedict was standing by the bedroom door. "Stop this, Sophie. You are not going anywhere. Okay, I might have been a bit ambiguous as to the reason for the rush for our wedding. I suppose that led certain people to think you tricked me. It was so sudden Sophie, I had no time to court you, to woo you. I had to get rid of Carlotta. I didn't want you to get away. I wasn't sure why. Well, I knew why. I just didn't want to believe it at first. It all came at me so fast."

Sophie thought about it. "I wonder, Benedict, if there was no steamer ticket—no rush—would we be happily married right now? Living in Bishopbriggs? Entertaining your friends in your big house?"

He walked into the bedroom and sat on the bed. He took hold of Sophie's hand, and she knew she could never pull it away. "I sometimes wondered that in the beginning, but really, I knew. I have said many times, the moment I laid eyes on you, I was yours forever. I have never, nor could I, consider touching any other woman. Tonight, I told Carlotta the truth. I told her you left me, and I followed you all the way to America, because I couldn't live without you. And Sophie, that is the truth. As for Fiona MacBride? Marsha and Audrey were putting stupid ideas in her head, and she isn't too bright. I'd have sooner become a monk. Martin and Nicholson always knew the truth, as did Sir Alfred, because I told them you had never been kissed before me."

Sophie, as always, softened. She knew she wasn't going anywhere. She sat down on the bed next to Benedict and said, "Carlotta is very beautiful, but she couldn't give you children. Was that why you went off her?"

Benedict said, "Okay Sophie, the whole truth and may we please never speak of her again. It makes my stomach turn."

Sophie was surprised by the disgust with which he made that statement.

He continued, "The opposite, my sweet Sophie Belle. I believe I have said this before. I was not a very nice man when you met me. I used women to suit my purpose and vanity. I thought of myself as untouchable. No woman could reach into a heart that wasn't there. Imagine my surprise—shock. An uppity little girl with a turned-up nose, who learned all her manners from self-improvement books and who spoke like a duchess—due to elocution lessons—completely consumed my body and soul. I wasn't happy about it. Me? Benedict Cochrane? A lovesick swain? I tried all manner of things to gain the upper hand. All my efforts were useless. I stayed away for days on end, sleeping in the lonely bed you are now seated upon—not so lonely anymore. I belittled you. I cringe at some of the things I said to the most beautiful girl in the world. The girl in the navy-blue suit."

Benedict took down Sophie's hair, as he had done so often, his piercing grey eyes looking so intensely into her sparkling blue eyes, with tears welling up in them, "Sophie, once I took you out of your tiny little world, you shone like a star, men falling over themselves to look at you. I never understood how you didn't notice that. The door was wide open for you. I knew it the night of that stupid City Chambers ball. I wrote my name all over your dance card, and I abandoned you. Any other woman would have thrown it away and made merry with the many young swains vying for their attention. Tell me, do you still have that dance card?"

Sophie was entranced, Benedict Cochrane was mesmerizing her as he so often did when he was like this, and as was her usual, she forgot why she was so hurt and angry in the first place. "Yes, it is the only dance card I ever had."

Benedict said, "Then aren't I the lucky one. Sophie, had you been born to your uncle and not your mother, you would be long since married to the American millionaire you dreamed of. Instead, you are stuck with the stupid Scotsman. That reminds me. Another fear I had, if you got on that steamer, still unmarried, you might have gone off me." He brightened, "Still it seems you find me captivating—for whatever the reason—and that nasty temper of yours has gotten most of the packing done. Well except my stuff, I suppose," and then he said, "Sophie Belle," he paused, and Sophie waited for more wonderful compliments regarding her beauty, but instead he said, "That food smells delicious. I'm starving."

Sophie kissed him happily, all thoughts of ever leaving Benedict Cochrane swept right out of her head. She said, "Beef wellington. It should be about ready but there is nothing to go with it. I was too upset to peel the potatoes."

He laughed and pulled her into his arms, "That's alright, your beef wellington is as delectable as you once described it. It will do on its own. I will let you have a little slice. Now off you go, wench, and serve me up my dinner."

Sophie ran off to the tiny kitchenette she had grown to love. She decided she was glad she met Carlotta Ramirez. She was glad Carlotta saw Benedict smiling, carrying all the presents Sophie made him buy. Benedict's way with words mesmerized her in the same manner they mesmerized the jury. Sophie's heart was, once again, brimming with happiness.

Benedict Cochrane poured himself a whisky. He could hear his wife, his Sophie Belle, singing in the kitchenette, happy and secure in his love for her. He pondered, *what did I ever do to inspire such love and devotion from an angel.* He smiled to himself, and mentally gave himself a pat on the back, Sophie Belle Cockroach would never forsake him—if she hadn't already. He took off his black coat, loosened his shirt and rolled up his sleeves and shouted, "Do you want me to set the table?" He then laughed at himself; *those are words I never expected to say to a woman. It seems you may have won, Sophie Belle.*

Sophie shouted back, "No, I will do it, just you sit down and drink your whisky."

Which he did, and said, "Happily," as he watched his Sophie Belle place a fresh tablecloth on the table and set the vase of flowers upon it, making it nice for him. Perhaps, she didn't win after all.

He started laughing, and Sophie began laughing too. She said, "I made that too easy on you, didn't I? Barrister Cochrane? You are lucky I don't pour that whisky over your pretty head. However, I know how much you pay for those nice silk shirts!"

CHAPTER 20

Three days later, the Cochranes and the Hickses were boarding the Olympic, for their return voyage to New York.

As the passengers waved to the crowds below, Sophie was struck with such a feeling of gratitude, tinged with a sense of disbelief. The others in her small party were so blasé about their first-class staterooms. Sophie was still in awe of hers. For all his bad behavior, Benedict Cochrane had made her into the fine lady she longed to be, even as a little girl, when such an idea was so out of reach to be rather ridiculous.

Sophie regarded her traveling companions. They all played a role in her success and yet, they said it was she who brought such happiness to them? How could that be? Simply because one day she was given the opportunity to purchase lunch for a woman whom she perceived to be such a fine lady, so far above Sophie's station in life.

Regardless, she was on her way home now, anxiously anticipating seeing her beloved son again, as well as her aunt and uncle Carlisle, Jack and even Sam.

Sophie Belle Cochrane finally had her long-anticipated honeymoon, albeit that she was the one to arrange the whole thing.

Suddenly, Sophie's reverie was interrupted by the sound of a rather posh male voice shouting, "Cochrane! As I live and breathe! What are you doing sailing to New York?"

Benedict shouted back, "By George, Merriweather?" and he

hurried off to join the gentleman, who was standing with two women; one possibly his wife, and another considerably younger. Benedict shook hands with and embraced the man. He also embraced the older woman, who was possibly Euphemia's age, and gallantly kissed the hand of the young lady.

Euphemia seemed astonished too. She said to her husband and Sophie, "Edward Merriweather—Eddy—they were famous friends at university. He was often in our home since his family lived in London. That is his wife, Miriam. She also attended Glasgow University. The couple married shortly after graduation. I don't recognize the younger woman. They lost touch. Of course, Eddy soon settled down as a married man—not so my brother!"

Euphemia waved over to her brother and his companions, and he called her over.

Sophie stood in shock, feeling ignored, and Sir Alfred said, "Let's go over and be introduced, Sophie."

But Sophie said, "No Alfred, you go. I will see you later. I need to fetch something from our cabin…er, stateroom."

Sir Alfred turned to persuade her; however, she was already lost amid the dozens of passengers still standing waving and greeting one another on the upper deck.

⁓

Sophie closed the door of the stateroom and pulled down her carefully coiffed hair. She gazed at herself in the mirror and decided upon a scented bath. The bathroom was beautifully appointed, and Sophie poured half a bottle of the rose scented bath salts, into the sumptuous bath. She thought, *honeymoon over, Mrs. Cochrane. However, no more tears. Two can play his game.*

⁓

Sophie was already slipping into her silk pajamas, the ones she bought at Copeland's on their last day in Glasgow, when she and Euphemia went shopping, when Benedict finally appeared.

Euphemia still had her account in the expensive department store and Sophie also purchased turquoise harem pants, the latest rage in Paris, along with the matching tasseled blouse and feathered headdress. The outfit was extortionately priced, and Euphemia tried to talk Sophie out of her purchase. At the time, Sophie thought of dressing up for Benedict. She had little intention of wearing the outfit otherwise—in New Chestnut? The very thought of it made her laugh.

Sophie spent over two hundred pounds that day and Euphemia also spent a considerable amount. Both ladies laughed merrily about the thought of Benedict's face when he received the bill, and Sophie remarked, "Well we both know he was grossly overpaid for his defense of Uncle Jimmy. My uncle was clearly innocent the way I see it!"

Euphemia heartily agreed and the ladies decided upon their last afternoon tea at the Willow Tea Rooms. The restaurant had been recently redesigned by Mr. MacIntosh and the ladies were cheerfully discussing ideas to update Sophie Belle's Tea Room in New Chestnut, in the same Charles Renee MacIntosh style, which was all the rage in Glasgow.

∽

Benedict said, "I expected to find you crying, Sophie Belle. They are old friends. We are having dinner with them this evening. I suppose I can introduce you at dinner, since you ran away today. What in God's name are you wearing?" He didn't wait for an answer, and said, "I see you have bathed. I think I will do the same."

Sophie said, "Oh yes, I am surely looking forward to meeting your friends this evening when I am rested. What kept you so long?"

Benedict said, "We all decided upon a cocktail in the bar to see us on our way. Shame you didn't join us. I was telling Merriweather and

Miriam how we met. The other lady is Miriam's sister, Miss Cynthia Smith."

Sophie thought, *and here was me thinking I had shed the girl selling ribbons image forever? Silly me.*

But all she said was, "Enjoy your bath," and turned her back on him to continue brushing her hair.

Benedict was about to say how much he loved her hair and how sweet she looked in her silk pajamas, but instead, he simply shrugged his shoulders and proceeded into the bathroom.

Sophie was smiling to herself as she heard him complaining about the wet towels and floor. She was remembering the way she found his flat before she obligingly cleaned it up for him.

Sophie Belle Cochrane decided she was indeed going to turn the tables on the good barrister that night at dinner. Enough was surely enough!

⁓

Sophie said, "White tie? Is there something special for dinner tonight?"

Benedict said, "Sophie Belle, why are you acting so petty. Afraid of a bit of younger competition? Anyway, there will be after dinner entertainment and dancing. Didn't you travel first class on your way to Liverpool?"

Sophie said, "Yes, but I returned to my room after dinner. Which one is younger? Oh, I presume Miss Smith. I am sure you will enjoy a fox trot with her. So, you told them all about me, didn't you? The shop girl story or the knocked-up story? Just so I know how to behave."

He merely said, "Sophie, I am not in the mood for moods. I am joining Merriweather for an aperitif. You can come down with Alfred and Euphemia. Do you intend to get dressed? Or are you wearing those pajamas?"

Sophie smiled, "No, I will be getting changed, dearest. See you in a bit."

Benedict was about to leave but said, "Sophie Belle, please behave yourself tonight."

Sophie smiled sweetly and threw her shoe at the door upon his exit.

∽

Sophie Cochrane took great pains with her appearance that night. She felt scandalous in her harem pants and telephoned the ship's hairdresser, who elaborately styled her hair high before affixing the feathered headdress.

She eventually knocked at Euphemia and Alfred's door, "Are you ready to go down?"

Sir Alfred burst into laughter, "Sophie Belle, are we about to enjoy an entertaining evening? Euphemia, what do you make of these…"

Euphemia finished for him, "Harem pants and all the rage in Paris. Sophie? Possibly a little scandalous for my brother?"

Sophie said, "I certainly hope so. Did he tell them the whole haberdashery story over drinks earlier?"

Euphemia said, "It was much abbreviated, his friends appeared more interested in our mutual enterprise in New Chestnut. I gather Mrs. Merriweather is rather militant. They now live in New York, and she is very involved with the Suffragist movement there. In fact, she asked if we might be interested in hosting an event at our restaurant and of addressing the ladies in her group."

Sophie was astounded. "Why didn't your brother mention any of this to me instead of complaining about wet towels in the bathroom?"

Sir Alfred said, "Because he said he doubted if you would be interested in such an endeavor. I think he was a little irritated, not to be the center of attention. His friends are so excited to meet you."

Sophie said, "Oh, he doubts if I will be interested? Euphemia, we must make haste with our plans of redecorating the tearooms. We will be hosting a very special event there soon—although possibly not until the spring."

Sir Alfred led both ladies into the elegantly appointed dining room and Sophie could easily ascertain that her mode of attire was causing utterances of both approval and disapproval from those already seated. She stood as she noticed her handsome husband approaching her. She was reminded of Carlotta's words. His frown was indeed most appealing.

She took his proffered arm, and he smiled a steely smile and said, "What in hell's name have you got on? Whose benefit is this meant to be for?"

Sophie said, "Oh, dearest, don't you like my little ensemble? I think you are showing your age. In that case I doubt you will like how much you have paid for it."

Dinner that first night was nothing like Sophie expected. She realized that she had come a long way from feeling lesser. Miss Cynthia Smith hung on her every word, as indeed did Mrs. Merriweather. Both ladies so very much-admired Sophie and Euphemia's successful venture. They also admired Sophie's harem pants and Cynthia begged her sister to purchase a pair for her in New York.

Sophie learned that Edward Merriweather had relocated to New York some years ago, along with his wife who was one year behind him and Benedict at Glasgow University. Edward was a Londoner, and his wife was from Edinburgh. Cynthia was Miriam's half-sister, and at twenty-one years of age, was hoping to marry a millionaire in New York.

She said, "Mama has lost patience with me, and I have two younger sisters that she also must see satisfactorily settled. Hence, I am off to New York for a year, having been given the orders to find myself a rich husband."

Cynthia was lively and spirited and Sophie liked her, not the least because she appeared to so admire Sophie. She was pretty with big baby blue eyes, and she was certainly more interested in Sophie than in Benedict. She said, "I wish I had the nerve to even begin to achieve what you have achieved, Mrs. Cochrane. What do you think are my chances of finding a rich husband in New York. I certainly do not want to be sent back to Edinburgh."

Sophie thought, *a spoiled, rich young girl with no doubt a dowry asking for my advice. What can I possibly tell her?*

She decided, "I was also once destined for New York with the very same intention, persuaded and influenced by my aunt and uncle who live in Manhattan. However, Mr. Cochrane wouldn't allow me on the ship without marrying him. Of course, that did not stop me from boarding the ship, along with my sister Euphemia, and brother, Jack Sullivan. Fortunately, the good barrister found life without me was not worth living and he joined me—eventually. However, he escapes back to Scotland every chance he gets."

Eddy Merriweather was much amused, and said, "I wondered if my friend would ever settle down. He certainly showed no signs of it the last time I saw him. Must be almost ten years ago."

Sophie laughed, "I suppose you could say I set my cap at him. Well, me and many others. I expect I was the most persistent."

Eddy said, "And I daresay the most beautiful."

Benedict said, "Alright, I will say this, and then may we change the subject. My pretty wife, dressed up tonight for the harem, is quite the little actress. She burst into tears whenever I tried to kiss her. She pretended she couldn't dance, just to show me up. She never wasted an opportunity to insult me. However, through all that, she was Cinderella, which meant in order to win her hand, I had to be Prince Charming."

Sir Alfred burst into laughter, "Prince Charming? I have heard the good barrister called many names but never that!"

Soon afterwards the dancing began, and Benedict was first to lead his wife onto the dance floor.

Sophie lovingly looked up at him, and said, "Benedict, I really didn't know how to dance. I had never attended such an event. It was the only dance card I ever had."

Benedict said, "Yes, I was such a bounder, to put it mildly. This year, we will go to New York City for New Year's Eve. I promise you. I need to get you another dance card so I can fill it in and keep to my word this time around."

Sophie was looking at her husband with a shocked expression on her face. He said, "What? Sophie Belle? You wore that bizarre get up to get at me? Well, it has backfired since I can't let you dance with any other men when you are so indecently clad."

Sophie said, "Benedict, I don't care to dance with other men."

He said, "I know that. Only when you want to make me jealous. Well, no further need for that. I watched you at dinner and realized something wonderful."

Sophie was still looking at him in shocked confusion, and he explained, "I am married to a very fine lady, beautiful, intelligent, indeed a temptress, and we have loved each other since first we locked eyes. Such good fortune. In my case undeservedly so. I love you Sophie Belle Cochrane—even wearing those silly pants which I will be removing later. I have already ascertained what your punishment will be."

Sophie laughed, "Does it involve black lace?" Then she added thoughtfully, "Do you realize, sir, that you just told me you loved me, right in the middle of the dance floor?"

And Benedict said, "Did I really say that? Of course, could just be infatuation."

Printed in Great Britain
by Amazon